THE TEMPLE
OF THE
THREE WHISPERS

BOOK ONE:

THE LADY OF
CEDRIC'S COVE

BRIAN HARMON

The Temple of the Three Whispers
Book One: The Lady of Cedric's Cove

Copyright © 2023 Brian Harmon
Published by Brian Harmon
Cover Image and Design by Brian Harmon

ISBN-13: 978-1-945559-21-1

Author's Note:

This book is the first in a SEQUEL SERIES. To fully enjoy the story that follows, be sure to check out *The Temple of the Blind* series, books 1-6, available wherever you purchased this title.

And for those of you familiar with the rest of my body of work, you might even find some more familiar faces in these pages…

Whenever you're ready, then welcome. And enjoy the ride.

~ Brian

Don't miss these other great books by Brian Harmon!

The Temple of the Blind series:

The Box (Book I)
Gilbert House (Book II)
The Temple of the Blind (Book III)
Road Beneath The Wood (Book IV)
Secret of the Labyrinth (Book V)
The Judgment of the Sentinels (Book VI)

The Temple of the Three Whispers series:

The Lady of Cedric's Cove (Book I)
Circles in Hermes' Footsteps (Book II)
Misplaced in Mysteria (Book III)
The Denselands (Book IV)
The Impassible Wall (Book V)
The City Beyond Memory (Book VI)
The Keeper's Dollhouse (Book VII)
Priestess of Ruin (Book VIII)
The Temple of the Three Whispers (Book IX)
Whispers in the Murk (Book X)

The *Rushed* series:
Rushed (Book 1)
Rushed: The Unseen (Book 2)
Rushed: Something Wicked (Book 3)
Rushed: Hedge Lake (Book 4)
Rushed: A Matter of Time (Book 5)
Rushed: All Fun and Games (Book 6)
Rushed: Something Wickeder (Book 7)
Rushed: Evancurt (Book 8)
Rushed: Relic (Book 9)

Hands of the Architects trilogy:

Spirit Ears and Prophet Sight (Book 1)
Pretty Faces and Peculiar Places (Book 2)
Broken Clocks and Amber Threads (Book 3)

For Collin

Prologue

It was a beautiful wedding.

It was *hot*. A little *too* hot, as almost everyone there had attested at least once. That much was undeniable. But beyond that, everything had been absolutely perfect. The sky was clear. The sun was shining. Not a single gust of wind dared to mess the bride's flawless hair. And everyone who'd had a role to play in the day's events had performed impeccably. Even the bride's father managed to not stutter his one line as he gave his beautiful daughter away, in spite of his obvious nervousness. Even the sunset was shaping up to be spectacular.

It was as perfect as a fairy tale.

And Nicole was very proud of herself for her part in that. After all, as the maid of honor, she'd made it her duty to ensure that the bride did nothing more than was expected of her on her special day. It was the very least she could do for her best friend. And quite a job that had been, too.

It wasn't that she was one of those overbearing demon brides who began frothing at the mouth at every askew flower. Quite the contrary, she'd been as happy as Nicole had ever seen her, gliding from place to place, practically floating in her lovely gown. But she'd wanted to help with everything and to talk with everyone. It'd taken all Nicole had just to make sure the woman ate the very dinner she spent so many weeks painstakingly planning!

But it was pretty well done now. The vows had been said, dinner enjoyed, cake served. The bouquet had been thrown, the garter flung, the couple's first dance recorded on every cell phone in the room. Toasts were made. Speeches were given. And now almost everyone was outside, either on the dance floor or under the shade of the tent.

She passed through the banquet room, weaving between the mostly empty tables, soaking up some of the air conditioning while she had the chance. Most of those remaining inside were the groom's family. The Narwits had pretty much remained gathered around their table throughout the day's festivities. They weren't the most sociable people she'd ever met. And they were a stark contrast to the bride's energetic Roushen family, which were pretty much monopolizing the dance floor and the bar. But everyone she'd met today was very nice.

Two little girls ran past her, laughing and squealing in their pretty party dresses and she smiled after them.

"Nicole, do you know if there are any paper towels?" asked a very thin, older woman with a face that was somehow both lined with wrinkles and at the same time remarkably youthful and girlish. An adorably pudgy four-year-old was trailing along after her. This was the bride's Aunt Rae and her grandson, little Will.

"There should be," she replied, smiling at the boy as he stared up at her with his big, wondering eyes. "Check the cabinets in the kitchen."

"Thank you."

The two hurried off toward the kitchen and Nicole turned and made her way across the room and through the doors, where the brilliant sunshine was almost blinding and the sweltering heat took her breath away.

It was a lot more crowded and noisy out here. There was music and chatter and laughter and the squealing of children freshly fueled with wedding cake.

Her gaze immediately fell on the formidable bulk of a very large and very familiar man standing in the scarce shade of the building and she immediately set upon him. "*Daddy*, you should be inside in the air conditioning!"

Stuart Smart didn't acknowledge his daughter with a look. He kept his gaze fixed stubbornly on the merry crowd, lifted his drink toward his lips and replied, "I'm perfectly capable of enjoying a few minutes of fine summer weather without dropping dead of heat stroke just because I happen to be *fat*."

"Fat" might have been a bit of an understatement. At well over four hundred pounds, and with a steady increase with each passing year of his life, he was positively *obese*. Nicole lived in constant dread of the heart attack he was slowly but inevitably approaching, but he was impossibly stubborn and couldn't be convinced to change his lifestyle just to "slim down a bit" as he called it.

She knew her own father, naturally. The more she pressured him to take care of himself the harder he would push back. He was a brilliant man. A genius, in fact. He was, after all, *Doctor* Stuart Smart, proud owner of *two* doctorates, and head of the physics department at the university here in Briar Hills. But he didn't like to be called "Dr. Smart." He'd always thought it sounded silly, like the name of some ridiculous comic book villain. It might seem like such a frivolous thing, for a man of his immense intelligence to be bothered by something like a name, but this was the way her father's brain worked. For all his impressive intellect, he was actually very easily embarrassed. And that, she knew well, was his greatest weakness. "Nobody said anything about being fat," she informed him. "But you're *sweating* through your shirt."

He paused in the middle of taking a sip from his drink.

"She's right, dear," said Lorilynn Smart as she stood at his other side, holding a glass of wine.

His face reddened a bit at his wife's affirmation of the situation.

"It *is* a *smidge* hotter than I care for," he muttered.

Lorilynn gave her daughter a knowing smile and sipped her wine. She, too, was a brilliant and accomplished academic, and a wonderfully generous and loving woman. But while she was nowhere near as large as her beloved husband, she was still quite heavy, with broad hips and a huge bosom. And she was as plain as she was plump. Her straight blonde hair was fine and shapeless, her clothes as dull and modest as they came. She refused to wear makeup, even to a wedding. Even her glasses were oversized and unflattering. It drove Nicole crazy that she cared so little for how she looked. But she was as stubborn about her vanity as her husband was about his fitness. "There's simply no point wastin' energy tryin' to look like somethin' I'm not," she would stubbornly reply in her faint southern drawl any time she found herself the target of her daughter's nagging. "Your father loves me just as I am and that's all that matters to me."

"Oh, Nicole!" A thin, energetic woman appeared before them, her long dress light and flowing, dripping with jewelry, her hair adorned with flowers. She was waving a small digital camera. "Let me get a picture of the three of you!"

Nicole smiled and crowded closer to her parents.

"You already got a picture of the three of them, Mom," said Andrea, who appeared at the woman's side as if from nowhere. She was slender and lovely in her bridesmaid dress. Like all the girls in the wedding party, her long hair was pinned back, better revealing all the glittering rings in her ears, eyebrows and nose as well as the little Virgo sign tattoo on the back of her neck.

"No I didn't," replied Frieda Prophett. "I got a picture of the three of them *with the bride*. I want a picture of just the three of them."

Nicole was fairly certain that Andrea was right. She *had* taken this picture before. Twice. But she smiled and posed for it anyway.

"It's fine!" Lorilynn assured her. "We don't mind."

"Seriously," said Andrea, "how many memory cards did you bring?"

"Plenty," replied her mother as she snapped the picture. "Now you get in there, too."

Frieda was as delightfully girlish and cheerful as her daughter, with the same fondness for jewelry (minus the piercings, though). She was a very lean woman—thanks to a strict diet and workout regimen—with a bronze, tanning bed tan, store-bought nails and expensive dyed hair (she was a natural brunette but preferred her hair to match her daughter's, which was currently dyed a bright and cheerful shade of red).

Above all else, she was a very kind woman and Nicole was always pleased to see her, which was good because she saw a lot of her. She and Andrea were roommates, after all. They shared an apartment near the university. And Frieda visited a *lot*. She got a bit lonely when her husband was away. Being married to a fireman meant a lot of nights sleeping alone in a bed made for two and there wasn't anybody to talk with since her daughter moved out.

Frieda caught sight of two of the groomsmen and set off again as quickly as she'd appeared, stalking them through the crowd.

"Those poor guys're gonna have nightmares about her tonight," sighed Andrea.

Nicole laughed. "I think it's sweet."

Andrea set off after her mother. In addition to the zodiac sign on her neck, the thin straps of the bridesmaid dress showed off the little angel wings on her back, one on each shoulder blade.

"Yes, I think I'm ready to go back inside for a bit," decided her father.

"Good idea," agreed Nicole.

"Yes, quite sensible," added her mother, casting her another knowing grin over the rim of her wine glass before turning and following her husband.

As they wandered back into the comfort of the air conditioning, Nicole set out to check on the bride.

She could just see her there, a vision in white twinkling like a star at the center of the colorful crowd.

This was where all the Rudmans had gathered, she realized. There was the bride's parents, Dwight and Charity, along with her aunt and uncle and their grown boys. They were a much smaller family than the Roushens on her mother's side.

Nicole knew all of them. She'd practically grown up with this family, after all. She used to get invited on family vacations, even. She was as comfortable with these people as she was in her own home.

And there was Brandy, herself, standing in their midst, beaming. She looked absolutely perfect, with her fair blonde hair up, a band of rhinestones glittering in the sun and her veil flowing down behind her. She'd put on a few pounds these past couple years, but not many. She still possessed a slender, girlish figure. If anything, she was just a tiny bit curvier, which didn't do her any disservice at all, in Nicole's opinion. She was a vision of loveliness, an unrivaled beauty, an angel to behold.

But she still thought she looked a little strange without her glasses.

Brandy had decided to wear contacts today, so she'd be extra pretty in her pictures—although her glasses had never in her life made her look any less beautiful than she was without them. Ordinarily, contacts irritated her eyes, forcing her to wear her glasses to see, but she could usually get away with wearing them for a day or two and had managed to avoid red and watery eyes for her pictures. Nicole, who'd always had perfect vision, despite that both of her parents were significantly nearsighted, felt blessed that she didn't need to worry about glasses or contacts. And yet, as she looked over her best friend's naked face, taking in the difference of her appearance as she'd done over and over throughout the day, she couldn't help but remember that there'd been a time, a few years ago, when Brandy's poor eyesight had saved her life.

But that was a long time ago. A lifetime ago, it seemed.

And Brandy wasn't Brandy Rudman anymore.

Nicole continued through the crowd, past friends and family members and...

(Wait...)

She stepped past someone, close enough to feel the air stir between them, and was suddenly startled. Something wasn't right. Her heart leapt in her chest. Her breath caught in her throat. She stopped and turned, confused, the hair on the back of her neck standing up...

(Who...?)

But no one was there.

She stood for a moment, looking back across the crowd, confused. She couldn't quite recall anything about the person who just walked by. She couldn't remember whether it was a man or a woman. She couldn't remember the color of their shirt. She could only recall that something didn't seem right...

She turned and continued on, dismissing it.

She was just tired, was all. It'd been a busy day.

* * *

"It's just perfect," exclaimed Aunt Collette as she gazed out across the lawns at the still surface of the lake. "I never even knew this was here."

"I know," replied Brandy. "It's so beautiful."

The Weirweather Country Club made a perfect backdrop for the reception and had tons of great photograph spots. And it didn't even cost as much as a lot of the smaller places she'd considered.

"I'm *so* stealing this place when I get married," agreed Cassandra Wechick in her bridesmaid dress.

"You have to find a man first," Nicole informed her as she emerged from the crowd.

Cassandra rolled her eyes. "Don't remind me."

Brandy looked out over the lake. She could barely believe the day had finally come. It'd been almost *five years* since Albert asked her to marry him. It felt like *forever*. And yet it also seemed like only just yesterday that she first locked eyes with him in that Chemistry classroom.

There was something surreal about it finally being the big day. She kept feeling as if she'd wake up at any moment.

"Can I get you anything?" asked Nicole.

"No, thank you. I'm good."

"*I'll* be good when I can finally get out of this monkey suit," grumbled the father of the bride.

"But you look so cute!" exclaimed Brandy.

"It's true," agreed Nicole. "You do."

"I don't want to look cute," Dwight muttered, blushing a little. "I want to be comfortable." He wasn't used to dressing up. He was a jeans and work shirt kind of man. He'd rather be dirty and covered in sawdust and grease any day.

"*I* like you all dolled up," said his wife, tugging on his lapel.

Charity Rudman, unlike her husband, enjoyed having an excuse to dress up. And she looked amazing in her blue evening gown, her long, blonde curls cascading over her shoulder. "Reminds me of *our* wedding day."

"See," said Nicole. "*She* thinks you're hot."

"Yes I do," chuckled Charity.

Dwight blushed even brighter and struggled to find a response to that.

"If you guys don't stop teasing him," giggled Brandy, "he's *never* going to forgive me for making him wear that."

"It's fine..." he muttered, still blushing. "Just hot."

"It's almost over," his wife assured him.

And it *was* almost over. Brandy turned and looked out at all the wedding guests. After five years of planning, it was going to be all over and in the past before she knew it. It was a little sad to think about.

But it wasn't the end of anything, really. It was the beginning. Today was only the first day of her life as Brandy Cross, the first day of her life as her husband's wife. And that was nothing to be sad about.

Everything was perfect.

"You look absolutely *gorgeous!*" exclaimed a very chubby old woman in huge, rhinestone-studded sunglasses and a wide, floppy sunhat.

"Thank you," replied Brandy. She had no idea who this woman was. She didn't remember seeing her until now in spite of the fact that she looked quite hard to miss in her bright yellow dress and that huge hat. She didn't even see her approach. She was just there, right in her face. But then again, that had been happening all day. Today was the first day she'd met a good number of her new in-laws. Not to mention all the friends of the family that had shown up. Unlike hers, Albert's family wasn't from Briar Hills. They came from all over Missouri. And many of them had even traveled from out-of-state to be here today.

"Simply *stunning!*" sighed the woman. "I still can't believe how much the two of you have grown up!"

Brandy smiled her best smile and tried not to look baffled

by that comment. She made it sound as if she'd known them both their whole lives, in spite of the fact that they never even lived in the same city until six years ago.

Perhaps the woman had her confused with someone else. An old, childhood friend of Albert's perhaps?

The old woman leaned close to her then and said, "Good luck on your new adventure, dear. And whatever may get thrown at you, always remember that the two of you together can accomplish *anything*."

"Okay..." she replied, bemused. "Um... Thank you."

"Can I get you a water?" asked Nicole.

Brandy glanced back at her, distracted. "What? Oh. No. I'm fine."

"Make sure you stay hydrated," warned her mother.

"I literally just finished a bottle," Brandy assured her.

"Just let me know if you need anything," said Nicole.

"Stop fussing over me. I'm fine." She turned back toward the old woman, but she'd already vanished back into the crowd. There was no sign of the floppy hat anywhere. Instead, as she looked out across the crowd, she met the gaze of an old man she didn't recognize. He was wearing a rather obnoxious-looking red suit jacket and a gawdy tie and his skin looked strangely pale and splotchy. He was staring right at her...almost *leering*...

She averted her gaze and pretended not to notice the old man.

She reached for Albert's hand, but as she did so, she heard his voice from the opposite direction.

"Wevenwert," he said. "In Tennessee, yeah."

She looked over, surprised. She thought he was standing right next to her, but he was several steps away, talking to his aunt and uncle about their chosen honeymoon destination.

"Oh it's *beautiful* there!" exclaimed his aunt. "Which resort?"

Embarrassed, Brandy turned to see whose hand it was she almost grabbed by mistake, but there was no one standing there.

"The Lucianna Mysteria," replied Albert. "We booked four nights."

"We stayed at the Forest Birdwynn when we went for our

anniversary," his uncle explained. "Very fancy."

"We considered that one, too."

Brandy stood there, confused. She was quite sure *someone* was standing there a moment ago.

"You're not driving all the way down there *tonight* are you?" asked Albert's grandfather.

"No, we're leaving first thing in the morning."

Brandy wiped her empty hand on her gown, though she wasn't entirely sure why. It wasn't as if she'd touched anything when she reached for the hand. There wasn't anything there *to* touch. And yet for some reason, she felt her skin crawl for a moment...as if she'd almost touched something *vile*...

"You okay?" asked Cassandra.

She looked up, surprised. "Yeah!" She forced a convincing smile. "I'm fine."

She glanced out across the crowd again, remembering the creepy old man, but he'd wandered off somewhere, too. There was no sign of the obnoxious red suit jacket anywhere.

"Don't let yourself get overheated," said Nicole.

"I won't."

Yes. The heat. That was probably it.

* * *

"Seriously," said Andrea, "how many pictures do you need? You don't even know most of the people here."

"They're not for *me*," replied her mother. She was trying to coax a smile out of a ten-year-old boy who looked understandably uncertain about the weird, overly cheerful lady with the bright red hair and too much jewelry and makeup. "They're for Brandy and Albert. I'm going to make them a nice album."

"They have a photographer, you know."

"That's different. That's for *professional* pictures. You also need regular pictures."

"If you say so."

Frieda turned and scanned the crowd again, searching for

her next victim.

Andrea fixed her gaze on the boy and silently mouthed, "Run for your life!"

The boy looked back and forth between the two of them for just a moment and then bolted.

"I can't keep track of the wedding party," complained Frieda. "Everyone's all scattered out."

"They're probably hiding from you."

"Oh *shush*."

"I think I saw the best man hiding in the bushes around front," said Stella as she stepped up beside them. She was carrying a plate with a piece of wedding cake, eating as she walked around.

"Who's side are you on?" asked Andrea.

"Nobody's. I'm a goddess of chaos, remember?"

"Right. I forget." Andrea met Stella Umbertan during her first semester at Briar Hills University. She was a cheerful and outgoing girl, not unlike herself, and they became fast friends.

Stella was fairly average, with long, curly, reddish-brown hair, thick eyebrows, a slight overbite, a bigger-than-average forehead and a great spattering of freckles painted across her cheeks and nose. Like Andrea, she liked wearing lots of jewelry and was adorned with several necklaces featuring a number of colorful stones and pendants hanging over the low neckline of her red party dress, as well as a large assortment of bracelets and rings on every finger, including her favorite, a large, iridescent white stone on her left forefinger. Andrea had long ago concluded that she was a genuinely good person at heart, but she had a curious sense of humor that more often than not amused only herself and frequently bordered on morbid. And she positively *loved* mischief. Nothing delighted her more than stirring up trouble. The more salacious the better. As such, at some point she decided to proclaim herself a "goddess of chaos" and it seemed like she was sticking to it.

"Is that your *fourth* piece of cake?"

Stella took a big bite and made a show of relishing it. "Ish *sho good*!"

"It should be illegal for people like you to be skinny. It's not fair."

"Shorry."

"No, you're not."

Stella shrugged and looked out across the crowd to where Albert and Brandy were still mingling with the guests. "It's crazy that they're finally tying the knot, isn't it? I mean, they've literally been engaged the entire time I've known you guys."

"I know..." They'd almost been engaged the entire time *she* knew them. Almost *five years* now. She stared at the two of them. They looked so lovely all dressed up. She was so happy for them. But seeing them like this felt so strange. She couldn't help remembering the first time she ever met them. What a bizarre and wild adventure that was! And now they were at a *wedding*. Was this really the same world? Was the Albert standing there looking so handsome in his tuxedo really the same man who opened the door that evening and took a mysterious envelope from her hand? That felt like a dream now. After all, he was just Albert. She saw him almost every day. And yet there was a time when she sat crouched in a thicket of brush watching him—a complete *stranger*—trying to understand what he had to do with an envelope that someone had taped to her bedroom window and the mysterious ruins of an old, never-completed men's dormitory.

She caught sight of Nicole making her way through the crowd again, talking with people. Could it really be true that the first time she ever spoke with Brandy and Nicole they'd all been *naked*? That just seemed absurd.

Didn't it?

It wasn't as if they all acted like it never happened. They still talked about it every now and then. Every few months the subject would come up. But overall, life had just gone on...as if they hadn't discovered some grand secret of the universe in those endless, black tunnels...

But then again, life didn't just go back to the way it was, either. Things were different after the Temple of the Blind. She met all her best friends because of that place. She barely talked to any of her old friends anymore. They'd all moved on with their own new lives.

She turned her gaze toward the lake. There, taking a break from the blazing sun beneath the branches of a huge oak tree with her mother and sister, looking absolutely *stunning* in her bridesmaid dress, was Olivia Shadey.

Of all of them, Olivia went through the most during those events five years ago. She had every right to walk away and pretend none of it ever happened. In fact, anyone else might have gone utterly mad after living through some of the horrific things she experienced. But in spite of all that, she always seemed so calm and poised. She was always smiling, always reassuring.

All the things that happened down in those tunnels that night felt like a distant dream. Then and now… It didn't feel like it could possibly be the same world.

Someone brushed up against her, jolting her from her thoughts.

"I'm so sorry!" gasped a surprisingly handsome man in a bright purple dress shirt. His hand closed on her bare shoulder, steadying her as if he'd nearly knocked her down when he'd only barely grazed her. "I wasn't watching where I was going. Are you okay?"

"I'm…uh… I'm good…" she stammered as she blinked up at him, distracted. She suddenly felt a little weak in the knees. He was tall and broad-chested, with muscular arms. And what gorgeous gray eyes he had…

He seemed to realize that he was too close and withdrew his hand, embarrassed. "I'm *so* sorry!" he said again, taking a quick step back.

"You're fine," she assured him.

"I'll just…" He gestured toward the crowd behind him. "…be on my way. Uh…see you around. I mean, probably."

"Sure…"

"Again, sorry!" The man hurried on his way and Andrea stared after him for a moment, distracted.

"So that's the kind of guy who opens your flood gates?" said Stella around another mouthful of cake. "Nice."

She blinked, surprised. "What? *No!* What're you talking

about?"

"I'm talking about those adorable doe eyes you were making at him."

"I was *not!*"

"Hey, I don't blame you. He was *yummy.*"

"I don't even know that guy!"

"What do you need to know about him? You saw him. Up close and personal, even. That's the kind of guy who raises the humidity in your panties, if you know what I mean."

Andrea wrinkled her nose. "Quit it."

"Like a *super soaker.*"

"Oh my god, *stop!*"

Stella shrugged.

"You're such a freak. What's gotten into you today?"

She gestured at her plate. "Sugar."

"Of course."

Stella gazed out into the crowd after the stranger. "Well *I* liked him," she decided. She lifted another forkful of cake and licked her lips. "He looked *fun...*"

"You're so weird."

"You know you love me," she replied, still watching the handsome stranger.

Andrea looked out across the lawn and saw that Frieda had found Olivia and was getting yet another picture of her with her mother and sister. "Ugh... She won't leave anyone alone for five minutes..."

"She's like Jason Voorhees with a camera," agreed Stella. "Unstoppable. *Terrifying.*"

She sighed and started to walk toward them, but she stopped mid-step.

In spite of the heat, the air around her suddenly felt as cold as ice. A strange shiver raced all the way through her body, raising goosebumps on her skin and making the hair on the back of her neck stand up.

For a moment, she stood there, frozen in place, her eyes wide. A terrible dread bubbled up from somewhere inside her.

Then, just as quickly, the feeling passed.

Again, she felt only the heat of the July sun beating down on her skin.

"You okay?" asked Stella.

"I'm fine," she replied, forcing a convincing smile. She glanced around once more, trying to understand what was making her feel this way, but all she found was a small, timid-looking woman staring back at her from the clubhouse doorway.

She smiled an embarrassed smile and turned away, trying her best to act like she hadn't just had some sort of mental episode.

Nothing more than the ghosts of old memories, she supposed. She shrugged it off and continued on.

* * *

Olivia smiled politely for the pictures and then watched as Frieda moved on in search of new prey.

"I like it," decided Elaina. "It's pretty out here. I'll bet the pictures are *beautiful.*"

"*Very* beautiful," agreed Olivia.

"That's true," said their mother. "And you girls can do whatever you want. I've just always thought a wedding should be in a church. For me, personally, I mean. I'm not judging at all. I'm just old-fashioned, I guess."

"Nothing wrong with old-fashioned," said Olivia.

"That's right," agreed Elaina.

Olivia and Elaina were four years apart in age, but looked so much alike that they could've been twins. And they both looked so strikingly like their mother, Leta, that there could be no doubt that they'd both sprung from her genes. All three were curvy and buxom and positively beautiful in their perfect tans, flawless skin and immaculate nails.

"I *did* like the flowers," said Leta.

"I *loved* the cake," said Elaina.

"It was *so* good. Do we have the name of that bakery?"

"We do," replied Olivia.

"That's good. I'm definitely making a note of it."

"Absolutely," agreed Elaina.

"Wish it wasn't so hot, though," complained Leta.

"I think it's fine," said Olivia. As far as she was concerned, the beauty of this magnificent day far outweighed the minor inconvenience of the heat. The sky was positively breathtaking. And everyone looked so happy. She was so thrilled for Brandy that her special day had turned out so gorgeous. She looked out across the winding greens, at the slowly stretching shadows of the surrounding trees, at the pink hue of the approaching sunset. It really was fairytale perfect.

She was still staring off into the distance, distracted, when she realized that someone had approached her. She snapped out of it to find a tall, very shapely woman standing before her in a long, silvery dress. Her hair was a cascade of long, black curls and her left shoulder was adorned with tattoos of bright yellow sunflowers.

"Excuse me," she said with a warm and cheerful smile. She held out a small, brown box, a little bigger than an engagement ring box. "We have this little tradition in our family for weddings. We give these to the bridesmaids on the special day. It's a sort of good luck charm."

Curious, Olivia took the box and opened it. Inside was a small, rust-colored pendant on a silver chain. It looked like a simple, painted stone, roughly spade shaped. It wasn't particularly pretty or dainty. Not really her style. But she wasn't one to turn her nose up at a gift, much less a good luck charm.

"I know it's going to sound kind of silly," the woman began, "but it's based off a little-known old Chickasaw legend. If you put this on before midnight and wear it for three days without taking it off, it's said to bring good fortune in all matters of love and family for the rest of your life."

"Oh," said Olivia. "Well, that's a nice thought, isn't it?"

"That's a sweet gesture," said her mother. "What a lovely tradition."

Elaina nodded. "It's so sweet. I like it."

"I know, right?" said the woman. "I'm not going to tell you

it works, but my mom swears by it. She says no woman who's ever put one of these around her neck on a wedding day ever divorces or has difficulty bearing children or loses a loved one too young."

"A *very* nice thought," amended Olivia.

"It is," agreed Elaina.

"I've never been very superstitious," said her mother, "but I've also never seen any reason to turn down a good luck blessing. I mean, why not?"

"Exactly," said Elaina. "If all you have to do is wear it for three days, what could it hurt?"

"Enjoy it," said the woman, beaming. "And all the happy tomorrows it promises." Then she turned and walked away.

"That's so sweet," said Elaina, taking the pendant from her hand and examining it in the sunlight. "What a nice tradition."

"It is," agreed her mother. "I wonder which side of the family has Chickasaw roots. Your dad's mother's side has some Osage blood."

"I remember him talking about that," she recalled.

But Olivia wasn't listening to them. As she watched the woman with the sunflower tattoos walk away, she was struck by a sudden and crushing feeling of such impending doom that it froze her in place and made her heart stutter in her chest.

She stood there for a moment, her dark eyes wide with mounting fear. She hadn't felt anything like this in years. Not since that burning mountain five years ago... But she knew the feeling immediately. It was pure and unmistakable dread, like watching a speeding truck bear down on her with nowhere to run, knowing that a bloody end was inevitable.

Her psychic mind was warning her of something. Inexplicable danger in her near future.

But what could it be? And *here* of all places? *Now?*

But there was nothing here. Everything was exactly as it was supposed to be.

And even as she scanned the crowd around her, looking for anything out of place, she realized that the feeling was gone, vanished just as quickly as it had come over her.

She blinked, confused, and looked around. No one else seemed to have felt anything.

A false alarm? Was that a thing when it came to psychic stuff? It *was* only for a moment…

She glanced across the crowd again and saw that the woman with the sunflower tattoos had disappeared while she was distracted.

She looked at the pendant her mother and sister were still examining. She never got the woman's name… But a good luck charm? *It's said to bring good fortune in all matters of love and family for the rest of your life*, she recalled.

But before she could process the thought any further, Brandy was there, trailing her brilliant white train behind her, a vision of beauty. She swept right up to her, took her by the hands and squealed, "Next time!"

"Next time!" agreed Elaina.

"That's right!" said her mother.

"Your turn!" said Brandy.

Olivia blushed, embarrassed by the attention, but she couldn't hide her smile. She looked down at her hand, at the twinkling diamond on her ring finger.

It was, after all, why her mother and sister were so hung up on cake and flowers and pictures. It was all they wanted to talk about for the past seven months. Next time they got together like this, the cherry blossoms would be blooming and it would be *her* dressed all in white and Brandy in the bridesmaid dress.

"Are you excited?" asked Brandy.

"I am." She looked out across the lawn at Wayne, who was slowly making his way along the side of the building behind a crowd of people, clearly trying to hide from Frieda and her relentless camera.

He looked so handsome in his tuxedo. Even though they kept getting separated, she'd been watching him all day. Broad shouldered and heavyset, he looked more like a bodyguard than a groomsman. It was hard to tell by looking what a gentle and sensitive soul he could be. Sure, he could be a little grumpy at times, but never to Olivia. He worshiped the ground she walked on.

And she told anyone who would listen that he was her big strong hero, though hardly anyone had any idea just how literally she was speaking. Like Brandy and Albert, the two of them had been inseparable since they returned from the temple that day.

She had to resist an urge to run to him right now.

He finally proposed to her on Christmas eve this past year, and for a while she was so happy she thought her heart might give out.

"I'm already nervous, though," she said, blushing a little brighter.

"That's normal," her mother assured her.

"Totally normal," agreed Elaina as she handed her back the pendant.

"You're going to be great!" agreed Brandy.

"I hope so." But she was nervous *today* and she was only a bridesmaid.

She glanced around at the crowd again. There was no sign of that odd feeling of dread.

That was probably it, she decided. Just her nerves.

* * *

Wayne remained wary.

At the moment, Frieda Prophett was preoccupied with some of Albert's hyperactive little cousins, but she could come after him again in a heartbeat.

He took another step back, doing his best to keep the bulk of the crowd between him and her.

"She won't bite you, you know," said Nicole, surprising him from behind.

He glanced over his shoulder at her, then looked warily back at Andrea's camera-happy mother. "I don't believe you."

She laughed.

"She's voracious, I'm telling you." Then he ducked and turned away. "Shit, she's looking this way!"

"You're okay. She's heading for Albert again."

29

"Better him than me," he grumbled.

"You'd better get used to it. That'll be you in a few months."

"I know." He glanced over at Olivia and caught a shy smile. God, she looked amazing today!

"You guys're driving to Dunnen tomorrow, right?" said Nicole.

He nodded. "Big family get-together. It's my grandpa's birthday. Backyard barbeque and everything."

"Sounds fun."

"Yeah. Fun." Although he might have been more nervous about being surrounded by his family tomorrow than he was about being dressed up and paraded down the aisle today. He loved his family, but somehow he always managed to feel like a little kid again when everyone got together like that. And not in that warm and fuzzy nostalgic kind of way.

And to make it worse, he couldn't seem to convince his grandfather that being a graphic designer for an advertising agency was an actual job. The old man seemed to be convinced that every artist was a penniless recluse living in a studio apartment in some slum. He wasn't sure how many times he could listen to the lecture about how everyone needed a job with a good pension plan. He was starting to sympathize with Van Gogh lopping off his own ear.

All things considered, he'd much rather be spending a beautiful Sunday at home with his fiancée.

"I know how much you hate to drive, too," said Nicole.

He nodded. His earliest memories were of endless months of painful physical therapy after a bad car accident when he was only four years old. He *hated* being in a vehicle. And he couldn't just ask Olivia to drive. The only thing worse than being behind the wheel was being in the passenger seat, with no control whatsoever. "We've got to be there early as hell, too," he grumbled. "My dad's down in his back again and hasn't been able to do *anything* to get ready for this party, so Mom wants me there at the crack of dawn to help get everything set up for her."

Nicole wrinkled her nose. "Yuck."

"I know. She wanted me there *today*," he added, "but I had a prior engagement." He gestured at his tuxedo.

"Don't you have a brother who lives a lot closer?" she recalled. "And like *three* sisters?"

"Yeah, but Wade's *so* busy right now with his *super* important *real* job at the accounting firm," he sneered.

"Yeesh…" muttered Nicole. "Drama."

"I know. And she's always acted like the girls are too delicate to do any kind of work."

"Okay, I've *met* Whitney and she is definitely *not* delicate."

"No. She's just *spoiled*."

Wayne had never once regretted staying in Briar Hills with Olivia after college graduation. If he still lived in Dunnen, he was sure he'd never get a moment of peace.

"I still think it's cute how you all have 'W' names," said Nicole.

"Yeah. Freaking *adorable*," he groaned. *Annoying* was what it was. If he had a nickel for every time someone mixed up his and his brother's names he could probably have bought his own private island by now.

A woman he didn't know called out to Nicole from the crowd and she turned away, leaving him to continue his watch for Andrea's relentless photographer mom.

"I love weddings," said a small, cheerful voice at his side.

He glanced down to see a young girl in a frilly, powder blue dress standing beside him, her long, brown hair pinned up in a series of perfect braids. She was looking out across the lawn at the bride and groom.

"Everyone works so hard to make it such a perfect day, but in the end it's not really about today at all, is it?"

Wayne frowned and glanced around. Was this girl talking to him? He didn't know her, but she was standing right next to him, as if she'd sidled up to him specifically for this conversation. And no one else was close enough for her to be speaking to.

"It's about the future," she went on. "It's a brand-new beginning. Today is all about closing the book on two independent lives and opening a new one all about a new life together, one that might just go on for the rest of their lives."

He stared down at her, still frowning. Those were some pretty big observations for a girl who only looked to be about nine years old. Was she repeating something she heard an adult say? Or something she saw on television?

"But we don't know what the future holds, do we?" The girl hadn't looked at him the entire time she was speaking, but now she lifted her face and met his gaze. She had remarkably pretty green eyes. "Every day is full of new beginnings. Some of them are just very small. We should embrace each and every one of them, don't you think? No matter how scary the future looks?"

He stared down into those strangely haunting eyes. "Um... Sure?"

The little girl smiled up at him. "There's going to be lots of scary things. There's no avoiding that. But being scared doesn't matter as much as what you choose to do with that fear."

He opened his mouth to respond, but wasn't sure what to say.

The girl lowered her emerald gaze and looked out across the crowded lawn. "Besides, sometimes the scariest roads lead to the absolute *best* places."

He followed those eyes and found himself staring at Olivia again. Was she talking about...?

"No one's taking her away, you know," said Nicole.

He glanced over at her, distracted. "What?"

She smiled and looked over at Olivia. "It's cute how you're always looking over where she's at when she's more than a few feet away from you."

"I don't..." He looked across the lawn again at his fiancée, embarrassed. Then he looked back down at the little girl, but she was gone, disappeared back out into the crowd as quickly as she'd appeared.

Before he could ask Nicole if she saw where she went, Andrea appeared from the crowd, hurrying toward them. "Hey, everyone's gathering in the front to see the couple off."

"Already?" exclaimed Nicole. It was still pretty early. "What's their hurry?"

She rolled her eyes and said, "Prolly 'cause they can't wait to get into each other's pants, as usual."

"Hush!" laughed Nicole, glancing around to make sure none of the family heard her.

"Well it's true. You know how those two are."

"I know," she whispered. Even after all this time, Brandy and Albert could hardly keep their hands off each other. It was adorable…if occasionally awkward… "But it's not like they haven't done it a million times before. What's gonna be so special about it now that they're married?"

"I don't know. Maybe they've never done it dressed as a bride and groom before?"

"Stop!"

"I'm just saying."

The girls started across the lawn, following the shifting crowd toward the front of the building where the groom's shiny blue Mustang sat adorned in "just married" decorations.

Wayne lingered a moment, still wondering about the little girl, then followed after them.

Someone was walking next to him, he realized. He could see them in the corner of his eye. Someone tall and thin. Someone with a strangely imposing presence. But when he turned to see who was there, he was alone.

He stopped and looked behind him, confused, but there was no one there either.

Strange…

There's going to be lots of scary things, he thought, remembering the unusual words spoken by the little girl. Thinking back on it, there was something eerie about her…

Maybe he'd been out in the sun too long?

When he turned back, Olivia was there. She swept right up to him, stood up on her toes and kissed him. "There you are," he said, smiling.

"Here I am," she replied, smiling back at him. Then her smile melted a little. "You doing okay? I know you hate these kinds of things."

"The only thing I hate about it is that we keep getting separated."

Her smile bloomed again. "Aw." Again, she stretched up and kissed him.

"That's new," he said, reaching out and touching the rust-colored pendant hanging around her neck.

"It was a gift. Some kind of tradition. Supposed to bring us lots of good luck or something."

"Cool."

"I thought so." Then she took his hand and tugged at him. "Come on. We don't want to miss them."

"I'm coming." But as he let her lead him away, he glanced back one last time, wondering.

* * *

Albert and Brandy endured a final round of hugs from family and friends and said their farewells, then drove off down the winding drive toward the highway and into their future.

"God, I'm hot!" gasped Brandy. She pulled her dress up, exposing her knees and letting the air conditioning blow between her thighs where the intense summer heat had left her skin damp with perspiration. "Aren't you hot?"

"I'm a little baked," he admitted. "But I'm okay."

On their left was the lush, rolling green of the golf course and on the right the lake shimmered in the bright sunshine. It had been an excellent choice, far better than any of the crowded hotels or the pricy bed and breakfasts they'd considered. There was an illusion of luxury, a spacious banquet hall and a gorgeous backdrop for the outdoor wedding Brandy had always dreamed of.

There was a skinny, middle-aged man tending to a flower garden bordering the drive. As he drove past, the man looked up at him. They seemed to lock eyes for a moment…and there was something odd about those eyes…something unsettling… It sent a strange shiver down his spine in spite of the heat and made him think for some reason of stone passageways stretching into endless darkness.

Then he was past the gardener and the intruding thoughts faded away like smoke.

"You don't think it was *too* hot, do you? Like all anyone's going to remember is that it was hot?"

"I don't think so," he replied, pushing the stranger out of his head completely. "I think the most memorable part was how beautiful the bride looked."

"Aw." She smiled at him. "Sweetie, it's your wedding night. You don't have to suck up."

He laughed. "I wasn't sucking up. I just think you're gorgeous." He reached over and gave her bare knee a gentle squeeze.

"You're so sweet!"

He loved her so very much. It was hard to imagine that she was actually his wife now. It had taken almost five years to get used to the idea that she was really her fiancée.

"It really was perfect, wasn't it?" she sighed. She'd fully expected it to rain and force them to move the ceremony into the cramped hall. Though her mother certainly would have made it beautiful, it couldn't possibly have been as lovely as exchanging their vows beneath a clear blue sky with the lake sparkling in the background.

"It really was," he replied.

As he neared the end of the drive, he passed through a shaded grove of trees. It was here, as the blazing sun became mottled by the swaying canopy of branches overhead, that he felt an odd chill wash over him and his gaze was drawn out into those trees.

An intense feeling of unease swam through him and he was suddenly struck by a distinct feeling of being watched.

His gaze swept from trunk to trunk, expecting to see someone peering back at him from behind one of them.

He recalled the gardener and his strange eyes… And then he found his thoughts rushing back to the temple, to endless, black corridors, mysterious shadows and unthinkable creatures…

Something about this place and time right here and now felt

the way that place felt…

There was an eerie *significance* about it all.

Without thinking, his hand crept toward his pocket. There, tucked away inside his wallet, was a coin given to him almost six years ago by a man with no eyes. It was a reminder of all the things that were lost that night. A connection to that place he could hold onto, lest he ever begin to forget that such fantastic things could truly exist.

For the first time in a long time, he found himself yearning to return to those places, to seek out the answers he never found back then.

But then Brandy took the hand that was resting on her knee and guided it all the way up her thigh and under her dress, tearing his thoughts thoroughly and completely away from whatever it was he was dwelling on a moment ago.

He looked over at her, surprised. "When did you take off your panties?"

"This is my honeymoon," she replied with a mischievous little smile. "I didn't *pack* any panties."

The only word that would come to Albert's lips was a very surprised, "Oh…"

* * *

Nicole stood on the sidewalk, bidding farewell to the guests passing by. A lot of people were leaving now that the bride and groom had gone. Most of the Cross family was already climbing into their vehicles. Albert's sister was crossing the parking lot with her husband and their four-month-old daughter, Kylie. (*Such a cutie!*) Olivia's mom and sister were heading for their car, too. Wayne and Olivia wouldn't be very far behind them. They had a two-hour drive ahead of them early in the morning, after all. But plenty of guests weren't done celebrating. The parents of the bride and groom were heading toward the bar together. The Roushens and the Rudmans were both very sociable families and could always be counted on to celebrate well into the night.

And she fully intended to join them. It was a party, after all.

But as she stood there, an odd sort of sadness passed over her.

She turned and looked up the winding driveway after her friends. The happy couple was well out of sight by now. They were off on a brand-new adventure together.

Just the two of them…

Like that night six years ago…

Without her…

She blinked and turned away, frowning at herself. What a selfish thing to think. Of course they were heading off without her. It was their honeymoon. In what messed-up world would they take her with them? Talk about being a third wheel!

And yet…that invading sadness was still welling up inside her, flooding her thoughts, drowning out the happiness she'd felt throughout the day.

She wished she could be headed off like that right now, nothing but a long night of romance and lovemaking ahead of her. To be going home with someone special… Someone who loved her the way those two loved each other…

Again, her gaze drifted toward the driveway and she stood there a moment, wondering what it must feel like…

Her thoughts drifted.

It had been a long day. She was tired. She felt oddly emotional. A loneliness was descending on her, a crushing, suffocating feeling.

Then someone was there. Warm hands closed around her bare elbows. Lips brushed the back of her neck, sending a soft shiver through her body. A deep, aching longing made itself known somewhere inside her.

"Let's go home," he whispered.

"Yes," she sighed.

Then she opened her eyes and shuddered hard. She turned to face whoever was there…except there was no one. She was standing alone at the edge of the parking lot.

Her thoughts scattered and dissolved. What just happened? Was someone there? Did someone…say her name or something...?

She couldn't remember. She looked around, but no one seemed to be trying to get her attention. She was just standing there, feeling mopey...daydreaming about... She turned and looked out across the lawns, then at the winding driveway that carried Albert and Brandy away. Daydreaming about *what?* Something about having someone to take her home, she thought.

What an odd thing to be thinking about. What did she care whether she had a stupid date or not? She didn't even have time for stuff like that. She was the maid of honor. She had responsibilities. And now that the bride had left, she was free to enjoy herself to her heart's content.

She was just tired, obviously. It'd been a long day. And such a hot one, too.

She turned and started back, following the sound of the music.

That strange feeling of being left behind had faded away completely. She supposed a small part of her still kind of wished she had someone to take her home, but that wasn't so unusual, she didn't think. It was a wedding. She'd been surrounded by lovey-dovey stuff all day. The queer, crushing loneliness, however, had ebbed again.

It was a happy day. A day of celebration and merriment. A day to have some wine and dance and be with people she cared about. This was no place or time for gloom.

But in the creeping shadows of the setting sun and the swelling darkness of the approaching night, something terrible and hungry watched her.

Chapter 1

It was still hot. The sun had set more than an hour ago, but the humidity wasn't letting up in the slightest. Andrea needed a break to catch her breath. She left the dance floor and found an empty seat at the back of the tent to sit and fan herself.

Brandy wasn't kidding about her family being party animals. In spite of the heat, both the Rudmans and the Roushens were still going strong. And in striking contrast, almost all of Albert's family had already called it a night, even though it was barely half-past nine. Family holidays for those two were going to be like night and day.

She glanced around. She didn't know a lot of people here. Wayne and Olivia left half an hour ago. Her mom left not long after them, having finally decided she'd taken enough pictures. Nicole had been hanging out with Cassandra most of the evening. (They and Brandy went *way* back, apparently. Like, all the way to grade school or something.) And Stella was still out on the dance floor, flirting with every guy who caught her eye. She might have been fishing for someone to take home with her, but it was just as likely that she was hoping to start some drama with someone's jealous girlfriend. That sort of thing never failed to amuse her.

She couldn't help feeling a little pang of loneliness.

It was always like this, though. People always had a way of just sort of...well, *forgetting about her*. At least that's how it always felt.

Maybe she should go drag Stella away from her unwitting victims and go get a drink at the bar. Although, she'd have to dig out her identification. *Again*. That was kind of annoying. She was going to be twenty-three next month, after all. But no one ever believed her when she told them how old she was. She just had one of those faces, she supposed.

She sighed and stood up, only to find her path blocked by the handsome stranger in the purple shirt who bumped into her earlier that evening. "Oh!" she exclaimed, surprised.

The stranger smiled. "Hey."

"Hi. Again."

"I just wanted to apologize again for earlier. I promise I don't go around trying to knock people over."

She stared up at him. Again, she felt strangely mesmerized by those piercing gray eyes. "You're fine..." she sighed. Then she blinked and blushed a little. "I mean *I'm* fine. *It's* fine. Really. You really, like...*barely* touched me. Really." She bit her lip, embarrassed. Why was she rambling like this? And how many times was she going to say the word "really"?

He smiled again. It was a lovely smile. Charming. A movie star smile. "I've always been a little clumsy, I guess."

"Yeah... Me too." She blushed a little more. What was she even saying? Why did she feel so fluttery inside? What was it about this guy? She didn't usually have such a silly reaction to pretty faces like this. Of course, she didn't usually see eyes like those, either... They were so hauntingly beautiful...

And he was so...*muscular*... She found herself imagining him working out, sweat glistening on his bare chest, and had to force the silly image from her mind. Where was her head today? She glanced over at the dance floor, hoping that Stella didn't catch sight of her. If she saw her talking to this guy like this, she'd never let her hear the end of it.

But her gaze was drawn right back to the stranger's gorgeous eyes.

"I'm just happy I didn't hurt you," he said.

"Yeah..." She blinked hard and tore her gaze away from his handsome face. "I mean, you didn't." She glanced around at the other people under the tent, half-expecting everyone to be watching her make a fool of herself, but no one seemed to be looking their way. "Like I said, you barely touched me. Really."

"That's good. I'm so glad. I'm Elias, by the way."

"Andrea."

Again, he showed her that charming smile. "How pretty."

She felt herself blush at the compliment. "Thanks…"

What was it about this guy? She never got flustered like this. Were her cheeks really burning because he complimented her name? It wasn't like she picked it out or anything. She was kind of just handed it when she was born. But that fluttery feeling in her belly wouldn't let up.

She wasn't sure why, but she *really* wanted him to like her.

He frowned and leaned a little closer. The scent of his cologne struck her and she felt strangely weak. She stared back at him, her heart suddenly pounding. For some reason, she imagined him kissing her and the thought made her breath catch in her throat. A far hotter heat than the humid night air swept up her body.

And those piercing gray eyes seemed to peer right into her soul.

"You look a little flushed. Are you feeling okay?"

"Yeah…" she sighed. "Just…humidity…" *Like a super soaker*, she thought, Stella's words circling back to her from somewhere in the back of her mind. Then she blinked, her eyes widening. Her face flushed an even brighter shade of red. "In the air, I mean!" She pointed up at the sky. "The weather. The…you know…the *hot*." She cringed and bit her lip again. What kind of gibberish was she spewing? Stupid Stella!

But the stranger didn't laugh at her foolishness. He only glanced up at the dark sky above. "It *is* hot out here," he agreed. "It might be a bit cooler closer to the lake. Would you care to take a little walk with me? See if that helps?"

"Um…" She glanced around, still blushing, still feeling weirdly weak in the knees. All the other wedding guests were talking and dancing among themselves. No one was paying them any attention. Everyone seemed to have forgotten she was there. Like always… "Sure," she decided. "Why not?"

He smiled that intoxicating smile once again and then turned and started walking toward the shoreline.

She walked beside him, out onto the grassy lawn and into

the deeper shadows where the music began to give way to the songs of frogs and crickets. A strange sort of giddiness was swirling around inside her. What was happening here? Her heart wouldn't stop pounding. A nervous knot was tightening deep inside her belly. And was she *trembling*?

She couldn't remember the last time she felt so flustered.

Was this going to turn into a date? Was that chance encounter earlier in the night going to lead to something she'd never forget? She'd never had one of *those* kinds of encounters. She'd had a few boyfriends here and there, but never anything serious. Most boys didn't interest her very much. They were never very fun. They never turned out to be interesting at all. They only ever seemed to have one thing on their minds.

The only guys she ever really found interesting enough to hold her attention were Albert and Wayne. They were the coolest guys she'd ever known. But that was probably only because she was there in the temple with them that night. Once you've seen someone face down true horrors to protect you, it was kind of hard not to put them on a pedestal.

But there was something *very* interesting about this guy. He was charming in a way she didn't see very often. He was *endearing*. The way he kept fussing over her even though he'd only barely brushed up against her. The polite way he spoke.

They walked to the water's edge and stopped. The surface of the lake was still. The chirping of the frogs and insects was much louder here. It nearly drowned out the music.

"It's better out here," decided Elias. "Out from under those lights." He looked up at the sky above. "They were washing out the stars."

Andrea glanced up to see that he was right. The dingy darkness had become a sea of starlight, accented by the fairylike glow of fireflies all around them.

"I've always liked looking up at the stars. They're so beautiful, don't you think?"

"Yeah. They are."

He turned and started walking along the shoreline, still gazing upward. "Have you ever stopped and taken the time to contemplate the sheer depth of the night sky? I mean *really* contemplate it?"

"Yeah…" she sighed. Then she frowned. "I mean…maybe? I'm…not sure…"

He chuckled and the sound gave her another of those nervous flutters inside.

At least he didn't seem to think she was a total idiot. Or maybe he did and he just found her amusing. Either way was good, she decided.

"It's unfathomable," he went on, his gaze still turned toward the heavens. "Everything humanity truly knows anything about lies here on the surface of this one planet. Our whole existence is nothing more than a speck of dust in an endless expanse of lonely darkness."

"Wow…" Slowly, she lowered her gaze and met those mesmerizing gray eyes.

"This whole world…everyone who's ever lived and died in it…and it's all just the pitiful light of a single candle flickering in the cold vastness of a deep, dark forest."

That was an odd metaphor. Not for the first time tonight, her thoughts drifted back to the temple and the endless black forest that surrounded it.

The thought gave her a slight shiver in spite of the heat.

"It's better over here by the water, isn't it? Cooler?"

"Yeah…"

"Do you feel a little better?"

She looked up at him, distracted. "Huh? Oh… Yes. I do."

"That's good."

She looked out over the lake, then turned and looked back toward the tent. They were getting farther from the light. Stars or no stars, she shouldn't wander too far away. She still didn't know anything about this guy.

But then he touched her arm and her heart leaped in her chest.

"Careful."

She looked down at his arm, surprised.

He bent forward a bit, peering down at the shadowy

ground. "No. My mistake. I thought you were about to step in a hole, but it was just a shadow. Sorry about that."

"It's fine," she said as he withdrew his hand. The warmth of his touch lingered there and she found herself clinging to it, willing it to not fade away.

She felt a little lightheaded. How many drinks did she have? She couldn't quite remember. But she didn't think it was that many. Having to dig out her ID every time was too annoying.

"It's a little too dark out here," he realized. "I didn't mean to take us so far away. Let's walk back toward the light."

She nodded. "Good idea..." But weirdly, a part of her wanted to stay out here in the dark with him. She didn't know a thing about him yet, but she was very interested in learning.

Somewhere in the back of her mind, she could almost hear Stella urging her on.

"As much as I like looking at the stars," he said as they started back toward the sound of the music, "I think I'd like to see *you* a little better." Then he reached up and rubbed awkwardly at the back of his neck, looking embarrassed. The innocence of the gesture sent another of those fluttery sensations rushing through her. The strongest one yet. "I don't mean to be forward, but if I'm being honest, I think you're absolutely enchanting."

"Oh..." she gasped, a wave of vertigo passing through her. "Okay..." was all she could think to say.

He cleared his throat and turned away. Was he *blushing*? "Sorry. That probably sounded corny as hell, didn't it?"

"No... It's... It's okay..." She was clutching at the fabric of her bridesmaid dress. Her body felt so hot. Her heart was *pounding*. She realized she was breathing hard and tried to force herself to calm down before he heard her. How much was she blushing? Suddenly, she didn't want to go back toward the party with all those lights, where everyone could see her acting like such a fool.

In fact, she wanted to turn around and keep walking the other way with him. Maybe even find a nice, private spot way out on the quiet greens...under all those stars...

What was happening? This felt like a dream.

She couldn't remember ever wanting someone so badly. He

was *perfect*.

He stopped walking and turned to face her. Those incredible eyes fixed on hers, freezing her in place. "Would you happen to be free for lunch tomorrow?"

She couldn't tear her gaze away from those eyes. "Uh huh," she replied, breathless.

He smiled that charming smile. "Awesome. Maybe for now we could go get a drink? Sit and get to know each other a little?"

She nodded.

Then he leaned closer to her, the scent of his cologne washing over her again, making her knees tremble beneath her. "Or...if you'd rather...we could sneak away from here right now."

Slowly, she nodded again. "Sure..."

That charming smile spread into something a little less charming, but she didn't really mind. That wasn't important.

"*My place* is quiet," he added. "We could spend *all night* getting to know each other *very* well."

Alarm bells were going off somewhere inside her head, but she ignored them. She was too busy taking in those gorgeous eyes.

"Does that sound like fun?"

"Uh huh..."

His smile wasn't charming at all, really. In fact, it was sort of slimy. Less a smile than a leer. But he was so *pretty*... And she *really* wanted to get to know him like that.

Her heart was thundering. She was practically *panting*. She was sure she must look like a total freak, but she didn't care. She *wanted* him!

Do it! she heard Stella whisper inside her head. *Do him!*

"Great," he sneered. "We'll do that. We'll have so much fun together." He reached out and touched her cheek. The sensation was intoxicating. She felt herself sway at the feel of his fingers against her skin. "But first, I wonder if you'll do a little something for me."

"Okay..."

"A package was delivered to you at some point in the past

few days."

"Package…" she agreed, nodding.

"It's a very important package."

"Important…" She wished he'd get on with it. She didn't care about any package. She wished he'd just shut up and take her somewhere and kiss her and undress her and do all the things that were racing through her mind right now with her.

"I really need that package," he told her.

"Okay…" she breathed. God, she was hot. Her body was burning up. She could feel herself sweating.

"Take me to the package."

She blinked up at him, confused. "Huh?"

"The package," he said again, the no-longer-charming smile vanishing from his face. "Take me to where it is."

"What package?" She glanced around, her thoughts breaking apart like clouds after a summer storm, and grimaced at a dull pain in her head. "Wait…" What was happening? A wild panic was slowly welling up inside her. What was she doing out here? Why would she venture so far from the safety of the lights with this man she knew nothing about?

The stranger withdrew his hand and straightened up. "You haven't got it yet," he realized. Then, to himself, he grumbled, "Damn. That would've made things so much easier."

She backed away from him as the strange conversation played over in her mind with fresh awareness. Did she really just stand there and agree to let this creep take her home? What was wrong with her?

She took another step back and stumbled as her heel sank in the mud at the water's edge.

There was nowhere left to go in that direction except out into the water.

"What did you do to me?" she gasped.

"Just some basic psychic manipulation," he replied as if that were the sort of thing one did every day. He didn't even look at her as he spoke. He was thinking to himself, pondering what to do now that she didn't have what he wanted. "Nothing permanent."

Psychic manipulation? Like the kind of psychic that Albert, Brandy and Olivia were supposed to be? "What do you want?"

"Obviously, I'm looking for a package," replied Elias. "That *is* what I asked you to take me to."

"I don't know anything about any package!"

"Clearly. If you *had* known about it, asking you to take me to it wouldn't have broken the psychic bond I placed on you."

She made her way out of the mud, circling around him, not daring to take her eyes off him.

Was it because she was thinking clearly again that he didn't look nearly as attractive as she thought he did a moment ago? Or was it just because he was apparently the kind of sicko that could manipulate girls' minds to make them agree to go home with him any time he wanted?

"What are you going to do to me?" she demanded.

"Nothing," he replied. "You don't have what I want. So I guess we're done here."

She glanced over at the clubhouse. They were still pretty far from the tent and the music was fairly loud. She wasn't sure anyone would hear her if she cried out for help. There was no way he was just going to let her walk away now that she knew what he was capable of. She needed to be running in that direction. But she was fumbling to get out of the mud without losing her shoes.

Was this his doing, too? Did he put the suggestion in her mind to get herself stuck in the mud? Was he planning to attack her before anyone could realize she was in danger?

But Elias—if that was even his real name—didn't try to stop her. He stood there, watching her as she stumbled back onto dry land and then hurried off toward the party.

What was going on? Who was that guy? How did he hypnotize her like that? And what was the package he was asking about?

She looked back over her shoulder as she crossed the lawn. She expected the man in the purple shirt to be following her. Or else that he would have vanished into the darkness surrounding the lake. But he was still standing right where she left him, still watching her.

Should she tell someone about him? What would she even say? What really happened out there? He never actually did anything to her, technically. He didn't hurt her. He didn't even try to kiss her. She had no proof that he meant her any harm. And she doubted very much that anyone would believe her if she said he was trying to jedi-mind-trick her into going home with him.

Except maybe for someone else who knew that psychic powers were real...

Maybe it had something to do with Albert, Brandy and Olivia and *their* psychic powers. And if it had something to do with *them*, she suddenly realized, then it might have something to do with the mysterious temple where they first learned they possessed those powers...

This whole world... she thought, remembering the strange words he said to her by the lake, ...*everyone who's ever lived and died in it...and it's all just the pitiful light of a single candle flickering in the cold vastness of a deep, dark forest.* Was that a coincidence? Or was he actually talking about the Wood? That literal vast forest that surrounded the entire world?

But Albert and Brandy had already left. As had Wayne and Olivia. The only one of them still here was Nicole.

Maybe *she'd* know what to do.

Except when she went to find her, Nicole was nowhere to be found.

Chapter 2

No one knew where Nicole was.

No one saw her leave. No one said goodbye to her. She was just gone. And when Andrea finally checked the parking lot, her little white Camry was gone, too.

She'd already left...

Andrea suddenly felt very alone and very afraid.

Did that Elias creep do something to her? Did he hurt her?

No... That wouldn't explain why her car was gone.

Or would it? He had some sort of freaky *hypnosis* power. He made her stand there like a lovesick puppy and stare at him while he made her agree to let him take her home, probably to do unspeakable things to her. Maybe he puppeted Nicole into leaving the party and driving away. With powers like that, he could have sent her off programmed to veer into the path of a truck or drive into the river. Or worse, he could've sent her somewhere where no one could find her, somewhere he could have her all to himself later...

She shuddered at the awful thought and called Nicole's cell phone, but like the last two times she tried, it went straight to voicemail. Either it was turned off or she didn't have it. Either way, it provided no peace of mind.

She tucked her phone back into her bra and forced herself to take a deep breath. She needed to look at this logically. If Nicole and her car were both missing, then she wasn't still here at the country club. She'd left. The first thing she should do was get in her own vehicle and leave. She needed to be as far from the creep in the purple shirt as possible.

He never tried to pursue her after she left him by the lake, but by the time she reached the safety of the crowd, he'd disappeared into the surrounding darkness. She hoped he'd fled the scene, but she couldn't be certain that he wasn't still around somewhere, watching her from the shadows like the creep he was.

First, she'd drive home to see if Nicole was there. Maybe the heat got to her and she wasn't feeling well. Or perhaps she'd merely needed something from their apartment. A change of shoes, perhaps. (She could use a change of shoes herself. Hers were now covered in mud. Plus they weren't exactly made for running from super-powered perverts in purple shirts.)

But the fact that no one seemed to know where she'd gone bothered her. Why would she just leave without telling someone? Shouldn't she have said something to *someone*? That just didn't seem like her…

Her red Ford Escape was parked farther down the sidewalk from where Nicole's Camry had been parked. She plucked her keys from her clutch and unlocked the doors as she hurried toward it, frustrated. She *needed* Nicole. Whether this had anything to do with the temple or not, she was clearly dealing with something supernatural. Ordinary men in purple shirts didn't generally possess powers of hypnosis or go around asking about mysterious packages. (Neither did ordinary men in other colors of shirts, as far as she knew.) Whatever was going on, she wasn't confident that she was brave enough to handle it on her own.

A stray cat darted out from under a car, startling a terrified squeal from her. She stopped and tried to get control of herself, but her heart was racing. She hadn't been this frightened since that night in the temple.

She should've grabbed Stella off the dance floor and dragged her along. Then at least she wouldn't be alone right now. But Stella wasn't the most dependable of people. She was usually too much into her own shenanigans to be of much help. And she absolutely wasn't going back there to look for her. She just wanted to leave. The faster she drove away the better. But when she opened the Escape's door, she froze.

There, lying in the driver's seat, impossible to miss, was an object wrapped in a dark-red cloth and tied with a length of fat, dingy rope.

A package was delivered to you at some point in the past few days, she thought, remembering the words the purple-clad creep spoke to her while she was under his strange spell. *It's a very important package.*

But it wasn't the package that sent her heart pounding as much as where it was sitting.

Six years ago, a whole year before she and the others became ensnared in that strange adventure deep in those scary tunnels, someone left a mysterious box and its key for Albert and Brandy to find.

Those objects were left in the driver's seats of their locked cars...just like this one.

She felt numb. It had already crossed her mind that perhaps there was some connection to the Temple of the Blind, but this wasn't just a fleeting similarity. This felt like a whole new beginning.

A feeling of absolute *terror* began to fill her as she stared at the mysterious bundle of cloth lying there in her seat. A part of her didn't want to touch it. She just wanted to slam the door shut and run away.

But there was another part of her as well, a foolish part of her, perhaps even a morbidly curious part of her, that kept her grounded to that spot.

It didn't make sense. The box was a sort of invitation to the Temple of the Blind. It was the map that led them to the Sentinel Queen. But the Temple of the Blind was gone, collapsed into rubble. And the Sentinel Queen was dead.

To her own surprise, she found herself reaching out and picking up the object.

It was heavier than she expected. There was something solid inside it. And the cloth felt very thick and velvety. Something about it gave her a shiver all the way down her body in spite of the humid night air.

Someone grabbed her arm and yanked her backward, wrenching a startled scream from her.

"I'll take that," said the man in the purple shirt as he

snatched the object from her hand and shoved her against the side of the vehicle.

Her clutch and keys dropped to the ground at her feet as she stared up at him, her blue eyes wide with terror.

That was dumb! She'd stopped paying attention. She'd let the surprise of finding the package distract her and he'd walked right up behind her while she stood there gawking at it. She knew he was looking for a package and now she'd led him right to it.

Was that his intention all along?

Elias—*if* that was even his real name—held the object up and looked it over. "That's the one," he said. "I knew it was here somewhere."

"I'll scream," she threatened.

He turned those gray eyes on her. "Go ahead," he told her.

She sucked in a breath, but before she could make a sound, he let go of her arm and seized her by her throat. With a terrible strength, he squeezed, cutting off her breath.

"Anun amum ut mu…" he said, practically spitting the strange words into her face. "Anun Goar Nangup."

She grasped at his wrist, trying to pry his hand away, but he was far stronger than her. It wouldn't budge.

Her chest aching, her eyes bulging, her pretty face turning purple, she struggled to fight him. She clawed at his arm. She kicked at his legs. But if he felt any pain, his face didn't show it. He stared down at her with those awful gray eyes as the world swam before her.

"You should be honored," he informed her. "Your death will be the catalyst that allows *Him* to finally return."

How could she ever think those eyes were beautiful? They were like the rotten eyes of a festering corpse. And this man was an absolute *monster*.

"For the *Patient One*," he told her. "He Who Waits in the depths of the void beyond all that is."

She was still trying to pry open his hand, but her own hands were trembling. Her chest ached. Her head was pounding. She let go of his arm with one hand and groped for her phone still tucked in her bra where she'd been keeping it all day, within easy reach for any pictures she might want to take. If she could manage to get it out while those awful eyes were focused so intensely on her face, maybe she could call for help.

Except, there was no way help would arrive in time. Already, darkness was closing in around her like a great, cold iris, enveloping her.

She was going to die.

And there was nothing she could do about it.

But then there was a resounding thump and the man in the purple shirt abruptly let go and dropped to the ground.

She fell to her knees, gasping and coughing.

"Are you okay?" asked a small, unassuming-looking woman dressed in a simple blue blouse, black skirt and sandals, looking more ready for an office party than a wedding reception. She was a few years older than her, about Wayne's age, she thought, with long, dark brown hair and sleepy eyes. She was clutching the handle of a golf club in her dainty hands.

Was she okay? She didn't *feel* okay. Her throat hurt. Her head and chest were still aching. Her body was shaking and there were tears streaming down her face.

That was terrifying. Just who the hell *was* that guy? What was that nonsense he was spouting about patient ones and voids and…whatever else that was? She was fairly sure some of it wasn't even in English.

"That was too close," said the woman, though her voice didn't quite match the statement. She had a very soft and timid voice that made her sound almost *bored*. She tossed away the golf club she'd used to bludgeon the would-be murderer from behind and then picked up the package and pressed it against Andrea's chest. "Hold onto this. Don't let go of it."

Andrea blinked through the tears and looked down at the velvet bundle, her mind swimming. Everything was happening so fast.

This woman… She'd seen her before. Several times throughout the night she'd glimpsed her. She was always standing off by herself, looking a little out of place. Their eyes had even met several times.

The woman gathered up her clutch and keys and handed them to her, too. Then she took her by her arms and helped her to her feet. "We have to go," she said, closing the SUV's open door. "We'll take my car."

Still coughing, still struggling to comprehend how her world had gone so utterly crazy, she let the woman lead her across the parking lot and into the passenger seat of a silver Honda Civic with Wisconsin plates.

"We don't want to be here when that guy wakes up," said the woman as she slid into the driver's seat and started the engine.

"Who was he?" coughed Andrea.

"I don't know, but his entire body was saturated in a *very* unpleasant energy. He barely felt human. And he had incredibly dangerous psychic powers."

"You could tell all that?"

"I could." She pulled out of the parking lot and sped off toward the highway beyond. "I have certain...*abilities*," she replied. "I know things. Like how we really don't want him getting his hands on that."

Andrea looked down at the package, barely realizing that she was still clutching it to her chest. "What is it?"

"Something very important," replied the woman in her sleepy voice. She sounded as if she weren't used to being up so late. "Something you're going to need."

"For *what*?"

"I don't have all the details. But five years ago, you played an important role in opening a vital doorway. Now it's time to finish what you started."

Andrea stared at the woman, her thoughts racing, a sick, burning sensation blossoming deep in her belly. Five years ago? As in five years ago when they went down into the depths of the temple? But nobody knew about five years ago except the six of them who went down there and returned. They'd all vowed never to speak of those events with anyone else. And not just because the whole thing sounded insane. People had died in those places. There were bodies. The legal ramifications alone of letting those secrets slip were unthinkable. But even worse was the danger. The temple might be gone, but if anyone else ever attempted to enter Gilbert House...

And yet, hadn't she just been thinking about how the appearance of this strange, cloth-wrapped object was just like the appearance of Albert's box and Brandy's key six years ago?

She glanced around at the Civic's interior. It was dawning on her now that she knew nothing about this woman. She'd saved her from the creep in the purple shirt, but that didn't necessarily mean she could be trusted. She *looked* harmless enough, but looks could be deceiving. For all she knew, she could be a whole different kind of crazy. "Who are you?" she asked.

"I'm Gina Sarrelli," replied the woman. "A goddess sent me. I'm here to help."

Andrea stared at her for a moment, bemused. "Oh..." she said at last when nothing else came to mind. "Okay..."

Chapter 3

Nicole stepped into her empty apartment, hung her purse on the hook next to the door and turned on the lights.

The clock on the wall revealed that it was barely past ten o'clock.

Across town, the party was still going on, the music was still playing, everyone was still having a good time, but she wasn't there. She was here. All alone.

She wasn't sure what happened. One minute she was dancing and having a fantastic time, the next, she was suddenly and inexplicably overcome with an overwhelming feeling of crushing depression.

She didn't even tell anyone she was leaving. She just collected her purse, walked to her car and drove home.

And now that she was here, she couldn't quite understand why she felt the need to do that.

It seemed perfectly silly now. It wasn't as if she wouldn't be missed. She should turn around and go back before people started spreading rumors that she got drunk and left with one of the groom's cousins or something...

Yet she merely pushed the door closed behind her and locked the deadbolt.

She felt so tired. Her eyes were droopy. Her feet hurt. Her back was aching. Even her stomach felt sour. And on top of it all, that strange sadness just wouldn't let her go.

Maybe the heat had made her sick.

She sighed and took off her shoes.

Around her, the apartment walls were practically papered with photographs. They were taped, pinned or poster-puttied to almost every vertical surface in every room, including the refrigerator and kitchen cabinets. Even the lampshades were glowing collages of smiling, laughing faces. They also covered most of the ceiling in her bedroom, where she could look upon them even while lying in bed. Everywhere she went, she was literally surrounded by precious memories of her and Andrea's friends and family.

She paused and stared at one of her favorites. In it, she was sitting on the couch with Albert and Brandy. He was in the middle and the two of them were scrunched up on either side of him, their cheeks pressed against his, smiling for the phone's selfie camera. It was difficult to tell whether he was more uncomfortable or delighted by the attention.

She smiled a little at the memory, but she couldn't seem to lift her heart out of the gloom she felt swelling inside her.

This was stupid. What was wrong with her brain tonight? She was perfectly fine all day long. It wasn't as if she were jealous of her best friend.

…was she?

She frowned. No. That was ridiculous. Sure, *sometimes*, when she was feeling a little down, she wished she had what Brandy had. She and Albert shared something special. Anyone could see that. Of course she wanted an Albert of her own. Anyone would. But that didn't mean she wanted *Brandy's* Albert. Those two belonged together.

She stared at his face in the photograph. That sort of goofy, awkward half-smile of his…

He *was* a really great boyfriend. She was beyond happy that Brandy found someone like him. In fact, she always found herself comparing the guys she met to him, as if he were the gold standard in boyfriend material. After all, how many men could climb to the top of a burning mountain with a broken arm? Or navigate an ancient labyrinth full of monsters with only a box full of junk as a map? Or open his eyes in a chamber of unimaginable horrors and face unfathomable terrors, risking his very *sanity* to save a woman he barely knew?

And there it was, that glorious image of Albert stepping from the mouth of the fear room, cradling Brandy in his arms like a princess. How many times had Brandy told the story? How many times had she watched her best friend's eyes soften as she remembered gazing up at him, knowing what he'd done for her, that he'd risked not just his life, but *endless madness* to save her?

But that was a little different... It was kind of dumb, but she'd always had a soft spot for the old cliché of being princess carried out of danger by the big strong hero.

There was just something so perfectly romantic about the story. So...she supposed that...*perhaps*...she *had* always felt a *little* envious of her... Just for that one little fairytale moment. It was a closely guarded secret that sometimes, when she was feeling particularly lonely, she liked to imagine what it would've been like if she'd been there instead of Brandy, if it had been *her* that he carried in his arms from the literal mouth of madness. Just to make herself feel a little of that warm tingly feeling inside.

She pushed these thoughts from her mind and turned away from the photograph. That was different. Everyone had little turn-ons like that. She also kind of had a thing for firemen, but that didn't mean she was hot for Andrea's dad.

She rubbed her eyes, weary, and then looked down at the heels she was still holding. Again, she wondered what she was doing? What was wrong with her head tonight? She should put these back on and go back to the party. Dance some more. Have some fun.

Maybe lay off the wine for the rest of the night...

Tomorrow she'd feel better and this whole thing would probably seem funny.

But her gaze drifted to a photograph of Wayne and Olivia.

Wayne was pretty awesome, too. Wayne, who once stood and waited until something unthinkable speared him right through his guts while everyone else scurried to safety ahead of him. Wayne, who walked a haunted tunnel and battled a horde of walking, clawing, snapping corpses with his bare fists to rescue sweet Olivia from an unspeakable forest.

Before she went down into those tunnels, she had a bad habit of latching onto the wrong kind of guy. It was a defense mechanism of sorts. She couldn't seem to find the kind of boyfriend she wanted, but she didn't want to be alone, so she made do with the kinds of guys she knew she wouldn't get too attached to. It wasn't very healthy behavior, to say the least.

That was because of Josh. He was her first love. Her high school sweetheart... But she was young and stupid back then. In her regretful naivety, she thought she needed to spread her wings, to see what else was waiting for her out there in the big, wide world, and she made the mistake of letting him go. Now he was married to someone else and was never going to be hers again.

It wasn't that she couldn't find the kind of boyfriend she wanted. It was that they were never *him*.

After that night in the tunnels, however, she stopped that toxic behavior. She just couldn't seem to look at those kinds of boys and see anything worth wasting her time with. Not after she knew that there were men like Albert and Wayne out there. Men who had literally protected her with their lives. Those other guys didn't even come close to measuring up. And that was good.

The problem was that *no one* ever measured up after that. There was something wrong with every guy she met. They were *never* good enough.

The closest she came was Keith Dorray. She met him at a party and really thought she'd found the one. He was funny and smart and attractive. And he was a very nice guy. Ironically, however, he was *too* nice. It was cute the way he always wanted to open doors for her and pay for things. Very chivalrous. But he was always draping his jacket over her shoulders when it was the slightest bit chilly out and insisting on covering her whenever it was raining. He wouldn't let her carry anything. He was always taking her hand when she walked up and down stairs. He was borderline *controlling*. She'd survived Gilbert House, the Wood and the Temple of the Blind. She could open her own damn beer! They dated for less than a year before she broke up with him and she hadn't been with anyone since. That was seven months ago. She was starting to think she wasn't meant to find someone.

There just wasn't anyone else like *them*, after all. Albert and

Wayne were the only two men who'd ever faced true monsters for her, and both of them belonged to someone else, someone luckier than her.

And then they all lived happily ever after.

Without her.

She sighed. It was just her luck, after all. The knights in shining armor rode away with their chosen princesses and left her standing there like an ugly stepsister.

She squeezed her eyes shut again. She was really tired. The long day and the heat had gotten to her.

She dropped her shoes in front of the closet. Forget the party. She unzipped her dress and made her way down the hallway toward her bedroom.

Memories followed her on the walls.

She wanted to take a shower, but the closer she came to her bedroom the more she just wanted to throw herself onto the bed and sleep.

She paused at a picture of all six of them, everyone who ventured into the tunnels that night and were fortunate enough to return. She reached up and touched the picture, letting her fingertips slide across the familiar faces.

There was Olivia, nuzzled up against Wayne, clinging to him…

There was Albert with his arm draped around Brandy…

She closed her eyes and sighed. A strange, aching yearning was slowly building inside her. She couldn't remember ever *wanting* something so badly…

Warm hands closed around her waist. Lips brushed the back of her neck.

She opened her eyes and shivered.

The air conditioning felt cold after spending so much time in the sweltering heat and sun. She hoped she didn't end up getting sick.

She looked back over her shoulder at the empty apartment. What was she thinking about just now? A fleeting memory danced through her brain and then vanished completely.

Nothing… Only a weary and strangely sad mind imagining

things…

Again, she fixed her gaze on the picture. Again, that loneliness came flooding back. It was funny how Albert happened to be leaning closer to her in that picture than to Brandy, almost as if…

She let out a wistful sigh and leaned a little closer.

His hand was even resting on her upper thigh. She didn't remember that… Or did she…? Now that she was thinking about it, she could almost recall the way it felt.

It was nice…

Arms reached around her, embracing her. Soft kisses blossomed on her cheek. Warm breath danced across her neck. Gentle teeth tugged softly on her earlobe.

One hand closed around one of her breasts.

She let out a soft gasp and blinked.

What happened? Did she almost doze off there? Was she that tired?

She was daydreaming about something and then… What was it she was thinking about?

She looked back at the picture. At Albert sitting there with one hand casually resting on her thigh and his other arm draped around her. Her head was resting against his shoulder.

She looked so happy…

Her gaze drifted downward to another photograph. Albert and her…just the two of them…their cheeks pressed together. That was from the little Christmas party they had last year. She was wearing a Santa hat. She was clinging to him, hugging him.

He had some of her lipstick on the corner of his mouth…

Something tickled the back of her mind for just a moment, something with a strange, frightened sort of edge to it…then was gone, as if snatched away by some invisible hand.

Her gaze swept across the wall, from one photo to the next. Her and Albert, together…over and over again…

A smile tugged at her lips as she remembered all the amazing times they shared together. What a much more pleasant feeling than that weird sadness she came home with…

She reached out and ran her fingertips over a picture of the two of them kissing.

New Years Eve, two years ago…

She closed her eyes, savoring the memory, and then turned and stepped through her bedroom doorway.

As soon as she was across the threshold, a sudden dizziness overcame her. She reached out, grasping for something to steady herself, but there was nothing there.

She started to fall.

A sharp panic shot through her.

But then he was there. Her hero. Strong arms enveloped her. She felt herself lifted and then held. Warm skin pressed against her.

She pulled him closer.

Then he was kissing her.

She felt her bridesmaid dress fall to the floor. The air conditioning was cool on her exposed skin.

A hand closed around her bare breast.

Wait…

She stood there a moment, blinking down at her discarded dress. Something was wrong. None of this was as it should be. An icy fear began to overtake her.

But then he was kissing her again and she couldn't remember how she could possibly think that all wasn't right with the world.

She let him push her back onto the bed.

He was on top of her, his body pressed against hers.

She welcomed his kisses.

She gasped when he stripped away her panties.

His body felt so good against hers. She wanted him so much. A moan escaped her lips as his hands caressed her skin.

Vaguely, somewhere in the distance, she heard a voice call out her name, but that wasn't important. Nothing was worth tearing herself away from this.

Albert kissed her again and she felt the world melt away around her.

That distant voice called out her name again, but again she ignored it.

She looked down at him as he lowered himself onto her and kissed her heaving breast. For the most fleeting of moments, she found herself thinking that there was something dreadfully wrong about his mouth…

But that didn't matter. Not now. Not in this perfect moment.

Nothing mattered.

Chapter 4

Andrea unlocked the door and burst into the apartment. "Nikki?"

Nicole wasn't in the living room or kitchen, but her car was parked outside and her shoes were on the floor where she always left them, strongly suggesting that she *should* be here.

She dropped the mysterious bundle and her clutch on the table and hurried down the hallway. "Nikki? Where are you?"

Nicole's bedroom door was standing open. Her bridesmaid dress was lying in a heap on the floor. But Nicole, herself, was nowhere to be seen.

"Nobody's home," said Gina. She was looking around at all the photographs, her sleepy eyes taking in the many smiling faces.

"I guess not..." she replied, confused. The bathroom door stood open and the light was off, but she stepped inside and checked behind the shower curtain anyway, as if perhaps she might have decided for some strange reason to sleep in the tub for the night.

She paused in the bathroom doorway for a moment, rubbing at her bruised throat, her thoughts racing. Where could she be? That was definitely her car outside. Sometimes she went out jogging, but it was far too late for that, even if it *were* even remotely likely that anyone in their right mind would want to go for a run after such a long and exhausting day. Her gaze was drawn back to the empty bedroom, the discarded bridesmaid dress, the disheveled bedspread.

Something wasn't right...

Gina stepped into the middle of the room, her drowsy gaze washing over every surface.

Andrea plucked her cell phone from her bra as she made her way back through the hallway to the living room. She needed to settle down. There was probably a logical explanation. Maybe Nicole met a guy at the party. Maybe she drove back here, changed and left with him in his car.

She was a grown woman. She could do things like that if she wanted.

She tried calling Nicole's cell phone number again, but again it went straight to voicemail. "Where the hell are you?" she muttered. Then she caught sight of Nicole's purse hanging by the door. She hurried over to it and peered inside. Her keys and wallet were still there. And so was her phone. That uneasy feeling in her belly swelled. "I don't think this is right…"

"It's not," said Gina, still looking around. "Something's happened."

"That creep in the parking lot…" He must've gotten to her somehow.

But Gina shook her head. "No. Not him. This is something different." She turned and met her gaze. "This place might not be safe. We should leave."

"What? *No.*" She glanced around the room again, panic welling up inside her. "I'm not going anywhere. What do you mean 'something's happened'? You mean to Nikki?"

"I don't know the details. Sorry. I only know that there's something wrong with the surrounding space here. It's been disturbed somehow. We should go."

But Andrea shook her head. "No…" She tucked her phone back into her dress and fled down the hallway again. "*Nikki?*"

"She's not here," insisted the woman. "I'd know if she was."

Andrea didn't listen to her. She checked her own bedroom. She checked the closets. She even threw back the curtains and pressed her nose to the windowpanes, half-expecting to see her wandering around in the dark out there.

There was no sign of a struggle. There was only the usual amount of untidiness. There weren't any broken windows or locks. She saw no sign of blood. The only thing out of place was the bridesmaid dress on the floor.

Unsure what else to do, she picked up the dress and turned it in her hands. The smell of Nicole's perfume wafted up from it. It wasn't torn or scuffed. Was it her imagination, or was the fabric still warm?

She didn't like this. Why was this happening? First that creep attacked her. Then this woman turned up out of the blue. And now Nicole was missing?

She tossed the dress onto the bed and buried her face in her hands, frustrated.

How did things get so wrong? It was such a *happy* day. The girls all looked so beautiful. The boys were so handsome dressed up. People were smiling and laughing. The sun was shining so brightly. Then Brandy and Albert drove away and night fell and the music blared and everyone was having so much fun on the dance floor. And for just a moment she thought she'd even met a really nice guy.

Why was this happening?

Again, she withdrew her phone. She'd call Wayne. He'd know what to do. She didn't *want* to bother him. He and Olivia had a long drive early tomorrow. She remembered hearing him complain about it. They were probably already asleep for the night. But this was an emergency. The kind of emergency that warranted waking someone up even though they had to get up early the next morning. There was a stranger here talking about the things that happened five years ago. And Nicole might be missing! Wayne would be mad at her if she *didn't* call him under these circumstances.

But Wayne's cell phone went straight to voicemail, too.

And so did Olivia's.

They'd either forgotten to unsilence them following the wedding or, more likely, they intentionally left them off to ensure a good night's sleep.

She didn't bother leaving messages.

She growled, frustrated. This wasn't fair.

"The goddess only sent me to find *you*," said Gina. "No one else is involved."

"I'm not leaving until I find Nikki!"

"I'm sorry," said Gina. "I know you're upset and that's understandable, but she's not here. I told you, I'd know if anyone was here. I'd feel them."

But Andrea shook her head. She couldn't just leave without knowing what happened to Nicole. This woman was a stranger. She could be lying about everything. She never should've let her drive her home.

"What we should be focusing on is that." She pointed at the wrapped object lying on the table.

Andrea turned her gaze to the mysterious package the guy in the purple shirt wanted so badly. She still hadn't opened it. She still wasn't sure she wanted to.

"It's probably not a coincidence that your friend went missing the same day that arrived. It might answer some questions."

Andrea stared at the dark red velvet and the dingy rope knotted around it. She *did* want to know what was inside. Somebody left that in the driver's seat of her car, just like someone left the box for Albert six years ago, even though she *always* locked her doors (just like Dad always drilled into her head). But she was also scared. What if this *was* another Temple of the Blind? What if it sent her back to Gilbert House? Without Nicole? Without Brandy or Albert? Without Olivia or Wayne? All alone, with just this woman she knew nothing about?

But then again, she didn't know any of *them* back then, either...

"The goddess sent me here to find you," said Gina. "She said you were in danger and would need my help. I know you don't trust me yet, but I'm here to keep you safe. That wedding was crawling with people who weren't what they seemed to be."

She blinked at her, surprised. "You mean more than just that creep in the purple shirt?"

"A *lot* more than just him. I don't know what's going on, exactly, but something's definitely happening. And if the goddess is involved, I'm guessing it's something much bigger than just the two of us. And it's going to start with that." Again, she pointed at the red bundle on the table.

Andrea didn't like this. Not one bit. She wished someone else were here. What if she screwed this up? She stepped over to the table and looked down at it. It felt so surreal, standing there in her pretty bridesmaid dress, her hair still all pinned up, staring at a mysterious package and wondering what horrors could be hidden inside.

What if it truly *was* something horrible? What if she opened it to find a bloodstained knife? Or a *severed head?*

Okay, it was much too small to be a severed head... But still!

She took a deep breath and let it out in a resigned sigh. Then she reached out and untied the rope. "Just remember if we end up naked in a sewer somewhere that this is all your fault."

Gina frowned, confused. "Um... Fair enough?"

As she unfolded the cloth, something gold glinted in the overhead lights. Some kind of jewelry? She recalled a golden necklace that Nicole took from around the neck of a one-armed skeleton on their journey to the top of the burning mountain. But as she unwrapped it, she found herself holding not a piece of jewelry, but some kind of *weapon*. "A dagger?" she pondered. "No... More like an arrowhead?" No, it was too big for that...

"A spearhead, maybe," suggested Gina as she watched her lift it from the cloth.

"I don't know. Looks like *some* kind of stabby thing." It was about ten inches long, triangular, with a short, blunt handle, too narrow and too pointy to be any kind of paddle or fan. There were strange little squares and triangles etched into its shiny surface, with odd little lines weaving through them. And there were more intricate markings that looked like symbols of some sort. Some were simple, little more than just various arrangements of overlapping lines and squiggles. Others looked more like pictographs. There was one that sort of looked like a bird, she thought. Another might have been a fish... "It's not very sharp," she observed, running her thumb along the blade. In fact, it looked as if it had been handled quite roughly. The edges were chipped away in places.

"Gold isn't a very strong metal," said Gina. "It doesn't

make good tools or weapons. If that's what it's made of, then it's probably ceremonial or symbolic."

Andrea turned it over in her hands, then lifted it closer to her face, squinting at the carvings on it. "Something's written here... It says, 'Pierce the gatekeeper's heart to open the way.'" She looked over at Gina, her brow creased. "I am *not* killing anyone."

But Gina shook her head. "I doubt you'll have to. It's probably a riddle of some sort."

"If it's riddle solving your goddess wants, then she should've given this to Albert. I'm no good at this stuff."

Gina tipped her head slightly to one side. "Who?"

"He's...uh..." She shook her head. "Never mind."

"There's a reason she chose you, I'm sure."

Again, she turned the blade over. "There's nothing else on here I can read. It's just that bit about stabbing someone in the heart. That doesn't exactly tell me what I'm supposed to do next."

Gina scrunched up her sleepy face and thought about it. "There should be something," she reasoned.

"Your goddess didn't tell you what we're supposed to do next?"

"No. Only the address of the country club and today's date. I don't..." She trailed off, as if distracted, and looked around the room. "Something's changing."

"What?" Andrea glanced around, concerned. "What're you talking about?"

"I'm not sure, but something's happening. We should get out of here. Now that you have that, things are going to be looking for you."

She made a pitiful whining noise in her throat and turned around, scanning the apartment. "I don't like this. Does this have anything to do with what happened to Nikki?"

"I don't know. But we should definitely leave."

"Fine..." She placed the spearhead back onto the cloth and backed away from it. "Let me change my clothes."

As she hurried off to her bedroom, Gina scanned the

apartment around her. Something was there, she realized. Something dangerously close, yet just out of reach. Another place was looming just beyond this one... And something was moving within it, sending out faint ripples, like a predator lurking beneath the surface of a murky lake. "Please hurry," she called after her.

Chapter 5

"Snap out of it!"

Nicole awoke with a gasp.

Who said that? Who was there?

She was lying on her bed in the dark, naked but for the garter she'd been wearing under her bridesmaid dress. She sat up, startled, her eyes wide open. A quick look around revealed that there was no one else in the room with her, but she was sure she heard a voice just now. A man's voice, no less.

Was someone else in the apartment?

She swung her legs over the side of the bed and listened, but everything was perfectly quiet. Was it only a dream?

She shivered and rubbed her shoulders. Why was it so cold? Was something wrong with the air conditioning? Her skin was covered in goosebumps. Her teeth were chattering.

She reached for the blankets, but paused as she looked down at the bed. Why was she sleeping on top of the covers? And for that matter…how did she get here? She didn't remember going to bed… Or taking her clothes off… She didn't even recall how she got home. The last thing she remembered was Brandy's wedding. She was on the dance floor. She was having a great time. Then…

She squeezed her eyes shut and tried to clear her head. Something wasn't right. Her head felt all foggy.

She was at the party and she started feeling sick…? Was that right? Did she have too much to drink? Again, she hugged herself against the cold. No…drinking too much had never given her chills like this before.

Could she have been drugged? There was a terrible thought. A *sobering* thought. Her eyes snapped open again. She recalled the voice that woke her up…

She stood up and swayed on her feet, dizzy. Her head was swimming. Where was her dress? She didn't see it anywhere. But she also didn't remember where she took it off… The world before her wavered in and out of focus. A heavy drowsiness descended over her like a warm blanket, lulling her shivering nerves.

"Come back to bed…"

But she shook her head. "Jus' a minute…" she yawned, rubbing her eye. "I gotta check the…the thing…the *thermostat*… S'cold in here…" Then she frowned and looked back at the bed again. What was that just now? Was someone there? She felt for a moment like someone was lying on the bed…

She stood there, listening to the silence, trying to blink away the drowsiness and clear her head. She could hear voices murmuring in the distance.

Probably the neighbors again. They were always shouting at each other.

She squinted at the bed. Why was she standing there staring at the bed? What was she thinking about just now?

Another shiver rushed through her and she turned away from it. Stumbling a little, she crossed the room and looked out into the hallway.

No one was there.

Everything was quiet.

Very slowly, the events of the night were beginning to trickle back to her. Nobody drugged her. She remembered leaving the party on her own. She remembered driving home alone. She even remembered entering the apartment and locking the door behind her.

It wasn't that she felt sick, exactly, she recalled. More like…weirdly emotional. She felt suddenly and cripplingly depressed.

One hand on the wall to steady herself, she made her way down the hallway to the living room. No one was here. She was home alone. The door was still locked. Andrea wasn't home yet.

She wondered what was going on over at the clubhouse.

Had anyone missed her yet?

For that matter, what time was it?

But when she looked at the clock on the stove, its display was black.

She frowned at it, confused. Was the power out? Looking around again, it finally occurred to her that none of the lights were on, yet it was still somehow light enough to see. The entire room was bathed in an eerie and slightly bluish glow that seemed to have no source.

Something wasn't right here. She could feel it. Something *slippery*. Every time she started to grasp it, it wriggled through her fingers. Something about this place…about the apartment… It didn't feel right. It didn't feel like *home*.

She was still leaning against the wall, still struggling against that odd dizziness. She looked at her hand, at the photographs staring back at her between her splayed fingers.

A mounting terror was welling up inside her. She never should have come back here. Not alone. She needed to leave. She should find her dress and hurry back to the party, to the crowded dance floor.

She wasn't sure how, but she knew that was the safest place for her.

It was dangerous to be alone.

But her body was so heavy. Every step, every *movement*, felt weighted. She was caught in slow motion, struggling to even turn around.

And her eyelids felt so heavy. With each passing second she grew wearier.

What was happening to her?

But then he was there. Strong arms slipped around her waist. Warm flesh pressed against her back.

"I've got you," Albert assured her.

She sighed as his lips brushed the back of her neck.

"Let's go back to bed."

"Mmm…" was all the response she could muster. Yes. Her warm bed sounded wonderful. And to be wrapped in his arms again…

Still leaning on the wall, she turned and started back toward her bedroom. Albert would take care of her. He'd take care of *everything*. Just like he'd always done. She wouldn't have to worry about why it was so cold in here... Or why the lights weren't working... Or why the carpet felt so strange and squishy beneath her feet... Or what that foul smell was...

Her sleepy gaze washed over the many photographs on the wall as she trudged past them, all those smiling, laughing faces she loved so much...

Except none of them were smiling now.

She looked around, confused. She knew all these faces, but all the joy had vanished from them. Every single picture was staring back at her with empty, soulless eyes and ominous, threatening scowls.

She stopped walking, her body stiffening. Where was she? What was this place? This wasn't her apartment.

The cold air on her bare skin...the strange, bluish glow...the horrible, squelchy floor beneath her feet... And that *smell*... A subtle reeking...faint, fleeting, but definitely there, like something dead and rotting...

And worst of all...those arms around her waist...

She didn't bring anyone home.

"It's okay," Albert whispered into her ear. Those hands crept upward. Fingertips caressed the undersides of her breasts, but instead of filling her with yearning, it sent a shiver of pure revulsion through her already trembling body. Icy terror gripped her, jolting her awake. "I can be yours," he breathed. "Just like you always wanted."

That wasn't Albert. Albert couldn't be here. Albert was with Brandy, where he belonged. Why on earth would she ever think, for even a moment, that he would be here with her instead?

She stood frozen with fear, her heart pounding.

Whose arms were those?

"I can love you forever..." sighed a voice in her ear in a breath that was ice cold and reeked of dead things.

She didn't turn to look at the thing that was pretending to be Albert. She didn't dare.

Summoning all her strength, she tore herself free of those arms and ran. She fumbled open the lock and fled the apartment...only to find that there was nowhere to run. What was once a short hallway with four numbered doors, two stairwells and an exit at either end was now an endless corridor of locked doors with no end in sight in either direction.

Just like in that mockery of her apartment, the lights were out, replaced with that eerie, blue glow that didn't seem to come from anywhere. The air was cold and putrid. The floor beneath her bare feet felt wet and slimy.

She stood there, confused, looking back and forth, her heart racing. What was happening? Where was she? What was this place?

Then the thing that wasn't Albert was there again.

Arms that weren't his...that weren't *any* man's...that weren't even really *arms* at all...slithered around her waist, encircling her, groping at her.

"Come back..." it whispered in a voice that was definitely not Albert's. How could she ever have thought it was him? No part of this thing was even remotely human!

She stood frozen, trembling with terror, still too afraid to look behind her, to look the truth in its monstrous eyes. All she wanted to do was run, but once again, her legs had gone heavy. She couldn't seem to move them.

The thing's lips—if that was what those things were— brushed her bare shoulder in a hideous mockery of a kiss. Something wet and slimy slid upward, creeping toward her neck and produced an awful tingling sensation on her skin.

"No..." she croaked, her voice broken and barely audible, as useless as her betraying legs. "Let me go..."

She remembered this thing now. It was with her at the wedding, as she watched Brandy and Albert drive away, whispering its strange lies to her, then it vanished as if it had never been there, not merely from the physical world, but from her very thoughts. She turned around and immediately forgot it. Then it found her again later, on the dance floor. It lulled her into that weird sense of despair and lured her away from the crowd, *lured her all the way home*, where it undressed her and pushed her onto the bed while pretending to be Albert.

Something sucked at the tender flesh of her neck. That tingling became a prickling. Then, slowly, it became a *burning*.

She remembered thinking that she was seeing Albert crouched atop her, lowering himself over her, and thinking there was something wrong with his mouth...

A great, shuddering sob escaped her. She closed her eyes as a tear streaked down her face.

"I said snap out of it!"

Startled, she opened her eyes. There, standing in front of her was Keith Dorray. His dingy blond hair was longer than it was the last time she saw him. He had a stubbly start of a beard that he didn't have when they parted ways seven months before. But it was him. She could never forget those stark blue eyes.

For a few baffling seconds, she was so surprised to see him there that she almost forgot the horror that was molesting her from behind.

"Don't just stand there and let it have you!" shouted Keith. Then he reached out and slapped her.

The pain was sharp. The sound felt almost deafening. The entire world seemed to radiate with the shock of it.

She pressed her hand to her face, her mouth agape, barely able to comprehend it. That was Keith. The guy who fussed over every little thing she did. The guy who wouldn't let her carry groceries. The guy who once tried to blow on her wonton soup for her so she wouldn't burn herself. He didn't *slap* people.

What the *fuck*?

But even as these things rushed through her mind, she realized that Keith wasn't there at all. And neither was the thing that was pretending to be Albert.

She turned around, confused. She was standing in the building's main hallway outside her apartment. The lights were back on. The floor no longer felt strange and squelchy. And it was no longer cold. In fact, it was hot and humid out here.

She could hear the neighbors across the hall talking in their unit.

She wiped the tears from her face and made another circle, scanning her surroundings, half-expecting that monster to snatch her away again. But she was all alone.

She was safe.

Then her heart skipped a beat as she realized that she was also standing out in the open hallway *stark naked*!

Before someone could step through a door and see her, she rushed back into her apartment and slammed the door behind her. Then she locked the deadbolt and pressed her back against it for good measure.

What the hell was all that? A monster? A nightmare version of her apartment building? *Keith*? Did all of that really happen? Or was she going crazy?

Then she realized that she wasn't alone. A stranger was standing in front of her, staring back at her. A smallish woman in a blue blouse and black skirt.

"Oh wow," said the woman in a soft and sleepy voice, her eyes sweeping down her bare body and back up again. "Look at you."

Chapter 6

Nicole blinked at the woman, confused and embarrassed, her mind racing. Did she just barge into the wrong apartment? *Naked?*

But she barely had time to process the situation when she heard Andrea's voice call out from the next room: "*Nikki?*" She burst from the hallway, barefoot but otherwise still dressed, her eyes wide with worry. "Is that y—*whoa! Why are you naked?*"

Nicole stared back at her, unsure what to even say. It seemed so surreal to see her still dressed in her bridesmaid dress, her hair still perfect, looking exactly as she had all day, as if this could possibly be the same world she woke up in this morning.

"Are you okay? Where *were* you? And again, *why are you naked?*"

She reached up and pressed her hands against her face. So many questions! And she had no answers for her. She wouldn't even know where to begin. *Was* she okay? Where was she, indeed? That place had looked like their apartment but it most definitely wasn't. The more she remembered of it, the more alien it seemed. She couldn't understand how she ever thought that awful place was her home.

"What are those marks all over you?"

She dropped her hands, confused, and looked down at herself. There were strange, reddish blotches on her chest, belly and shoulders. They were arranged in circles, in groups of seven. Some of them were beading blood. And now that she'd seen them, she realized she could feel them, too. They stung like friction burns, as if she'd been rubbed raw with coarse fabric or even sandpaper. She could feel one burning on the side of her neck and shoulder blade, too.

Her gaze was drawn to one on her left breast, just above her nipple, and she recalled with sickening clarity the kiss from the not-Albert with the dreadfully wrong mouth...

Teeth marks, she realized with a shudder of revulsion.

"What *happened?*" pressed Andrea.

But Nicole shook her head and stalked toward the kitchen. She needed to get her head straight. She needed to *prioritize.* "I need beer," she decided.

Andrea watched her walk away. "You sure you don't need clothes first?"

"Beer first," she insisted.

"Okay..." She glanced over at Gina. "Sorry, my roommate is kind of a nudist."

"I don't mind," she replied as she watched the shapely brunette cross the room.

"If you say so..." said Andrea, wrinkling her nose at the lacy garter that was the only stitch of clothing her roommate was still wearing. With her hair still up and her makeup still mostly perfect, her toned body tanned and clean-shaven, she looked more like a bachelor party stripper than a maid of honor, but she decided to keep that observation to herself. "This is Gina, by the way. In case you were, you know, wondering."

Nicole flapped a hand at her without looking back. "Nice to meet ya." She didn't try to hide herself. She never did. She wasn't really a *nudist*, as Andrea claimed. She didn't walk around naked all day. She wasn't an exhibitionist. She just simply wasn't modest when it came to her body.

"Yeah," said Gina. "You too..."

Five years ago, when the six of them ventured into the depths of that frightful labyrinth, they were all naked in front of each other, even though most of them were complete strangers at the time. Albert and Wayne saw every inch of her and she saw every inch of them. It was mortifying at first, but it was surprising how quickly everyone got used to being like that. It made her realize that there was nothing to be embarrassed about. It was only their bodies. And after all they went through down there, she absolutely refused to be bashful about her own skin. She couldn't count the times she'd changed clothes in front of them all since then. She and Albert had probably seen each other naked dozens of times. It was just how they were. There wasn't anything sexual about it. They just didn't have anything to hide. And in all honesty, she found it refreshing to be so close with her friends.

When she realized that she was naked outside in the hallway, she panicked a little, but that wasn't about being seen so much as being reported to the police. Public nudity was a crime, whether she cared if anyone saw her or not. But this was her own home. This Gina woman, whoever she was, had already seen her naked. What did it matter if she didn't rush off to find some clothes? She didn't look offended, so what did she care?

"Seriously," pushed Andrea, "what happened to you?"

"*Beer*," Nicole pushed back. She opened the fridge and snatched a can from the top shelf. She'd had several glasses of wine tonight already, but she was fairly sure the not-Albert thing scared her sober. She needed something to help her stop trembling.

Also, she kind of wanted a few more seconds to process everything before she attempted to explain anything. If she tried to talk about it now, it was all just going to come pouring out in one big, crazy-sounding flood.

She opened the can and took a long drink.

That wasn't just some dream. She was sure of it. She didn't just sleepwalk naked into the hallway. Andrea would have found her when she came home. And that monster left *real* marks on her body. *It* was real. That weird, alternate version of her apartment was real.

And it happened right here in her own home. In her own *bedroom*...

The only thing about that awful experience that wasn't real were those weird delusions of getting freaky with Albert. The very thought made her cringe. There was no way she was telling anyone about that. How embarrassing!

Why Albert? She was quite sure she didn't have any kind of deeply buried sexual attraction to him. Sure, he was kind of cute, and she thought he was a great person and she totally respected how smart he was and she even flirted around with him a lot because it amused her when she made him flustered, but she didn't have any kind of crush on him or anything. She definitely didn't *fantasize* about him like that. That was…well it was kind of *ew* wasn't it? He was *Albert*. He was like a *brother*!

God, the more she thought about those weird delusions the more she wanted to crawl in a hole and *die*.

And then there was Keith… Like Albert, he couldn't have been real. He *slapped* her. Granted, she apparently *needed* a swift slap to snap her out of it, but Keith would never do that! Not the Keith she knew, anyway.

"Will you just talk to me already!" snapped Andrea.

"She was attacked," said Gina.

Nicole turned, the beer can still lifted to her lips, and raised an eyebrow at her.

"What?" gasped Andrea. "By *who*?"

"Not who. What. I told you there were other things at that party. Not just people who weren't what they seemed to be. Things, too. Barely-there things that most people can't see. One of those followed her home. Got inside her head. Filled her with false emotions. Then took her away."

"Took her away?"

Gina nodded. "To another dimension right next to ours. That's what I felt when we first arrived, why the space felt disturbed. And why I couldn't feel her presence until just before she came through the door. It's astounding that she managed to find her way back. She's very lucky."

"Is that true?" asked Andrea.

Nicole stared at Gina, surprised. "How did you know all that?"

"I just know things," she replied.

"Is that what happened?" pressed Andrea.

Nicole took another swig from her beer, then said, "All I know is I got weirdly emotional and came home feeling confused. Then I…" She shook her head. "I don't know. Fell asleep, I guess. Woke up in some kind of weird, twisted version of this apartment. It was cold. And the carpet felt weird under my feet. *Squishy*... And all the pictures were wrong." She glanced around at the photographs around her, confirming they were as they should be. Smiles, not scowls. *Brandy's* lipstick on Albert's face, not *hers*. (God, how could she think such things?) "And there was this...*thing* there...trying to keep me from leaving." She didn't dare mention Albert. The very thought of sharing that detail was still mortifying. "What did you call it? A barely-there?"

Gina shrugged. "I don't know if it has a name. Like I said, most people never see things like them."

Nicole scratched absently at one of the blemishes the monster left on her neck. "Why did it look like our apartment?"

"That's just how those kinds of places are sometimes. They don't exist on their own, so they mimic the space nearest to them in the real world, borrowing their properties, sometimes in weird, twisted ways."

"And there's one just hanging out next to our apartment?" said Andrea, glancing around as if it might start bleeding through at any second.

"Chances are the thing that attacked her made that place. The barely-there, if you like. Some things can do stuff like that. When the barely-there goes away, so will the place."

Nicole stared at her, confused. "*Who* are you again? How do you know all this stuff?"

"Gina Sarrelli," she replied. "And I kind of just do."

"She knows things," affirmed Andrea. "Apparently."

"The same way I know it's still not safe here. We should go."

"Go where?" asked Nicole.

"Anywhere. I can't say exactly what that thing was that attacked you, but I know it's very old and very dangerous. It'll be back. It'll be watching. It preys on people when they're alone."

"Oh good..." grumbled Nicole. "And here I was worried it was gone." She glanced around, nervous, almost expecting to see the horrid creature peering back at her from behind the couch or under the table with Albert's eyes. She remembered thinking for a moment between muddled, alien thoughts that she never should've left the crowded dance floor, that it would've been safer there. Did she know somehow, deep down inside, what sort of thing she was dealing with?

"We should stay close together," suggested Gina.

Andrea nodded. "Uh, *yeah*. No getting separated, for sure."

"No shit," said Nicole. "Looks like the three of us are going to the bathroom together until further notice."

"That would be best," agreed Gina, "yes." Then she turned her gaze to Andrea. "This thing's different from the man at the golf course. It had a different purpose. If it wanted to kill her, I'm sure it could have. Easily."

Nicole had started to take another drink, but lowered the can again at this. "What man? What's she talking about?"

Andrea tipped her head to one side. "You sure you don't want to put some clothes on?"

"I don't give a shit about that. Did something happen? Are you okay?"

"I'm fine, but..." She scratched awkwardly at her elbow. She hadn't wanted to tell her about the creep in the purple shirt. She didn't want to worry her. Not just yet, at least. "Yeah... While you were doing...uh...whatever it was you were doing in the hallway *naked*...some really weird stuff's been going down."

"A man with psychic powers tried to strangle her," said Gina.

"*What?* Oh my god! Are you okay?"

"I'm fine," insisted Andrea. She shot Gina a dirty look. Did she really have to blurt stuff out like that? "It was just some creep. *She* was there. She saved me from him."

"Thank God..."

"Apparently, that's why she was there," she went on. "To watch after me. She says a *goddess* sent her."

"A goddess," said Nicole, blinking at the mysterious little woman.

"That's what she said."

"The goddess," explained Gina, "is the Great Beholder who knows everything about everyone."

"Oh..." She looked back at Andrea, bewildered.

"Three days ago," Gina went on, "she gave me today's date and the address for Weirweather Country Club. There, I'd meet the person I needed to find. I'm supposed to stay close to her and make sure no harm comes to her."

Nicole rubbed at her eye with the heel of her free hand. This was a lot to take in after what she'd just gone through. "And does this 'goddess' tell you to do things often?"

"Not very often, no."

"Oh."

"I know how it sounds," Gina assured her. "But I also know that you've both experienced things far crazier than the notion of an all-knowing goddess, so can we maybe skip the part where we all act like the new girl's a few crayons short of a box?"

"Touché," said Andrea.

"Sorry…" sighed Nicole. She was right. Five years ago she discovered that psychics, monsters and even parallel worlds were real. And she was literally just attacked by some kind of mind-manipulating creature. Why *not* a bossy goddess? "So this 'goddess' of yours…sent you here today, straight to Albert and Brandy's wedding, to find someone." She glanced up at Andrea. "Where all of us were. Everyone who came back out of those tunnels that night. That doesn't sound like a coincidence."

"That's what I was thinking," agreed Andrea. "But she says she's only here for me."

"No one else is involved," affirmed Gina.

"But I'm not leaving without Nikki."

"Fine. I can't stop her from coming with us. The goddess might even have intended it so. I'm sure she would've known you wouldn't come with me alone. But I also can't promise she won't be in danger."

Nicole was frowning down at her beer. "I'm surprised she wasn't here for Albert. Or Brandy."

"I know," said Andrea. "I kind of thought the same thing." Five years ago, everything started with Albert and Brandy. They knew about the Temple of the Blind a full year before the rest of them ever laid eyes on it. "But *that*…" She pointed at the golden spearhead lying on the table. "…was waiting for me in the front seat when I went to my car earlier."

Nicole looked over at the strange, golden object for the first time, surprised. "You mean like…?"

"Uh huh. Exactly like Albert found the box that night. And Brandy with the key."

"That's…kinda unsettling."

"I know, right? I mean, the temple's gone." She glanced over at Gina. "Isn't it?"

But Gina only shrugged. "I don't know anything about any temple. Sorry."

Nicole walked over to the table and set her beer down beside the cloth. Then she picked up the strange, golden weapon and examined it. "Is it supposed to mean something?"

"No idea," replied Andrea. "You're really not going to put clothes on, are you?"

"In a minute," she grumbled, looking closer at the spearhead.

"Sorry," she said to Gina.

"It's fine. I really don't mind."

"So you're supposed to stab somebody in the heart with this thing?" said Nicole, reading the message carved into the spear's surface.

"I already said I wasn't killing anybody," insisted Andrea. She plucked it from her hand and looked it over again, frowning at the words carved there.

"If you say so. But how are we even supposed to know where to start with that thing?"

"No idea. I keep wishing Albert were here. He's the puzzle guy."

"Well you must be able to figure it out yourself, right? I mean if her goddess only asked for *you*…"

She shook her head. "Well I don't have a clue, so I guess the goddess was wrong."

"The answers will come," said Gina. "But we should still leave here as soon as possible. The barely-there might not come back if we stay together, but there are other things in this city tonight. And sooner or later, something else is going to come here looking for you." Then her gaze dropped to the spearhead. "Or for that."

Andrea groaned. "This sucks." She snatched the cloth and rope off the table. "Why did it have to be *me*?" But as she gathered up the fabric, she caught sight of something. "Hey, what's this?"

Something was written on the inside of the cloth.

She laid it back on the table and spread it out. Someone had scrawled a sloppy message across it in what appeared to be white paint.

The three of them gathered around it.

FIND THE LADY OF CEDRIC'S COVE.

"Well *that* doesn't tell us anything," growled Andrea. "Where's Cedric's Cove? I've never heard of it."

"Neither have I," said Nicole.

"I have," said Gina.

Andrea looked up at her. "Where is it?"

"Nobody knows."

"Oh…"

"It's rumored to be somewhere on the Great Lakes, but people say it moves around. No one knows how to find it."

"So how are *we* supposed to get there?" asked Nicole.

She pointed at Andrea. "It most likely has something to do with *her*. That's probably why the spear was given to her. And why I was sent here to protect her."

Andrea crossed her arms and considered it for a moment. "Well, it *was* me who got all of you out of the temple that night. Maybe you can only get there using that portal thing I did? That might explain why no one else can find it."

"I can't say for sure," said Gina. "The goddess didn't explain it. But it's likely that at least one of your special abilities is key to finding Cedric's Cove."

Andrea frowned. "At least one…? I mean I was able to open a portal a couple of times, but that was pretty much it. I'm not even sure I could do it again." Admittedly, she'd tried it a few times in the weeks following her trip to the Temple of the Blind, but nothing ever happened. After a while, she decided that it wasn't something she could just do on a whim. And that was probably a good thing, really, considering that they hadn't been alone in that tunnel. Journey of the Dead, as the Keeper called it, was guarded by something terrifying. The living weren't supposed to be there, after all. "I'm not really good for anything."

But Gina shook her head. "No. You're special. You have a very strong connection to the spirit world. You can sense things that others can't. The fact that you're essentially a bridge between the living and dead makes you exceedingly rare."

Andrea stared at her, bewildered. "I'm what now?"

"Your goddess told you that?" asked Nicole. "Or is that one of those things you just…knew?"

"I just know." Then she turned her sleepy gaze back to Andrea, "I'm sort of like you, except instead of a connection to the spirit world, I have a connection to my environment. I can feel things about the space around me and the people interacting with it. I know when someone's more than they appear to be. I know when people are near, even if they're hiding. I even know who's on the phone as soon as it rings."

"Cool," said Nicole.

"Yeah," said Andrea. "Very cool." But she sounded distracted. She was staring off into space, her thoughts dwelling on what Gina said about her having some kind of connection to the spirit world. Could it really be true? If so, it sort of made sense that she was the one who was sent to that tunnel with all the traveling spirits. And now that she was thinking about it, she recalled that she was the only one of the group who could sense the spirits in that place. No one else seemed to be able to feel them at all. And even before that, when she was on the path leading up the burning mountain, it was *she* who first sensed the ghosts that had gathered there. The others heard and felt things, too, but not nearly as many times or as clearly as she did.

"I know it sounds hard to believe," said Gina.

"No, I think I can believe it," said Nicole. "I mean, we know Albert and Brandy were psychic. The Sentinel Queen told us so, remember?"

Andrea nodded. It was the reason they were chosen to receive the mysterious box that led them there. They were the perfect amount of psychic, in fact, enough to feel the subtle energy of the temple but not so much that they'd fall victim to its terrifying traps, the way poor Beverly did. "And Olivia, too," she recalled. "She knew the right path to take up the mountain." Then she frowned. "When there *was* a right path…"

"Don't remind me," sighed Nicole. If you looked closely, you could still see the faint scars the night tree left around her neck that night. There were more like them all over her body, faint but visible to anyone who looked closely enough. Marks left by the tree's *teeth*.

"It's not really uncommon," explained Gina. "Lots of people actually possess some kind of psychic ability. But only a very few are ever even remotely aware of it. And far fewer still can actually use those abilities consciously."

Andrea tipped her head to one side, curious. "So does Nikki have some kind of psychic power, too?"

Gina turned her sleepy gaze on Nicole. "No. I don't get anything from her at all."

"Oh…"

Nicole rolled her eyes. "Yeah, that totally tracks." She was, after all, just the tag-along best friend that night. Everyone else was chosen to go down there in some way or another. Albert and Brandy were given the box and the key. Wayne and Olivia were given those envelopes. And Andrea was given that file on Gilbert House with Albert's name and address scrawled across it. But *she* just sort of showed up uninvited. She was lucky she made it back at all. If it had been a horror movie, she would've been the first to die.

"Sorry," said Andrea.

Nicole waved the issue aside and fixed her gaze on Gina. "But is it really related to the night we met? After all this time? I thought that stuff was all over after the temple collapsed."

"I don't know anything about any of that," replied Gina. "I don't know what happened to any of you. The goddess only told me that the person I was looking for played a role in opening a vital doorway and that now it was time for her to finish what she started."

Andrea nodded. That was almost word-for-word what she said to her when they first met. But it was weird to her that she seemed to know both so little *and* so much.

"I'm just able to tell that you've all been through something significant."

"Significant..." said Nicole, thoughtful. That was Albert's word. He kept saying that about things. He'd speculated that it was his psychic mind's way of alerting him to things it sensed about the temple. She drained the rest of her beer and grimaced. Then she turned and walked back to the kitchen to toss it in the recycle bin.

"I like your tattoo," said Gina, her gaze fixed on the tree on her lower back.

"Thank you."

"It's something meaningful, isn't it?"

"It's a night tree," said Andrea. "We ran into those five years ago when..." She glanced over at her. She knew that something happened five years ago, but she claimed to not know what it was. How much would she understand without someone explaining the whole story to her? "When things happened the first time," she finished.

Nicole nodded. After nearly a year of Andrea trying to talk her into it, she'd finally agreed to go with her to get a tattoo. Andrea got the little zodiac sign on the back of her neck and she, herself, got the tree. The actual artwork was Wayne's. She asked him to draw it for her and he did a magnificent job. He wasn't there when that one grabbed her and began dragging her up into its deadly canopy. He was dead during that part of the journey. (Long story.) But he saw his fair share of them when he rescued Olivia from the forest surrounding the flipside of Gilbert House.

Not long after, Andrea convinced all of them—Nicole, Brandy *and* Olivia—to go with her to get her other eyebrow pierced and all three of them had come out with shiny new bellybutton rings. Only just recently did Andrea acquire the angel wings on her shoulder blades. Olivia went with her that time, but she chickened out and didn't get one for herself.

"I thought it was kind of a morbid choice at first," recalled Andrea. "I mean one of those trees almost killed her. I had *nightmares* about those things."

"It's a reminder," explained Nicole as she opened the refrigerator and plucked another beer off the shelf. "Not of almost dying but of the fact that I *didn't*. Of just how much I owe all my friends. I wouldn't be here today without them. *All* of them."

Andrea smiled. "Yeah, definitely not as morbid as I first thought."

Of course, to anyone but the six of them who ventured into those tunnels that night and returned, it was only a curious-looking tree. Whenever someone asked her about it, she couldn't tell them the truth. They wouldn't believe her if she did. For those people, she typically just told them it was a tree of life, a symbol of good fortune, a sort of good luck charm.

Nicole took another long drink, then grimaced and stifled a burp. "So what does any of this stuff have to do with the temple? I mean it can't just be a coincidence that you came looking for Andrea."

"Yeah," said Andrea. "You said something about finishing what we started?"

"The temple collapsed when Brandy opened the door," said Nicole. "It's a pile of rocks. What's left to finish?"

"I don't know what you went through last time," replied Gina, "and I can't begin to guess what you'll go through next, but the goddess takes care of those she calls on. You can trust her."

"Sure," grumbled Nicole. She took another swig. She was starting to feel a little better, but if this was going to be anything like what happened five years ago, she might need another two or three to properly prepare herself.

"I'm not leaving without Nikki," insisted Andrea. "Things got *way* scary last time I did this sort of thing. There's no way I'm brave enough to go by myself."

"I told you, that's your choice," replied Gina. "If she's willing to come, I can't stop her."

Nicole sighed. "Well there's no way I'm just letting you take her on some dangerous trip to God knows where, just the two of you, with some psychopath strangler hunting you."

Andrea seemed to wilt with relief to hear her say that.

"Besides, I'm not staying *here* alone. What if that thing comes back? I mean it attacked me once even though you came here for *her*."

"It might," admitted Gina. "I definitely can't promise it won't. But I also can't promise it'll be any safer for you where we're going. I have no idea what's going to happen next."

Nicole took another gulp from her beer and then reached up and started taking down her hair. "So this place we're going… Cedric's Cove, was it?"

Gina nodded.

"Right. How do we go about finding a place that no one knows where is?"

Gina spoke very softly and seemed very timid, but she met Nicole's eyes unflinchingly. Underneath her shy mannerisms, there was obviously a very brave woman. "I know some people who've researched it. That's how I originally heard about it. They might be able to point us in the right direction."

Nicole shook out her hair and sighed. "So what do we do first?"

"You can put some clothes on," suggested Andrea. "That'd probably be a good start."

Chapter 7

Nicole sat in the back seat of Gina's Civic, watching the trees speed by in the dark. It felt strange leaving Briar Hills behind, especially without telling anyone where they were going.

While the two of them packed a travel bag and dressed—Nicole in denim shorts and a gray tank top, Andrea in a pair of athletic shorts and a black tee shirt, and both of them in their most comfortable sneakers because they were almost certainly going to find themselves running from something scary before this ordeal was over—Gina made a phone call to her friends. According to her, these friends traveled the country investigating portals, dimensional rifts and alternate universes, which Andrea, for one, didn't even know was a career option. As it happened, they actually lived right here in Missouri, but way up north, in Tunipet.

But they weren't going to Tunipet. They were going to Michigan. All the way up near where Lakes Huron and Michigan touched. Somewhere in that area, according to Gina's friends, was a place they called All Trails Crossing. That was where they recommended beginning their search for Cedric's Cove.

Not exactly how Nicole wanted to spend the remainder of her weekend.

At least she didn't have to worry about work. She was a special education teacher for one of the city's public elementary schools and was currently enjoying the summer off. But she did have a few things planned over the next few days that she went ahead and canceled. She had a feeling they wouldn't be home anytime soon.

Andrea, however, worked part time at a local ice cream parlor and was supposed to be back to work after tomorrow. She was trying to find someone to take her Monday and Tuesday shifts. She also texted her parents, claiming to have gotten a ride home from the reception after a few drinks—like a responsible daughter who followed her dad's advice and was in no way taking an impromptu road trip somewhere likely very dangerous with a total stranger—and asking of they'd mind picking up her Escape from the country club parking lot in the morning.

Gina had assured them that she was good to drive and that they wouldn't have to worry about that, at least. She'd arrived in Briar Hills the day before and slept comfortably all night in a hotel. Of the three of them, she was by far the most well-rested.

Nicole had spent the first hour of the trip trying to get some decent sleep in the Civic's back seat, but although she was certainly tired enough, she couldn't seem to nod off. Her thoughts kept returning to that twisted version of her apartment where all the smiles in her pictures had been replaced with evil scowls and she couldn't help fearing that if she nodded off she might wake up in that place again.

Andrea, on the other hand, didn't seem to be concerned with sleep in the least. She'd pretty much been talking nonstop since they departed Briar Hills, barely even pausing to read and respond to all her incoming texts. She talked about the wedding, about Brandy and Albert, about her camera-happy mom and her crazy friend, Stella. Then she talked for a while about Gilbert House and the Temple of the Blind, about how she met everyone five years ago.

She'd always been a bit of a chatterbox. Especially when she was nervous. And this business with the man in the purple shirt and the mysterious package had made her *very* nervous.

Gina, in stark contrast, didn't have a lot to say. She answered questions when Andrea asked them, but didn't go into very much detail. So far during the conversation she'd revealed that she grew up in Indiana, had no living family and was currently living in an apartment in the Milwaukee area with two roommates.

"So tell us about this goddess of yours," said Andrea, barely pausing for a breath between sentences. She was sitting in the front seat, brushing out her hair. "Does she, like, descend from a brilliant light or something?"

"Nothing so glamorous, no." Gina's voice remained soft and sleepy. She sounded almost bored every time she spoke, as if she'd done this sort of thing a million times. "She appears in my dreams, actually. A lot of it is really fuzzy when I wake up. Like, I can't remember exactly what she looks like, only that she's very beautiful. And I can never remember where we are when she talks to me. I remember it being really bright and kind of hazy, and that we're surrounded by lots of stuff…but I can't recall what any of the stuff is. The things she tells me, though, I remember word for word when I wake up."

"Huh." She tied one side of her hair up into a pigtail and then wrapped it around itself, forming it into a small bun. "I had something like that once, except it was just this creepy voice inside my head." She fussed with the one bun for a moment, then turned her attention to the other side. "And this wasn't the first time she spoke to you?"

"No. A few years ago she gave me a job. A literal one. With a graphic design studio."

Andrea scrunched up her face, confused. "Oh. That's a little different. *I* got sent into the stinky sewers and almost died a bunch of times in this really huge, creepy, monster-infested maze… Did it pay well?"

"It did, actually. But it wasn't really what I wanted to do."

"So are you an artist? Like Wayne?"

"I am. But I don't know him."

"Oh, right. You wouldn't." She talked about him a little while telling her what happened five years ago, but she didn't really go into any detail about him. "I'm still in college, but I change my major, like, every semester. I just can't decide what I want to do with my life. It's driving my dad nuts." She finished tying up the second bun and then looked herself over in the vanity mirror, making sure they were straight. "But why an actual job? I don't get it."

"It was kind of a cover. I was really there to keep an eye on a girl who worked there. Sort of like how I was sent today to keep you safe. I eventually got fired for helping her sneak into the boss' office."

"Bummer. Sorry."

"It's fine. He was literally a monster."

"Oh…"

"That's really cute, by the way. Your hair."

"Thank you!"

"She's *always* cute," grumbled Nicole. "It's like having a puppy that hogs the bathroom."

Andrea looked back and poked her tongue out at her, briefly revealing the silver stud embedded there. Nicole, for one, couldn't quite figure out how she remained so cute with so many piercings. How did you pull off badass punk rock *and* adorable cutie-pie at the same time? Even after knowing her for five years, she still couldn't quite wrap her head around it.

"You two remind me of some friends of mine," said Gina.

Andrea glanced over at her. "Yeah?"

She nodded, but didn't elaborate.

Nicole took out her phone and stared at the screen. There were no messages there tonight, which didn't exactly surprise her. Almost everyone who ever texted her was there at the wedding today. They'd all be almost as tired as she was. Or flat on their faces drunk, she supposed.

She wanted to text Brandy and warn her about the barely-there. She couldn't stand the thought of something attacking her on her special night. But the last thing she wanted was for them to spend their honeymoon looking over their shoulders and worrying about her and Andrea heading off to some mysterious traveling city with a strange, soft-spoken woman who talked to goddesses.

Besides, if it were *her* wedding night, there was no way she'd have her phone on.

She took solace in knowing that Brandy and Albert would be *together* all night and then off to Tennessee first thing in the morning. If Gina was telling the truth about the barely-there only attacking people when they were alone, then it wouldn't be able to get them. And hopefully that was the only monster on the prowl in Briar Hills tonight.

Wayne and Oliva would be together, too. They were *always* together. Olivia had barely left his side since the two of them came back from the tunnels that night. He saved her life several times, even literally *dying* to keep her safe and then miraculously coming back to them. She could barely blame her for falling head-over-heels. But she couldn't stop wondering if she was doing the right thing not contacting them.

On the other hand, Olivia had a very special talent that none of the rest of them had. Her psychic ability gave her an early warning for peril. If something like the barely-there were to enter their apartment, it would almost certainly set her on edge.

But she wished she knew for certain that she was doing the right thing. Her gaze drifted to Gina. They still didn't know anything about this woman. Sure, she'd saved Andrea from that creep at the wedding, but that didn't necessarily mean she could be trusted. She and her so-called "goddess" could have their own agenda. Or she could've been working with the creep in the purple shirt the whole time and saving Andrea could have been nothing more than a ruse to gain her trust.

She certainly didn't seem dangerous. If anything, she seemed utterly harmless. She was small, timid and looked like she wanted to have been in bed hours ago.

But she intended to keep a close eye on her.

She looked down at her purse beside her. Inside was the spearhead, again wrapped up in its velvet cloth and tied with its rope. It didn't fit inside Andrea's clutch, so she'd volunteered to be in charge of it for the trip. It didn't seem wise to just carry it around in full view, not even wrapped up like it was. Not when they already knew at least one maniac was out there looking for it.

What had they gotten themselves into? Who was this mysterious Lady of Cedric's Cove they were supposed to find? And was all this really related to the Temple of the Blind somehow? Was she another Sentinel Queen, perhaps? Or maybe something even stranger? Could what happened that night really be what all this was about? Old memories kept seeping up through her mind. Endless black corridors. Cold, flooded tunnels. Unearthly things prowling unseen in the darkness. Eerie, lifelike statues full of lust and fear and hate. Dead bodies collecting dust in a silent dormitory.

She shuddered and tried to force those thoughts back down. But they were stubborn. Especially the memories of her and Albert naked together...

She buried her face in her hands and stifled a groan.

What the hell was wrong with her brain today?

"So these people who told you where we should go next..." said Andrea. "What were their names again?"

"Violet and Corey," replied Gina.

"Right. Them. What're they like?"

"They're nice."

"Oh..." she said when she realized this was all the response she was getting. "That's good."

"Sorry, I've only actually met them a couple times. But they've always been very nice to me."

"How'd you meet them?"

"Through friends," replied Gina.

"Oh. Okay."

"And they research portals to other worlds?" prodded Nicole.

"That's right."

"Have they *found* many of these portals?"

"They have. Corey's mapped the locations of several gateways since they started researching. And he's theorized the existence of dozens more all over the Midwest."

"Gateways as in doorways to other worlds?" asked Andrea.

Gina nodded.

"Wow." She already knew that there were worlds other than this one *and* that they sometimes overlapped in strange ways. There was that hellish forest, for one. And that tunnel she ended up in after the carrion eater knocked her over that cliff. And as she recalled, Wayne had told them that the old man he met on Road Beneath the Wood spoke of even more worlds waiting out there. But it seemed surprising to her that these friends had actually hunted down portals to some of these other worlds.

"They believe that most of them aren't really whole worlds, though," Gina clarified. "The vast majority are what Corey calls 'pocket dimensions.' A finite area of space folded within physical space. Like a wrinkle in a blanket."

"Like that eerie version of our apartment?" asked Nicole.

She nodded. "That's how I knew about those places mirroring the elements of the outer world surrounding it, making them look like warped versions of whatever was just outside it. Corey described them to me once."

Andrea shivered. "That still sounds *so* creepy."

"Not a place I'd recommend visiting," agreed Nicole.

"There are different kinds of pockets. Not all of them are scary like that. Some are just empty. Corey thinks most of them are so subtle you wouldn't know you'd stumbled into one. People just sort of wander in and out of them all the time, completely unaware. I don't understand how it all works. I don't know if anyone does, really. But they're a lot more common than people realize."

"Yeah…" She recalled seeing someone who looked like Keith in there. Was that merely a manifestation of her own subconscious kickstarting her flight response? Or could someone have really been in there with her? She supposed she might never know…

"But there are *whole* universes, too, right?" asked Andrea, her thoughts drifting back to that enormous black forest that loomed outside Gilbert House's windows and surrounded the Temple of the Blind. "Like, full-sized worlds out there?"

"Definitely," said Gina. "Those are much rarer, but some of them have entire ecosystems with their own flora and fauna. Violet has an entire journal of crossers."

"Crossers?" said Andrea, confused.

"Creatures from other dimensions that cross into ours," she explained. "Crossers."

"Ah. Gotcha." She nodded. Like those dangerous hounds and gross carrion eaters. "Catchy."

"It was Violet's word. She made it up to distinguish those

kinds of creatures from other kinds."

"What other kinds are there?" asked Andrea.

"All kinds."

"Oh…"

"And they've researched this Cedric's Cove place, too," said Nicole. "But they've never found it?"

"They haven't. But they've uncovered some interesting lore surrounding it. And Corey's convinced the key to finding it is in this one area where all the maps overlap or something."

"All Trails Crossing…"

"Yeah."

"I'm surprised they didn't insist on coming," said Andrea. "If it's something they've done so much research on."

"They wanted to," replied Gina. "But I told them to stay away. They're not involved."

"Right. Your goddess told you so. Like with Nikki."

"Yes."

Andrea exchanged an uneasy look with Nicole. She hoped she did the right thing by going back for her. But she couldn't imagine any scenario where leaving her alone for the barely-there to find again was the right thing to do.

"You two should probably try to get some sleep. I'm not sure what tomorrow's going to bring."

"You sure you'll be okay by yourself?" worried Nicole.

"I'll be fine. I'll know if something dangerous gets too close to us."

"Wake us if you start to get tired at least," said Andrea.

"Sure."

But as the miles passed by on the other side of the glass, sleep came easy to neither of them. They both found themselves staring out into the passing wilderness, wondering what dangers might be waiting for them where they were headed.

Chapter 8

When Nicole finally managed to fall asleep, she somehow didn't have a nightmare about the barely-there Not-Albert with the dreadful mouth and the mesmerizing voice. Instead, she found herself standing alone in a dark corridor of smooth, gray stone, staring out into an open, black chamber where the cold floor gave way to bare earth. There was a single dead tree inside, looming over a small pond of eerily still water.

There was something dreadful about that looming blackness.

Something ominous.

And something frightfully *familiar.*

But before she could recall where she knew this place from, she was jolted awake by the sudden deceleration of the Civic.

"We there already?" mumbled Andrea as she struggled up from her own shallow slumber.

Nicole looked around, confused. The dashboard clock told her it was only a little past four, much too early to have arrived at their destination, and they were still on the interstate. There was no traffic, no construction, nothing to impede them, but they'd slowed to a crawl. "What's up?"

"Something's not right," said Gina. There was a hint of concern in her sleepy expression now. Her face was pinched, her lips tight, her eyes alert. She was sitting up stiff in her seat, her small hands gripping the wheel.

"The barely-there?" asked Nicole.

"No. It's something different."

Now Andrea was wide awake, too. She was sitting up in her seat, her blue eyes scanning every shadow in the passing trees and fields.

Nicole squinted into the harsh glare of her cell phone screen, but wherever they were, she didn't seem to have any cell service. "Are we off the grid? This is still the interstate, isn't it?"

"I started having a really bad feeling a little while ago," explained Gina. "Then my phone stopped giving me directions. No reception. It's like we're in a dead zone."

Andrea checked her own phone, with the same result. "Well *that's* disturbing... Did we drive into one of those gateways you were talking about?"

"Anything's possible."

"So what do we do?" asked Nicole.

"I don't know. But there's something up there."

"Ahead of us?" asked Andrea. She and Nicole both squinted into the darkness ahead, but there was nothing to be seen.

"We need to get off the highway as soon as possible."

"How far to the next exit?" wondered Nicole.

"Too far." She checked her mirrors, then glanced over her shoulder. There was no one else on the highway with them. "I passed a county road about two miles back," she recalled.

"That doesn't do us much good," said Andrea.

But Gina stepped on the brake, dragging the car nearly to a stop and forcing them into their seatbelts. "Hold on."

"What're you doing?" gasped Nicole.

She cut the wheel and swung hard to the left, crossing the fast lane and the shoulder. Nicole and Andrea both cried out in surprise as the inertia threw them against the passenger-side windows. Then the Civic dropped onto the grassy median with a heavy thump and an alarming grinding noise that made Nicole utter a rather unladylike curse. Andrea let out a long, high-pitched squeal. They bounced through the weeds and over the ditch. Then, finally, the vehicle lurched up onto the southbound lane, where Gina stomped the accelerator and sent them speeding back the way they came, the wheels screaming on the pavement.

"I don't think that was a legal U-turn!" gasped Andrea, her eyes wide and her hands pressed to the dashboard.

"Definitely not!" agreed Nicole. This wasn't exactly an off-road vehicle. They were lucky they didn't bottom out and get stuck. Then what would they have done?

"Trust me," said Gina, her voice still strangely calm and quiet for someone who just turned their leisurely drive into a *Dukes of Hazzard* rerun. "We really didn't want to be going in that direction."

Andrea turned and looked back through the rear window at the highway behind them. She couldn't see anything but the chasing red glow of their own taillights. "Are we safe now?"

Gina looked up at the rearview. "Not yet. Whatever it is, I can still feel it back there."

"Do you think it'll come after us?"

"I don't think it's a coincidence that it was there. I felt a distinct intention about it, whatever it was. It was waiting for us. It knew we were coming. When we don't show up, I'm sure it'll come looking for us. The only question is how long will it be before it realizes we've turned around?"

"And how far away we can be before that happens," reasoned Nicole. She turned and stared out the back window, her heart sinking. She didn't like this. It didn't feel the same as it did last time. Last time, *they* went to all the scary places. When they left, the nightmare things inside those places stayed behind. They didn't have to worry about them as long as they never went back. But *these* things weren't confined to temples or labyrinths or multidimensional dormitory ruins. These things were out in the world. They blocked the highway. They invaded her bedroom. This was an entirely different kind of bad situation, the kind they weren't allowed to just walk away from.

Gina was already going well over the speed limit, but it didn't feel like it. The seconds dragged on. That ominous darkness followed behind the bloody glow of the taillights.

Andrea caught herself holding her breath, waiting for something terrible to leap from the darkness. What was it? What did Gina feel back there? She remembered the absurdly lethal hounds down in the labyrinths of the temple with every inch of their alien bodies evolved to slice, tear, carve or rend the flesh from their victims' bones. She remembered the hulking brute that was the Caggo and its psychotic love for murder and torture. Was it like those things? A violent abomination of nature? A bio-logical killing machine? Or was it more like the mysterious, shad-owy thing that pursued them after they ignited the flames in the temple's belly? The one that pierced Wayne's body and plunged him into the cold depths of darkness until the Keeper miracu-lously returned him to them hours later.

It was probably something altogether different. And proba-bly even more terrifying.

Had the world always been this way? Had there always been this many terrifying things out there? It was almost weird to think how perfectly normal her life used to be. Once upon an almost forgotten time. She remembered that fateful night. She was upset because her best friend at the time, Rachel, had recent-ly started snubbing her at school. Such petty problems looking back on it, but soul-crushing to that eighteen-year-old girl who didn't yet know how big and strange the world was... Then the envelope appeared. Albert's name and address. Gilbert House's deceptively unassuming ruins. Everything suddenly became so deliciously *mysterious*. Strangers acting suspicious. Secret meetings in the woods. A hidden cellar door.

She couldn't resist it. She had to know more.

But then, just as suddenly, there were monsters. Mysterious voices. Endless, dark passageways. Before she knew it, she was naked and vulnerable, embarrassed and afraid. Scary noises in black tunnels. A dead city of blind people and their faceless queen.

It was all plenty frightening. She had her share of night-mares after that, just like everyone who made it back from that place. But for the most part, those memories were less scary than *thrilling*. She *enjoyed* thinking about the Temple of the Blind and the Sentinel Queen and all the other crazy things she discovered were out there.

But that was because she knew those things were all buried forever down there. No one could ever make her go back there again. And even if there were more places like that in the world, why would she ever go to any of them?

She didn't expect these things to come to her.

Gina reached the county road and made another hard turn onto it, dragging them toward the driver's side of the vehicle with twin screams of surprise. A moment later, she was speeding away from the interstate.

"Did we lose it?" gasped Andrea.

"I don't know," replied Gina in that same, sleepy tone. "I hope so."

"More importantly," said Nicole, "is this detour going to end up getting us lost?"

"We should still be okay," replied Gina. "We just need to keep heading northeast."

"Unless that thing just keeps blocking our path the whole way there."

"That's also a possibility, yes."

"Can you tell if it's still back there?"

She shook her head. "It's faded now. I don't feel it anymore."

Andrea relaxed back into her seat. "Thank God… That was the scariest—"

"Oh no," gasped Gina, her hands tightening around the wheel. She looked up at the rearview, her sleepy eyes wide awake again. "It's here."

Chapter 9

Nicole and Andrea both turned, hearts pounding, and looked back through the rear window. In the eerie glow of the taillights, they could see nothing but the unraveling road they were leaving behind.

"Are you sure?" asked Nicole.

"Positive," replied Gina. For the first time, her voice began to sound a little more panicked. "I don't know how it caught up so fast."

"I don't see anything," said Andrea. But then she did. Her gaze drifted up to the treetops on either side of the road. They were being battered back and forth as if caught in a stiff wind. And as soon as she saw this, she realized that there was something unnatural about the sky back there. A dark mist seemed to have rolled in. It was crowding around them, reducing the visibility in spite of the bright moon hanging in the sky.

"What's happening out there?" shouted Nicole.

Gina pressed the accelerator all the way to the floor, pushing the Civic to its limit, but the strange storm continued to overtake them as if they were standing still.

Outside, it grew darker and darker.

"I don't like this!" squealed Andrea.

"I don't know what to do..." whimpered Gina. That perpetual sleepiness was gone. Her eyes were wide open. For the first time, she looked afraid.

Ahead of her, visibility was beginning to diminish. The headlights faded into the growing gloom, making it more and more dangerous to be driving this fast with each passing second. So far the road had been straight, but if it turned on her without warning, she soon wouldn't have time to react.

Nicole stared back at the moon as the gloom tarnished it from silver to rust before her eyes. This wasn't just some monster, she realized. This was a force of nature. How were they supposed to escape something like this?

Gina assured them back in their apartment that her goddess looked after those she called upon, that they could trust her. So where the hell was she? Now would be a good time to get her holy ass off her heavenly throne and do something!

She turned and looked at Andrea. "You're supposed to have some kind of connection to the spirit world or something, right? Can't you do something?"

Andrea looked back at her as if she were crazy. "*I* don't know how any of this works!" Then she looked over at Gina. "What about you?"

She shook her head and glanced over at her, her mouth open to say again that she didn't know what to do, but the words stopped in her throat and her eyes widened at something over Andrea's shoulder.

Andrea twirled around in her seat, startled. There, just on the other side of the glass, was a pair of very long, black legs running in pace with the Civic.

They looked like horse legs, except they were far too tall to be any kind of horse she'd ever seen before. They stretched *way* up into the darkness. The knees were almost as high up as she could see. Even giraffes weren't nearly that tall.

She looked back over her shoulder at the rear legs of whatever freakish thing was towering over them, only to find that there were more than four. There seemed to be several of these things running with them. And when she turned and looked the other way, she found several more on that side.

"What are they?" shouted Nicole.

Gina shook her head. "I don't know. But they're *evil.*" It wasn't a word she used lightly. There were things in this world that were *dangerous*, and there were dangerous things that were not of this world, but true evil was rare. These things, however, were *oozing* with it. It was like an overwhelming stench. It flooded her brain, muting all of her senses. Visibility was becoming perilously low, but she didn't dare slow down. A suffocating feeling of impending peril had seized her heart and she knew without a doubt that if she paused for even a moment, these things would kill them.

Andrea leaned closer to the window, peering up higher and higher, trying to see what the freakish legs were attached to, but there was nothing to see except more of that unnatural gloom.

Then, before she could look away, a pair of shining eyes blossomed somewhere high up in that darkness, like the blinding glare of a distant lighthouse, and looked right back at her, meeting her gaze. At the same moment, a feeling of such intense terror pierced her heart that she would have screamed if her throat hadn't locked up with fright.

Nicole leaned forward, toward the middle of the back seat, as far from any of the windows as she could position herself. "We've already established that *I* don't have any kind of special powers so it has to be one of you!"

"Didn't the goddess tell you anything about this?" cried Andrea.

Gina shook her head hard, her long hair whipping across her face as she did so.

"I thought you said she was all-knowing? Shouldn't she have seen this coming?"

"She doesn't tell me everything."

Then one of the monstrous things swerved in front of them. Gina cried out in surprise and tried to veer out of the way. Something slammed against the passenger-side door with a jarring thud. The only thing out there was those freakishly tall legs, but it felt as if she'd just bounced the Civic against an immoveable iron post.

"They're running us off the road!" squealed Andrea.

"Hold on!" cried Gina. She dared to push the accelerator down and struggled to keep the car between the crowding monsters.

Something slammed against the driver's side of the car, making it veer and wrenching terrified screams from all three of them. Then something collided with the rear fender on the other side of the car, sending the vehicle fishtailing for a few heart-stopping seconds.

A forest of freakishly long legs surrounded them. Dozens of them, a flurry of thin, hairy limbs on either side of them and in the rearview, some of them even flashing across the road in front of them, barely missing the Civic's speeding bumper.

The wheels dropped off the side of the pavement and churned up gravel.

They were going too fast for this. At any second they could lose control. Or the unfamiliar road could make a sharp turn. But there was nowhere to go. They were trapped. It was only a matter of time before they were forced into the ditch. And then what? What would these monstrous things do to them once they could no longer flee?

Of course, that was only assuming they survived whatever crash they were inevitably speeding toward...

Ahead of them, in the shriveling beam of the headlights, another set of those impossible legs blossomed into view, this time standing perfectly still, just waiting for them in the darkness.

Gina cried out in surprise and stomped the brake.

Then one of the monsters slammed against the rear fender again, sending them spinning around. She twirled the wheel, turning into the skid like she was supposed to, but they were still going too fast. The right side of the car came up off the ground, threatening to roll.

All three of them screamed.

Then the back of the car dropped off the shoulder and it slammed back down again before jolting to a stop.

"*That was not fun!*" squeaked Andrea, her hands pressed to the dashboard in front of her, still holding on for dear life.

Gina stomped the gas and tried to speed back the way they came, but the tires spun uselessly in the dirt and gravel of the ditch.

They were stuck.

The monsters were everywhere. Great, hairy limbs darted past every window, circling, swarming, until it seemed less like a herd of four-legged monsters and more like one massive thing with countless legs.

And perhaps, thought Andrea through her stifling fear, that was precisely what it was. She couldn't see what was really atop those towering legs, after all.

"I'm sorry!" squealed Gina. "I don't know what to do!"

Something slammed against the driver-side door. Then the front fender on the passenger's side. Then something crashed against the roof of the car, denting it.

Nicole stared up at that dent as she shrank down in her seat, terror overwhelming her. The dark reality of the situation was rapidly sinking in. "Oh my god…" she blubbered. "Oh my god oh my god oh my god…" Another crash pushed the dent in farther, wrenching a terrified scream out of her. *Somebody help!* she thought through her terror. *Somebody please get us out of here!*

But no one was there. No one was coming to help.

They were going to die out here.

Chapter 10

Gina's little Honda Civic was under siege. Powerful hooves lashed out, jolting the car in every direction. The roof was slowly being beaten down on them, inching lower and lower with each passing second. The windshield cobwebbed and folded inward. The rear driver-side window shattered, sending bits of safety glass raining down around Nicole as she freed herself from the seatbelt and slid down into the foot space. Andrea and Gina were clinging to each other over the console between the front seats, trying to make themselves as small as possible.

Everything was chaos and screaming. There was nowhere to run. Getting out of the vehicle certainly wasn't an option.

The front passenger-side window shattered, followed by the rear window.

The airbags activated and exploded outward, tearing the dashboard to pieces, filling the upper half of the vehicle.

It was all closing in on them. Soon they'd be crushed to death. Or perhaps they'd only be buried alive in a suffocating tomb of broken, twisted metal, a far slower and more agonizing death. Or maybe those horrible things with the impossibly long horse legs would drag them all out of the mangled wreckage and end them in far more brutal ways.

Caught in the confusion and terror of the moment, all three of them were convinced of their impending doom. There wasn't any other possible outcome. They couldn't fight these things. No one was coming to help them. No one even knew where they were.

But then something changed.

Gina wasn't entirely sure *when* it changed. She didn't notice it at first through the crippling terror that flooded her mind. But the bombardment had stopped. The only sound within the car was their own terrified screams.

Slowly, one by one, they each seemed to reach the same realization and began to quiet.

Gina dared to peer up at the broken window, fully expecting there to be something terrifying waiting there for her, something that would no doubt tear her very head from her shoulders the moment she locked eyes with it.

But there were no predatory eyes staring in at her.

For a moment, she glimpsed those monstrous horse legs as the creatures darted around the vehicle, but then they were gone, vanished as quickly as they'd appeared, leaving only an eerie silence behind them.

"What's happening now?" whispered Nicole. She was peering up from her cowering place in the rear floorboards, her lovely eyes wide and glistening with terrified tears. Her makeup, so lovely all day in spite of the heat and even that weird encounter with the barely-there, was now smeared.

Andrea could only manage a terrified squeak in response. There were streaks under her eyes from crying and a lock of bright red hair had fallen free of one of her buns, but she wasn't hurt.

Somehow, *none* of them were hurt.

There was a light outside, Gina realized. She sat up, wary, and looked the other way, through the somehow still-intact driver-side window.

At first, she thought it was another car, but it was the wrong color. It was a strangely *gray* light, dingy, dull, less like the glaring headlamps of an oncoming car than a murky reflection of moonlight off a muddy river. And it *moved* like a reflection off water, too. It sort of shimmered. In fact, it practically *oozed*. And unlike the headlights of a car, which would be pointed toward them, this light was moving *away* from them, slinking off into the distance, slowly vanishing into the haze.

"When did it start raining?" asked Nicole as she turned and peered out into the steady drizzle. Wasn't the sky clear just before those things attacked them? She distinctly remembered watching the moon change colors as they approached.

Andrea looked up through her own window. Now that she was aware of it, she could feel it. A cold mist falling onto her bare arm. She wiped the tears from her eyes and sniffled. "Is that what made those horse things go away?"

The darkness the things brought with them had vanished along with them. In its place, the world around them had become bathed in a soft and gloomy haze.

Gina stared off into the rainy fog where the strange, gray light had already faded away. "I don't think so," she replied. It was only for a fleeting moment, but she thought she sensed someone over there just before the light disappeared. Someone...or some*thing*...that filled her with a strange, inexplicable feeling...almost like an overwhelming *sadness*.

"Can we still drive this thing?" asked Nicole.

Gina glanced over her shoulder at her, distracted. "Wha...? Oh. Uh..." She turned her attention back to the car. It seemed to be working. It was still idling. It was still in gear, even, just as it was when those monsters bombarded it.

She gripped the wheel and pressed down on the accelerator, attempting to pull back onto the road. But the tires spun uselessly in the mud. She cut the wheels back and forth, trying to find some grip, but they were stuck. She shifted it into reverse and tried again, but the Civic stubbornly refused to budge. It was wedged into the ditch.

"No use," she sighed at last. The panic that had overtaken her during the attack had already vanished again. With her emotions back under control, she managed to sound almost bored with this new predicament. "It's not going anywhere."

"Does that mean we have to go out there?" whimpered Andrea.

"We can't stay here," replied Nicole as she swiped at her cell phone screen. "I don't have a signal to call for help. What if those things come back?"

"What if they come back and we're out there instead of in here?" she countered. "We don't even know how far it is to the nearest house."

But Gina didn't wait for them to finish debating the subject. She opened her door and stepped out into the rain.

"Hey, wait up!" said Andrea.

"Be careful!" gasped Nicole as she slipped the strap of her purse over her head and shoulder.

Gina didn't seem to hear them. She walked out into the road and then stood there in the rain, squinting at the misty world around her. "We've moved..." she said after a moment.

Andrea leaned across the seat and peered out the open door at her. "What?"

"We've moved," she said again, a little louder.

"Moved how?" asked Nicole.

Gina glanced back at them. "This isn't the same place we were. Everything's different."

Nicole's door didn't want to open. It groaned and creaked in protest. But she was able to force it enough to squeeze through and step out into the rain with her.

Andrea was more reluctant, but she left the vehicle, too, cringing a little at the feel of the cold rain on her arms and neck.

She was right. The road they were standing on now was all gravel and mud. The one they'd been traveling when those horse-things attacked was paved.

"Then where are we?" asked Andrea.

"I don't know," replied Gina. "But it feels wrong." She turned all the way around, slowly scanning their surroundings, trying to peer through the haze. "I don't like it..."

Andrea's eyes fell on the vehicle. "Oh no! You're car." It looked like someone had taken a sledgehammer all the way around the Civic. There didn't appear to be a single surface left undamaged.

Gina's gaze washed right over it as she turned. "It's just a car."

"Yeah, but... I mean, still..." If that were *her* car, she'd be beside herself. What would she do? How would she explain it?

But the vehicle was the least of Gina's worries. She'd either deal with it later or she wouldn't. And if she dealt with it later, she'd be *thankful* to still be around to worry about it. What mattered right now was finding a way out of whatever new trouble they'd found themselves in.

Nicole took a few more steps away from the battered Civic, still squinting into the rain. "What's that over there?"

It was a light of some sort. Faint and bluish in the haze. She began moving toward it.

"Careful," begged Andrea.

The light wasn't very bright, but it was there. A beacon in an otherwise empty grayness. And as she approached it, she spotted a large shadow looming beside the light. A few more steps revealed the light to be a streetlamp and the shadow to be the side of a building.

"A house?" asked Andrea. "Maybe someone there can help us."

As they moved closer, another shadow of a building emerged from the mist. And between the two stood an open gate.

A driveway?

Gina stared at the gate, uncertain. That was about where she saw that mystery light fading into the mist. Was it showing them where to go? And did that mean they should go there or that they should stay away? The goddess never gave her any instructions about anything like this.

Nicole continued on, still clutching her purse and the wrapped spear against her. Was that why those things attacked them? Were they trying to get their hooves on the spear? Or were they just trying to kill them?

Another of those dim, bluish lights blossomed in the darkness, followed by another, and with them more of those shadowy shapes. The two buildings were only the first of many, it seemed.

Not a house, but *lots* of houses. An entire neighborhood?

As they stepped through the open gate, the dirt and mud gave way to a narrow, cobbled street. More gloomy streetlamps dotted a winding path down a shallow hill lined with closely packed buildings.

It was a cute place, Nicole thought. All brick and wood and cobblestone. It looked like something out of a movie. But the rain and the mist made it look strangely *dreary*.

Andrea paused and looked up at a street sign mounted atop one of the gate posts. "'Tristesse Lane,'" she read. Then she glanced over at Gina. "Ever heard of that?"

She shook her head. She was fairly sure she'd never heard that name before. But that uneasy feeling was only growing as they drew closer. Something about this place just didn't feel right.

Nicole looked down at her phone, but still she didn't have a signal. "I can't look up anything about it, either..." What kind of backwater town didn't have cellular service? Where were they? She didn't like the idea of being so completely cut off from the rest of the world.

They continued on, hugging themselves against the cold as the drizzling rain continued down around them, slowly drenching their clothes.

There wasn't a light shining in a single window, Nicole saw. Although she supposed that shouldn't surprise her. It was still very early in the morning, according to her phone. Everyone was probably asleep.

But there could usually be seen at least *some* sort of light visible at night in any given home. Most people used some sort of nightlight.

No. She was probably just being paranoid. She'd had two pretty big scares in the past few hours, after all. She was looking for things that were wrong at this point. Watching for anything that might warn her of the next fright.

Gina stopped and shook her head. "This is wrong," she decided. "We shouldn't be here."

Andrea looked over at her. "What do you feel?"

"I'm not sure. It's like there's this...weight on my chest... Just...this *crushing* feeling...like I can't breathe..."

Nicole and Andrea exchanged a worried glance.

"We should leave. Right now."

Nicole nodded. "Yeah. If you say so."

"You're the boss," agreed Andrea.

But when they turned around, the gate was gone. There was no sign of the dirt road.

Tristesse Lane wound its way up the hill behind them, stretching on and on into the mist.

"Well, shit…" sighed Nicole.

Chapter 11

The three of them trudged through the endless drizzle, wispy curls of fog drifting across the cobblestone at their feet. They passed silent doorways, empty, black windowpanes and streetlamps whose dreary, bluish light barely reached the ground beneath them. There were no decorations to be seen, not a single splash of color, not a sign of *cheer* in sight.

Around them, that dreary, endless rain continued to fall, never hard enough to impede them in any way, but constant enough to keep them wet and cold and miserable. In fact, none of the joys or comforts of summer seemed able to reach this place. The flowerbeds were barren. The grass was patchy and sickly. The few trees that grew along Tristesse Lane all appeared to be dead.

The buildings on either side of them seemed to be small apartment buildings, all of them three or four stories tall, with perky little signs in front that gave them each deceptively happy names like Sunny Rosegarden Terrace or Joyful Bliss Estates or Jubilant Radiance Plaza. Each one had its own, personal touches, its own unique identity, so that no two were exactly alike, but still they were all the same. Each one was silent, gloomy and dark. And each one gave off a distinctive aura that Gina, for one, could feel all the way to her bones.

This was a bad place.

She sensed no real violence here. No radiating malice or hatred. No predatory hunger or perverse lust. No *fear*. All she could really feel was a deep, lingering sense of *sadness*.

It reminded her of the street where she grew up, although she wasn't entirely sure why. It looked nothing like Marigold Street back in her old Indiana hometown, but something about this unhappy feeling it gave off was eerily reminiscent of the life she had back then.

She was becoming more and more certain that there was something very *wicked* about this street. And there was no way off it. They could go downhill or up, seemingly forever, but that was all. The buildings were crowded right up against each other. No other streets branched off this one. There were no alleyways to slip into. It was just the one endless lane...

"We can't just keep going on like this forever," said Nicole as she paused to look behind them again.

"I think this street begs to disagree," grumbled Andrea, her lip quivering from the cold of her soaked clothes.

Nicole's teeth were chattering, too. She couldn't believe she was actually *cold*. It was so hot all day. It was more that her clothes were wet than the actual temperature, she thought. Her tank top had gone nearly transparent, showing off almost every lacy detail of her bra. And she wasn't going to be able to change into something dry anytime soon. Their bags were still in the trunk of Gina's car, on the other side of the gate that apparently didn't exist anymore.

She couldn't help being reminded of the Temple of the Blind and those pools of frigid water they'd been forced to cross on their weird journey into the heart of the labyrinth. At least this rain didn't seem quite as cold as that water. But their clothes were soaked. Back then, down in those dark passageways, she didn't have that. They were all naked the whole time. They dried much more quickly that way. And Albert had speculated since then that perhaps that was the whole point of making them pro-ceed naked into that terrible labyrinth, to allow them to swim easier and dry faster and spare them the discomfort of wet, chaf-ing fabric.

The very thought of Albert sent a strange, almost sickly sen-sation through her, a jolt of embarrassment and guilt that was almost revulsion.

Why did it have to be *him* that thing pretended to be while it was toying with her mind? Albert was one of her closest friends, one of her favorite people in the entire world. She didn't want to feel like this whenever he crossed her mind. It was wrong.

She remembered being down there in those tunnels... For a long time, it was just the three of them. She and Albert and Brandy, alone together in the darkness... Vulnerable... *Intimate*... She remembered emerging from one of those frigid pools and the three of them huddling together for a while for warmth, naked and unashamed. It wasn't sexual. Not at all. That was the *last* thing on her mind at the time. And in the weeks and months that followed, those memories had never been carnal, either. Those moments had only brought them closer together as friends. He was like *family* to her.

And he was right where he belonged. In a warm bed somewhere, next to his new bride...their naked bodies pressed together... happily snoozing...blissfully unaware of these new horrors.

Again, she found herself feeling sorry for herself.

The one left behind.

The one nobody took home...

She pushed the thought away, disgusted with herself. What was wrong with her? Now certainly wasn't the time for those kinds of stupid thoughts. "Stupid barely-there..." she muttered.

Andrea looked over at her, her lips still quivering from the cold. "What?"

"Nothing." She turned her gaze toward the nearest of those silent doorways. "Seems like these buildings are the only way off this damn street."

Gina shook her head. "I don't like the buildings. They feel wrong."

"I don't like *any* of this," countered Nicole. "But we can't stay out here in the rain forever. Just look at you."

Gina's blouse had gone transparent, too. Her hair was plastered to her face. She was sniffling.

Andrea stared at the darkened doorway. The sign identified this building as Glimmering Sunrise Place, though there was nothing "glimmering" about it and she highly doubted you could ever see the sunrise from any of those gloomy windows. "I don't know... If Gina says they feel bad..."

"It's either that or just keep following this stupid street until one of us catches pneumonia." She glanced over at Gina. "I mean, unless you really think this is actually taking us somewhere."

Gina shook her head. "No. I've heard of places like this before. Places that stretch on forever. With no cell service. And no clear way out. This is the kind of thing my friends investigate."

"You mean one of those pocket dimension things?" said Andrea.

She nodded. "Or something bigger. Either way, this definitely isn't our world."

Nicole remembered the endless hallway she found when she tried to flee that monstrous mockery of her home and immediately pushed the thought from her mind. "Can you feel anyone in here with us?"

"Lots of people." She pointed at the doorway. "Inside." Then she looked back the way they came, up the winding street at all the buildings lined there. "Inside all of them."

"So maybe there *is* someone who can help us," reasoned Andrea.

"No. There's something wrong with them. I don't think they can leave here." She turned and met Nicole's gaze. "Just like us."

Nicole shuddered and hugged herself against the cold. "Okay, so that *does* sound pretty awful… But I'm still not hearing any other ideas."

"What about the spear?" suggested Andrea. "Do you think it could help us out?"

Nicole glanced down at her dripping purse.

"I don't think so," replied Gina. "I think we're supposed to take it to Cedric's Cove. This place doesn't feel like somewhere we should be. I think we've been dragged off course. Probably by someone or something that doesn't want us to get where we're going."

"You never know," reasoned Nicole. "Maybe whoever sent it meant exactly for us to end up here."

Gina shrugged. "Maybe. But I can't think of a way to use

it." Her sleepy gaze drifted toward the buildings again. "Unless you think one of those people might be the gatekeeper you're supposed to stab in the heart."

"No way!" snapped Andrea. She wasn't killing anyone.

"Then that just leaves us the one choice, doesn't it?" decided Nicole. "Inside."

Andrea groaned and looked back at that nearest doorway. Glimmering Sunrise…with no glimmer *or* sunshine… "Do any of them feel better than others at least?"

"They're all exactly the same," replied Gina. "Too exactly the same, in fact." She turned and looked at the building across the street from Glimmering Sunrise Place, puzzled. "It's like they're all just different doors leading to the same place."

Andrea groaned again. "I don't like this. *At all.*"

Nicole didn't like it either, but it was becoming clear to her that they were going to have to go inside one of these buildings eventually. They might as well get it over with. She walked up to the door of Glimmering Sunrise Place and looked it over. There was no bell. With names like "Plaza," "Terrace," and "Estates," these buildings should be apartment units, not single-family homes, and there weren't any mailboxes anywhere to be seen, suggesting that this door opened onto a common hallway, not into someone's living room, but she knocked anyway, just to be certain. The last thing she wanted to do was surprise some gun-happy homeowner watching television in his underwear.

"This place makes my belly hurt…" groaned Andrea.

"It's wrong here," agreed Gina. "We should be careful."

"So you keep saying…" She turned and looked back up the winding cobblestone lane. "I told you guys we never should've gotten out of the car."

But Gina shook her head. "That doesn't matter. By then, we were already here."

"Oh…"

Nicole knocked again.

"No one's going to answer," Gina informed her. "No one in there can hear you."

She glanced back, uncertain, then tentatively tried the knob.

It was unlocked.

"Hello?" She eased the door open and peered inside. A long, dark hallway waited beyond. She bit her lip, cringing at the thought of all the scary things that might await them there, and looked back again. "Creepy…" she groaned.

But at least it was dry in there.

"Why's it so dark?" asked Andrea as the three of them stepped inside and let the door close behind them.

It was a good question. There were light fixtures in the ceiling, but they were like the streetlamps outside, dim, dingy and barely bright enough to reach the floor beneath them. And the far end of the hallway was utterly lost in the gloom.

Again, she remembered the hallway outside that nightmare version of her own apartment. More and more, she was realizing that this place was just like that one. She looked down at the floor and wondered if the carpet here would feel squelchy and strange if she weren't wearing shoes.

A set of stairs beside them led up to a second floor that was no brighter than the first. If anything, it was even darker up there.

Other than that, there wasn't anything particularly ominous about the hallway. It wasn't decayed and covered in cobwebs like so many horror movie settings. The walls weren't splattered with blood. All things considered, Nicole decided it could be worse. She survived Gilbert House. She could certainly handle this.

But Gina shrank back against the closed door, her hands clutched against her chest. "Not good…" she whimpered.

Nicole glanced over at her, concerned. "What's wrong?"

"It's really bad here…"

"Bad how?"

She was staring into the darkness that swallowed the far end of the corridor, her eyes shimmering with unshed tears. "It feels like…"

"Like *what?*" pressed Andrea.

Gina turned those weepy eyes on her. A tear streaked down her cheek as she said, "It feels like hopelessness in here."

Chapter 12

Nicole held tight to one of Gina's hands while Andrea clung to the other.

They lingered for a long time in the front doorway of Glimmering Sunrise Place, too spooked by Gina's ominous observation to venture any deeper into these gloomy hallways. But spooked or not, they each understood that eventually they were going to have to move. They couldn't stand around like this forever. And going back out into that endless rain was no better an option. Eventually, they were going to have to move forward.

Finally, they mustered the courage and set off down the hallway into that waiting gloom together, Nicole's cell phone light illuminating the way far better than those useless overhead bulbs. But as they pushed into that darkness, past one closed door after another, they discovered that the ground-floor hallway of Glimmering Sunrise Place was every bit as endless as Tristesse Lane outside.

And the deeper into that darkness they went, the more ominous the place felt.

It feels like hopelessness in here... Nicole shivered as those words drifted through her mind again and again. What did that mean? Hopeless how? Hopeless like the gates of hell? As in, "Abandon hope all ye who enter here"? Was that the sort of place they'd found themselves in?

"Are there people in all these apartments?" wondered Andrea as they passed what must have been at least the twentieth closed door.

Gina nodded.

"There's that many people here?" marveled Nicole.

"I don't know how many there are. Not all the doors go to

different places."

"How does *that* work?" wondered Andrea.

"Probably the same way Gilbert House worked," guessed Nicole. "That place wasn't much for following the laws of physics, remember."

"Oh yeah..." Gilbert House was one thing on the outside and an entirely different thing on the inside. One part of it existed in their world and the other existed out in that freaky forest. She never went inside it, herself, but she'd heard everyone else's stories. It certainly wasn't on her destinations bucket list.

"This place isn't what it appears to be," said Gina. "It's not a building at all. It's something a lot more complex. Space is all twisted up here. Direction is an illusion." She looked back over her shoulder. "We might not be going anywhere at all right now. Or we may have already gone a hundred miles."

Andrea looked back at the dimly lit doorway they were leaving behind. "Really?"

"Things get weird in places like these."

"Doesn't seem like it's the same as the temple, does it?"

Nicole shook her head. "I don't know. The temple was pretty weird, too. Remember how messed up time was when we got back? All our watches were different. I think I actually had jetlag for a few days after that."

"Time gets weird in places like this, too," agreed Gina.

They walked on, passing door after door after door. Every now and then another of those uselessly dim lights would appear ahead of them and they'd trudge beneath it, only to pass back into the darkness beyond it.

Nicole's mind kept wandering. She kept thinking about Brandy and Albert, off on their night of wedded bliss. She wasn't jealous. That was just a stupid fake emotion planted by that nasty barely-there, but she couldn't deny that this just didn't seem very fair. Why did Brandy get a night in paradise while *she* got a stroll through the ninth circle of hell?

Was it really so much to ask that God or the universe or that creepy little Keeper guy or *whoever* the hell was behind all that nonsense five years ago pick a cute guy to send down into those tunnels for *her* to go home with? Then she could've dragged *him* along on this nutjob adventure to find some imaginary traveling Great Lakes city.

It wasn't that she felt like she needed a big strong man to take care of her, of course...but one had to admit that they were pretty handy for things like this. They liked being all macho around pretty girls in scary situations. It made them feel useful.

(Albert and Wayne had both admitted as much, after all. Apparently, it was a guy thing.)

All joking aside, though, she couldn't seem to shrug off this lingering loneliness.

Why was she even thinking about things like this? It wasn't as if she didn't have plenty to keep her mind occupied. And yet here she was, feeling sorry for herself because she still didn't have a boyfriend.

What was wrong with her? She seriously needed to get her priorities in order!

Eager for a distraction from her own idiotic thoughts, she glanced over at Gina and asked, "Can you really feel everyone who's here?"

"Everyone who's nearby. They're suffering. All of them."

"Oh," squeaked Andrea, cringing.

"Can we help them?" asked Nicole.

"No. They're too far gone. The misery of this place is all they know now. And that's what'll happen to us, too, if we can't figure out how to leave this place."

"Aren't you just a happy little ray of endless sunshine..." she grumbled.

"Sorry."

"It's okay." She stopped and looked back and forth. There were more of those uselessly dim lights glowing up ahead of them, but no end in sight for this stupid hallway. "It's like the street outside," she realized. "We either walk on and on forever or we pick one of these doors and see what's behind it."

"Can I have a few hours to think about it?" whimpered Andrea.

"The longer we're here, the less likely we are to ever leave," warned Gina.

"Oh…"

Nicole took a shaky breath. It was starting to feel like the air was getting heavy. A weight seemed to have settled on her chest. "Okay…" she sighed. She walked to the nearest door and lifted her fist to knock.

"No one will hear you," said Gina.

She paused, her hand still raised, uncertain.

"Just saying…"

Nicole knocked anyway. It just seemed rude not to. Even in whatever this freaky, endlessly looping dimension was. But there wasn't much effort behind it. She doubted anyone inside would've heard it anyway. Then she turned the knob and opened the door, revealing a gloomy, cluttered living room.

It wasn't trashed by any means, just sort of well-lived. There weren't even any dirty dishes or empty cans lying around. There were books and magazines piled carelessly on every available surface, some spilled off onto the floor. A few socks and a sweater had been tossed lazily around the room. A jacket was draped over the back of an overstuffed chair with threadbare armrests.

It didn't look like the sort of place they'd find someone trapped and languishing in endless suffering.

It was a surprisingly modern room, even. A big, flatscreen television was mounted to the wall in front of a lightly worn sofa. A cell phone was charging on a glass coffee table. There was a desk in one corner with an open, snoozing laptop. She could see the red and blue lights of a router and a modem glowing on one of the lower shelves along with other, less-recognizable devices. In fact, this scattered spattering of little electronic lights was the *only* light emanating from within the apartment. The overhead lights, like most of the ones in the hallway, were all dark, and there didn't appear to even be a switch for turning them on. Most of the light illuminating the space came through the single, rain-streaked window, from one of those dreary streetlamps outside.

Other than the eerie darkness, it wasn't very unlike her and Andrea's apartment, really. Just a bit smaller. The far corner of the room acted as a small dining area, with a table and two wooden chairs. A short counter separated the space from a cozy kitchen. And next to that, an empty hallway stretched deeper into the darkness.

But she couldn't help noticing that what little light passed through the window was the same sort of bluish color she saw in that hideous mockery of her home the barely-there dragged her into.

Was that what had happened? Did the barely-there get them all? Did it snatch them away while they were distracted with those horse monsters? Was that why they couldn't find a way out?

She pushed the thought away, unsure what to do with it even if it *did* turn out to be true, and called out into the silence. "Hello? Is anybody home?"

No one answered.

Gina tugged at the back of her shirt, then pointed at a set of folding closet doors next to the hallway.

She hesitated. Now that she'd muscled past her trepidation and entered one of the apartments, only to find it empty, she found her fear creeping back in. She wasn't eager to go poking around, opening doors, looking for something that would give her more nightmares like the ones that followed her home from the temple that night.

They'd all had nightmares. It was fairly inevitable after the things they went through. Hers had mostly been about all those monsters they encountered coming back and murdering the people she cared about. She seriously wasn't looking forward to going through anything like *that* again. But it didn't seem like she had much choice in the matter. As she kept reminding everyone else, they were obviously going to have to do these things eventually anyway.

Reluctantly, she crossed the room and approached the closet.

She heard something as she reached for the handle. A very soft sound from inside. A muttering? Or was it more of a whimper?

Bracing herself for the worst, she gripped the knob and slid the door open.

Inside, a man lay curled up on the floor beneath a sparse selection of hanging coats and jackets. He appeared to be in his late twenties or early thirties, with dirty black hair in need of a cut, a stubbly beard and a pale, almost pasty complexion. There were dark bags under his watery eyes and he was staring off into space, seemingly unaware that he had visitors.

"Hello?" tried Nicole.

The man made no indication that he heard her.

"You, um…okay in there?"

Still, the man didn't move. His lip was quivering. He looked for all the world like someone who's life had utterly fallen apart.

She knelt down and peered closer at him. "Do you need help?"

Those eyes never moved from that far off place.

"He can't hear you," said Gina. "He's gone."

Nicole looked up at her, confused. "He's right *here*," she replied. "He's *awake*. He's just…" She turned and looked back down at him.

"No… There's nothing left inside that man but despair."

"Drama queen much?" muttered Andrea.

"It's not a mood," she explained. "It's not that he's depressed. It's not that his despair is overwhelming. It's like…there's nothing else left. Like his mind has been completely and permanently emptied of everything that's not sadness and grief."

Nicole felt the hairs on the back of her neck prickling at these words.

"You mean…like something *ate* all this guy's happiness or something?" asked Andrea.

Gina frowned. "Maybe something like that, I guess… I mean I don't know, but…"

"That's *seriously* messed up…"

Nicole watched a tear slip down the man's face and drop to the floor as a suffocating dread began to spread deep inside her belly.

What was this place?

Chapter 13

Tristesse Lane couldn't be seen through the gloomy mist and the rain streaking down the windowpane, only the dingy glow of those useless streetlamps. This, in itself, was weird since there shouldn't have been any windows in this room. There were at least two dozen apartments between this one and the front of the building. Given that all the buildings were mashed right up against each other, the only windows that should've been able to look out onto those lamps were the ones in the very first unit. But of course, that was applying real-world logic to a place that defied the very laws of nature.

Gina did warn them that this place wasn't what it seemed to be.

The window didn't open. Andrea considered breaking it. If she leaned out into the rain and got a better look at the street out there, would she be able to tell if anything was different? She doubted it. And she didn't care for the thought of breaking the window and pointlessly letting in the dampness only to make the guy in the closet's miserable existence that much worse.

Gina tried turning on the television, but there was only static. And while it cast a somewhat brighter light into the room, there was something unsettling about the white noise and the snow. It reminded them all of too many horror movies. She switched it back off and returned the remote to the coffee table.

Nicole looked in all the drawers and cabinets, even in the refrigerator and the microwave, searching for anything that might help them better understand their situation and perhaps puzzle their way out of it. Most of the cupboards were completely bare. There was a scattering of basics. A few dishes. Some coffee mugs. A depressingly small amount of silverware. Flour and salt.

Sugar. Half a bag of rice. A few cans of soda and some very questionable-looking leftover containers. (In case the guy's wallowing in abject misery on the floor of his closet wasn't evidence enough that he didn't do much entertaining here at ever-so-cheerful Glimmering Sunrise Place.) But she never really expected to find anything. This wasn't one of those cheesy escape room games. She didn't know what this place was, but it was undeniably *real*. The truth was that she was only stalling.

They were *all* only stalling.

Going back out into that hallway felt as useless as going back outside and walking around in the rain again. But the only other place to go was into the other hallway, deeper into Mr. Sad's unhappy home.

She didn't want to be here. There was something dreadfully *wrong* about this apartment. But at the same time, she was just as wary of the endless hallway outside. At least this place had some semblance of comfort. A part of her wanted to just plop down on that couch and stay a while.

Maybe everything would just take care of itself.

(As if.)

Gina made the decision for them. She stepped into the oppressive gloom of the interior hallway and shined her cell phone's flashlight into it. Like the one outside, it stretched much farther than the architecture of the building warranted.

Andrea peered into the corridor as well. "Do you feel anything down there?" she asked, her voice hushed.

"More of the same," she replied. "Sadness. Misery. Hopelessness."

Andrea glanced over at the folding door as the man hiding behind it let out another pitiful whimper. "You think there's more people like *him* in the *bedroom* closet?"

"There's no bedroom," Gina informed her. She was already moving, plunging headlong into the darkness.

"Wait up!" hissed Nicole. "Don't run off on your own!"

But she didn't slow down. By the time the two of them caught up with her, they were fully enveloped in the gloom.

Andrea looked back, but already, the dimly lit apartment

had disappeared back into the darkness. They appeared to be in yet another endless hallway. She frowned and shined her cell phone light all around her. Had they finally managed to get themselves lost somewhere they couldn't escape from? Was this endless darkness the last thing she was destined to ever see again?

But then two more doors appeared. One on either side of the hallway.

Gina shined her light at one and then the other, her small features scrunched into a look of unsettled concern. "Stronger here…"

Nicole didn't bother knocking this time. She grabbed the knob of the door on the left and pushed it open. Another apartment lay sprawled out before her. The architecture was completely different than the last one. Most of the walls were bare brick. Iron beams stretched across the ceiling. The furniture was modern minimalist. Again, the room was untidy, but not filthy. Instead of magazines, there were art supplies scattered around the room. Sketchbooks and pencils. Paints and brushes. Canvases and drop cloths. There was a fireplace against one wall, but the fire had long gone cold and again the only light was the depressing glow of those streetlamps outside, this time casting through the rain-streaked panes of two large windows.

In the middle of it all, a tall, shirtless and barefoot man in paint-stained blue jeans lay sprawled on his back on the scarred wood floor, his hair gray and thin, his body doughy and pale. He looked like a *literal* starving artist. In fact, she would have mistaken him for dead if not for the fact that his glistening eyes were wide open, staring blankly at the ceiling, and his lips were trembling, as if he were trying to speak.

"Hello?"

Like the younger man in the previous apartment, he didn't answer. He didn't even seem to hear her. Even when she walked up to him and nudged his cheek with the toe of her shoe, he didn't move.

"Nothing left," whispered Gina.

Andrea shivered. "These people are seriously harshing the

mood in this place. *Total* downers."

"This is fucking *creepy* is what it is." Nicole turned and walked back through the door, only to find that the hallway they'd just come from had changed. Instead of emerging from one of two doors facing each other, she was now standing at the very end of a hallway, staring straight down it into more gloom. "Wait...what?"

"I told you space was messed up in here," Gina reminded her.

"This building is *way* wonky," whispered Andrea.

Nicole shined her light back into the artist's apartment, confirming that it hadn't disappeared too, then she set off down the new hallway. She wasn't going to let this stupid building beat her. She'd survived Gilbert House. She'd survived the Temple of the Blind. She'd scaled the burning mountain all the way to its blistering peak. She wasn't going to let *this* stupid, depressing place be the thing that broke her.

And yet she jerked to a startled halt as someone somewhere in that looming darkness let out a terrible, mournful wail that sent a chill all the way to her soul.

She actually *felt* it. The depths of that person's endless despair. It pierced her heart like an arrow and sent shockwaves of emotional agony through her entire body. She felt a tear streak down her cheek.

She looked back, her eyes wide in the gloom. Andrea and Gina stood staring back at her, their eyes shimmering with mirrored tears.

They'd felt it, too.

Reluctantly, she faced the darkness again and continued forward, slower this time.

"I don't understand any of this," whispered Andrea. "Why are we here? How did we even *get* here?"

"Someone brought us here," replied Gina.

"*Why?*"

She shook her head. "The goddess warned me that obstacles would stand in our way."

"What's so special about Cedric's Cove, anyway? Why is it

so important for me to go there?"

"She didn't tell me that."

"Of course not…"

"But I do know for a fact that there've been things happening in the world recently. Things having to do with the lifecycle of the universe. Like the door you helped open five years ago."

Andrea nodded. She *did* say that all of this had something to do with "finishing what they started." Whatever that meant.

Ahead, only more darkness unfolded before them, threatening to keep them trapped here forever.

"I wish I knew how to do that portal thing again," said Andrea.

Nicole glanced over at her. "Right. That thing with that creepy ghost tunnel."

"Ghost tunnel?" asked Gina.

"It was called Journey of the Dead," explained Andrea, remembering the words spoken to her by that mysterious voice all those years ago. "I guess it's what the dead use to travel from this world to the next or something. Apparently, it was the 'tunnel of light' that some people say they see when they have near-death experiences, but there wasn't any light down there. It was pitch black."

"Sounds like a spirit highway," said Gina. "I know the fringe roads are supposedly built on some of them, but I've never heard of anyone alive entering the spirit highway, itself."

She'd never heard the term "spirit highway" before. Nor did she have any idea what a fringe road was. But she already felt a little overwhelmed and she didn't really feel like asking. "I don't really know anything about it," she said instead. "I'm pretty sure it was that creepy Keeper guy who actually sent me there."

"Oh," said Gina. "Him. That kind of makes sense."

"You know the Keeper?" asked Nicole, surprised.

"I know *of* him. Some friends of mine had some business with him a few years back."

"Oh…" She glanced at Andrea, surprised. "Small world."

"Sometimes," replied Gina.

The three of them fell quiet and continued on.

But Nicole didn't care for the silence. It felt strangely disturbing. "Personally," she said, "I'm not sure I'm quite desperate enough to use that tunnel again anyway. We almost got trapped there last time."

"Believe me," said Andrea, "I remember." For a moment there, she really thought she was going to be left behind when the tunnel closed. She didn't know how to hold it open and leave at the same time. If it hadn't been for Wayne... Well, she didn't really like thinking about it.

Inevitably, they fell silent again.

Nicole was trying to think of something else to say, anything to help chase off this oppressive silence, but after a few more tentative steps, two more doors appeared from the gloom, one on either side, just like the last pair.

She chose the one on the right and opened it.

This third apartment was different from *both* previous units. Small and cozy, carpeted, with several overstuffed chairs draped with blankets and pillows arranged around a glass coffee table scattered with sewing supplies. There was fabric and unraveled yarn strewn all around the room. Like the previous two, it was completely dark, lit by nothing more than the same, weak streetlamps shining through the same rain-soaked window panes.

A very thin old woman sat in one of the chairs in the dark, the same empty expression on her face, the same pasty complexion, the same dark bags under her eyes. An unfinished quilt lay wadded up at her feet.

She was muttering something beneath her breath, a barely audible whisper, over and over again.

Andrea knelt down beside her and gave her a gentle shake. "Hey..."

"You can't reach them," Gina reminded her. "None of them. They're all gone."

What was it she kept saying? Was it a name? Danny, perhaps? Or Andy? Mandy? She couldn't quite make it out. "We can't just leave these people here like this."

"We can't do anything *else*." Gina shivered and crossed her arms against the lingering cold of her damp clothes. She was uncomfortable. Not merely because of the cold, but also because she didn't like having to keep telling them these things. She felt like the bad guy. "I know it sounds cruel, but it's just the way it is. I'm sorry."

"It's *heartbreaking…*"

"I know. Believe me, I know."

Andrea squeezed the woman's hand. "It's like she's waiting for someone she knows is never coming."

It was, indeed, like that. She could feel it. There was a crushing sense of desperate loneliness and longing emanating from her.

"Do these people think they're at *home*?" wondered Nicole as she glanced around. There were decorations on the walls and mantle. Dusty silk flowers, scented candles in fancy glass holders and framed needlepoint pictures of cats and chickens and goldfish were carefully arranged around the room.

"Maybe," said Gina. "At one time, I guess… I'm not sure they're capable of thinking anything at all now, though. Not on any conscious level."

Nicole glanced back at the open door, thinking. She recalled the dejected artist's home, then the first guy's place. She hadn't seen a single photograph in any of them. She knew that her own personal preference for plastering every inch of her walls with pictures of her friends and family wasn't common, but it seemed odd to her that none of these people had *any*. Did these people not have any happy memories to look at before they came here? Or were those taken away by whatever heartless force trapped them all here?

Andrea stood up and shook her head. "There has to be *something* we can do for them."

"We should just go," said Gina. "We have to keep moving. There's something awful at work here and the longer we stand around, the quicker it'll get into our heads."

"Definitely keep moving," agreed Nicole.

Andrea didn't want to go. It seemed wrong to just walk away. But if what Gina said was true, then there really wasn't anything they could do for the woman.

Nicole stepped back out into the hallway to find that it had changed again. It wasn't quite as obvious as it was last time. She wasn't suddenly standing at the end of it. But the door across from this one had disappeared.

She shined her light right, then left, uncertain of which way to go. If this had been the same corridor as before, then going left should take them right back to the dejected artist's place. But if the door across the hall had vanished, then *everything* was probably different.

Another wail broke the endless silence, but it sounded different this time. It was farther away. And the voice was deeper. Huskier. And it didn't seem to cut quite as deeply as the first one. It didn't seem to quite reach all the way to her soul...

It was hard to tell, but she thought it came from the left, so she picked right and set off into the darkness once again, hopefully in the opposite direction.

More doors appeared from the gloom. One on the right. Then the left. Staggered instead of mirrored.

She didn't bother opening any of them, and Andrea, for one, was glad. She didn't want to see any more of these people. She couldn't seem to get that old woman out of her thoughts. The loneliness in her voice as she called out that name they couldn't even properly hear... Was she calling out for her child? A sibling? An old friend? A long-lost lover? Someone who promised to return soon, but never did?

It was frightening just how easy she found it to empathize with such a thing. That could be her someday, after all. What if she never found her happy ending like Brandy and Olivia? What if everyone drifted away from her? What if no one ever came looking for her?

What if, in the end, she found that no one loved her anymore?

She forced the awful thoughts from her head and pushed on. There were more of those dim overhead lights up ahead, like in the outer hallway, barely bright enough to reach the dreary carpet below them. She squinted up at them. Or were they the *same* lights as before? Had they somehow circled back to that first hallway? Did *all* the doors open onto the same corridor?

This was all so confusing. And she was getting tired. How long had it been since that nightmare with those freaky horse-legged things? How far had they walked?

From behind one of the doors came the haunting sound of a woman sobbing.

Nicole and Andrea both glanced at Gina as they approached it, but she only gave them a sad shake of her head.

They could go in there and follow the sound of that crying to its source, but nothing they could say or do would save the woman from her sorrow. There was nothing else inside her.

"They can't *all* be lost causes, can they?" asked Andrea. "I mean *we're* not like that."

"Not yet," said Gina. "But we will be. If we don't find a way out soon." Her gaze fixed on the door as they walked past it. "All these other people have been here a long time. A lot longer than they realize. A lot longer than should be possible."

Andrea made a frightened squeaking noise in her throat. Why did she have to make everything sound a hundred times more creepy than it already was?

As the sobbing receded into the darkness behind them, their lights revealed a door waiting for them that was partially open. They peered through the crack to find not a living room, like those before it, but an office. A cluttered desk stood against the wall, surrounded by bookshelves. A computer monitor sat atop it, dark but for the single red light in the bottom-right corner. An unlit lamp stood beside it, an empty promise of light in the oppressive gloom. It was silent inside but for the soft pitter-patter of the unending rain on the glass.

The chair lay overturned on the floor, surrounded by a scattering of papers and file folders, and behind it, a middle-aged man in a crumpled dress shirt was curled up in the leg space beneath the desk, his back to them, his body shaking with the force of silent sobs. He was clutching his head in his hands, his fingers clawing at his hair as if he meant to tear it out by the roots.

They continued on past the door, leaving the man undisturbed.

Andrea rubbed at her stomach. A sour ache had begun to spread in there, like the unpleasant burn of indigestion. Except this wasn't anything as mundane as buffalo chicken salad. This was something *emotional*. A sick *dread* was growing inside her. It felt as if the phone had just awakened her in the middle of the night and she just *knew* it was terrible news.

Was it this place? Was it the crippling hopelessness that had afflicted all these poor people seeping into her own brain, slowly enveloping her? Or was it only her own fear, the mere idea of some kind of infectious misery that she was certain to catch, either from these people or from the very building itself?

Ahead of them, the hallway abruptly opened up into yet another apartment and they found themselves standing in a rustic dining room with polished oak furniture and stuffed deer heads mounted to the walls. Hunting rifles were leaned against the wall and ammunition boxes were piled on the table.

Once again, the endless rain streaked down the windowpanes.

Gina stopped in the doorway and clutched at the front of her shirt. A startled gasp escaped her.

Andrea glanced around, her own heart racing. "What's wrong?" But even as she uttered the words, she found that she already knew something was dreadfully off here.

It was the *smell*.

There was a very subtle but unmistakable lingering odor of gunpowder...

And *blood*...

Gina's eyes were fixed on a high-backed chair someone had turned to face the window. Between the ever-present gloom, the angle and the size of the chair, she couldn't see anything, but she knew nonetheless that someone was sitting there. Someone who wasn't moving at all.

Someone who wasn't ever going to move again...

"Did someone...?" croaked Andrea. It was difficult to see in the gloom, but there appeared to be a single trail of blood trickling down the back of the chair.

"Oh no..." sighed Nicole.

Gina turned and fled back into the endless hallway.

Nicole and Andrea ran after her without hesitation. Neither of them wanted to linger in that room.

"Wait up!" called Andrea.

"Don't get separated," Nicole reminded her.

Gina stopped and leaned against the wall. Her heart was pounding. She was breathing hard and grasping at her shirt again. "I don't like this…" she wheezed.

The hallway had changed again. This one was much narrower than the others. And the doors were different, too. They seemed smaller and flimsier. And much *older*. The paint was peeling off their surfaces. But the wrongness was much more than the mere appearance. She could feel it.

"It's okay," Nicole assured her. "We'll get through this."

But she shook her head. "We just keep going deeper and deeper."

Andrea shined her light back and forth. "We'll find our way."

"No…" She turned and met their gazes. A tear streaked down her face. "I can feel it We're just like them…" Then, in a tiny whimper of a voice, she said, "We're lost."

Chapter 14

Nicole refused to believe that they couldn't escape this place. There had to be a way. If Wayne and Olivia could find a way out of that zombie-infested forest five years ago, then the three of them could find their way out of one stupid apartment complex, no matter how many dimensions it was stretched across.

And yet they walked on and on, through a subtly shifting landscape of empty hallways, gloomy apartments and dejected tenants.

Time passed. Everywhere they went, the people of this gloomy place—the *downers*, as Andrea called them—wept. Some softly. Some silently. But some wept *hard*. Some sobbed. Some wailed. And some *screamed*. Some *shrieked*.

They stopped trying the doors. They figured out quickly that nothing good ever waited behind the closed doors. But some of them, like the one to that office behind them, already stood open as they passed them, usually offering more glimpses into the vast array of styled apartments, seemingly plucked from buildings all around the world, from cramped city lofts to spacious country condos.

And sometimes the hallway simply emptied into an apartment like a culvert into a cistern, as in the case of the hunter's lodge, giving them no option but to pass directly through whatever unpleasantness lay waiting for them inside.

The only thing worse than the constant weeping of the suffering downers was the silence of those whose suffering had stopped. As they passed through a room with an entire wall of big, rain-smeared windows on one side, Nicole was certain she caught a glimpse of a morbid shape dangling from a rafter in an adjoining bedroom. And Andrea couldn't miss the askew curtain in a dark bathroom that revealed a glimpse of pale, naked toes sticking out of a tub of blood-tinted water. But by far, Gina had the worst of it. Because her strange, psychic power made certain that she felt every person behind every door that she passed, living or dead, and every horror that Tristesse Lane had carved into their broken minds. A fate Gina was increasingly certain was all that awaited them in this miserable place.

She could feel it. A deep, sickening dread deep inside her, as if all were wrong with the world and even the very *thought* of escape were meaningless. It rooted itself deeper and deeper with each passing minute they spent trapped here, tightening its grip on her, slowly strangling her, literally making it harder to breathe.

She didn't even understand why she was here. Hadn't she served her duty? Hadn't she done what the goddess wanted her to do when she went to work at that awful tower, under the cruel gaze of the lying monster that tore her friend's life apart?

The job, itself, wasn't all that bad. She was being paid to make art. And paid well. But designing product packaging and magazine advertisements wasn't exactly what she wanted to do with her talents. She wanted to make her own art. She wanted to do her own thing. What she really wanted to do, what really made her happy, was comic book art.

Sure, it was a little *dorky*. It was a *lot* dorky, in fact. And she wasn't often quick to admit it to people because she knew what it sounded like. And now, as she found herself wading deeper and deeper into the depths of this God-forsaken, melancholy nightmare, it seemed like such an unobtainable dream.

Why should she be able to do what she really wanted to do? Who did she think she was? What made her think she deserved to be happy? She was just Weird Gina.

You don't even try to be normal, do you?

She stopped and turned around, distracted.

"You okay?" asked Andrea.

Gina stood there a moment, blinking into the darkness at their backs, her heart still pounding in her chest. The voice in her head just now... It was only an old memory, she knew, but it seemed so real for a moment there that she thought…

No. Just more of Tristesse Lane's cruel tricks.

This place had sucked the joy out of everyone who came here, leaving them with nothing but burning anguish. Why *wouldn't* it trudge up painful memories and make them feel fresh again?

"Gina?" pressed Andrea, worried.

"I'm okay…"

"Do you need to rest for a little while?" asked Nicole.

"No. We can't stop. If we stop…" She pushed on, still clutching at the front of her blouse. She'd already undone the top two buttons. Why did it feel so hard to breathe in here? "We just can't stop," she finished.

Nicole and Andrea said no more. They continued on, keeping pace with her.

How long had they been here? Nicole's phone said it was nearly seven o'clock, but that didn't feel right. She sensed that it should be much later than that.

Gina warned them that time could get weird in here. It almost made sense. She knew that there were places out in space where time could be distorted. Black holes were said to do things like that. Why not rifts between dimensions?

Nicole wondered, not for the first time, what her father would think of places like these. Would Dr. Stuart Smart's genius intellect be able to understand the weird behavior and make sense of what, to her, was utter nonsense? But of course she'd never dare tell him. He was the kind of man who would be driven to seek knowledge and demand proof, which of course she didn't have. He probably wouldn't believe a word of it. He'd think his daughter had gone crazy. And that was the best-case scenario. If he *did* believe her, even a little, he might go searching for proof on his own. And she couldn't bear the thought of him entering someplace like Gilbert House. It was far too dangerous.

Maybe if Albert were here… Like her father, he was always thinking. And he had a way of talking through the weird stuff, coming up with hypotheses to try explaining the seemingly unexplainable. He was the one who solved the riddles on the box and found the map. He was the one who examined the layout of that endless maze and patterns of scratches on the floors in different areas and figured out that the labyrinth hounds were bound to certain passageways, long before they learned the beasts couldn't jump or climb. And he was the one who came up with the idea of using sidewalk chalk to mark their progress in such a way that it not only prevented them from unwittingly retracing their steps, it also allowed Wayne to catch up to them, even though he was hours behind them. If he were here now, she had no doubt his brain would be hard at work theorizing how a place like this could exist. In the process he'd throw back the curtain and make it all at least a little less scary.

But then again, this place wasn't like the Temple of the Blind or Gilbert House. This place had literally rearranged itself while their backs were turned. It defied all logic. It was possible—likely, even—that even Albert couldn't hope to wrap his head around something like this.

Maybe Wayne would be the better choice. He was a creative type, an artist, like Gina. He was good at thinking outside the box. He was smart, too. And well-read. Perhaps *he'd* have a better chance of understanding this kind of weirdness.

Not that it mattered in the least. Neither of them were here. And they weren't going to show up, either. No one knew where she was. *She* didn't even know where she was. And for that matter, would either of them even bother looking for her? Why should they concern themselves with her? She wasn't the one either of them chose. And could she really blame them? There wasn't anything special about her. Gina had pretty much told her as much. She didn't have any psychic abilities like Brandy and Olivia. She had no connection to the spirit world like Andrea. She was nobody. *Less* than nobody. She was just the loser tagalong. What did they need with a third wheel like her anyway? She was only ever in the way.

Everyone would be better off without her.

She squeezed her eyes closed and rubbed her temples. What the hell was wrong with her? Why was she thinking like that? She knew better. Sure, Albert and Wayne made their choices, but she could hardly blame them. She wasn't even there when Albert and Brandy first discovered the temple. And Wayne was always meant to go find Olivia. But they were her friends. They all cared about her as much as she cared about them. She was certain of it.

It was this place... She looked around at the endless hallway, at those pointlessly dull bulbs scattered so far apart that the light only succeeded in making the scene *more* scary...

It was getting in her head, she realized. It was trying to do to her what it had done to all the poor people already trapped here.

As if in reply, another of those awful wails cut through the eerie silence, sending another icy chill sweeping through her.

God, she hated this place.

"Be careful, you guys," she said, trying to focus her thoughts. "It seriously feels like something is messing with our heads."

Gina nodded. "I think you're right."

"Definitely stay close together," said Nicole.

But when she reached out for Andrea's hand, she was gone.

She turned, her heart stuttering in her chest. "Andrea?"

Gina shined her light around. "Where'd she go?"

"*Andrea?*"

Around them, the hallway had changed again. They were standing at an eight-way intersection, each corridor empty and dark and silent.

And Andrea was nowhere to be seen.

Chapter 15

Nicole hated the thought of leaving that spot. She was convinced that whichever way they chose would only take them farther and farther from wherever Andrea had gone and they'd never find their way back.

But standing in one place wouldn't get them anywhere, either. She'd shouted for a long time—at least an hour, it felt like, though her sense of time didn't feel very reliable—with no response. She could have gone anywhere. How big was this place? How many dark apartments? How many trapped and joyless souls? It felt as if they'd walked for miles and yet they hadn't yet revisited any of the ones they'd seen. There could be thousands of them. *Millions.* The odds of finding a single person in all this madness was *infinitesimal.*

Eventually, it became painfully apparent that they had no choice but to pick a direction and hope for the best. Except, of course, that there *was* no hope in this place. Gina had already informed them of that. Hope had long ago abandoned everyone here, including them, it seemed.

How long ago was it now since they left that intersection? An hour? Two? Ten? Her phone said it was past nine, but that couldn't be right. It was still dark outside, but of course that didn't mean anything. Her feet and legs were tired, but not exhausted. And she hadn't yet felt hungry or thirsty or felt any need to find a bathroom (which was especially good, since every room she'd seen had been occupied and she didn't care much for sharing an awkward moment like that with a sobbing downer...or worse, a *dead* one). But in spite of all these things, she was quite sure that much more time had passed than was otherwise apparent.

"Time is weird when it breaks," Gina explained when she asked her about it. "It doesn't necessarily just slow down or speed up. Sometimes it fragments. Sometimes different things in the same place will move through time at different speeds. You could age an entire year and never run the batteries dead in your phone."

"And I thought the whole 'one Gilbert House, two dimensions' thing was hard to wrap my head around."

"Things do get complicated."

The two of them were walking side-by-side, clinging tightly to each other's hand, not daring to let go lest they, too, be swept away into the darkness of the *very* poorly named Glimmering Sunrise Place, where nothing glimmered, the sun never rose and they didn't seem to be anyplace at all.

Gina had put away her phone, opting to save the battery for now.

"I can't leave without her," said Nicole after a while. "I won't. We have to find her."

"We do," agreed Gina. "We need her. The goddess told me to protect her. I have to make sure she gets to Cedric's Cove safe."

"Oh yeah…" She'd forgotten all about Cedric's Cove.

"Not that the job I was given is the only reason I care about finding her. That wasn't what I was trying to say."

Nicole glanced over at her. She hadn't thought anything of the sort, but she supposed it would've been easy to take it that way. This woman wasn't the most tactful person she'd ever met. But her honesty was rather refreshing, she thought.

"I only mentioned my job because I find it suspicious that it was Andrea who was taken."

"You think someone snatched her away on purpose because of the spear?" She tightened her grip on her purse, suddenly more aware of its weight at her side.

"I do. And it worries me."

It worried her, too. This was no longer about merely escaping this depressing hellhole. It was a rescue mission. Even if Andrea weren't some kind of key for locating the traveling city, she'd never leave here without her friend. But where did she even begin? She couldn't comprehend how to get *herself* out of here. She couldn't even comprehend how to get *around* in this gloomy labyrinth.

This was all so frustrating.

The two of them walked on. They no longer had the luxury of walking past the doors and letting them keep their terrible and gloomy secrets. Andrea could be behind any one of them, perhaps already sinking into a bottomless pit of despair.

One by one they opened each and every door they passed and peered inside.

Behind one, a man wallowed on the floor beneath a kitchen table littered with cookbooks and baking supplies. Behind another, a woman lay face-down on an unkempt bed, surrounded by stuffed animals, her sobs muffled by pillows. Farther along, an old man lay stretched out in a worn recliner, his crooked hands pressed to his face. And behind yet another door, unseen behind a clutter of overturned chairs and tables, a young man was uttering the words, "…sorry… …so sorry… …I'm so sorry…" over and over again.

With each scene, Nicole felt her heart sink a little more.

Where was Andrea? What was happening to her? Was she still herself? Was she still resisting the soul-crushing atmosphere of this awful place? Or was she already sinking into its infectious despair? With each of these awful doors she opened, she was becoming more and more afraid that she was going to find her dear friend already gone.

What if she couldn't save her? What if she was lost? What would she do?

Even if she somehow managed to escape this place, would she ever be able to feel happiness again, knowing that she'd left Andrea to this terrible misery?

She didn't deserve to leave if she couldn't find her. What kind of friend would she be if she just left her here?

And what would everyone else say? How would they look at her if they found out she crawled out of this intolerable nightmare and left her here to suffer? How disgusted would they be by her? How much would they *hate* her?

More tears streaked down her face. She wiped them away with the back of her hand and shoved the ugly thoughts away.

No. She couldn't let this place poison her mind.

She squeezed Gina's hand. "You were *so* right about this place," she said. "We have to keep our heads straight."

But when she looked over, there were tears streaming down Gina's face, too.

"They never wanted me…" she whimpered. "Never…"

"What? No. Stop."

"No one ever wanted me…"

"That's not you," gasped Nicole. She turned and faced her, grasping her other hand. "That's just this shit place talking. Don't listen to it."

But Gina was shaking her head. "It's true, though… They told me so. They never wanted me…"

"Who told you that?"

"My sisters. My family… I never belonged there…"

"That's…" Nicole shook her head. It was startling to see so much raw emotion pouring out of her. She'd been so reserved all this time. How much was she holding in? How much was she keeping bottled up inside her? And for how long? "Even if someone *did* say that…"

"I never belonged," wept Gina. "Never…"

"You *did*. I'm sure of it."

"Not *anywhere*…"

Nicole wrapped her arms around her and hugged her tight. She could feel her own tears spilling down her cheeks. "You belong *here*. Right *now*. I *promise*."

There, in that unglimmering, sunless noplace, surrounded by gloom and doors and misery, Nicole and Gina wept in each other's arms.

Chapter 16

Andrea stood alone in the darkness, staring through the rain-streaked windowpane at the dingy streetlamps looming beyond.

She didn't remember there ever being streetlamps out there before, but they were there now.

Slowly, she turned and looked around. She was standing in her bedroom. Her *old* bedroom. The one back at her parents' house. Everything was right where it used to be. Her bed. Her desk. Her nightstand and lamp. Even her jewelry boxes and stuffed animals.

Except most of this stuff wasn't in this room anymore. She'd taken most of it to the apartment when she moved in with Nicole. This was a guest room now.

How weird...

She walked over to the bed and sat down.

She felt strange. *Empty.* As if she'd lost something very important to her. But she couldn't quite remember what that something was.

In fact, she couldn't quite remember what she was doing. She felt like it was something important...

Her cell phone was lying on the comforter next to her. She looked down at it and frowned. Odd...she thought it was in her hand for some reason... She was using it for something...

(Flashlight.)

She rubbed at her eye and sniffled. No... Why would she need a flashlight? Sure, it was dark in here right now, but it was her room. She didn't need a flashlight to move around her room.

She picked it up and illuminated the screen.

No messages.

No calls.

No one seemed to want to talk to her anymore.

Again, she turned her gaze toward the window. She wondered if the rain would ever end. It seemed like it'd been raining for so long. She could barely remember it *not* raining. But that was odd. She was sure she'd seen sunlight shining through that window before.

She also remembered something else.

A manila envelope wrapped in plastic, stuck to the outside of the screen with duct tape.

Again, she frowned. That was an odd memory... It felt like a very old memory. But it also felt like a very important one. Something about that envelope... Something about...

(Albert.)

She scrunched up her face. Who?

But the name was gone almost as quickly as it had surfaced.

Still...there was something important about that envelope. She was sure of it. Something *fascinating*. Something she wanted to tell Rachel about.

Again, she looked down at the phone.

But Rachel didn't want to talk to her.

"*Ugh!*" groaned Rachel. "I already told you, I'm *busy*."

Andrea blinked, distracted. She was standing in a busy high school hallway. People were bustling about, trying their best to get between classes.

She knew this hallway... This was *her* high school. She was here every day. She was just here yesterday, in fact. And yet...somehow, it felt like she hadn't been here in a very long time...

Rachel closed her locker and fixed her with that obnoxious, bossy stare that she always had. She'd forgotten how pretty she was, with her flawless skin and deep, brown eyes. Why did she look so *young?* Did she always look so young? But how else would she have looked? "I have things to do."

Andrea glanced around, confused. Were the lights always off here?

Rain beat against the windows at the end of the hall.

"It's seriously time to grow up," snapped Rachel.

She rubbed absently at her chest, at the painful pang that just shot through her heart. What was she just thinking about? She was sitting on her bed, holding her phone in her lap, staring out at that endless drizzle.

Oh yeah... Rachel. She was thinking about Rachel.

Once upon a time, Rachel was her very best friend. But Rachel went away. She moved on.

She *outgrew* her.

Just like *everyone* eventually outgrew her...

Mindy Trebner outgrew her and moved to California with her husband. Frannie Gutrine outgrew her and went off to college in New York. Emily Lopledder outgrew her and opened a bakery in Memphis. Even her childhood friend, Helen Omberst who used to live just down the road and loved daring people to do scary things outgrew her. Helen didn't even leave Briar Hills. She just slowly drifted away and eventually stopped talking to her altogether.

Why did all the people in her life leave her alone?

And how long before the friends she had now grew tired of her? How long before Nicole outgrew her? Or Olivia? Or Brandy? Or Stella?

"I'm free like the wind," said Stella.

She stood up, surprised. Did that voice just come from the hallway?

"Someday, I'll just blow away and maybe I'll never come back."

Andrea tucked her phone back into her pocket and stepped out into the hallway.

"You can't stop a force of nature."

This wasn't right. She turned around, scanning her surroundings. This wasn't the hallway outside her bedroom door in her parents' house. This hallway was much bigger. And much *darker*. She couldn't see anything.

She couldn't even see the door she just stepped out of.

"Hello?"

No one answered. The only sound was the soft, constant

patter of the rain.

"Is anyone there? Stella?" It *sounded* like Stella. That was the kind of weird stuff she was always spouting. But now that she was standing out here, she couldn't quite understand why Stella would be in this house at all. She'd never been here before. "Mom?"

She turned and looked behind her. Actually...was this even her parents' house anymore? Had it ever been? Was that her old room she was just in? She tried to remember, but her thoughts were all hazy.

Like those streetlights outside the rain-streaked windows...

Wait...

Something was wrong. What was she doing before she was in her old bedroom? She felt like it was something important.

(It's wrong here.)

She closed her eyes and rubbed her temples. Her head hurt.

(Don't get separated.)

Was she with Nicole?

(We're lost.)

Why did her head hurt so much when she tried to remember things?

(It feels like hopelessness in here.)

She gasped and opened her eyes. Gina!

But she was suddenly standing in her bedroom. Not the bedroom she just left, not the one from her childhood, but the one she had now. In the apartment she shared with Nicole. The lights were out again. The window sprinkled the room with the fairy lights of those rain-soaked streetlamps.

Again she squeezed her eyes closed. What was happening? Why did everything keep changing?

But when she opened her eyes again, she found that things *hadn't* changed. She was still in her apartment bedroom, sitting on her bed...right where she'd been all day...

...or had she?

"I think I'll go out west for a while," said Stella. She was looking out the window, watching the rain. "See what kind of trouble I can stir up there. Then maybe I'll tour Europe."

"Won't that cost a lot of money?" asked Andrea.

"I've got enough saved up."

She frowned. Stella had been telling her almost since the day she met her that she was leaving as soon as she was done with school. Just one more person in a hurry to leave her behind...

She should be used to it by now, but it still stung.

Why did everyone always leave her?

Tears had suddenly welled up in her eyes. She wiped them away with the heel of her hand and sniffled.

When she looked up again, she was back in her parents' house. Except everything had changed again. She was in the living room this time, sitting on the couch. Everything was dark and dusty. Half the familiar furniture was missing. All the family photos had been taken down off the walls.

Nobody had lived here in quite some time.

She stood up and turned around, taking it all in.

Where did the time go?

As the baby of the family, she always knew she'd someday be the only one left, but it seemed to her that those days had passed into memory far too fast. They were all gone. Her dad. Her mom. Her brothers. Everyone she loved...just gone...

She was all alone.

Her gaze fell on the mirror, on the sunken face that stared back at her. When did she get so old? When did all those years slip away from her?

Her breath caught in her throat and tears streamed down her cheeks.

"No..." she wept, shaking her head. "No... Please..."

She didn't want to be alone!

Chapter 17

"...not you..." Nicole muttered to herself. "...it's not you..." She raked her face across the back of her wrist, wiping away the never-ending stream of tears, not daring to let go of Gina's hand for even a second. "...this isn't you..."

But it was so hard to keep herself grounded. Those awful, self-destructive thoughts just kept washing over her. They came faster and faster, lasted longer and longer, like waves washing up on the shore as the tide rolled in. And she was utterly helpless against it, unable to escape, as if buried up to her neck in the sand and left to die a slow and tortured death. All she could do was catch her breath at the last second, hold it...and hope for another.

The next one rolled over her. An agonizing certainty that she was nothing more than a burdensome disappointment to everyone she loved. The pain was excruciating. It cut her all the way to her core, wrenching away her breath, bludgeoning her heart so that the unbearable ache in her chest was like the desperate suffering of one on the very verge of drowning.

But it wasn't her.

She clung to that fact with every ounce of her strength. It was her one lifeline. It was the one glimmer of hope in this otherwise utterly hopeless gloom. These feelings she felt...these thoughts inside her head... *They weren't her own.*

It was this place. Glimmering Sunrise Place. Tristesse Lane. This evil, rain-drenched street in the middle of a torturous, emotional nowhere.

"...none of it is true..." she grunted through clenched teeth. "...none of it is *real*..."

But it was all so exhausting. She was so tired. She didn't

think she could keep the hopelessness at bay much longer. Soon she wouldn't have the strength to keep reminding herself that it was all a lie. Soon, it would be easier to just give up and let the anguish swallow her.

She simply couldn't last much longer.

"Really?" said a familiar voice. "This is all it's going to take to beat you?"

She blinked up at the figure standing over her. Was that…Keith?

"I thought you were stronger than this," he scoffed. "I thought you didn't need anyone."

She wanted to tell him to fuck off, but it were as if the words were too heavy to push past her own lips. She didn't have the energy.

And perhaps he was right… Perhaps she wasn't strong enough. She had no idea how she was going to find the strength to pull herself out of this mess. In fact, if not for Gina, she was fairly sure she would've already given up.

Gina… The girl sobbing in her arms, who kept blubbering about how no one ever wanted her or loved her…no doubt the lies that Tristesse Lane was telling her with each suffocating wave that washed over her.

One hand was tightly enlaced in hers. Her other arm was draped around her, holding her close, desperate to not loosen her grip for even a second lest she be torn away into the painful gloom.

It wasn't just about her. If she lost her grip and slipped into that endless sea of despair, then Gina would be swept away by it, too.

Just like poor Andrea…

How could she have let that happen? How could she have lost her dear friend like that? And how could things have turned so sour that she couldn't even pick herself up off this filthy floor to continue searching for her?

She was no kind of friend.

She was useless.

All she was good for was getting the people she cared about

killed. Or worse.

She uttered a frustrated scream through her clenched jaw and hugged Gina tighter against her.

Again, that wasn't her. That was the building. That was Tristesse Lane. She had to fight it. She had to stay alive.

But...she was so tired... It was getting so hard to push these terrible thoughts away.

"Snap out of it," shouted that unkind, imaginary version of her ex-boyfriend.

And she wanted to snap out of it. She *needed* to snap out of it. She would've snapped out of it just to spite him. But she couldn't seem to lift herself above it.

She was inevitably sinking into the horror of this awful place...deeper and deeper into that inescapable despair...

It was only a matter of time before she drowned.

Chapter 18

Gina was lost in a vast sea of self-doubt and emotional agony. Occasionally the pain would ebb for a moment, just a little, not enough to give her any relief, but just enough that she became aware of someone clinging to her in the darkness.

She couldn't remember who this other person was. And she had no idea why anyone would be holding her like that. Was she being held down? Was this the person who brought her to this awful place?

No one cared enough about her to actually come into this hideous darkness to save her. No one had ever really wanted her, after all. Anyone who pretended otherwise was just trying to be polite.

She'd always been alone. And she'd die alone, too. Right here in this God-forsaken building.

No... It wasn't even a building. It looked like hallways and doors and rooms with furniture and appliances, but it was only an illusion. She could see it now for what it was. This wasn't wood and brick and concrete. This wasn't carpeting she was sitting on. Those strangely spaced, too-dim lights in the ceiling weren't bulbs. Even the rain wasn't what it seemed to be. Tristesse Lane wasn't a street at all. All of it, this whole, hideous place...was *alive*.

She was inside a living thing.

And it was going to slowly *devour* her.

Somebody said something—a long time ago now, it seemed—about this place *eating* people's joy. She couldn't remember who said it...but she understood now that they were right. This place *did* eat people's emotions. It ate everything but the really painful stuff, leaving nothing else, not even the desire to escape.

Again, her thoughts scattered and her head was filled with the mocking voices of a painful past, telling her that she didn't belong, that she wasn't wanted...

She looked up at those dim, useless lights in the ceiling that weren't lights at all. They were *eyes*. They'd been watching her this whole time.

She was never getting out of here.

The hopelessness would literally consume her.

And it would do so for a very, very long time.

Chapter 19

Andrea wanted so badly to give up. She'd lived far too long already, day after endless day...year after endless year...all alone... No one ever came to see her. No one checked on her. No one cared about her.

But she didn't even know *how* to give up.

She couldn't even get up out of this bed anymore.

A frown creased her shriveled face. *Was* this even a bed? Or was she merely lying on the cold floor?

Maybe she'd fallen. It wouldn't be hard. She couldn't see to find her way around anymore.

Could she *ever* really see? She thought she remembered being able to see, but her memories were all so hazy... And it seemed to her that this place had been dark for as long as she'd been here. Only a little light reached in through that rain-streaked window. Everything else was shadowy and cold and damp.

She reached out with her crooked fingers and felt for a blanket, but there didn't seem to be one. Her nails raked across coarse fabric.

Was that the bare mattress? Or was that a rug?

"You never were cut out to make it on your own," said Nicole.

Except Nicole wasn't there. She never was. It was only a memory from her unhappy life.

"Should've gotten married," said Brandy. "Had some kids."

"She would've had to grow up, first," sighed Olivia.

She turned her head and stared into the dingy glow of the streetlamps outside. Did she really remember her old friends saying those things to her? Or was that just something she overheard them saying behind her back? She couldn't remember. And she couldn't decide which scenario was worse.

Not that it mattered. They were right, of course. She'd wasted her life. Everyone left her, one way or another. And now she was going to die alone. And it was her own fault for being so...*unlovable.*

"Wow," said Stella. "You're a sad case, aren't you?"

Andrea turned her head the other way. Stella was there, sitting in a dusty chair with her legs casually crossed, perfectly visible even in the oppressive darkness. She looked exactly the same as she did back when she knew her, right down to her oversized Rolling Stones tee shirt drooping over one freckled shoulder.

"Pitiful, really."

She supposed she *was* pitiful. Did she ever really think that she deserved any better than this?

"You're so *boring*," complained Stella.

Andrea turned away again. She didn't even have the energy to tell this rude hallucination from her past to leave her alone.

Of all the people who haunted her, why was Stella the most stubbornly persistent? She'd had other friends she knew longer and better, yet *she* was the one who always seemed to be lingering in the shadows, watching her suffer, needling her as she wallowed in despair. Did she best represent the life she failed to live? Or was she just the cruelest of those mocking voices, the better to remind her that she'd always been an unlovable loser?

Why couldn't her hateful mind just leave her alone?

Then a flash of blinding light pierced the darkness, stabbing at her half-open eyes. She cried out, surprised, and covered her face.

"Ooh!" chirped Stella. "Something interesting for a change!"

Chapter 20

Glimmering Sunrise Place shuddered around them and something like an unearthly scream shook the floor beneath their feet.

Nicole gasped as the latest wave of misery suddenly washed away, leaving behind a rapidly swelling panic that she didn't, at first, fully understand.

Where was she? What was happening? Why was she so terrified?

"Oh god," cried Gina.

The two of them were clinging to each other in the darkness, desperately fighting to stay together. Their hearts were pounding. They were struggling to catch their breath. Their bodies were shaking. They were cold and they were wet and they were terrified.

How long had they been here? It felt at the same time like mere moments and entire lifetimes.

Something had changed, Nicole realized. Her slow and steady descent into that mad hopelessness had ceased. It was as if she'd been slowly suffocating inside a sealed chamber and then something broke the seal, letting in a sudden rush of fresh air.

But she was still trapped in this place.

Gina pulled her closer, hugging her, tears still streaming down her face. "We have to get out of here," she gasped.

"I know!" Her cell phone was lying on the floor next to her, its light still shining, illuminating their immediate surroundings. She snatched it up and pointed it one way, then the other.

The hallway didn't really look like a hallway anymore. It wasn't square, for one. Gone were the man-made ninety-degree angles. It was rough and rounded. And its walls were no longer the smooth texture of plaster and paint. It looked more like a cavern than a corridor. The floor looked more like moss than carpet. The doors appeared to be little more than crude etchings carved into porous stone. And every surface was *wet*.

Did it always look like this? Did she just not see it for what it was?

Careful not to let go of each other, still half-expecting something to snatch one or both of them away, the two of them struggled to their feet, trembling.

Gina tugged impatiently at her hand. "We're not alone," she whispered.

Nicole shined her light in the other direction, but it all looked the same to her. "What do you feel?"

"I don't know. It's weird. Things are appearing and disappearing all around us, causing weird distortions." Her panicked gaze darted back and forth and yet her voice never lost that quiet, sleepy quality. "It's like there're these ripples passing through every surface, making it hard to tell what any one thing might be." She wiped at her tears, visibly frustrated. "But there're things here now that definitely weren't here before."

"So something's getting in? From outside? As in a way *out*?"

"From *somewhere* else. I can't say where. Could be somewhere worse."

Nicole looked around at the eerie, oozing walls of the fake apartment hallway around them. "I think I'm willing to risk it."

"We don't have a choice. If we don't leave here now, we never will."

Nicole felt an icy panic welling up inside her. She wanted nothing more than to be out of this nightmare. But she couldn't leave yet. "Andrea," she breathed. "We have to find her! Can you feel where she is?"

"I can only feel rapid-fire glimpses of things all around us. The closest I can describe it is like a strobe light effect."

Nicole looked back and forth, still trying to force down the rising panic inside her. Which way did she go? How were they supposed to find anything in this awful place?

"Look out!" cried Gina, shoving her up against one of those

damp, cave-like walls.

"What—?" she yelped, but then she felt it, too. Something huge passed by them in the passage, something unseen in the glow of her light, but with an unmistakable presence that sent a chill all the way through her body.

"Everything's being thrown into chaos," gasped Gina. She was speaking calmly, but there was a distinct edge of panic in her voice and her usually sleepy eyes were wide with fear. "We have to get out of here now."

"Not without Andrea!"

"I know that. But we have to hurry."

But how could she hurry when she didn't even know which way she was supposed to start running?

But then she heard a cry from somewhere in the surrounding gloom. She turned, her heart leaping. Was that her? Where did it come from? That way? Or was it over there?

Gina seized her arm with both hands and pulled her toward the ground. "Get down!"

The thing that passed over them wasn't the same as the thing that brushed past them a moment ago when she shoved Nicole against the wall. This one had a feel that sent electric jolts of terror jumping through their nerves. It was similar to the kind of chill that crept up your back or raced down your arms, but it had an intensity that was like a string of firecrackers going off inside her veins.

"What was that?" breathed Nicole when the thing had moved on and she could find her voice.

Gina could only let out a terrified squeak in response. She'd never felt anything like it before. And she hoped to never encounter it again.

Shakily, Nicole rose to her feet and glanced around. "Andrea?" she called, though she didn't quite dare raise her voice all the way to a shout for fear of what it might attract. "Where is she?"

Then she heard another cry.

"That's her!" She squeezed Gina's hand, careful to not let go for even a second, and hurried toward the sound. At least, she *thought* she was hurrying toward it. It was impossible to know for sure. Glimmering Sunrise Place had come alive. The walls seemed to be moving. They broke apart around her, then stitched themselves back together again. The false hallway became a false living room with oozing rafters and melting walls. Then that became a bedroom with strange, tumor-like growths rising from the floor that sort of resembled poorly painted furniture.

There were noises now, too. Gone was the steady, eerie silence, replaced by unsettling utterances that crept through the gloom from indistinct sources, distant, muffled and muted, like screams from deeply buried coffins. (Although why in the hell *that* particular analogy should come to her, she didn't know!)

Strangest of all, it was raining again. She could feel it falling down around her. And oddly, it seemed to her as if it had never *stopped* raining.

She cried out for Andrea, desperate to hear a response.

Gina yanked her hand back, halting her just in time to avoid another of those strange and enormous presences as it rushed across her path like a freight train.

Or perhaps it was the same one as before. She didn't know. She couldn't really see them. All her eyes were able to pick up was a great, shimmering, barely glimpsed distortion crossing her path.

"Careful!" pleaded Gina.

But she didn't have time to be careful. She had to find Andrea. As soon as the thing was gone, she rushed forward again, practically dragging Gina behind her. "Andrea!"

The downers were still here. She kept glimpsing them from the corners of her eyes as she passed through the ever-shifting landscape. They didn't seem to realize that the world was coming apart and reforming itself around them. They didn't seem aware of anything but their own despair.

She'd only gotten a brief taste of what that was like and it was horrible. But these people were fully enveloped in their misery. Gina told her that they'd all been here a long time. She couldn't imagine what their existence must be. Or if you could even call it an existence.

What was this place? Why did something so awful even exist?

Somewhere ahead of her, Andrea cried out again.

Nicole pushed forward, shouting her name.

And then she was there, stumbling through the gloom in those stupidly adorable space buns, one of them half-unraveled, soaking wet, makeup smeared, tears streaming down her pretty face, looking lost and terrified.

Nicole didn't so much embrace her as collide with her, knocking her backward and practically off her feet. "Don't scare me like that!" she cried.

Andrea hugged her back, her chest hitching with the force of her sobbing. Her mind was still trying to unravel itself from those awful illusions. Her life hadn't passed her by. She wasn't old and frail. And most of all, she hadn't lost everybody she cared about. She wasn't an abject failure at life and she wasn't alone.

No matter what that horrible hallucination of Stella might've told her.

"Oh my god…" cried Nicole. "Are you okay?"

"I think so," she replied, her voice muffled against her shoulder. The things she saw in that horrible gloom were already fading, like the haunting images lingering after a bad dream. She lifted her hand and looked at it over Nicole's shoulder. Her skin was soft and smooth and unblemished, her nails were even still perfectly manicured for the wedding, yet she couldn't get the image of those crooked fingers and that shriveled, wrinkled skin out of her head.

What a terrible nightmare. Not that she was old. Growing old didn't frighten her. It never had. What terrified her, she now clearly understood, was the thought of life passing her by and leaving her all alone and full of regret for all the things she didn't say or do.

"You guys, we have to go *now*," warned Gina.

Nicole nodded and wiped the tears from her face. "Right. Yeah." She glanced around, unsure of what to do next. "Which way?"

But Gina didn't know. She, too, was looking around, trying to make sense of all the madness flooding from this gloomy place.

Then a flash of light pierced the gloom behind them.

Andrea thrust her hand toward it, pointing. "That's what I was trying to follow," she managed through her sniffles.

That was good enough for Nicole. She squeezed Gina's hand and linked arms with Andrea, determined not to lose anyone else, then she pushed toward the place where she saw the light.

Everything was especially broken here. Things were getting all mixed together. Bits and pieces of different rooms and hallways were scattered everywhere. Part of a bed was protruding from the floor. A portion of a brick wall had merged with one of the hallway doors. There was a stove sticking out of a bathtub. And the floor was slick and muddy and uneven, making it more and more difficult to run.

"Where was it?" asked Nicole.

"It looked like it was around here somewhere," replied Andrea.

"Farther up, maybe?" guessed Gina. But after pushing on a few more steps, she gasped and yanked them back.

"Holy shit!" yelped Nicole as she jolted to a stop in front of a huge, gaping chasm.

"Not that way!" cried Andrea.

But the floor was rapidly disappearing all around them, opening up into that vast, black emptiness.

"Not good!" squealed Andrea.

Nicole cursed. This wasn't even fair.

"It's not going to let us go," breathed Gina.

Nicole wanted to tell them it was okay, that they weren't beat yet, that they were more resilient than this. But she couldn't see a way out this time. She didn't know what to do.

What would happen if they fell into that darkness? The laws of nature weren't exactly predictable in this place. Would they hit the bottom at terminal velocity and dash their brains across whatever surface awaited them down there? Or would they just keep falling forever? Or would they just end up back in that awful darkness, separated, suffering wave after wave of anguish and despair?

She'd never been one to just give up, but right now she felt as if she'd rather die than go through that kind of torture again.

The chasm in front of her swelled. It didn't crumble and cave in like a sinkhole. It seemed to flex and fold in on itself, more like a great, fleshy orifice yawning open.

This place was literally going to swallow them whole!

They backed away from it, but the ground was wet and slimy. And were they always standing on an incline? Their feet slipped, threatening to spill them over the edge.

Panic shot through each of them as they struggled to back away.

A great, ominous rumble rolled over them, as if all of Tristesse Lane had awakened and was angry with them. And those creepy, muted sounds had become almost-audible shrieks and wails. They seemed to be drawing closer, as if the whole place were slowly closing in around them.

Then a blinding light pierced the darkness at their backs.

They turned to see a great, shimmering hole ripping open in the empty air. A shadowy silhouette loomed on the other side, peering back at them.

"This way!" boomed a man's voice. "Hurry! He won't let me hold it open for long!"

Nicole might not have possessed the same level of awe-inspiring intellect as her overachieving, scholarly parents, but she wasn't dumb by any means. She knew better than to just blindly accept an invitation from a strange man, whether he was calling out to her from the back of a suspicious-looking white van or from a dimensional rift in spacetime. But she didn't need to sleep on it to know that their situation couldn't get much worse than it was right now. Which was good, because there wasn't going to be any time for thinking about it.

She could feel the ground moving beneath her heels.

She began to fall backward.

She wasn't going to make it!

Then a hand pressed against her back, giving her a much-needed push. At the same time, she imagined that she heard Keith's voice whisper, "Be careful over there."

But Keith wasn't there. He couldn't be there. It was only another of this place's lying illusions.

Holding onto Gina's hand and Andrea's arm, she leapt forward and into the blinding light beyond.

Chapter 21

The transition from the darkness to the light was jarring. Brilliant sunlight stabbed her eyes. There was a sudden and startling change in pressure that popped her ears and made it feel as if something sucked all the air out of her lungs. And the ground met her much sooner than she expected, much sooner than *any* of them expected, sending them all sprawling face-first onto musty smelling, green-tinted tiles.

Breathless, disoriented and wet, her hair plastered to her face and tears still streaming down her cheeks, a pounding pain deep inside her weary head, the only thing Nicole wanted to do was collapse onto the dusty floor and rest. But she didn't dare let her guard down yet. She pushed herself up onto her knees and then turned and looked back, her hands raised to defend herself from whatever might still be pursuing them.

A great, gaping darkness loomed before her terrified eyes, a cavernous, *pulsating* emptiness, crawling with otherworldly shadows that twisted and writhed and squirmed. Shapeless, half-seen things reached out for her, worming their way through the opening, dripping and squelching and oozing.

Was that really where they just came from? Were they really *inside* that awful, slimy darkness? How did they not see it for what it was? How could they think for even a second that they were inside some ordinary *apartment building*?

She shouldn't be kneeling here like this. She should be running away from here as fast as her weary legs would carry her. But...what was the point? Where could she go? She was only human, after all. How could she ever believe that she could actually *escape* something like that?

She watched the oozing, darkling shapes as they slithered

closer and closer to her.

They didn't escape anything... It was all just a cruel trick... A sick joke...

She was so *useless*...

But then, with a strange crackling noise, the rift collapsed on itself and vanished as if it had never been there at all. At the same time, all those strange, alien emotions inside her mind evaporated so quickly that it sucked a startled gasp from her.

What the hell was wrong with her? Was she really ready to just give up and let those things drag her back inside?

But she didn't have time to wrap her head around it. As she knelt there, her heart still pounding, she realized that a tall, muscular man in a dirty white tee shirt and faded jeans was suddenly standing in the space where the strange, oozing hole had been. He bent down, gently took her still-raised hands and helped her to her feet. "Hello there," he said.

"Hi..." she sighed, her thoughts still swirling inside her head. Where did all that terror go? Where was all that self-doubt? It was as if this man had swept it all away. A strange warmth swam through her belly. A nervous, giddy sort of feeling. Was he the one who saved them? Was he her knight in shining armor? She stared into his eyes, so beautiful and gray. "I'm Nicole..."

He smiled the most charming smile she'd ever seen. "Hello Nicole. I'm—"

"Hey!" Andrea scrambled to her feet and yanked Nicole away from the handsome stranger. In the same motion, she stepped between them and buried her knee in his unsuspecting groin.

The stranger's handsome face twisted into a mask of agony and he turned away with a painful groan, clutching at his injured baggage.

"Andrea!" gasped Nicole, shocked.

She jabbed a finger at him. "That's the creep who attacked me!"

"*What?*" She shook her head, confused. What the hell was wrong with her? Why were her emotions running so wild?

"Bad guy," affirmed Gina as she stood up and wiped at her

dripping face. Her blouse was still wet, the thin fabric plastered to her modest chest.

"Elroy or something," recalled Andrea.

"*Elias*," he groaned. "Fucking…*ouch*…"

"Whatever! He tried to hypnotize me into to sleeping with him!"

"And he tried to strangle you," Gina reminded her in her usual, sleepy tone, as if she were only pointing out that he'd changed clothes since they last saw him instead of that he'd tried to murder her. He was the same creep in the purple shirt that she knocked out with the golf club in the parking lot of Weirweather Country Club.

"He's after the spear!" said Andrea. "Don't trust him!"

"Oh god…" he groaned, turning to face them again. "For the record, I—" But before he could finish, Nicole stepped forward and planted her own knee in his crotch. This time, he dropped all the way to the floor, clutching at himself.

"*That's for laying your hands on my friends!*" she shouted. That distracted, fluttery, lovestruck feeling was gone as quickly as the hopeless self-loathing before it. Now all that she felt was a seething *fury*.

"Jesus…fucking…nnnnnnn…" he grunted, his face bright red. "*Fuck me that hurt…*"

"Now get up so I can give you another one for fucking with my head a minute ago!"

"*I just saved all of you!*"

"Probably so you can brainwash us and be all pervy with us!" snapped Andrea.

"It doesn't work that way!" he shouted.

Nicole glanced around, really taking in their new surroundings for the first time. They were in another hallway. But this didn't look anything like the gloomy apartment hallways of Glimmering Sunrise Place. It was a lot brighter here, for one thing. Sunlight was shining down through skylights in the ceiling. But it wasn't as bright as it first appeared. In fact, the more her eyes adjusted to it, the more she realized that everything here was sort of dingy. The walls were cold cinderblock painted a murky sort of beige. And this hallway didn't go on forever like those others. It was only about forty feet long. There was a metal handrail running the length of each wall. A single door stood at each end, both with full-length frosted windows that offered only a blurry, tantalizing tease of what might lie beyond. It didn't exactly appear to be falling apart around them, but it had a dusty, neglected sort of emptiness about it, strongly suggesting that people no longer came here every day.

Slowly, the man who called himself Elias pushed himself up onto his hands and knees. "*For the record*," he said again, his voice cracking with the strain, "I never intended to trick you into going home with me. That was just to test whether your mind was fully bonded to mine. If you'd resisted that suggestion, I'd have known I couldn't make you take me to the package." He groaned and rose up onto his knees. "And I can only use the psychic trick *once*. As soon as I instructed you to do something you couldn't physically do, the bond was broken. And once the bond was broken, I was never going to be able to do it again."

"He's telling the truth," said Gina. "I can tell. That particular ability is triggered by physical touch." She glanced at Andrea. "When he 'accidentally' bumped into you at the reception."

And several other times, too, she realized. Like when she started to feel weird about wandering too far from the party and he pretended he was trying to protect her from stepping in a hole.

"And when he took my hand to help me up," Nicole realized.

"And it only works on people as long as they're unaware he can do it," added Gina.

"See?" he sighed. "Now can we please *stop kicking the guy who just saved you from a fate literally worse than death in his nuts?*"

The three of them stood there for a moment, staring down at him. Then Nicole kicked him in the groin again.

He let out an agonizing scream and collapsed back onto the floor, writhing in pain, tears streaming down his face.

"I was totally going to do that, too," said Andrea.

"I'm glad I beat you to it," said Nicole.

"Fu-hu-hu-hu-hu-*hucking hell*!" he cried.

"Big baby," grumbled Andrea.

"Totally had it coming," said Gina. She was rubbing at her head again. It was still pounding, making it hard to think clearly. She felt strange. She was still reeling from the effects of that last place, but there was something else as well, something about *this* place. She felt off balance here, dizzy, as if everything were very slowly spinning.

Nicole stood over the man, scowling. "What did you say his name was? Leroy or something?"

"*Elias*!" he snapped. He was dragging himself across the floor, trying to put distance between himself and the violent women who seemed determined to cause permanent damage to his future lineage. "My name...is *Elias*."

"Probably not his real name," reasoned Andrea.

With another agonized groan, he pushed himself back up onto his knees again. "Actually..." he grunted, "...it is. Elias Hochog."

"Did you say *hotdog*?" said Andrea.

He glared over his shoulder at her. "It's '*Hochog*.'"

She made a face at him. "Aw, the big pervo's sensitive about it."

"What do you want, Hotdog?" demanded Nicole.

"*Hochog*."

"What the fuck ever. Like I give a shit. Why are you stalking us?"

"I just told you, I was *saving you*! If it wasn't for me, you'd still be trapped on Tristesse Lane with *him*."

"Yeah right," snapped Andrea.

"Who's 'him'?" asked Nicole.

"Glum."

"What?"

"*Gwilym Glum*. He's the one who snatched you away to Tristesse Lane."

"That's who owns that place?" It was weird to think that there was a name behind the nightmare she'd just endured, much less that the name was "Glum" of all things...

"Not *owns* it so much..." replied Hochog. He turned and leaned his back against the wall, wincing, his hands still pressed to his aching groin. "More like...Glum *is* that place."

Nicole shook her head, confused. "Huh?" Was he *trying* to mess with her head now?

"It's complicated, I know. And the more I try to explain it to you, the more complicated it gets. Glum is less a person than a concentrated mass of unnatural energy and will."

"A what?"

"He's not human," he explained. "Not even close. That *place* you were trapped in, for example. That's actually a manifestation of his own physical form. A universe *within* his own body, if you will. A perfect, inescapable prison *and* a sort of stomach."

Andrea wrinkled her nose. "Ew..." She was suddenly entirely too aware of that slimy, damp feeling on her skin.

"Yeah. Best not to think too much about it."

"He's telling the truth about that, too," said Gina. "I could feel it when we were inside. More and more the longer we were there. There was an intelligence about that place. It wasn't just alive. It was sentient." Tristesse Lane was less a place than an *entity*. She recalled again what Andrea said about something *eating* people's emotions and felt a shudder of revulsion at the thought. How close did they come to ending up just like that? Was that why her head was still hurting? Did that place damage her in some way? Had a part of her *already* been devoured?

"Glum wants you because you're *important*," he went on. "The job you were given. That package you're carrying around."

Nicole clutched her purse closer to her. She could feel the spear inside. The bulk of its velvet wrapping, the weight of the metal.

"You're connection to the Keeper," he went on. "*Important.* And his kind can't resist a chance to get their claws on something important."

"His kind?" said Nicole.

"He's one of twelve incarnations of an ancient evil that control different aspects of the living universe. Most of them manipulate the events of the world through various and sometimes downright sinister means."

"*What?*" This conversation just kept getting stranger.

"It's fucked up, I know. Welcome to the *real* world. And all the things most people never see. Glum literally controls a significant portion of the world through depression, hopelessness and despair."

"You're making stuff up," said Andrea.

"How would that even work?" asked Nicole.

With a painful groan, he straightened his legs and pushed himself up the wall until he was upright, but remained leaning against it, as if he didn't trust his legs to hold all of his weight. "It sounds convoluted, I know, but it's effective. I mean, think about it. What happens if someone who's destined to make the world a better place suddenly becomes too demotivated or anxious to achieve that destiny? Or worse still, what if they suddenly become so depressed that they commit suicide?"

"That's awful!" gasped Andrea.

"Yes. It is. But that's how the world really works. Mankind thinks he's in charge, but he has no idea what's really out there. Governments aren't the ones who decide how the world turns. The ancient Greeks and Romans were closer. Deities. Entities. Sentient forces of nature. Ancient and *monstrous* things from worlds long dead still lingering in the shadows. All of them playing games with human lives. All of them butting heads and squabbling among themselves. Most of them greedy, selfish or downright malevolent."

Nicole couldn't deny that there was at least a grain of truth in that. In addition to monsters, she'd met a creepy little goblin-looking thing that called itself the Keeper and a freakishly tall woman with no face who called herself the Sentinel Queen. Why not a massive creep named Gwilym Glum who manipulated the world's history by making people *depressed?*

"Why should we believe anything you say?" demanded Andrea. "You tried to *kill me!*"

He shook his head. "No. That wasn't me."

"Of course it was you! I was kind of *there*. What, you gonna to tell us you have an evil twin?"

He let out a snort of a laugh. "Not exactly, no. You really have no idea of all the things going on out there, do you? Do you think I was the only one who showed up to that wedding hoping to get my hands on that package?"

Andrea looked over at Gina. She *did* say that the party was crawling with things other people couldn't see and people who weren't what they seemed.

He turned those gray eyes on Nicole. "Some of them get inside your head, you know. Make you think and do things you'd *never* think or do."

She narrowed her eyes at him. Was he talking about the barely-there? Did he *know* what that thing made her see? The very thought made her want to kick him again.

"So you expect me to believe you were *possessed?*" scoffed Andrea.

"Is that so hard to believe?"

"Kind of, yeah."

Gina squeezed her eyes closed and pressed her hands to her face. That strange, dizzying sensation was still with her. Something wasn't right here, but she couldn't put her finger on it. If only she could think more clearly.

He sighed and stood up straight. "I know you don't trust me and I don't blame you, but you're lucky I showed up. You don't realize it, but a lot's been going on lately. Events are in motion. Wheels are turning. *Changes are coming.* You three are a part of all that, whether you want to be or not. That means there are a lot of eyes on you. When you just disappeared off the face of the earth after the horsemen attacked you…well, it got a lot of attention."

"Horsemen?" Nicole recalled those freaky things that looked like ridiculously tall horse legs. Who was in charge of naming these things?

"Everyone knew someone was interfering with things, but no one was certain who or why. But *I* knew." He turned his gray gaze on Gina now. "I have abilities of my own. I felt Glum's presence prowling around at that party." He looked back at Nicole. "It took a particular interest in *you.*"

"The barely-there…"

"Whatever you want to call it. But it's just another part of Glum."

She stared at him. It was true. The place the barely-there took her that looked like her apartment but wasn't…it was the same as Glimmering Sunrise Place. It was *all* Tristesse Lane.

Gina opened her eyes and looked around. It was this place. It was all wrong somehow. She couldn't feel anything beyond this short corridor. There was nothing on the other side of these walls, nothing above or below them, nothing beyond those doors… It was like they were adrift in the vacuum of space.

"I know you don't want to trust me," pressed Hochog, "but I'm here to help. Really."

Andrea shook her head. "We don't need your help."

"Oh, I'm pretty sure you do. How far do you think the three of you are going to get on your own? Without me, you'd still be back on Tristesse Lane, wallowing in Glum's despair. Or *worse*. I felt something else in there when I tore open that hole. Something a lot stronger than me. I wasn't the only one who came looking for you. And you can bet there'll be more." He met Andrea's gaze and held it. "How will you do when *gods* come looking for you? Hm? Act as tough as you want, but you *need* me."

Andrea glared back at him. "No, we don't."

"We won't trust you," agreed Nicole.

"But you'll trust *her*?" he countered, nodding at Gina.

Both of them looked at her and she blinked back at them, confused. "What…?"

"*She* saved me when *you* tried to murder me!" snapped Andrea.

"That's convenient," he said. "Very convincing."

"Shut up," growled Nicole.

"Are you aware of what kind of monster *she* answers to?"

Gina shook her head. "No. The goddess is good. She sent me to protect her from you."

"Is that what you tell yourself?"

"I said shut up!" snapped Nicole. She seized Gina's hand

and squeezed it. "You're not driving us apart."

Hochog turned his gaze on her. "Give me the package. I can get you where you need to be."

"Go to hell!"

He sighed. "Why won't you understand that I'm trying to help you?"

Nicole didn't take her eyes off him. He was big. He was muscular. But there were three of them and she was fairly sure he couldn't just take the spear from them. They'd already proven that they could hurt him. And he wouldn't be wasting his time talking if he was armed.

Maybe he was telling the truth. Maybe he really was here to help. He did, after all, pull them out of that awful melancholy hell. And maybe he *was* being manipulated when he attacked Andrea. It really wouldn't be that much different from what Glum did to them back there on Tristesse Lane. But even if that were true, it was only that much more reason to not trust him. If he could be controlled once, he could be controlled again at any time.

Something could be pulling his strings right now.

Besides, she just didn't believe anything this guy said. There was something about him that set her on edge.

"We shouldn't be here," said Gina.

Nicole glanced over at her, concerned.

"Something's very wrong about this place."

"What kind of something?" asked Andrea.

"I don't know, exactly…but he's doing something to it. He has us sealed in. We can't get out."

Nicole glared at Hochog. "What's she talking about? What did you do?"

He shrugged. "I didn't do anything. It's just a little stopover."

She took a step toward him. "Let us go," she growled.

He took several steps backward and covered his crotch. "Now hold on! Don't go getting violent again. I told you, I'm protecting you. This is a safe place. Somewhere Glum and anyone else who might want to get their hands on you girls won't be able to find you. I just need to rest a little longer before sending us the rest of the way home."

But Gina shook her head. "No. He's hiding something from us."

"What are you really doing?" demanded Nicole.

Again, he sighed. "I'm *protecting* you. Why won't you believe me?"

"Because you're a slimy, perverted, murdering pig?" suggested Andrea.

"That's just hurtful," he replied. And he *did* manage to look wounded.

Nicole glared at him. "Where are we?"

"We're between dimensions, if you must know. I didn't have the energy necessary to get us all the way home, so I erected this place while I rest."

"He's lying," said Gina. "Whatever ability he has to move between dimensions doesn't work that way. He's holding us here intentionally."

With a tired sigh, he turned those gray eyes on her again. "My god you're annoying."

"Rude," she replied.

"Let us out," growled Nicole.

"Sure." He turned his attention back to her. His entire demeanor had changed. All the charm had vanished. There was something very *sinister* about those gray eyes now. "Just as soon as you give me the package."

"Not happening."

"You don't seem to understand the situation you're in. That object is more important than all of us. You can't get it where it needs to be on your own. If you try to do it alone, you'll fail. And I can't let you let it fall into the wrong hands. I've been doing my best to be nice about this, but you don't have a choice in the matter. If you want to live through this, you have to trust me. *Now stop being stubborn and give me the package.*"

"Fuck you," snarled Nicole.

He glared at her. "Fine. Have it your way. But when things go south, don't say I didn't give you a chance." He took a step backward. "I should warn you, though. On the other side of those doors is a place where even the Keeper, himself, won't be able to find you."

"There's his true colors," sneered Andrea. "Total creep."

"There are places out there that you can't even imagine," he said, ignoring her. "Places that have seen such tragedy, that have absorbed so much hatred and cruelty that they've taken on a life of their own. And this one…" He gestured at the door behind him. "It's one of the very *worst*."

"Shut up!" shouted Nicole.

"They called it a hospital," he plowed on. "But it was never intended for that. No one was ever sent there to get *better*. Most of the people weren't even sick when they were brought there. It was where people were sent to *disappear*. In a hundred and seventeen years, no one admitted through the front gates ever came back out. It was a place where abuse and neglect were standard practice, where countless people suffered hideously inhumane treatment, gruesome medical testing and torturous surgical experimentation. It was a place of endless suffering. A hopeless hole of misery where death was the only thing anyone could look forward to." He glanced around at the dingy walls, those gray eyes shining with an eerily sadistic delight. "Places like this, places with so much evil…so much *despair* soaked into their bones…for so many years… They don't go away when you shutter them. They don't even go away when you tear them down. They take on a life of their own. They bleed beyond the borders of the 'real' world and become someplace new. They *grow*. Like a poisonous mold." Again, he met Nicole's glaring gaze. His smile this time wasn't charming by any means. It was positively *vile*. "*No one* leaves this place. Not even the dead."

"You're fucking sick," Nicole told him through clenched teeth.

"Last chance," he warned. "Give me the package."

"Don't trust him," whispered Gina.

"Not a chance," snapped Andrea.

"Burn in hell," spat Nicole.

He smiled another slimy, evil smile. "Anun Goar Nangup."

Nicole blinked at him, confused. "What?"

"Have fun in there," he said. Then he took another step backward and vanished as if in a dense fog. In the same instant, the hallway changed. The doors at either end disappeared, revealing a much longer corridor stretching on in either direction. There were suddenly doors all along each wall. And everything was much older than it was before. The dusty green floor was suddenly filthy and littered with debris. The ceiling above them was cracked and sagging, with large gaps exposing naked pipes and rotten wiring. The walls were dingy and peeling.

"Not cool, Hotdog Jerk!" shouted Andrea.

Chapter 22

"Stupid Hotdog…" grumbled Andrea. She'd plopped down cross-legged on the dirty floor and was sitting with her hands buried in her face, trying to calm herself. So much had happened… It felt like weeks ago that she was at the wedding. How did she end up in this place, shivering in her wet tee shirt, feeling as if she'd been dragged through a filthy river? "I really hate that guy."

"Fucking *psychopath* is what he is," growled Nicole. She opened the nearest door and peered into the room beyond. It appeared to be a patient room, with an old, rusty bedframe and an overturned tray table. The space was tiny and cramped, with only a tiny slit of a frosted window letting in any light. It didn't look like the sort of facility she'd ever want to be admitted to. It looked more like a prison than a hospital, which she supposed was exactly how the sicko described it to them. "What was that nonsense he said just before he left? That…amen gore…whatever?"

"He said some stuff like that when he was trying to strangle me, too," recalled Andrea. "I don't think it was English."

"I don't know what it meant," said Gina. She was leaning against the wall, her hands propped on her knees, her eyes closed. "It gave me a really creepy feeling hearing it, though. I don't think it was just meaningless nonsense."

"The guy's batshit crazy if you ask me," grumbled Nicole. She crossed the hallway and opened the next door, but the room was identical to the first, except instead of a tray table on the floor, there was an IV stand in one corner. "All that talk about gods? Seriously?"

"He wasn't wrong," said Gina.

She glanced over, surprised. "What?"

Without opening her eyes, she said, "There are real gods out there. Or at least, very godlike things that call themselves gods. Lots of them."

"Like *your* goddess?" guessed Andrea.

She nodded. "And a lot more. And that stuff he said about the twelve incarnations of an ancient evil was true, too. I've met one of them."

"Really?"

"It's a long story." She opened her eyes and met her gaze. "We can talk about it later, but right now we should focus on where we are."

"I guess you're right." Andrea leaned back on her hands and took a slow, deep breath. It was all so much to take in. First Hotdog Creep and that mysterious package. Gina and her goddess. The barely-there. The horsemen. And of course Tristesse Lane… God, but that was weird to think about. It felt like a distant dream now, but for a while, she was convinced she was trapped there for an entire *lifetime*.

And they hadn't even reached their destination yet!

"The way that man described this place…" recalled Gina. "He's not wrong about places with that much bad history expanding beyond the boundaries of the world they start in. It's kind of like a blister."

"So another pocket dimension," reasoned Andrea. "Like Tristesse Lane."

"I told you they were more common than people realized. If we're in one of those, we could be trapped here until he lets us out."

"Which isn't very likely." Nicole stood there a moment, her gaze fixed on Gina, curious. "Back in that apartment building…or whatever that place was… You said you could feel the people that were trapped there. You said the doors didn't all go where they were supposed to or something."

"I can sense things about my immediate surroundings. I can feel the layout of buildings I'm in and near. I can tell if there are people around, where they're at and what they're doing. Not every detail. Not all the time. I just automatically know lots of stuff."

"Cool. That seems like it can be pretty useful."

"Sometimes. Other times not as much. I could do without knowing exactly when all my neighbors are having sex."

"Ew," said Andrea. "Yeah, that's definitely too much information."

"Uh huh."

"So what can you feel about *this* place?" asked Nicole.

She let her gaze drift lazily from one door to the next. "I don't like it. I can feel things around me, so we're not still trapped in the pocket that man was holding us in.. That disappeared when he did. But where we are now feels very wrong."

"Wrong how?" pressed Nicole.

"Everything's wonky here. Compacted. Distorted. It's like space is folded over on itself. Multiple times. Some parts feel backward. Some parts feel upside down. But mostly…" She hesitated, uncertain, but finally she met Nicole's gaze and said, "Mostly it feels like decay here."

She wrinkled her nose. She was sorry she asked. "So the creep wasn't just trying to scare us, then."

"No. It's like everything's all tangled and knotted up." Everything beyond what she could see felt twisted and skewed and blurred, like warped reflections in a funhouse mirror. It didn't all seem to even go together, like puzzle pieces that all came from different boxes. "All I know for sure is that we need to find a way out of here fast. It has a really bad 'shark-infested waters' kind of feel to it."

Andrea let out a tired whimper. "Did you really have to put it that way?"

"Sorry."

"So which way's the exit?" asked Nicole.

But Gina could only shake her head. "I don't know."

She cursed under her breath.

"Sorry."

"Don't be. It's not your fault."

Andrea looked up at the shining skylights. "Well there must be a way out if we can see sunlight through those. I mean, outside is kind of right there, isn't it?"

"That sort of thing doesn't really mean much in places like this," explained Gina. She'd closed her eyes again. She looked exhausted. "Sometimes things are just weird."

"Oh…"

Nicole frowned up at the skylights. Tristesse Lane didn't have any sunshine. It was a rainy night the entire time they were there. And the Wood, which surrounded the Temple of the Blind and Gilbert House, existed within an endless night with no moon or stars in the sky. It seemed odd to think that it was a bright and sunny day in any of these nightmare dimensions, even if it was some kind of *fake* sunshine…

"No cell service," reported Andrea. She was staring at the screen of her phone, her lip curled in an expression of mild disgust, as if the device had disappointed her.

Nicole didn't bother reaching for her own phone. It made sense. If they were in another world, then it probably didn't have any cellular towers.

Gina stood up straight, her hands pressed to her thighs, frowning.

"You okay?" asked Nicole.

She turned around, scanning the floor around her feet. "Lost my phone…" she replied, her voice as flat and emotionless as ever.

"Oh no." Andrea glanced around, too, but it was unlikely it was merely overlooked. There was nowhere for it to hide. They were standing in a completely empty hallway. "First your car, now your phone?"

"Must've dropped it somewhere on Tristesse Lane…" She dropped her hands from her pockets and sighed. "Wouldn't do us any good anyway."

"Sorry," offered Nicole.

"It's fine." And it was. It was only a phone, after all. She sure as hell wasn't going back for it, even if that *were* an option. "I still have my wallet, at least. And my keys."

"That's good," said Andrea. She recalled their lost overnight bags in the trunk of the ruined Civic and felt a twinge of regret for her lost belongings. But Gina was right. They were only things.

Gina leaned against the wall again, weary. "All that matters right now is finding a way out of this place." She looked toward the end of the hallway, to the doors standing at the far end. "If there is a way out."

"There is," insisted Nicole. "There has to be."

She looked away and said nothing, but it was clear she knew better.

"Somebody'll come looking for us, though, right?" said Andrea. "Eventually?"

"Nobody knows where we are," countered Nicole. "Except the creep who put us here."

"What about your goddess?" pressed Andrea.

Gina looked up at her, those sleepy eyes widening a little. "The goddess..." she sighed. "Yeah. She looks after us." She stood up straight again. "I'm sure she knew this could happen."

"That could mean there's a way out, right?"

It wasn't an entirely hopeless line of reasoning, now that she was thinking about it. Unless, of course, she'd failed the goddess somehow... But the goddess knew how everything was going to turn out, didn't she?

Nicole turned and faced Andrea. "Any chance you can use that wormhole trick of yours again? Like how you rescued us back in the temple?"

Andrea looked up at her. "I still don't know how I did that. It just sort of happened. I was falling off a cliff, remember? Then, the second time I did it, *you guys* were the ones falling... Both times I just kind of panicked."

"But after that. The *third* time. When you brought us all back home."

Andrea frowned. She was right. The third time she used her mysterious power, she made it work on command, not just as a reflex. But it wasn't just her doing it. "Wayne..." she recalled. "I could feel his presence, back when he was dead...or whatever... It was like he was reaching out to me. I'm pretty sure that was the only reason it worked."

"So you need a near-death experience or a dead Wayne to make it work? That's not a very convenient superpower."

She scrunched up her nose at her. "Sorry?"

Nicole glanced over at Gina. "You knew what kinds of powers Hotdog had. Do you know how *hers* works?"

But Gina shook her head. "I can tell you have that kind of ability, but I can't quite tell how it works. I'm not sure why I knew how his worked. Maybe because he knew how they worked? Or maybe his powers are more similar to mine than they are to yours? I don't know. Sorry."

"Nothing's easy," sighed Andrea.

Nicole stared down the corridor. Everything was so messed up. They only had one task. Find the Lady of Cedric's Cove. That was all. Gina even knew someone who could tell them were to start looking. All they had to do was drive to Michigan. But they hadn't even made it that far yet. Instead, they were run off the road somewhere in Illinois by those horsemen things, stranded on Tristesse Lane, lost in Glimmering Sunrise Place and now dropped in this filthy abandoned hospital in some new and even more twisted dimension. It was a wonder they'd survived this long.

"Yeah, no kidding," groaned Andrea.

Nicole looked over at her, confused. "What?"

"I was agreeing with you."

"With what?"

"You said, 'We're lost.' I said, 'No kidding.'"

She frowned and glanced at Gina. "I...didn't say that. I didn't say anything."

Andrea stared at her for a moment, letting that process. "Well, *somebody* said—" She turned suddenly and looked behind her.

"You okay?"

"Do you hear that?" she whispered.

"Hear what?"

"Voices!" She pointed down the hallway. "There's some-body over there somewhere."

Nicole listened, but there was nothing. In fact, the place was eerily silent.

"You really don't hear that?"

"I don't hear *anything*."

And neither did Andrea, now. The voices had gone silent. But she could hear them plainly a moment before. Someone was in here with them.

"Spirit activity," said Gina. "She's extra sensitive to it, remember?"

Andrea buried her face in her hands. "I can't deal with that right now," she groaned, her voice muffled.

"Sorry..."

"We'll be okay," Nicole assured them. But of course, she knew no such thing. It seemed to her that they were thoroughly lost.

Gina stepped away from the wall and looked back down the hallway, her sleepy features scrunched into a look of concern.

"What's wrong?" asked Nicole.

"Something's coming."

"What kind of something?" squeaked Andrea.

"Something bad. We need to move." She turned and hurried in the other direction.

Nicole and Andrea exchanged an uneasy look, then followed her.

Chapter 23

Gina led the way forward, her mysterious inner eye wide open, trying to wrap her head around this fractured, directionless world and stay as far as possible from the thing she felt lurking in these gnarled corridors.

She was twenty-six, plenty old enough to have learned to use the abilities she was born with, even with so many of those years spent trying to ignore and suppress those very abilities. She knew by now how to focus her mind to better feel these things. The hardest part was learning to tell the more subtle things she sensed from the physical. Confusing the two was the most common mistake she made growing up. And nothing labeled a young girl a freak and an outcast faster than being caught interacting with things that weren't there. Replying to voices no one else could hear. Staring at things no one else could see. Being afraid of things no one else believed in. At best, the adults around her would say she had an overactive imagination and needed to learn to focus. More often than not, she was simply labeled a liar. She was merely acting out for attention. But sooner or later people would start to say she was just a weirdo. A nutjob. A *freak*.

If only those people had known what she knew. The world wasn't nearly as simple as it seemed. That man walking on the sidewalk outside the school every morning during first recess wasn't a man at all. Nor was that dog heard barking in the distance every evening as the sun went down really a dog. There were things crawling around in the walls of the church. There was something awful lurking in the stagnant waters of the little pond behind the playground at the end of the street. And the man sitting behind the news desk on the channel her stepfather watched every night was quite obviously a thing with blood-red skin in a mask.

She envied the world everyone else lived in. A world where unseen things didn't scream in the dead of night in empty cemeteries. A world where viscus sludge didn't ooze up from storm drains and creep through the neighbors' lawns and up into the trees. A world where yellowish storm clouds didn't sometimes roll in, unnoticed by everyone but her, bringing with them strange, crawling shadows and slimy black worms that sprouted from the earth and wailed with the awful voices of frightened babies.

This was why she was so reserved with her emotions, why she always came off so sleepy and bored. She taught herself not to react to anything that might happen around her, reducing the risk of revealing her weirdness to those around her, as happened so many times when she was a girl. And it was why she distanced herself from people, even those she knew she could trust. She was afraid to get too close to anyone, only to have them push her away again.

Hers was a lonely world. She'd met a lot of people with extraordinary abilities, but she'd never met anyone else quite like her. And that, she'd always supposed, was why the goddess chose her. She was the only one like this, the only one who could do these things.

But even after all these years, it wasn't easy. Every time she thought she had a handle on it all, this strange universe would throw something new at her. Like this place, for example. And it wasn't merely the place. There was something nightmarish lurking in these silent corridors. A *presence*, unlike anything she'd ever encountered before. She couldn't remember ever sensing anything that filled her with such crippling *dread*. Although much of what she perceived with her special senses was relatively harmless, she'd encountered plenty of things that were genuinely frightening. *This* thing, however, was beyond any of those. This thing scared the hell out of her. There was something particularly awful about it. It set her nerves on end every time she tried to focus on it. It was as if some primal instinct carried deep inside her DNA were telling her that it was to be especially feared.

But she was increasingly afraid that she wasn't going to be able to escape it. All of the doors they tried were either patient rooms, storage rooms or offices, with no way out. The only windows she saw were all small, wire-reinforced and set high in the walls out of reach. And she very much doubted that they went anywhere, anyway. Like the skylights above them, she couldn't feel any real sunshine beyond the glass. And when they finally reached the doors at the end of the hallway and opened them, there was only another long hallway waiting on the other side. This whole place went on and on in a straight line, with no turns, no intersections…no *end*…and yet somehow it didn't *feel* like they were going in a straight line. As soon as she stepped through the doorway, the orientation of those warped surroundings changed. It felt for some reason as if they'd turned a corner.

Andrea gasped and twirled around, her wide eyes staring back the way they came.

"What's wrong?" asked Nicole.

"Something pulled my hair," she whimpered, grasping at the loose strands trailing down from her unraveling bun.

"We should keep moving," advised Gina. "We're not alone in here."

"Can you feel what she's picking up on?" asked Nicole as they passed through the doors and into the next hallway.

"No. I've seen ghosts before. I'm pretty sure anyone can see them if the spirits are strong enough and make themselves known. But I'm not sensitive to them like she is. I won't be able to perceive them as easily as she does. Or any of the other things."

"What other things?" asked Andrea.

"Lots of things. The spirit realm isn't just ghosts. There's a whole universe out there that belongs exclusively to the dead."

She groaned. She didn't like the sound of that.

Gina looked back down that unsettlingly endless corridor stretched out behind them. "What I feel right now definitely isn't a ghost. It's something much worse. We can't let it notice us."

Nicole looked back over her shoulder, too, nervous. "Is it getting any farther away?"

"Sometimes. Sometimes it's closer. It moves around in strange ways. I can't really describe it. Honestly, I don't know how long we can keep away from it."

Andrea let out a startled cry and stopped, her hands pressed to her mouth, her wide eyes fixed on the dirty window of one of the doors they were passing.

"*What?*" gasped Nicole.

"There's someone in there!" She thrust a finger at the dirty window. "Someone was just there! Looking out!"

"Spirit activity," affirmed Gina.

Nicole pushed open the door and looked inside, but there was no one there. It was a tiny room, with no way out and nowhere to hide. The only thing there was another rotten wheelchair and some scattered bottles.

Andrea shook her head. "I saw it..." she insisted. "It was a man." She gestured at her face and said, "Big, bushy eyebrows and beard. Plain as I'm seeing you right now!"

"I believe you," Nicole assured her.

Gina nodded. There was no reason *not* to believe her.

Again, Andrea turned and looked behind them. "Voices..." she whispered.

"Just keep moving," advised Gina. "The vast majority of ghosts can't hurt you. But there's something here that can. We have to get out of here before it finds us."

She nodded and started walking again.

"I guess it does kind of make sense," reasoned Nicole. "Remember when we were outside the temple? You were the first one who heard the voices there, too."

"I know." She'd thought the same thing when Gina first told her she had a connection to the spirit world. But it was still weird to think about. She frowned, "I thought they were just picking on me because I was the youngest."

Nicole tilted her head to one side, confused. "Why would they do that?"

"Don't people say kids are more sensitive to ghosts than adults? I figured maybe they thought I'd have a better chance of hearing them."

"Olivia's not even a full year older than you. That's not much of a gap."

"I don't know! Nobody ever told me I was some kind of ghost whisperer until yesterday!" She paused as they passed an open doorway, her gaze fixed on the space beyond it.

Nicole peered inside. It was yet another small patient room. The rusty frame of an old bed stood to one side. An old rolling table lay overturned on the floor. The ceiling was crumbling and the floor was warped in one corner, but it was only rot and decay. "It's just voices and shadows. Nothing real."

"Seriously…?" said Andrea, her voice cracking a little.

"Just keep telling yourself that. Come on."

They moved on, but Andrea's gaze lingered on that room as they walked away.

Clearly, no one else could see the blood splashed all over the floor and walls.

"They're going to hurt you," whispered a voice from somewhere inside the blood-soaked room.

Chapter 24

If Andrea had been able to choose a superpower of any kind, she wouldn't have picked the ability to see and communicate with ghosts. Or *anything* having to do with ghosts, for that matter. And now that she had that ability, she desperately wished she could give it away. Because this *sucked*.

They made their way to the far end of the second corridor and opened the next pair of doors, only to find another hallway waiting for them there, followed by another, and then another, hallway after endless hallway, desperately searching for an exit that probably didn't exist. And all the while, strange and unsettling things went on around her that only she seemed to notice. Footsteps that didn't belong to any of them. Elusive things that lurked in her peripheral vision. Faces that peered back at her through windows and cracked doors. Unseen things that reached out and touched her. More than once, she could have sworn there was a fourth person walking among them. And then there were the voices. Unintelligible whispers from empty rooms. Gasps and moans and sobs from every direction. Words in languages she didn't understand. And now there was a constant, barely audible murmuring that seemed to come from every direction at once.

But the worst, by far, were the things that she *could* understand.

"Shouldn't be here…" whispered a woman's voice.

"Please let me go…" wept a man's voice.

"They get inside your skin…" gasped a deeper-voiced man.

"Everyone disappears eventually…" sighed another woman.

"I want to go home…" whimpered what she was quite sure was a child.

She tried covering her ears, but the voices still found her. If anything, it only made them *easier* to hear.

"Help me…"

"Crawling all over me…"

"There's no way out…"

"It hurts so much…"

"Don't go to sleep…"

"Leave me alone!"

"Where's my mommy?"

"Don't touch me!"

She had to make a conscious effort by now not to cry. It wasn't just the voices. It was the emotion behind the voices. It was the pervading sense of helplessness and pain that seemed to ooze from the very walls around her. It was the crushing terror of all who were locked up in here, the despair of slowly coming to understand that they would never see their homes or anyone they loved ever again.

This was a far more visceral hopelessness than Tristesse Lane. That was misery. That was pure sorrow and despair. But this place was *brutal*. This place was *terror*. And she desperately wanted to be far away from here as soon as possible.

"You okay?" asked Nicole.

She nodded. She didn't quite dare speak. She was afraid she'd start sobbing.

"You sure?"

Again, she nodded.

"It's invasive," said Gina. "Feeling things others can't. You can't turn it off. No matter how much you want to. And it feels like no one else can ever understand you."

Andrea looked back at her, surprised. "Is that what it's like for you?"

"Every day," she replied.

"Last time, outside the temple…" recalled Nicole, "…the rest of us could see and hear stuff, too. Not just you. You just seemed to get the brunt of it."

"Different places have different rules," explained Gina. "As do different kinds of ghosts. It could be that she's just tuned into these better. Or that they're targeting her, specifically. Maybe *because* she's sensitive to spirits."

Andrea pouted. She didn't care for the idea of being targeted…

But she'd been thinking about the temple, too. That was the only other time in her life she'd experienced these sorts of things. And there were a lot of similarities. Like now, there were voices, many of them even speaking strange, unfamiliar languages. There were also shadows and barely glimpsed figures. She remembered more than once glancing back and seeing, for just an instant, more people than were actually with her. But if Gina was right and she really did have some kind of psychic connection to the spirit world, why was it that she never heard ghostly voices like that when she was growing up? She didn't remember ever having experiences like that in her home. Was it something she grew into? Was it something that was limited to places like these? She didn't understand.

Not for the first time since all this started, she found herself thinking of her childhood friend, Helen. Helen Omberst was *obsessed* with scary stuff. She used to collect creepy stories and seek out the scariest looking places in the city. She loved daring people to sneak into abandoned buildings.

Andrea did her share of exploring. She followed Helen into quite a few creepy places and felt the hair stand up on the back of her neck. But that was only play. All the stories about those places, the ghost tales, the spooky legends, it was all make-believe. Helen either heard the story somewhere and embellished it or she made it all up herself.

Never once did she experience anything at any of Helen's spooky dare locations. She never heard disembodied footsteps or caught sight of any shadows moving across the floors.

But she supposed she could've just been lucky.

Helen once found a large, concrete storm culvert hidden deep in the brush near the river and made up some gruesome story about a satanic cult that used to torture and cannibalize kidnapped children inside it. Somehow, she convinced Amber Cobberton to crawl inside and see what was there. The poor girl found candles and satanic symbols and freaked out, much to Helen's rather sadistic delight. To this day, Andrea wasn't sure if Helen put those things inside to screw with Amber or if it was merely the work of some morbid teenagers who just happened to be fooling around inside sometime before Helen found it, or even if the symbols she claimed to have seen were actually satanic or just random graffiti, but she was sure, even as a kid, that there was nothing supernatural about a storm culvert.

Then, years later, she met Albert and the others and it gave her a chill to think about a little girl crawling inside *any* of the tunnels in Briar Hills. Because it turned out there *were* things down there.

Bad things.

She let out a startled gasp and pressed herself against Nicole hard enough to knock her off balance.

"Hey!"

"Sorry!" She turned around, clutching her hands against her chest, her wide eyes scanning the empty space behind her. "Something grabbed my wrist."

"There's no one there."

"No one we can see," Gina reminded her.

"Sorry…" whimpered Andrea.

"It's fine." Nicole's gaze lingered on the gloom of the corridor behind them for a moment, nervous.

"It feels like it's getting worse."

"You could be attracting them," offered Gina. "They sense you can hear them."

Andrea made a frightened squeaking noise at the idea and crowded closer to Nicole again. "I don't wanna attract anything…"

"I'm sure it's fine," Gina assured her.

"Easy for you to say," she grumbled. "They're not in *your* head."

"That's true. Sorry."

They reached the next door at the end of the corridor and pushed it open. Yet another hallway waited beyond it.

"We're not getting anywhere," groaned Andrea.

"We'll figure it out," Nicole assured her, though she wasn't fooling anyone by now. They were thoroughly lost this time. And no one was coming to save them.

But a voice in Andrea's ear made her pause.

It was a faint voice. Soft. The voice of a young girl, she thought. She could barely make it out, but she thought it said, "This way."

Her gaze was drawn to the doorway they were passing. It was no different than all the rest of the doors. And yet, there was something strangely compelling about it.

Hesitantly, she reached out for the door, her hand trembling a little, and pushed it open.

It wasn't the same as the other rooms. It looked more like a waiting room. There was a reception desk in front of her and another doorway in the left corner. The door stood open, as if waiting for them. It was the only room she'd seen with another door in it.

"Here," sighed a voice from somewhere beyond it.

"Andrea?" pressed Nicole.

She pointed at the doorway. "I think…maybe that way?"

"Why that way?"

She bit her lip, uncertain. "Because a ghost just told me to?"

"And you trust it?"

"I don't know…" The voice didn't sound scary or mean. It just sounded like a soft-spoken girl. But she supposed that didn't mean much.

"Ghosts can't usually hurt you," Gina reminded her, "but they aren't always nice. Sometimes they're bitter. Sometimes they're mean. Sometimes they lie."

The three of them stood there a moment, hesitating. This *was* the first room they'd found that wasn't a dead end. That second door waiting inside was at least something new. And they weren't getting anywhere just following this same stupid hallway.

Then, finally, Andrea made her decision and entered the room. "I'm going this way," she decided.

"If you say so," said Nicole. It wasn't as if they were making any progress on their own.

Chapter 25

Andrea led the way for a while, following the mysterious voice that Nicole couldn't hear no matter how hard she tried.

Could they really trust any of the spirits here? Everywhere they'd gone had been filled with monstrous things that tried to lie to them or kill them or devour all the joy in their hearts. But if there really were ghosts in this place, was it all that hard to imagine that some of them might want to help them avoid whatever terrible fate they might have endured?

But it was undeniable that something had changed. The hallways here were different. They no longer stretched on and on in a pointless straight line. This part of the building looked more like a normal hospital, albeit an impossibly enormous one. There was still no sign of an exit of any kind, or even an elevator or stairway. But there was more than just the one hallway. There were intersections. They had choices now, which sort of *felt* like a better situation to be stuck in, even if every direction they turned just seemed to lead to more intersections and more wrong choices.

If this place was really like Hotdog described, if this was some kind of manifestation of that evil hospital within an entirely new world, then it probably explained the impossible layout and labyrinth-like feel. And if the original structure was really some sort of deranged prison that only *pretended* to be a hospital, a place no one who was admitted to ever checked out, then it even made a twisted sort of sense that there were no exits.

They stepped into an intersection of hallways and Andrea cringed. She pointed to the right. "Definitely not that way."

"What's that way?" wondered Nicole.

"No idea, but a voice I *seriously* didn't like just told me to go that way... Gave me the creeps *really* bad."

"Bad spirits," agreed Gina. "Trust your judgment. It's usually right."

She nodded and turned left. "The not-creepy voice says this way."

Nicole followed her. She very much hoped that Andrea was right about which ghosts were good and which were bad.

"That scary presence I keep feeling is getting closer," reported Gina. "I think it's starting to realize we're here."

"Fantastic," grumbled Nicole. "How far away is it?"

"I'm not sure. It feels like the concept of distance here is only an illusion. But I *am* sure it knows how to get around this place a lot better than we do."

Andrea let out a startled, "Eek!" and swatted at something next to her head. "Stop doing that!"

"Something touch you again?" asked Nicole.

"Voice. Like, a *super* creepy one. Right in my ear."

"What did it say?"

"I couldn't tell exactly... Something about wanting my skin, I think."

"*What?*"

"I know! Stranger danger much?"

Nicole shuddered and took her hand. "Let's definitely not get separated again, okay?"

She couldn't stop thinking about Glimmering Sunrise Place and how easily Andrea was taken from her. She only turned her back for a second and she was gone. How close did she come to losing her forever?

Gina told them that she was sent to find and protect Andrea. Was that the only reason they were able to get her back? Because she was important to whatever this twisted mission was that they were on?

What would have happened if it had been *her* who was snatched away, Nicole wondered. Could Gina and Andrea have ended up leaving her there? Would that Hotdog creep have bothered saving her with the rest of them? She wasn't important, after all. She was always just the tagalong...

She pushed these pointless thoughts from her head and focused on the path before them. That kind of thinking wasn't going to help anything.

Besides, she was the one carrying the spear. They probably would've had to come back for *that* at least… Right?

Andrea paused and opened another door. Inside was an office with a large, wooden desk surrounded by built-in bookshelves and filing cabinets. There was another door in the back. "She says this way."

"She?" asked Nicole. Focusing on their ghostly guide felt like a better use of her idle thoughts than how expendable she might be. "So it's a girl."

"Yeah. She sounds pretty young."

"Can you ask her name?"

Andrea crossed the office, tiptoeing through a carpet of yellowed papers. "Yeah. What's your name?" She pushed open the door and peered through it. Another hallway waited there, but it wasn't like the others. It was shorter and narrower, with only one other door at the far end.

Nicole picked up one of the papers as they passed the desk and glanced over it. It looked like handwritten notes written in faded pen, but she couldn't read any of it. She didn't even recognize the language.

"Can you tell me your name?" Andrea tried again. She stood there a moment, listening, but then she shook her head.

Nicole let go of the paper and let it flutter to the floor. "No answer?"

"She's not telling me." She crept forward, through the short hallway, still listening.

"Lots of ghosts are limited in what they can do," explained Gina. "She might have to conserve her energy."

Nicole glanced at her, curious. "Why do you know so much about ghosts if you're sensitive to different things than her?"

"When I was trying to understand who I was…why I was the way I was…I tried researching it. I couldn't find anything that seemed to match the things I could see and hear and feel…but there was a lot about paranormal phenomenon and research. It seemed like as close as I was going to get. I was hoping to find a connection, but all I learned was that I was even different from all the other people in the world with psychic abilities."

"That's a bummer," said Andrea. "I can see where that would sort of suck."

"Yeah…"

"But *I* think you're pretty awesome."

Gina looked down at the floor, embarrassed. "Thanks…"

"I'm just glad you're with us," said Nicole. "We wouldn't have made it out of Briar Hills without you." Somebody would have found poor Andrea strangled in that parking lot and she probably would've been dragged back to the barely-there's twisted perversion of her apartment, never to leave again.

Nicole followed Andrea through another door and into a larger space than any of the rooms before. There were several rows of chairs lined up in front of a large window on the right, each one slightly lower than the one behind it, like theater seats, overlooking a spacious room with what appeared to be a gynecological examination chair mounted in the center of the space, with a number of large, directional lamps mounted over it. There were heavy-duty leather straps hanging from the arms, stirrups and headrest of the chair.

It was a disturbing scene. Hotdog described the place more as a prison than a hospital, meaning no one was likely here by choice. It was entirely too easy to imagine people dragging some poor woman to that chair and strapping her down, naked and on full display for everyone in this room.

The angle of that chair… The very thought made her feel sick. She wasn't shy about her body. She didn't mind being naked in front of people. But she couldn't imagine being forced into something like that. The thought of being strapped down by a bunch of men in lab coats while strangers sat staring at her forcibly exposed body… What kind of twisted pervert would want to witness something like that? Was this where those in charge of this place came to watch the patients suffer? Or was it simply some perverted form of entertainment? A peep show to exploit and humiliate the female patients and amuse the twisted staff? Somehow, that sort of thing seemed equally plausible in a place like this.

Maybe she was overthinking it. Maybe this was where those in charge oversaw the doctors under their supervision. Or maybe it was where they brought medical students to observe examinations in real-time. Even so, she found herself doubting very much that any woman who ever found herself strapped into that chair was there of her own free will. And the thought disgusted her.

This place was evil, after all. Not only did Hotdog tell them as much, but Gina had pretty much confirmed it when she told them the entire place existed in another of those freaky pocket dimensions.

Places like this, places with so much evil... she recalled Hotdog saying, *...so much* despair *soaked into their bones...for so many years...*

She turned away from that window, trying not to think about the things that must've gone on in this horrible place to earn it such an evil reputation that it transcended reality itself, and started toward the next door.

"Not that way," said Andrea. "The other one."

Nicole paused, confused. The only other door was the one that they entered through. There wasn't anywhere else to go.

But Andrea was walking toward the farther corner of the room rather than the nearer one.

"What're you doing?"

"We go this way," she said. She pointed toward the wall. "The voice said so. Through this door."

Nicole glanced at the wall there. "*What* door?"

Andrea stared at her. It was her turn to look confused. "This one...?" She was reaching toward the wall, her open hand closing, as if around a handle, but still there was no door there. "Right here?"

Sure enough, she pulled open a door.

It was enough to send a wave of vertigo through Nicole's head. She actually swayed a little as she processed the fact that there was, in fact, a door there. It didn't appear there. It was always there. She could even *almost* remember it being there, even though she was quite sure it wasn't...

God, why was everything so fucking confusing?

She glanced over at Gina. She had her small hands pressed to her temples as if she suddenly had a headache. "Did you see that door before she opened it?"

"I didn't. I think only she could see it."

Andrea blinked back at them. "You guys couldn't see this door?" She looked back at it. "Wait... I thought I could only see ghosts. Why would I see doors? Can *doors* be ghosts? I'm confused."

Nicole shrugged. "Don't ask me."

"The vast majority of the spirit world is a complete mystery. We can't know everything about it without being dead. Maybe not even then."

Andrea jumped and swatted at something near her ear. "Ew! Go away! Stupid dead people!"

"You okay?" asked Nicole.

"Yeah," she replied with a revolted shudder.

"Voices again?"

She nodded. "Some old creep wanted me to touch his ghost junk."

Nicole wrinkled her nose. "Gross."

"I know, right? *As if.*"

"Well, I guess we know there're *perverts* in the spirit world. That's awesome. Glad to clear *that* up."

"Seems that way," said Gina. She looked back the way they came, still rubbing at her head. "But right now we have bigger problems."

"Oh good," grumbled Nicole. "We need bigger problems. The ones we're dealing with aren't nearly shitty enough."

"What's wrong?" asked Andrea.

"The presence I've been feeling... Opening that door really got its attention. It's coming this way. Fast. We don't have much time."

Nicole cursed and turned back to Andrea. "Lead the way. Hurry."

Andrea nodded and stepped through the doorway. There was another hallway waiting here, but again, everything looked different. Gone were the beige walls and the green tiles. These walls were red brick. These floors were a dingy gray. The rooms they passed were more prison-like than the ones in those first hallways. The doors all had small windows with wire mesh inside them. The remains of the beds all had leather restraints.

"Homey," grumbled Nicole.

"Why does it smell so bad here?" asked Andrea.

Nicole sniffed at the air. "I don't smell anything."

"Seriously?" She had her hand over her mouth and nose. "You can't smell that?"

"It smells like the rest of the building," observed Nicole. "Just…musty."

"Phantom smells," said Gina.

"Oh come on!" gasped Andrea.

"What does it smell like?" asked Nicole.

She lowered her hand and grimaced. "It's like…*sewage*…? I think? Rotten garbage?"

"Inhumane living conditions were disturbingly common in old hospitals and prisons," Gina informed them. "You might be getting a spiritual memory of what this place smelled like when people were kept here."

Andrea wrinkled her nose. "That's just *wrong*."

"I agree." Gina looked back over her shoulder. "But we really have bigger things to worry about right now."

"How close is it?" asked Nicole.

"Closer than I like."

Andrea pointed at her temple. "I know it sounds crazy when I start sentences like this, but that voice in my head says we're almost there."

"Tell her thanks for us," said Nicole.

"I think she can hear you." Andrea reached the end of the hallway and opened the door. This next room was the largest they'd found so far. There was a row of long-rotten bedframes lined up against the wall on either side. On the ceiling directly above each bed was mounted a large, adjustable, disk-shaped light. Several rusty metal cabinets were arranged around the room, many of them still containing an assortment of dust-covered bottles, jars and boxes. There were moldy papers and debris from the crumbling ceiling strewn across the filthy green tiles. Two metal desks stood on the far side of the room, both of them piled high with dirty folders.

She turned and looked back at Nicole. "She says this is it."

But Nicole only frowned at the room around them. "This is *what?*" She eyed those strange lights mounted above each bed. Was it only her morbid imagination, or did this look like the sort of place where horrible things once happened in the name of science and medicine? She couldn't help thinking about all the stories she'd watched on television about barbaric treatments and experiments performed on unfortunate patients. Wasn't that the start of every ghost story surrounding a hospital or sanitorium?

"She says this is the way out," replied Andrea.

"How is *this* the way out? There's no door." The only way out of this room was the way they came. "Unless there's another one here that only you can see."

"Unfortunately not..." She turned and searched the walls around her. "I don't understand it either."

"It's coming," warned Gina. She closed the door behind them and backed away from it. "We're trapped here."

"Oh no..." whimpered Andrea. "What do we do?"

Nicole stared at the door. Was it only because Gina told her there was something there, or could she feel it, too? Something on the other side that was rapidly filling her with a suffocating dread. A heavy, weirdly oppressive sort of presence.

Andrea let out a terrified squeak.

"What does Ghost Girl say?" asked Nicole, desperate.

"She's not saying *anything!*"

She cursed. "Was she lying to you?" The thought made her sick. "Was she just trying to back us into a corner?"

"I don't know..." She shook her head, her eyes glistening with frightened tears. Did she make a mistake. Should she not have trusted the voice?

"We don't have much time," warned Gina. She was still

backing away from the door, her brown eyes wide with fear.

Again, Nicole cursed. How could this happen? It wasn't fair.

"I don't know what to do!" cried Andrea. "I don't—" She gasped and clasped her hand over her ear. Then she wrinkled her nose, confused. "*What?* I don't...? I don't understand!"

"What'd she say?" asked Nicole, panicked.

"She said to use the spear."

"Use it for *what?*" She glanced back at the door. Surely she wasn't suggesting they use the spear to *fight* whatever was coming for them. Whatever was out there, she very much doubted that a dull spear with no handle was going to do anything to it.

"She says, 'The spear is the door.'"

"That makes even less sense!"

"I know!"

Nicole pulled the spear from her purse and unwrapped it. The gold glinted in the dull sunlight that filtered in through the dingy skylights. It was a strange contrast to these grimy surroundings. Nothing about it seemed to belong in this place. But if their ghostly guide said it was the key to getting out of here, she wasn't going to argue. She turned and held it out for Andrea to take.

But Andrea only stared at it. "What am *I* supposed to do with it?"

"You're the one she's talking to!"

"It doesn't mean I know what she's talking about!" She took the spear and looked at it, but she had no idea what to do.

"If the spear is the door, then it must be our way out," reasoned Gina.

Andrea held it up closer, right up to her face, scanning the various etchings in its surface for a moment. "Yeah... This isn't a door. It's a stabby thing. I don't know how to use a stabby thing as a door."

Gina stared at her for a moment, her expression blank. Even the rising panic melted away as she processed this comment. "That sounds idiotic...but I can't think of any way to argue with your logic..."

"I know, right?"

She turned and looked back at the door, her typically sleepy eyes filling with worry again. "You have to figure it out. It'll be here any second."

Nicole followed her gaze. Was it her imagination, or was the door changing. It was as if the light were fading in just that one place. It was getting *darker*.

"Whatever you do with it," said Gina, "it should probably be soon."

Chapter 26

Andrea's heart was pounding. Panic was quickly building up inside her, overwhelming her. How was she supposed to know what to do? She was no kind of expert on mysterious golden spears. Was she supposed to stick it somewhere? Was one of the things carved on it supposed to point to a hidden passage? Should she wave it around like a magic wand and shout, "Alohomora!" like Hermione Granger?

Not for the first time, she wished Albert were here. He was the puzzle guy. He was the one who decoded the messages on the box and unlocked the map to the temple. Maybe he'd know how to use the spear.

"It's right outside…" whispered Gina.

She looked back at the door again. Why was it turning *black*? Strange shadows seemed to be oozing through the cracks around it.

And now that she was looking, she could *hear* it, too. There was an awful moaning sound, like something from a creepy zombie movie.

"Now would be a good time to open the door," whispered Gina.

"No shit," agreed Nicole.

"No pressure then," grumbled Andrea. "Good to know."

"Just figure it out quickly!"

"Please," added Gina.

She turned the spear over and over in her hands, but she had no idea what she was supposed to do. What if she couldn't make it work in time? What if the thing at the door got to them first? It would all be her fault!

Why would anyone trust her with something as important

as this?

Something was wrong with the space around the door. It was bending and twisting as if she were looking at it through trickling water. That darkness gathering around it looked like boiling smoke and slithering tentacles. Even the paint on the walls around it seemed to bubble, as if something were wriggling just beneath it. A strange, overwhelming dread radiated from it, washing over her like an icy fog, raising the hairs on her arms and neck and filling her belly with molten terror.

She felt like she was going to puke.

But worst of all were the voices. Screams of terror and agony were drifting from somewhere behind the door, as if thousands of tortured souls were bound just on the other side.

"Any time now!" squealed Nicole.

"I don't know what to do!" She gave it a shake, as if the silly thing might just need its batteries jiggled or something.

The door was beginning to open. That living darkness began to ooze through like a great, black cloud.

She turned and looked at the room around her. There was nothing here that looked even remotely like an exit. There was no way out. They were utterly trapped.

Then that soft voice spoke to her again, over those awful screams and wails, right into her ear: "Don't look with your eyes."

She blinked down at the spear again. What?

"Look for the light in the darkness."

What light? What darkness? Why couldn't anyone just tell her what she was supposed to do in plain English?

"Close your eyes."

Close her eyes. She nodded. "I can do that," she muttered. It didn't make any sense to her, but she wanted instructions and she was given them. So she closed her eyes and took a shaky breath.

Now what?

But then she saw it. A light... Or was it more of an afterimage? Either way, it was bright. Like a burning star looming right in front of her. And there was something surprisingly compelling about it.

Still focusing on the light, she opened her eyes and found that there was a small hole in the wall right where that light was burning.

She hurried across the room and looked at it. It was just a hole, little more than the sort of place where an anchor bolt had once been inserted to hang a picture or something, right about eye level. It was hardly a fire exit. But now that her attention had been drawn to it, she couldn't help thinking there was something different about the tiny space inside that hole.

She didn't understand it in the least, but it felt like it should be a lot bigger than that...

"Use the spear."

She looked down at it again, confused. Use it for *what?* It was too wide to fit through the hole. She couldn't just shove it in there.

Behind her, Nicole and Gina were backing away from the door. It was swinging open, revealing more and more of the black mass gathered behind it.

Shadows crept into the room, forming shapes like skeletal hands on the walls, floor and ceiling.

"Andrea!" cried Nicole.

But she couldn't afford to panic. She closed her eyes again and focused on both that strange, burning light and the heavy golden object in her hand.

It wasn't really a spear, after all. It looked like a spear. It was shaped like one. But it had never been a spear, not in all the ages it had been around. It had always been something else. And in that odd bit of knowledge, she glimpsed just a glimmer of understanding.

Her eyes still closed, she turned the spear so that its tip was pointing down and then brought it close to her, pressing it against her heart.

It was similar to the sensation she felt five years ago, deep in that mysterious tunnel where the spirits zoomed by her in that utter darkness like horizontal rain. When she opened the portals that saved her friends. But it wasn't the *same* as that. This wasn't *her* portal. She was merely opening one that someone else left here, someone who knew they were going to need it.

Was this the Keeper's doing? Or was it Gina's goddess, whoever she might be? Or was it possible this was something the Sentinel Queen set up for them before she died? She didn't know. But she suddenly felt very certain that everything that was happening to them was by no means random. Someone, somewhere, for some reason, meant for them to reach this place.

All she had to do was open the door.

She couldn't say how she did it. It wasn't as if she turned some magic key or said some magic word. She just sort of willed it to open.

Chapter 27

Nicole was staring at those skeletal shadow hands as they crept across the floor, reaching out for her.

This wasn't happening. It wasn't real. It was just an illusion. This whole place was an illusion. This whole frightening ordeal. It had to be. This was all just some kind of bad dream.

She kept telling herself that, but she knew she was full of shit.

The thing oozing through the doorway in front of her was as real as she was.

"This way!" shouted Andrea. "Hurry!"

She looked back to find that a portion of that back wall had been pulled back into a long, receding tunnel, as if the bricks there were nothing more than a cleverly painted rubber sheet and something behind it was drawing it backward like the string on a bow. Andrea was standing in front of it, her back turned to it. She was clutching the spear between her small breasts, the loose hair from her unraveling buns whipping backward in a stiff wind that looked strange because Nicole couldn't feel any wind from where she was standing.

It was difficult to wrap her head around it.

"That's the way out!" cried Gina.

Andrea was already beginning to slide backward, as if slowly being sucked into the strange tunnel.

Nicole shook it off and hurried after her. It wasn't like this was the first time she'd ever seen Andrea standing at the center of a dimensional wormhole, after all. She could take a break and try to wrap her head around how fucked up all this was when she was well and safely away from Hotdog's nightmare hospital.

But before she could reach her, something seized her trailing hair and yanked her to a painful stop.

Those shadowy claws had ensnared her.

Andrea cried out for her, her bright blue eyes wide with terror. She reached out for her, but she was too far away. And she was moving farther away with each breathless second that passed.

Then she was just gone. It was like watching someone get sucked through an airlock in some science fiction thriller. In the space of a single frantic heartbeat, she was yanked backward and out of sight.

An icy terror enveloped her heart as another black, skeletal hand wrapped around her thigh. An arm slithered around her waist.

It was too late for her. She was going to be left behind.

All that she'd been through since the wedding... Did she even really make any difference? Was she better off never escaping the barely-there and that cold, squelchy, joyless mockery of her home? Would they have been better off without her from the start?

She really was just a useless tagalong...

But Gina didn't vanish into the tunnel like Andrea. She stopped herself a step short, turned back, grabbed her arm and held on with all her strength.

But small, timid Gina wasn't nearly strong enough to pull her from the monster's grip.

More skeletal fingers curled around her ankle. Another hand closed around her neck. Her feet were sliding across the filthy floor in the wrong direction. She was being dragged backward, away from the safety of Andrea's magic tunnel.

And Gina was being dragged back with her.

Nicole could see more of those shadowy arms reaching past her, skeletal fingers ready to close around Gina's wrists. In another second they would ensnare her, too. They'd both be dragged back into whatever awful, endless hell awaited her.

She didn't have time to think it through. She reached out with her free foot and used it to shove Gina backward, breaking her grip. In an instant she was gone, pulled through the portal and out of the monster's reach forever.

And then she was alone.

That stark terror descended over her again.

There was a moment of hope there. A few desperate seconds of it, anyway… But this was the best outcome. Of that, she was certain. Gina was sent to protect Andrea, after all. Not her. She was only the tagalong. She was *always* just the tagalong. Maybe this was what she was always here to do.

At least she was able to protect her friends. That was all she ever really wanted.

Those strange, shadowy arms wrapped around her. Bony claws dug into her wrist. Something pierced the tender flesh of her left side. A hot burning sensation crept across her right thigh. She caught just a glimpse of blood trickling down her arm as an inky darkness descended over her, blinding her, *suffocating* her.

This was going to hurt. A *lot*. And death was only going to be the beginning.

She could hear them clearly now. The voices of the dead, screaming and howling and wailing in the boiling black mass that was swallowing her. All those lost souls who fell victim to this thing before her.

She was going to be one of them soon. Whatever this thing was, she knew with absolute certainty that it wasn't just going to take her life. It was going to take her very *soul*. And it would never let her go. She was going to spend the rest of eternity trapped inside it. And every second was going to be nothing but torment and suffering.

I'm sorry, she thought as tears streaked down her face. She wished she could've at least had the chance to say it aloud to all the people she was leaving behind. To Andrea. To Gina. To her parents. To Albert and Brandy. Wayne and Olivia. To all her friends out there.

She was so sorry…

"*Why are you so much trouble?*" hissed a voice in her ear.

She gasped.

Strong arms were suddenly wrapped around her, holding her. Not the skeletal arms of a monster, but the warm, strong arms of a man.

A body was pressed against her back.

A familiar presence shined through the screaming, squirming shadows all around her, shielding her from the monster.

Keith?

The blackness blinding her parted. The tunnel that swallowed Andrea and Gina was right in front of her eyes.

"Go!" shouted Keith.

Before she could look back at him, he pushed her away.

She felt herself yanked forward. In an instant, everything drastically changed. The light. The sound. The air pressure. The temperature. The *gravity*. She felt herself turned upside down. Her ears popped. Her breath caught in her chest. A searing light blinded her. Her feet struck the ground without warning and she stumbled and fell.

Someone caught her. Strong arms enveloped her again before she could hit the ground.

"Keith…" she gasped.

But when she looked up, a stranger was holding her. A large, pudgy man loomed before her eyes.

Startled and disoriented, acting purely on reflex, she punched him in the face.

Chapter 28

"Again, I am *so* sorry," said Nicole.

The big guy lifted his huge hand in a dismissive wave. "M'fine," he insisted. His voice was muffled a bit by the damp towel the skinny woman was pressing against his nose, but there was no hint of anger or resentment in either his words or the gesture. In fact, he sounded positively cheerful for someone spouting blood.

"Really, I feel just *awful.* I didn't know who or where or..." She shook her head. She was still so embarrassed. "I just...I panicked."

"Totally understandable," replied the woman. "We startled you."

"My bad," he agreed. He was sitting with his considerable bulk squeezed into an outdoor folding chair, his head tilted back as the skinny woman tended to him.

They were in a small clearing, surrounded by trees. The air was hot, but breezy. She could hear birds and bugs singing all around her. There was a campfire smoldering inside a circle of stones and a tent pitched in the shade to one side. It looked like these two had been camped out here all night, but there was no sign of any vehicle. Wherever they were, they must've hiked in on foot.

"He's a tough guy," the woman assured her. "He'll be fine. Trust me."

"I'm impressed you even hurt him," said Andrea. She was kneeling in front of Nicole, tending to the painful claw marks the monster left on her wrist and forearm. She had more on her legs and abdomen. Fortunately, they hadn't dug in very deep. They were painful, and they were bleeding enough to warrant bandages, but they weren't serious. "He's, like, twice your size."

"*Awesome* punch," he said, grinning under the towel. "*Nice.*" He was at least six and a half feet tall, pudgy, round, with a sizeable gut, but not excessively flabby, an entirely different kind of big than Nicole's father, more solid than fat. He looked quite strong. Had he actually intended her harm, she wasn't sure she could have fought him off. But he really didn't seem even a little bit angry about being punched.

"Just keep that held right there," the woman told him, stepping back.

He gave her a thumbs up and pressed his other huge hand over the towel, holding it in place.

"He's hard to hurt," she promised. "And even harder to make mad. Almost impossible, really. He's big, but he's a gentle roly-poly."

Nicole rubbed at her forehead. She could barely keep up with all that was happening. One minute she was being attacked by that monster in that disturbing deserted hospital, utterly convinced that she was going to die a terrible death and end up trapped forever with all those ghosts. The next minute, that fake Keith was there again, berating her for getting herself into another sticky situation—as if it were *her* fault all these things kept happening—and shoving her through that strange tunnel in the wall. And then she was here in the middle of this campsite with Andrea and Gina and these two strangers. It was a lot to process and her processor felt like it was exceeding capacity. "So you guys are Gina's friends? The ones who study portals to other worlds?"

"Violet Snubb and Corey Vano," introduced Gina. She was sitting on the ground next to them. Like Corey, she was holding a towel against her face. "This is Andrea and Nikki." She frowned. "Sorry, I don't think I ever got your last names."

"Prophett," said Andrea.

"Nicole Smart," said Nicole.

"Sorry," Gina said again in her small, sleepy voice. She'd never been very good at social interactions. When was it even appropriate to ask someone for their last name if they didn't volunteer it? And was it presumptuous of her to call her "Nikki" like that? That was just what Andrea called her. She never even considered that it was only a nickname.

"Is that too tight?" asked Andrea as she taped down the gauze around Nicole's forearm.

"It's fine. Thank you. I'm more worried about *her.*"

"I'm okay," Gina insisted.

The portal that Andrea opened spit her out right in the middle of Violet & Corey's camp. She just sort of dropped out the sky with a terrified scream and landed on her butt right between them, disoriented, confused and half-hysterical because she thought she lost her friends. The last thing she remembered, after all, was that monster grabbing hold of Nicole's hair and yanking her backward. A few seconds later, while Violet and Corey were still trying to figure out where the little pierced redhead even came from, Gina landed face-down at Violet's feet with a painful yelp. The landing left bloody scrapes on her cheek and forehead as well as her elbow. Seeing her hurt was the reason Corey was so quick to jump up and grab Nicole when she appeared.

"It's feeling better already," she insisted. "Really."

"I can take care of the rest of these," said Nicole, ignoring her. She was already dabbing at the scratches on her thigh with a disinfectant wipe.

Andrea turned and seated herself cross-legged on the ground in front of Gina. "Let me see it."

Gina lowered the towel.

"Ouch."

"It's fine," she said again. It was a little embarrassing being fussed over like this. All she did was fall on her face like a klutz. She didn't break any bones or anything. She was sent here to keep Andrea safe, but she felt like more of a burden than a help. Was she really good for anything beyond her awful psychic senses? She would've been killed by that monster in that awful hospital if Nicole hadn't physically shoved her through the tunnel. For a moment there, she was certain that she'd cost Andrea's friend her life. But somehow Nicole must've managed to escape the creature's grasp because within seconds she was here, too, delivering a sucker punch directly to poor Corey's face.

"So where are we, exactly?" asked Nicole as she began bandaging her leg. She still didn't understand how they ended up in this campsite, but she was happy to finally be back in the real world. Although she supposed "real" probably wasn't the right word. It was all *very* real. She had the cuts and bruises to prove it.

"Michigan," replied Violet. She was sitting on the ground next to Corey's chair now, leaning back on her arms. She was a small woman, only a little bit taller than Gina. And she looked even smaller compared with Corey's impressive bulk. She had raven black hair that was short and unkempt. She was wearing black leather boots, *very* short blue jean shorts and a black, cropped tank top that showed off her lean belly. She wasn't wearing much in the way of jewelry, only a long chain around her neck that dipped way down into the neckline of her shirt and a chunky black watch on her dainty wrist. Nicole thought she appeared *way* too cool to be hanging around with three girls who looked like they'd been rolling around in the dirt.

"Michigan as in where we were trying to get to from the start?" asked Andrea as she gently dabbed at Gina's wounds. It seemed like forever ago that they set off from Briar Hills.

"Yep," confirmed Corey. He reached out with his free hand and gestured somewhat dramatically toward the surrounding forest. "Welcome to All Trails Crossing."

"It's actually Felvetter Park," corrected Violet.

"Right. Yeah." He reached farther back and pointed at the general area of the woods more behind him. "Technically, All Trails Crossing is about half a mile in that direction. Three quarters, maybe."

"All Trails Crossing isn't really a thing," Violet explained. "It's just what Corey calls it."

"Where all the trails cross," he added, sounding rather proud of himself.

"What trails?" wondered Andrea.

"From all the accounts," he replied.

"All the recorded reports we've ever been able to find from

people claiming to have seen Cedric's Cove," Violet elaborated for him. "Going all the way back to the early eighteen hundreds."

"Earlier, even," said Corey.

"The earliest *documented* accounts we were able to find were from the early eighteen hundreds," she clarified. "There are only rumors of anything before that. It wasn't until a news article in eighteen-oh-nine that there was a detailed eye-witness description of the town. After that, the story popped up every twenty or thirty years or so. The weird thing is that each of these reports claimed the actual location of Cedric's Cove to be in completely different areas, anywhere in a hundred-mile stretch of coastline. The people who found it started off in places nowhere near each other. That's what earned it the reputation as a wandering city."

Nicole moved to the scratches on her other leg. A wandering city… Gina told them about it way back when all this first started. That felt like forever ago.

"Our guess is that it actually exists in another dimension," explained Violet. "One that's not completely tethered to a counterpart location in this world. It drifts. Or maybe only the *entrance* drifts. That would explain why people hunting and fishing in areas a hundred miles apart seemingly stumbled across it."

Andrea wrinkled her nose. "Yay. More scary worlds to explore. Like we haven't seen enough of *those* already." She tipped her head to one side, thoughtful. "Is it weird that that portal thingy spit us out exactly here in you guys' camp? I mean, that can't be a coincidence."

"Well, yeah," agreed Violet. "I mean, we were waiting for you. You said you were coming."

Nicole glanced up. "We did?"

"Well, *Gina* did."

Gina stared back at her, confused. She didn't tell them to come. She specifically told them *not* to come, in fact. She didn't want them getting hurt. "When…exactly did I say that?"

"When you texted us," said Corey, his voice still a little muffled by the towel pressed over his face.

"But I never texted you."

Now it was Violet's turn to look confused. "What?"

"See?" Corey held up his phone to show her his screen. There were several incoming text messages with her name on them. They did, indeed, seem to be texts from her, asking them to meet her in this exact spot.

"That's my phone…" said Gina, not understanding at all.

"Yeah… *You.*"

But Gina was still shaking her head. "But I didn't…"

"You lost your phone," recalled Andrea. "Somewhere on Tristesse Lane."

Corey creased his thick eyebrows as he turned the phone and looked at it. "This wasn't you?"

"Someone must've picked it up," reasoned Nicole.

"On Tristesse Lane?" asked Andrea, doubtful. "Who could've picked it up there? Everyone in that place was too far gone to even see us, much less get up and hack into someone's phone."

"What's Tristesse Lane?" asked Violet.

"Maybe you dropped it *before* Tristesse Lane?" suggested Nicole, still trying to wrap her head around it. "But…then it'd just be in your car, wouldn't it?"

"Which we *also* left on Tristesse Lane," Andrea reminded her.

"Right…"

"I had it on Tristesse Lane," Gina reminded them. "I was using the light to see when we first went inside."

Nicole recalled that, now that she mentioned it. She only put it away to save the battery when it became clear they might be stuck there a while.

"Besides, there wasn't any cell service on Tristesse Lane," Gina reminded them.

"Seriously," said Violet, frustrated, "you keep saying that. *What's Tristesse Lane?*"

"Bad place," said Gina, distracted.

"Think *Night of the Living Dead*," explained Andrea as she pressed a bandage against Gina's cheek, "but replace the shopping mall with a really gloomy apartment complex and the zombies with really, really *sad* people."

"Night of the Living *Depressed*?" said Corey, confused.

"The *Walking Dejected*?" said Violet.

Andrea nodded. "Sort of, yeah."

Violet creased her neat eyebrows as she tried to imagine it. "That doesn't sound as scary."

"You'd be surprised," muttered Nicole.

"Oh."

Nicole finished up with her leg and turned her attention to the claw marks the monster left on her side. These were more painful than the others. They were really burning. But they didn't look too bad, all things considered.

"I got to *fight* zombies once," said Corey, his enormous chest puffed out.

"Cool," said Andrea. She pressed a second bandage over Gina's forehead and then moved to her elbow. "Us too. Except we mostly just screamed a lot and ran away. Wayne was the one who actually fought with them. You guys have been to the Wood, too?"

He blinked back at her, confused. "What's the Wood?"

Now it was her turn to look confused. "Uh...?" Where did she even begin. She thought these guys had been to all sorts of worlds. But they hadn't been to the Wood? Wasn't that the one that encircled all of the worlds, including *this* one? She thought you had to go *through* the Wood to get anywhere else. Was that...not how it worked?

Thinking about it now, though, it wasn't as if they passed through the Wood to get to Tristesse Lane. Or that hospital.

Nicole turned to face Violet, intent on getting back on track. "So *somebody* found Gina's phone and sent you guys a bunch of texts pretending to be her?"

Violet nodded and looked at Gina. "I really thought it was you. That's kind of concerning that it wasn't."

It was, indeed. Did those texts really come from Gina's phone? Meaning someone had picked it up wherever it landed inside Glimmering Sunrise Place? Or did those texts just mimic Gina's name and number? Either way was kind of unsettling, really.

"But they asked you to help us," reasoned Andrea. "I mean, we had no idea where we were when we came out of that portal. And you guys even had first aid supplies that we kind of needed." She gestured at Gina's elbow she was carefully disinfecting.

Nicole sat pondering this for a moment. "Did they say anything else?"

"Only to meet you here. And that you were running late. I didn't think anything about it, really, but it's kind of creepy now that I know it wasn't you..." She shook her head, bemused. "When you first called us, you said you didn't need us to meet you there. Something about your goddess saying we weren't invited."

"You weren't involved," corrected Gina. It wasn't that she just didn't want to invite them. That sounded mean. "I didn't want to endanger anyone."

"Well, we were worried about you," said Violet. "So we packed up and headed out anyway." She cocked her head and smiled. "Because, goddess or not, she doesn't tell *us* what to do."

"Also," said Corey as he lifted the towel and checked to see if he was still bleeding, "we wanted to be here in case you actually found Cedric's Cove."

Violet scowled at him.

"What? We've been looking for it for *years*. We weren't gonna pass up a chance like that."

"Yes, but *mostly* because we were worried about Gina."

"Of course. Definitely that too."

Violet turned her attention back to Gina. "We arrived early the next morning, but I couldn't get you on the phone. We waited for you all that day and all the next night, but you never showed up and we couldn't get you on the phone. It was scary. We didn't know what to do."

"Wait..." said Andrea. "So it's already Monday?" She'd suspected they might have been gone that long, but it was still surprising to hear it.

Violet stared at her for a moment. "No... It's *Wednesday*."

"*What?*" gasped Nicole. She pulled out her phone and looked at it, only to find that she was right. It was almost ten o'clock in the morning on Wednesday.

And she had a ton of missed calls and texts, too…

"You guys have been missing for *three and a half days*."

"No way…" sighed Andrea. She finished bandaging Gina's elbow and then took out her own phone. Her mind was racing. Three and a half days…

"I told you guys time works funny in places like those," said Gina.

"'Course, we didn't *know* you were missing," said Corey. "'Cause of the texts."

Violet nodded. "That next morning—Monday—we finally heard from you. Or…we *thought* we did, anyway…" She frowned, thoughtful. "I *was* wondering why you weren't answering any of my questions… Who could it have been?"

Andrea was still trying to wrap her head around the fact that they'd lost three whole days. "I'm supposed to work today…" she recalled. She felt oddly numb at the thought… What was she even supposed to do about it at this point? She settled for a quick text, letting her boss know that an emergency had come up and she didn't know when she'd be able to come back or even check in. At this point in time, it was all she could do. If they fired her, they fired her. It didn't seem to matter all that much right now.

"Olivia was looking for us," Nicole saw. She had several missed texts and calls from her. "Sunday evening. Must've been after they got home from Wayne's family thing."

"She blew up my phone, too," Andrea saw. Then she sat up a little. "Oh, right! Probably because I tried calling her when I couldn't find you Saturday night."

She nodded. "That would be why she wanted to know where we were so badly, I guess." She frowned. "I don't even know what to tell her."

"Nothing," said Gina. "We don't want to risk drawing any attention to your friends if they aren't involved."

Andrea wrinkled her nose. "We don't want to *involve them*, just let them know we're safe."

"It might worry them more if they knew you were caught

up in stuff like this again," she argued. She remembered the name Olivia. Andrea talked about her way back when they were still in her car, part of a considerable chunk of her unsolicited life story. She was one of the friends who were involved five years ago when they opened that doorway. She was apparently very nice and a little bit psychic. Also, she was getting married in a few months and studying to be a nurse. (Gina was good at listening and Andrea was good at chattering.) "You wouldn't want anyone coming to look for you."

"I suppose so," sighed Nicole. But she didn't like it. It felt like lying. And she hated lying to her friends.

"I'll just text her that we're fine and not to worry about us," decided Andrea, already tapping at her screen. "I mean, she'll already be able to see that we read her messages."

Gina shrugged. It wasn't up to her. They could do as they pleased. She just didn't want anyone getting hurt.

Andrea sent the text and then frowned at the screen. "I hope she doesn't get mad at me later." She wasn't sure she'd like it if *they* went off on some dangerous adventure and didn't tell *her*.

"She'll understand," Nicole assured her. Of all their friends, Olivia would get it.

"What happened to you guys?" asked Violet. "Where were you all that time?"

"God, where to even begin..." sighed Nicole.

"We were at a wedding," said Andrea. She laid her phone in her lap and then started taking down her unraveling space buns. "That's where it started. Someone left *that* in my car." She nodded at the spear lying next to her. She hadn't dared let it out of her sight since she arrived. "And that guy, Hotdog, tried to take it from me. He attacked me in the parking lot." She glanced at Gina. "But then you showed up and saved me."

"Hold on," said Violet, confused. "The guy's name was 'Hotdog'?"

"Yeah. We thought it was weird, too."

"Huh," said Corey.

"And he attacked you?" asked Violet, appalled. "Physically

attacked you?"

"Choked me." She winced a little at the memory and wondered if she had any bruises on her throat as proof. "Then we tried to drive to Michigan, but those monster horse legs attacked us."

"Horse...*what?*" said Violet.

"Then Tristesse Lane," she went on. "That place *seriously* messed with my head. And as soon as we found our way out of there, we had to deal with Hotdog again and got dumped in that stupid haunted hell hospital. And then the spear opened the portal thing and now we're here."

"Good thing none of that sounds crazy at all," grumbled Nicole.

"Yeah, I'm confused," confessed Violet.

"I'd be worried if you weren't."

"It didn't *feel* like three and a half days," said Andrea. She finished taking down her hair and then pulled it back into a simpler ponytail.

"Can we rewind a little?" asked Violet. "It started with that spear?"

Chapter 29

Andrea started from the beginning. Her friends' wedding. The creep in the purple shirt. The spear. Gina. And all that followed. She wasn't the best storyteller. She wandered off topic a few times. And it was hard to explain some things without getting into the *other* story from five years ago. But it gave them time to rest. And it gave them time to eat, too. Violet had deli sandwiches, chips and soda waiting for them.

"It's honestly not the craziest story we've ever heard," confessed Violet.

"Really?" asked Andrea.

"Up there, though," said Corey.

"It is," agreed Violet. She turned her pretty green gaze on Gina. "Speaking of which, do Seph and Pi know where you are?"

"They aren't involved," replied Gina. She was still sitting in the grass, adhesive bandages on her forehead, cheek and elbow, dirt smeared on the breast of her blue blouse, staring down at her feet, looking like she'd just lost a fight. She looked oddly guilty, as if she'd just been caught in a lie.

"Oh…"

"Who?" asked Andrea.

"My roommates," said Gina.

Violet frowned. "I mean, they're kind of familiar with some of this weird stuff, too…"

"The goddess said not to involve them. When people who aren't involved get involved, bad things can happen to them."

"Oh… Okay. If you say so."

Andrea glanced over and met Nicole's eyes for just a moment. Gina said that *she* wasn't involved, too, when this all began, but she insisted on her coming along. The thought gave her a nervous lump in her belly. What if something bad happened to her? It would be all her fault. But on the other hand, they couldn't have just left her behind for the barely-there to attack again.

"Won't they miss you, though?" pressed Violet. They *had* just confirmed that she'd been missing for the past three and a half days.

"I told them I was going to a convention. They won't be expecting me home until at least the weekend."

"Those two're pretty capable," said Corey. He no longer had the bloody towel pressed to his face. The bleeding had stopped. He'd stuffed it into his chair's cupholder.

Now Gina looked up at them. "If they knew, they'd insist on coming. And I couldn't let them. The goddess said it wouldn't be safe for them. Not this time. And they're…" She looked down again. More softly, she said, "They're important to me."

Violet stared at her for a moment. "Okay. You know best. And I get it. We wouldn't want anything happening to them, either."

Corey nodded agreement.

"So, there's a story there, I'm taking it?" said Andrea.

Violet smiled. "A pretty good one."

Gina drew her knees up close to her chest. She looked uncomfortable. "I told you, the goddess gave me that job… I wasn't really involved much beyond that."

"Well I don't blame her for wanting to protect her friends," said Nicole. There were now several larger adhesive bandages on her otherwise flawless legs in addition to the gauze wrapped around the deeper gouges on her wrist. "If her goddess said it wasn't safe for them, then she probably knows better than we do."

Gina nodded. She looked relieved.

Andrea glanced over at Nicole and wondered again if she'd made the right decision.

"So how do we find this Cedric's Cove place?" asked Nicole, wrenching the conversation back to the task ahead.

"All accounts describe a formation of rocks deep in the

woods," said Corey.

"Like, *three* of the accounts described a formation of three rocks," clarified Violet.

He shrugged. "Close enough."

"The most recent account was from only about thirty years ago," she went on. "It described the area in greater detail, along with its exact location. And we were able to find it."

Again, Corey pointed out toward the woods behind him. "Right out there. 'Bout half a mile's hike. Three quarters, maybe."

"That's where we think the path to Cedric's Cove starts. But we've never been able to find any more of the landmarks described in the accounts."

Gina turned her sleepy gaze on Andrea. "That's probably where you come in."

Andrea stared at her, unsure what to say. It was still odd to think that she was in some way the key to this mystery that was apparently hundreds of years older than she was. Surely there were other people out there that could do it. Better qualified people. You were always hearing about psychics and mediums on television who were supposed to have some mystical connection to the other side. She didn't even know she had powers like that until Gina told her. It wasn't as if ghosts regularly talked to her or anything.

"What's so special 'bout her?" asked Corey.

Violet smacked his knee. "Don't be rude."

He looked down at her, confused, then back at Andrea again, frowning. "Sorry."

"I think he means why you, *specifically*," said Violet.

But Andrea was nodding. "Yeah. No offense taken. I'm kinda with you. I don't really get it, either."

"She has a connection to the spirit world," explained Gina. "A very strong one. The goddess sent me to find her. The same night we met, she was given that spear and a message telling her to go to Cedric's Cove."

Violet nodded. "So it kind of adds up. Got it."

"Does it, though?" wondered Andrea. She still wasn't so

sure. She looked down at the spear again.

"So tell us about Cedric's Cove," said Nicole. "How do these accounts you've read describe it?"

"It's actually really weird," replied Violet. "No one ever stays long. Twenty or thirty minutes at most, not long enough to really explore. Then they're suddenly spit back out. But what's been described in that short time is always a fairly *modern* city, despite the legend being around so long. You'd think it'd be some Colonial-era settlement, but it's supposed to be surprisingly big. The last account described lots of buildings, including shops and church towers. Paved streets. Even electric lamps. But every account describes it as completely and eerily deserted."

"And partially flooded," added Corey.

"Flooded?" Andrea didn't care for the thought of ending up wet again... Why couldn't they go somewhere *nice* for once?

"Like Atlantis," he added.

"I don't think Atlantis would've been in Lake Huron," said Violet.

"Prob'ly another pocket dimension," he reasoned, ignoring her. "Mimicking a real city somewhere."

"But those places mimic the surrounding areas closest to them," said Violet, thoughtful. "Cedric's Cove is supposed to move around."

He shrugged. "Different places, different rules."

"Maybe..."

Nicole stood up and sighed. "Let's get this over with. Where're these stupid rocks again?"

Corey stood up. "We'll gear up. Take you there."

"No," said Gina. "We have to do it on our own."

Andrea stared at her, surprised. "We do?" She glanced up at Corey. "Because I kind of like the idea of taking him with us. He's *huge*."

Corey nodded. "M'good for hidin' behind if you need to," he agreed.

But Gina was insistent. "The goddess said so."

Violet crossed her arms and huffed. "I don't care if she *is* a goddess. I don't care if she's fucking *Beyonce*. No one tells us where we can and can't go."

Corey nodded.

"Please," said Gina. "It's not safe for you."

Violet made a face at her. It was an unhappy face. But it was a surprisingly cute face. She looked like the kind of woman who wasn't used to being told no. "I don't like it."

"I'll be fine. The goddess has kept me safe so far."

She and Corey looked at each other, uncertain.

"Safety comes first," he reminded her. "Your rule."

"You've been looking for this place forever," she reminded him. "Are you really okay just letting them go by themselves?"

"There'll be more places. Like she said, the goddess keeps her safe. Us, maybe not."

She sighed and shook her head. "Fine. But you'd better come back. Don't you dare make me tell Seph I let you go off and get yourself killed."

"And let us know what you find," added Corey.

She frowned at him. "And that, I guess… But mostly just come back safe, okay?"

"We'll do that," promised Gina.

"So tell us how to get to All Trails Crossing," sighed Nicole.

"Actually, before we do that," said Andrea, fidgeting. "Um…where's the bathroom out here?"

Violet gestured out at the woods around them.

She groaned. "Of course."

Chapter 30

Violet stood there and watched the three of them disappear into the forest. She didn't like it. Not one bit. But the world was a bizarre place. She'd seen a lot of crazy shit. And heard a lot of even crazier stories. If Gina said a goddess was watching over her, then a goddess was probably watching over her.

But she still wanted to grab her pack and set off after them. There was safety in numbers.

"They'll be fine," said Corey. He was staring after them, too, his big head tilted thoughtfully to one side. "Somethin' 'bout those two she's with. Can't put my finger on it, but it's there."

She nodded. He was right about that. They weren't Seph and Pi, but they reminded her of them a lot. She had a feeling Gina was in good hands.

Corey's cell phone chimed in his pocket, alerting him to a new text message. He pulled it out and looked at the screen.

It chimed again while he was looking at it.

"Hm," he said, his eyebrows creeping upward with interest.

"What is it?"

He turned the phone so she could read it.

"Huh," she agreed.

Their eyes met for a moment. Then they both looked out into the woods where they last saw Gina and her new friends.

"Okay then," she said. "Let's go."

He nodded.

The two of them turned away from Cedric's Cove and began packing up their campsite. They had a long drive ahead of them.

Chapter 31

The path wasn't very well worn. Within a few hundred feet of where they lost sight of Violet and Corey, it shrank down to little more than a game trail. And a few hundred feet beyond that, there wasn't any discernible trail at all. The directions Gina's friends gave her said to follow a low ridge until it flattened out, then look for a large, dead evergreen. The three rocks were supposed to be in the area just beyond the next hill.

Andrea led the way, per Gina's suggestion. In case there was something along the path that her special senses might pick up. She *was* the one the goddess summoned here, after all.

Gina, meanwhile, took up the rear behind Nicole and kept her own senses open for anything that only *she* might feel. It was a relief to be back in the real world after spending so much time in those other places. The familiarity was refreshing. Gone was that twisted, funhouse mirror effect. These woods were only woods.

Although there was *always* something just a little off in the woods. *Any* woods. Every woods she'd ever been in. There were things hiding in the trees that couldn't be detected with normal senses, things most people spent their entire lives blissfully unaware of. Things she knew had the potential to be quite dangerous, but very rarely did anyone any harm, as far as she knew. There was one here now, in fact. They passed by its hiding place just a few minutes ago, a dense cluster of gnarled trees a little ways off the path. She could feel its strange eyes following them. But it had no interest in them.

Not today, anyway.

There was almost always something like that. Not just in the forest, but everywhere, from crowded city streets to lifeless de-

serts. She'd traveled most of the country, visited so many different places, looking for somewhere peaceful without things that
frightened her. But there was always some mysterious, not-quite-
there thing that didn't belong, that no one else could see. Like
that strange entity circling high overhead right now. It moved
like a bird, but it wasn't one. A bird didn't flicker out of existence
and then pop back in again in a different place. Nor did birds
have serpent tails that slithered through the sky in their wake.

These were the things she'd learned long ago to just ignore.
They didn't bother her as long as she didn't bother them. But
these were the sorts of things that normal people refused to believe in. It was *them* she really feared. *People.* They had a way of
turning against those who were different, after all. Sometimes
violently. It was astounding how much hatred people kept hidden deep inside them.

But every now and then, people surprised her.

She kept finding her gaze drawn to Nicole as she walked
ahead of her. She'd never been good at communicating, but there
was something she needed to say before things turned weird
again and she lost her chance.

"Um…" she began. "I just…" God, she hated how hard it
was to talk to people. "I wanted to say thank you," she forced
herself to say.

"For what?" asked Nicole.

"For back in that hospital. For…you know… Saving me.
Pushing me through that portal."

Nicole grimaced a little. It was actually more of a kick. She
practically punted the poor girl out the door. "You tried to save
me, too," she reminded her. "You turned around and grabbed
my hand."

She wasn't sure what to say to that. *Of course* she tried to
save her. She couldn't just let that thing take her. And she supposed that was the point. But it wasn't just that one time. "You
also saved me on Tristesse Lane. You didn't let go of me the
whole time that place was in our heads. I've been wanting to say
thank you for that, too."

"We're kind of a team," said Nicole. "We look out for each

other. That's how we survived last time we went through this kind of stuff. It's how we'll survive this time."

Gina walked on, her thoughts churning.

Andrea was a little farther ahead, focused on the path. She wasn't paying attention to them, which was good. It made it a little easier to say what she needed to say without someone else listening.

"We're friends, aren't we?" said Nicole. "I mean I really don't think you can do stuff like this with someone and not be friends. It kind of bonds us together, don't you think?"

"I've...never been very good at being someone's friend." She was so afraid of getting pushed away again.

"You're not very good at letting people in, I can tell. But I can also tell you're a good person."

"I'm not so sure..."

"I *am*. I can tell."

"When you were trapped in that pocket dimension version of your apartment, Andrea insisted that we find you first. But I tried to get her to leave without you. I could tell something had happened, but I didn't know what. I was worried she'd be in danger if she didn't leave." She watched Andrea up ahead of them. It had been bothering her for a while now. She felt awful about it. "But if she'd listened to me, we would've been gone before you escaped. And I...I just keep thinking that if you'd still been alone there..."

"Sounds to me like you were doing everything right," reasoned Nicole. "You were there to protect Andrea, not me. And I'm *so* thankful for that. If you hadn't been there for her...if that creep had actually killed her... Oh my god... I can't even stand to think about it. Besides, you said you couldn't feel me when I was trapped in there. You just knew that something wasn't right. You were trying to protect her. That's nothing to be sorry about."

"But I just do what the goddess tells me."

"And it all worked out in the end. Maybe that's what she meant to happen all along. Maybe that's even the real reason she chose you. Not because of what you can do, but because of *who you are.*"

"But how do I know? What if I end up getting one of you hurt? What if I get *everyone* hurt? Or *worse?*"

"I think we were already well past the point of no return as soon as the barely-there got its claws in my brain and Hotdog got his creeper hands around Andrea's neck. If the only thing we've got to go on in this fucked-up world is the instructions of some lazy goddess who won't get off her holy ass and do all this shit herself, then that's just what we have to work with. Personally, I'm happy to have you and your psychic, trouble-avoiding brain with us."

Gina smiled a little at that. It was nice to be around people who appreciated her for the thing that had always made other people push her away.

They really *were* like Seph and Pi...

Nicole paused and looked back at her. "Five years ago, I followed my best friend and her boyfriend into an abandoned dormitory. Hours later, when I finally got home, I had *five* best friends and I've cherished every moment with each of them every day since. Things are scary now, but I'm convinced this is just a new chapter in that adventure, and I'm looking forward to you being number six."

Gina felt herself blush a little. She couldn't help it.

Nicole smiled at her before turning back. "It's nice to hear you open up a little, by the way. You should relax more around your friends."

"I... Yeah. I'll try..."

Andrea pointed up ahead and called back, "There's the dead tree they told us to look for."

A towering dead evergreen loomed ahead of them, just as Violet described it. The three rocks, then, should be just over the hill beyond it.

Chapter 32

It was clear to see what made the three rocks stand out as a landmark. They were as big as pickup trucks and the only ones like them in what they'd seen of the forest so far. They were arranged roughly in a circle and while the forest's trees and brush were crowded all around them, there were only sparse weeds and a few bunches of tall grass growing between them. It looked as though someone had intentionally placed them there for the sole purpose of acting as some kind of marker.

But now that they were here, what were they supposed to do?

Andrea walked around the rocks, examining them from every angle. Her first thought was that perhaps there was some kind of marking etched into one of them somewhere that matched one of the symbols etched onto the spear, but she didn't see any such clues, nor did she see anything that stood out to her in the surrounding forest, although, admittedly, she wasn't sure what she should even be looking for.

She'd been carrying the spear since they escaped the thing in the hospital. This was where they were supposed to start their search, the road to Cedric's Cove that Gina's friends had christened All Trails Crossing. She'd been thinking that the markings on the spear might have been like those on Albert's box. Perhaps it was a map, and all she had to do was figure out how to read the stupid thing. And, of course, where to begin.

Now, she stopped and examined it again. How would Albert think his way through this? Six years ago, he found the way to the Temple of the Blind by sorting out that the messages carved into the box were pointing to an entrance to the university's steam tunnels located behind the music building. The symbols on the spear might work the same way, if she could only figure out what it was they meant.

Pierce the gatekeeper's heart to open the way, she thought, reading the mysterious words carved on one side. She didn't see any gatekeepers standing around out here... Although she wasn't sure what a gatekeeper looked like... She didn't think there'd just be some olden-days dude in chainmail just standing around out here with a pike, waiting for them to show up. Gina was probably right when she said it was more likely a riddle of some sort.

She looked up at the three rocks again. They were *sort of* arranged in the shape of a heart, but not exactly. That felt like something of a stretch. She couldn't imagine that she was supposed to just plunge it into the earth.

This was hard... Why was *she* chosen to do this? It felt like whoever was behind all this was seriously overestimating her.

Did the three rocks and the spear even have anything to do with each other? How was she supposed to know if she was in the right place? What if Violet and Corey made a mistake? What if their theory about these rocks wasn't even close and they were a hundred miles from where she was supposed to be?

She turned the blade over and looked at the other side, as she'd done countless times already, as if there were more than two sides to the stupid thing, but still nothing made sense. Was it something to do with the symbol that looked sort of like a bird? Was it that little squiggly thing? Those overlapping lines near the handle?

What was she supposed to do?

She didn't want to keep doing this. It was exhausting. And it was so hot and buggy out here in these woods. She just wanted to give up.

She closed her eyes and stood there a moment, listening to the singing of the birds in the trees all around them.

"Maybe we should take a break," suggested Nicole. She was already sitting herself down on the ground. Gina followed her example. "Just relax for a little bit. Maybe that'll help."

Andrea nodded. Maybe that *was* what they needed. It felt like they'd been moving nonstop since the wedding. And that was apparently *four days ago*!

But it wasn't really four days. They couldn't have really gone that long without sleep or food without knowing it, much less water.

Time was funny in those places. Gina said so. And so far, she'd been right about pretty much everything.

The spear...

She looked down at it again. A part of her just wanted to throw the stupid thing as far out into the forest as she could. She never asked to be in charge of it, after all. It wasn't fair that she should have to deal with it. But that probably wouldn't solve anything. It'd probably only make things a lot worse.

She was staring at one of the symbols. It looked like three rough circles with some kind of dot in the middle of them...

She held it closer to her face. Three circles... Arranged sort of like... She turned and looked at the rocks. No...arranged *exactly* like the rocks.

Map...

Her heart was beating a little faster. Was that it? Had she actually figured out one of the symbols on the spear? Had she actually found a piece of the map?

But...what was that dot, then? She turned and looked at the open space surrounded by the rocks, but there wasn't anything there.

Unless it was covered up?

She walked over and raked through the grass and leaves with her foot, but there were no more rocks to be found. Had the forest floor covered it over? If Cedric's Cove had existed since at least the early eighteen hundreds, then there could be several feet of dirt settled over whatever might have once been here.

But that didn't seem right. They couldn't be expected to find something buried deep in the earth.

No... The dot was something else. Were they supposed to put something there?

She looked at the symbol on the blade again. It should be right about here. Right where she was standing...

You...

Was it *her*? Did *she* go where the dot was?

She looked out at the forest. From this angle, there were three paths leading out between the rocks. Maybe if she pointed the spear straight out in front of her and faced whatever direction the rocks and the etchings lined up.

No.

She frowned at the blade. That...didn't feel right...

She held it up and looked at it. At the symbols carved into it. At the shape of it. At those careless chips in the blade...

Yes.

For some reason, she felt the hairs on the back of her neck stand up.

Something felt strange. There was an odd chill in the air. But she didn't have time to think too hard about it. Her eyes were focused on those notches along the blade.

Were those really just careless chips? She lifted it closer to her face. Now that she was really looking at them, they looked oddly intentional. Almost *filed*.

She turned the blade around and held it in front of her face, studying it, her eyes widening with dawning realization.

If she held it just like so... And if she lined it up with the gap between the two rocks closest together... And moved it a little farther away from her face...

And there it was.

"Guys!" she gasped.

Nicole stood up and peered over her shoulder. It wasn't lined up from her angle, but she could see it. The shape of the gap between the two rocks was the exact shape of one of the notches in the blade. "Nice. So we have to go through there?"

There wasn't much room to squeeze through that particular space. And the forest there was overgrown. Andrea doubted that anyone would ever bother trying to fit through it. Not when you could just walk around it. Which was probably exactly the point.

"It makes sense," said Gina. She was still sitting cross-legged on the ground, staring at the narrow gap between the rocks. "Sometimes it's not about where something is, but how you approach it. There are paths you have to take. Step off that path and you'll have to start over." She glanced up at Andrea. "Or worse, sometimes stepping off the path might land you somewhere you can't come back from."

"Oh good," grumbled Nicole. "More scary shit."

Andrea pouted. She didn't want to deal with any more scary stuff. She wished they didn't have to do this alone. Why was it just them? Why did it have to happen while Albert and Brandy were off on their honeymoon? Why didn't Gina's goddess send her to find Wayne, instead?

But Gina had already told her that it wasn't about her strength or size. It had something to do with her weird connection to the dead, which of course only made this whole ordeal sound that much worse. Did that mean they were going to have to deal with more of those awful ghosts?

"Let's get this over with, I guess," sighed Nicole.

She was right. Stalling was only going to make this unpleasant business take longer.

Andrea squeezed through the gap between the rocks and pushed her way through the branches beyond. Almost immediately, she felt the sharp sting of thorns biting into her right shin.

Yes. Definitely unpleasant.

But there *was* a path back here, she found. A very faint one, leading away from the three rocks and down into the thicker part of the forest. It probably was only visible from this one angle.

The path to her...

She frowned. The Lady of Cedric's Cove... So much had happened since she found that message scrawled on the cloth the spear was wrapped in that she never had much time to think too much about it. But now she couldn't stop wondering who the Lady of Cedric's Cove was. What did she want with them? With *her*?

And now that they'd found the path to Cedric's Cove, was it only going to get more dangerous?

Be careful...

She pushed through the path and frowned. It wasn't quite a voice in her ear, like back in those creepy hospital hallways, but things kept popping up inside her head. Were those her own words, or were there ghosts in this place, too?

She's waiting...

She shivered in spite of the heat and looked around. There was no one else out here. The forest was empty but for the three of them.

Somehow, she felt like this was going to be a very long journey.

Chapter 33

Now it was starting to feel like the Temple of the Blind.

Nicole watched as Andrea led the way, holding the spear in front of her, slowly unraveling the map from the clues etched into its surface.

A few hundred feet into the forest, they found five more of those big, out-of-place rocks looming ahead of them, laid out in a pattern that Andrea quickly found mirrored on another of the etchings on the blade, just like the first three. This time, instead of a simple dot showing her where to stand, there was a line drawn through them, showing her the precise way she was supposed to weave between them to remain on the path.

That seemed to be all there was to it. Sometimes the shapes etched into the blade showed her the path in relation to a specific formation of rocks. Other times, she lined up the tiny notches in the blade with the unique shape of the space between two rocks from a specific angle to point the way. In both cases, the rocks were the key. They were the markers that revealed the exact path that Nicole assumed was leading them to Cedric's Cove. Without a map to tell you which rocks to walk between, it wouldn't be possible.

She couldn't help wondering how long ago these rocks were placed here. They definitely weren't natural to this area. Was this like the Temple of the Blind? Was this all arranged by the sentinels countless ages ago when the world was still new, for the sole purpose of this very day? Was this really still a part of all that stuff the Sentinel Queen told them about ensuring the survival of mankind by paving a path to a new world before this one died?

That was a lot to process. She didn't think she cared for the thought of being responsible for any part of something as profoundly important as the survival of all humankind.

She pushed those thoughts away and focused instead on the spear Andrea was carrying.

It was a lot like Albert's box. That mysterious wooden cube with Brandy's name scrawled on one side. At a glance, that was all it was. Just a wooden box full of random junk.

But it was a *map*. And an extraordinary one, at that.

She was never going to forget the night they first sat her down and showed it to her. She and Brandy were best friends, after all. They'd never kept any secrets from each other in all their years together. Brandy insisted on letting her in. Albert was a bit more reluctant, but then again, he hadn't even met her when he and Brandy started dating. He didn't know anything about her. And the feeling was mutual. After all, the first few times she met him, she'd actually had her doubts whether they'd even last. Sure, he was attractive, and he seemed very nice, but he was a year younger than Brandy, and she'd never really been into younger guys. And he was so much different than the other guys she'd always been into. He was nothing at all like her previous boyfriends. She didn't really get it.

But fairly quickly it became clear that Brandy wasn't just playing around. She really seemed to be in love with the guy. And then, as she got to know him, she began to understand why. He was sweet. He was kind. He was *very* smart. And, according to *Drunk Brandy*, who typically came out after about three margaritas and was known to share more than was strictly necessary about her sex life, he was apparently *extremely* satisfying in bed.

It was only a few weeks after they started dating that they showed her the box and told her the story. She wouldn't have believed it if it came from anyone else. But Brandy had never lied to her. She wouldn't try to prank her. She just wouldn't. And she couldn't deny that there were certain things about the story that sort of made sense. It explained why she and Albert became so serious so quickly, why their relationship turned *sexual* so quickly, even though Brandy had never been one to rush into *that* part of a relationship. It also explained why they sometimes seemed a little hesitant to talk about how they hooked up, beyond the fact that they met as lab partners in Chemistry. And of course it explained those odd little moments when they seemed to be sharing some big secret. Offhanded comments about a rash of nightmares. Brandy suddenly deciding that she didn't like horror movies anymore just as Halloween season was approaching. An odd habit of carefully peering into her car windows before opening the door. And she was *jumpy*. For a while there, the slightest thing would give her a fright. Nicole had actually begun to worry that there was something dreadfully wrong. It was something of a relief to finally hear the story and put it all together. Just like that, it all made sense.

And yet at the same time it was so *fantastic*... Could all that stuff actually be real? Could *any* of it?

Then she saw it all for herself. And so much *more*.

Now, watching Andrea lead the way with the spear, she couldn't help wondering how disappointed Albert might be when he found out he missed out on this. This was kind of his thing, after all. He loved a good puzzle. That was the whole reason he didn't immediately just toss the box in a dumpster and forget about it.

"I really hope I'm doing this right," said Andrea.

"I'm sure you're doing fine," Nicole assured her.

The landscape had changed. The dense deciduous trees and the underbrush thinned out, replaced by towering pines and a thick carpet of fallen needles. Those large rocks were everywhere now, jutting up out of the earth all around them like giant, crooked teeth. Even the atmosphere was different. It was cooler here, and not just because it seemed to be clouding up. It felt like the air was thinner, as if they'd climbed high up into the mountains.

There were no paths to speak of by now and nothing that resembled any of the markings on the blade, so Andrea turned to the notches again, scanning the landscape until she matched one of them to the shape of the gap between two of the rocks, right down to that little knobby bit jutting off the one on the right, perfect enough to leave no room for doubt that this was the intended purpose of the spear.

"We're not in the same place we were before," Gina warned them. "We've definitely transitioned into someplace new."

"So…does that mean I'm doing it right?" asked Andrea.

"I think so."

Nicole scanned these new surroundings. She didn't know much about the forests of the Great Lakes, whether it was common for the terrain to change like this. She wasn't even all that familiar with the forests of Missouri. Her parents weren't exactly outdoors people. They'd never taken a family camping trip in her life. Her uncle had taken her out a few times when she was growing up, showed her the forest, taught her a little bit about fishing and hunting. Most importantly, he'd taught her a little about survival in the wild. But she was never all that enamored with the outdoors. It was dirty and buggy and sometimes there were snakes, which was pretty much a deal breaker.

Somehow she didn't think Uncle Howie's advice would quite cut it in *these* woods. There was something about these surroundings that was just a little off. Even *she* could feel it. There was something about the sky out here. It seemed oddly *dingy*. And it was quieter than she thought it should be. It wasn't quite devoid of wildlife. She could definitely hear the occasional cawing of crows somewhere in those high branches. But that was all. There were no other birds or frogs or bugs to be heard.

Ahead of her, Andrea paused and looked back.

"Everything okay?" asked Nicole.

She nodded. "I think so… I mean, I'm pretty sure we're still on the path and everything. But I feel like I keep hearing this voice in my head…" She glanced back at Gina. "Do you think this place could be haunted, too?"

"Anyplace can be haunted."

"What's it saying?" asked Nicole.

"It's just… I guess it's sort of…helping? Maybe?" She shook her head. "It's kind of hard to explain."

"Well that doesn't sound so bad."

"I guess not…"

"That one ghost in Hotdog General back there was okay."

"That's true. She showed us the way to go. And she helped

me open the portal."

"She did?"

She nodded. "I thought maybe it might still be her, but like I said, it's different. That voice sounded like it was someone whispering right into my ear. This one's just...thoughts in my head, I guess?"

"Different places, different rules," Gina reminded her.

"Right..."

"Typically, the more you listen, the easier it is for them to communicate. That can be a good thing or a bad thing, depending on the spirit. But if it really is helping, then it might be good to open yourself up to it."

Andrea sighed. "This is all still a little freaky."

"Understandable," said Gina.

"It's not like we've never been helped by a ghost before," Nicole reminded her. The dead had helped them on their journey to the top of the Temple of the Blind and back. But it was still weird to think that *that* ghost was Wayne...who ended up surviving the trip with them...

She still couldn't wrap her head around how you could be a ghost *and* get out alive.

She followed Andrea as she continued along the spear's path, but now she couldn't help looking around at these scary woods. All this talk about ghosts was making everything feel a lot creepier. Did it always look so hazy around those distant trunks?

She was starting to get that uneasy feeling in her gut again.

Chapter 34

The haze in the distance only grew thicker. An eerie fog quickly rolled in around them like an ill omen, reducing visibility to only a few yards. In an unsettlingly short period of time, the landscape around them had transformed again, this time into a sea of gray mist and shadowy, towering pine trunks.

It was becoming harder and harder to stay on the path. Andrea struggled to see the marker rocks around them. Most of them were little more than faint shadows in the haze. Others, she was certain, were completely hidden in the fog. How was she supposed to find the way if she couldn't even see the markers the map intended for her?

"It's not really a fog, is it?" Gina observed.

Andrea looked back at her, confused. "What?"

"Fog is just clouds. Water vapor. If this were fog, everything, including us, would be damp. But everything's completely dry."

She looked down at herself. She was right. There was no dew on the grass or on her shoes. Her clothes weren't damp.

Nicole frowned. "What is it, then?"

"It's the boundaries of the world, itself," explained Gina. "It's less than a world, really. More like...a passage *between* the worlds. A road through whatever exists in the spaces between them."

"That sounds terrifying," whimpered Andrea.

"It kind of *is*," she warned. "The outer edges of this path we're following...of this tiny little space we're walking through...are really close. Perilously close. If we lose our way and wander too far off course... It's like I said before. There's a good chance we could be lost forever."

Nicole wrinkled her nose. "What, like falling off the edge of the world?"

"Yes, actually."

Andrea groaned. "So no pressure then. Got it."

"Sorry."

She gave her a dismissive wave and focused on the spear. So far, the rocks had been the key. They were scattered all throughout this hazy forest. And the notches on the blade required her to view the spaces between the rocks from just the right angle to match them. What if she missed one? And what about all the rocks she couldn't see? And then there was the matter of the other things etched into the surface of the spear, things she still didn't understand. Little symbols and shapes that didn't appear to have anything to do with these rocks. And if Gina was right about them falling off the edge of the world, or whatever, then she might only have one chance at this. It felt like whoever sent her this thing was putting an awful lot of faith in her ability to get these things right on the first try.

What if she'd already missed one?

What if the reason the "fog" had gotten so thick was because they were *already* off course and wandering dangerously close to the edge?

And why, exactly, did it have to be *her* doing this? Gina said way back when they started that her goddess must have sent for her because only she could find Cedric's Cove. But she knew for a fact that there were other people out there who could've figured this out. It didn't seem all that difficult. Albert, for example, probably would've already found his way there by now.

It didn't make sense.

"Can you feel anything about our surroundings?" Nicole asked.

Gina shook her head. "It feels like it looks. The farther away things are, the less…solid it seems? I'm not really sure how to describe it."

"As long as there's no monsters out here," said Andrea. "I've had enough of those for a while." It hadn't escaped her that the mysterious haze made it impossible to see if anything was creeping up on them.

"I haven't felt anything yet. Just some birds." She looked up into the haze above them, at the faint shadows of the pine branches high overhead, where the cawing of crows continued to be the only sound of wildlife. "At least, I think those are birds…"

Andrea glanced up, nervous. "Don't tell me things like that!"

"Sorry."

She sighed. She wished she could just go home and crawl into her own bed again. This was exhausting.

She pushed onward, scanning her surroundings, trying hard not to miss anything. She kept telling herself that whoever sent her this map must have expected her to be able to follow it. It seemed like a stretch that she would have to wander around in this fog, searching for just the right angle. If she wandered too far off course, even if she didn't fall off the world or whatever, she'd probably never be able to find her way back to where she left off. So she tried to keep to a straight line each time the map turned.

She lifted the blade and lined the notches up between two rocks ahead of her and a little to the left. She had to get a little closer for the right angle, but they lined up.

That way.

There were a total of nine notches cut into the edge of the blade. She'd already used five of them. There were only four remaining. Did that mean they were more than halfway there?

She felt a spark of pride. "This is easier than I expected. I thought it was going to be a lot harder than just matching stuff." She glanced back at Nicole. "Was Albert's box this easy? Did he just let us *think* he was super smart?" She never actually saw him solve any of those riddles, after all. She wasn't there for that part. By the time she caught up to them they were done with the box and way off the map.

"I don't think it's exactly the same thing," replied Nicole.

Andrea made a face at her. "Whatever. You know I rock."

Nicole chuckled.

Seriously, though, she was pretty good at this. Who needed Albert? She could've solved the riddles of the box. The Sentinel Queen should've sent it to her instead of him.

But then she remembered what happened to Albert and Brandy in that sex room and she changed her mind. That...wouldn't have worked. She would've had to receive the *key*, not the *box*.

Then she realized what *that* would've meant and she felt herself blush at the thought. That wasn't better! How embarrassing! And she would've been, like, *seventeen* at the time! *Barely*!

What was with her brain?

She needed to focus. She gripped the spear in her hand and looked around.

But there weren't any more rocks to be seen. There was nothing but that ominous, dry fog and the endless, towering pines.

Had she made a mistake? Did she misread that last clue?

She *needed* the rocks. They were the only things guiding her. There were no other landmarks to compare with the map. There were only trees, and trees weren't permanent. Trees grew and died and fell over and were replaced with new ones. They probably didn't make good points of reference for finding places that had been around as long as Cedric's Cove. And even if they did, she couldn't possibly be expected to line up exactly the right two trees. There were hundreds of them. It was utterly impractical.

Then something new appeared from the mist.

Not a rock, but a stone. Upright and flat. About two and a half feet tall. Heavily weathered. She tried to tell herself it was some kind of marker, left perhaps by whoever sent her the spear, but she knew a headstone when she saw one. And it didn't fail to send a shiver down her back.

Fantastic.

That was just what this stupid, spooky forest needed. A cemetery.

As she approached it, more appeared from the gloom. They seemed to rise straight up out of the forest floor among the pine trunks, as if the forest had simply sprouted up around them long,

long ago.

"Seriously?" she sighed, pausing to look at the first stone. Any markings had already been erased by time. It was impossible to tell if there was a name or a date. The base was half-covered in moss and it was tilted slightly to one side.

"Seriously what?" asked Nicole.

She walked on, past the stone, toward the others that were slowly emerging from the haze ahead of her. "Now there are *graves?*"

"What're you talking about?"

Andrea looked back at her, baffled. "What?" But as she watched, Nicole walked right through the tombstone, as if it were only a part of the fog. "Um…?"

"*What?*" stressed Nicole.

She stood there a moment, blinking at the headstone that was now behind Nicole's legs. It looked real enough. "You don't…?" Then she turned her attention to Gina. "Can *you* see them?"

"See what?" was her reply.

Andrea stared at her. Why was she the only one seeing headstones?

Careful…

She gasped and turned around, quickly scanning her surroundings. She still wasn't sure if that voice in her head belonged to a ghost or if it was only her own brain calling out to her somehow, but she didn't intend to ignore a warning to be careful, no matter where it came from. Especially not with the way *this* day had been going.

"Talk to me," said Nicole. "What's wrong? What're you seeing?"

"A cemetery," she replied.

She looked around, lost. "Where?"

"All around us." And it *was* all around them. There were tombstones dotting the landscape behind them that she knew for a fact weren't there a moment ago. "What's happening? Why am I the only one seeing this?"

More than one world overlap here…

"What?" She turned around. Was that still inside her head? It was getting harder to tell. And what did it mean? More than one world overlapping?

The dead know the way...

She didn't feel any malice from the voice. It really seemed to be helping her. In fact, the more she listened to it, the more she felt that it was the same voice that helped them escape Hotdog's freaky hospital. It communicated the same way. Short, brief sentences. It felt very soft and timid. But she was seriously starting to wish she'd spell this stuff out for her. She didn't want to deal with any more riddles.

The dead know the way... Her weird connection to the spirit world... Was that what this was about? Was it the *spirit world* that was overlapping here? Was *this* why it had to be her? Because getting here didn't merely require following the map, but also being able to see something in this creepy cemetery?

"*Talk to me!*" snapped Nicole.

Andrea turned and met her gaze. She was pouting. "Dead people..." she whimpered.

Chapter 35

Nicole looked around, uneasy. "So we're really standing in the middle of a whole *cemetery* we can't see?"

"It's not like there's a fence or anything," Andrea tried to explain. "Or, like, mausoleums... It's just...lots of *headstones*..." Her wide eyes swept across her surroundings and in a dramatic whisper, she added, "*Everywhere*..."

Nicole turned and looked at the spot behind her. According to Andrea, she walked right through one of them. But she couldn't see anything there. It looked like every other part of the forest floor. There was nothing on the ground there but pine needles and wisps of fog. And she didn't recall feeling anything when she walked through that space, either. There simply wasn't anything there.

But she didn't doubt Andrea. If the Temple of the Blind had taught her anything it was that nothing was ever necessarily impossible. If her friend said there was a tombstone there that she couldn't see or feel, then it was there. She had no doubt.

Andrea stepped over to the spot and knelt down, her gaze seemingly fixed on something in front of her.

It was perfectly easy to *imagine* that she was kneeling in front of a headstone, but it wasn't there, no matter how hard she looked.

"Is there anything carved on it?" inquired Gina.

But Andrea shook her head. "It's really old. I can't make anything out." She reached out with her hand, as if to touch something.

At the same time, a strange sensation swept through Nicole's body. It seemed to come up from the very ground beneath her. It was extremely brief, little more than a passing thought.

Like one of those shivers that the old people in her family always used to say meant someone had walked over your grave. Thinking about that particular idiom now, in this situation, made her feel incredibly uneasy. She glanced around, making sure they were still alone out here. And when she looked over at Gina, she saw that she, too, must've felt it, because she was looking over her shoulder as well.

But the forest had remained unchanged.

Or *almost* unchanged. When she looked back down at Andrea, she saw that she was running her fingers across the weathered surface of a very old gravestone.

"Holy shit! Where'd that come from?"

Andrea looked up at her, surprised. "You can see it now?"

"Something about you interacting with it, probably," reasoned Gina.

She looked back down at the stone, confused, then withdrew her hand. Nicole half-expected it to vanish again, but it remained where it was. "Can we not call it 'interacting'?" she said, wrinkling her nose. "It makes it sound like it's alive or something."

Gina shrugged. "Something about you *fondling* it, then?"

Andrea pouted. "Yeah, that's not better, is it?"

"Not really."

Nicole turned and scanned the forest again. "I can only see the one you touched, though. No others."

"Really?" She turned and looked out at the surrounding forest, apparently at all the other countless stones only she could see. "That's weird…"

"I wonder how you made that one appear."

"She's connected to the spirit world in ways I've never seen before," said Gina. "Something about her being halfway between the two might make certain things cross from one side of the veil to the other."

"I don't want to be connected to the spirit world," groaned Andrea. She stood up again, wiping her hand on her shorts as if she might have dirtied it on the stone. "I just want to be normal."

"I understand that completely," Gina assured her, "but right now we kind of need the thing that makes you different."

Nicole nodded. "She's right. Get those freaky superpowers of yours on and show us how to get the fuck out of this place. It's really starting to creep me out."

Reluctantly, Andrea turned and continued onward.

Nicole watched the way she walked. She didn't go in a straight line, but rather veered a little as she went, apparently avoiding more invisible tombstones.

Andrea said she watched her pass right through one, meaning they weren't merely invisible. It was like they didn't exist to her. She couldn't bump into one if she wanted to. Still, she tried her best to follow in her footsteps. It seemed like bad luck to walk through someone's headstone, after all, whether it was tangible or not. The thought of it sent an uneasy sort of feeling racing through her.

"See anything?"

Andrea shook her head. "It's all the same. For as far as I can see. Just gravestones and trees."

"Well there has to be *something* else. Can you read the inscriptions on *any* of them?"

"No. They're all the same. Old and worn down." She stopped walking and propped her fists on her hips as she looked around again. "What?"

"I didn't say anything," replied Nicole.

"Not you." She gestured at her head with the point of the spear. "Her."

"Oh."

"She just said, 'Not what they appear.' What does *that* mean? *What's* not what they appear?"

Nicole watched her. "The graves?"

"I think so? I mean, there's nothing else out here, so…I mean, she can't be talking about anything else? I guess?"

"So they're not really gravestones?"

"No, I feel like they are. It's something else." She shook her head. "It's hard to explain…"

Again, Nicole turned and looked behind her. The longer

258

they were out here, the more uneasy she felt. She didn't like this strange haze. And she didn't like how still it was. And she *really* didn't like the sound of those cawing crows high up in the pine canopy.

Why did it have to be crows? She couldn't count how many horror movies had portrayed them as ill omens. *At least, I think those are birds...* she recalled Gina saying as she described what she was feeling in these woods. Something about the way she said it sent a shiver down her spine, both when she said it and now.

Andrea tipped her head to one side, thoughtful, and stared at what Nicole could only assume was another stone. "Okay, this is probably going to sound kind of crazy...but I just have this weird feeling...like..." She crossed her arms as if cold and shifted her gaze to a different stone, then to another. "...I feel like there aren't any graves here."

Nicole frowned at this. "You're the one who said it was a cemetery."

"No, that's not what I mean. There's a cemetery... I mean, there are grave *stones*. But I don't think there are any actual *graves* under them."

"What the hell's the point in *that?*"

"How should *I* know?" She turned all the way around, scanning their surroundings again. "I mean it's not a *real* cemetery...right? You two can't even see it."

"That doesn't make it not real," Gina reminded her. "It just makes it something only you can interact with."

"It doesn't make any sense, though. How would I even know something like that?"

"Sometimes with abilities like these, you just know things. All you can do is try to figure out what you're supposed to do with that information."

Nicole watched for a moment as Andrea continued forward through the hazy trees and the gravestones that only she could see. What was this place, really?

"Wait..." Andrea turned and walked toward another of the stones. "I see something." She knelt down, presumably in front of one of the stones again. She reached out and touched it.

Again, a wave of vertigo washed over Nicole. She shuddered hard. At the same time, she blinked. In that brief instant while her eyes were closed, another stone had appeared out of nowhere.

"That is *so* fucking weird…"

Gina nodded.

"Look," said Andrea, running her finger over the stone. Unlike the last one, something was visible there, carved into the aged surface of the stone. It looked like it had been there a long time, but not nearly as long as the stone, itself.

"What is it?" asked Nicole.

Andrea traced the shape with her finger, from left to right, three sweeping arches, the middle one shorter than the other two. And two smaller curves beneath it. "Sort of looks like a bird…"

"If you say so."

Then Andrea lifted the spear and pointed to one of the symbols carved there. "*This* bird."

"Oh. Okay."

Andrea sighed and stared at the stone. "This is why it had to be me?"

"Looks like it," replied Gina.

"That just means it's a good thing we have you," said Nicole.

"I guess…" She was still staring at the stone, frowning. "They go deep," she sighed.

"What?"

"The headstones," she explained, her gaze sliding down from the stone to the needle-carpeted forest floor beneath it. "Deep. Into the ground. Very, *very* deep… All the way into…" She hugged herself against a sudden chill. "…into…" She struggled with the words for a moment, then settled on simply, "Somewhere *else*."

Chapter 36

It was strange, this feeling inside her as she walked among the mysterious stones, searching for more of the spear's hidden symbols. It was an *alien* feeling, one she couldn't recognize, as if a brand-new sense had been awakened inside her and she didn't yet know how to use it. And yet, there was also something eerily familiar about it. It was like the broken and faded memory of an old dream, long forgotten, yet still lingering somewhere deep inside.

Andrea could see the stones, that they *looked* like stones. She could feel the stones, that they *felt* like stones. But there was something *else* about the stones, too, something she didn't fully understand. They were simple monuments, taller than they were wide, rounded on the top, only three or four inches thick. And yet she felt very much that they were far more than that. They were much *larger* than they appeared. Not two and a half feet tall, but *towering*, like those surrounding pines. Bigger than those, even. But not stretching up into the air. Nor even down into the ground, exactly. Just...

Elsewhere... sighed the voice inside her head.

She turned and looked out into the trees again, at those more distant stones half swallowed by the strange haze. She was strangely aware of each and every one of them. They weren't the same. And they didn't feel like grave markers at all. Each one gave off an aura of *individuality*, as if they weren't stone at all, but living creatures. Or living *people*.

Although "living" was probably the wrong word...

The dead know the way, she thought, remembering what the voice in her head told her. Was that what these were? Was she surrounded by the dead? Did the stones represent spirits? What kind of sense did *that* make? Why would spirits present themselves as cold headstones? They'd already proven they could speak to her and touch her. Some of them had even revealed themselves to her, if only briefly.

You have to go deeper... said that voice inside her. *Find the courage to look beneath the surface...*

"This is so confusing!"

"Sorry," said Nicole. "I'd help, but I have no fucking clue how to do it."

Andrea gave a tired chuckle. "Thanks. I just..." She shook her head. "I just don't know what to do."

She walked on, weaving her way through tree trunks and gravestones. Every time she was almost convinced that she'd gotten lost, she caught sight of another symbol carved into one of them. One by one, she located all of them, tracing out a path through this strange cemetery that wasn't a cemetery, filled with gravestones that weren't gravestones, where the dead weren't buried and certainly weren't resting.

But as she walked away from the last of those symbols, she didn't feel as if she'd accomplished something. After all, she was still in that unearthly cemetery. What was she supposed to do next? What would mark the path now?

"I feel something," said Gina.

Nicole glanced back at her. "I'm guessing it's one of those, 'I feel a *bad* something,' kind of thing and not like a, 'I feel an open bar and crab leg buffet up ahead,' kind of thing."

"I'm not sure what it is. I've been feeling it since that last marker, but I couldn't understand it. It's not like the presence I felt in that hospital or anything like that. I don't sense any kind of imminent danger. It's something about these woods. Something..." She looked back over her shoulder, then out into that surrounding haze. "It's weird... It's... It's like this place exists in *layers*. But..." She met Andrea's eyes. "But some of those layers are missing."

Nicole stared at her, her brow furrowed, trying to understand it all. "You mean like holes in the ground or something?"

But Gina shook her head. "No. Not physically missing. I

think there are layers here that I just can't sense." Again, she turned her gaze on Andrea. "Like the way I can't sense the cemetery, maybe?"

Andrea stared back at her as she processed that.

"The spear was given to *you*," Gina reminded her. "This place right here is probably why it had to be you. Try to focus on the things only you can see. There might be something deeper."

She wrinkled her nose at her and pouted. Go deeper… That was what the voice inside her head told her. She looked at the stones around her.

Were they stones? Something deep inside kept insisting that she wasn't seeing them for what they really were. But what else could they be?

Something shimmered in the corner of her eye. She turned to see what was there, but it was only another stone. Her weary imagination playing tricks on her.

Or was it?

She tipped her head to one side and stared at it. It looked…*off*…but she couldn't determine *how* it was off. It was like a poorly photoshopped picture. It simply didn't seem to go with its surroundings somehow.

Focus on the things only you can see, she thought. Maybe Gina was right. There *did* seem to be more than what her human eyes were showing her.

She started walking toward the stone. But the stone was farther away than she first thought. In fact, it was *much* farther away than she first thought. And it was much *bigger* than she thought. She continued walking, past tree after tree, toward a headstone that was no headstone at all, but a looming stone structure.

An above-ground vault? A mausoleum?

It had the same shape as the headstones, taller than it was wide, with a rounded top. But it was an entire structure, about twelve feet tall at the top of its arched roof. And it was at least as long as it was tall, and about nine feet wide.

She walked around the side to the back, which turned out to be its front. There was a heavy iron door waiting there, already slightly open, as if someone were expecting her…which didn't exactly give her a warm hospitality kind of vibe, if she were being honest...

"Is this where I'm supposed to go?" she wondered. Then she remembered that no one else could see these things. She was going to have to describe it. "It's like a..." but when she turned around, Nicole and Gina were gone.

She was standing all alone in a mist-shrouded sea of weathered headstones.

She turned around, her heart pounding. "Nikki?" she called. "Gina?"

Even the forest had vanished. There wasn't a pine tree to be seen. Or even a single needle on the ground. Beneath her feet was bare, lifeless earth.

"Hello?" Her gaze drifted back to that ominous iron door. "Anybody?" she added. The word came out in a frightened squeak.

Where were Nicole and Gina? Did something take them? Or was it *she* who'd been taken? What was this place? She hoped they were still okay. But she glanced down at the spear she was still gripping in her hand. Would they be able to find their way out of that forest without her? Without *this*? It made her sick to think that they might be stranded back there. Gina warned them that if they wandered too far off the trail they could be lost forever. What was going to happen if she couldn't find her way back to them?

Go inside...

She groaned. She didn't *want* to go in there. She never agreed to do this, much less to do it *alone*. But what choice did she have? If she tried to walk away, would she even be able to leave? She had no idea where she was or if it was even possible to get back to that pine forest from here. What if she only ended up getting lost in the endless fog of this cemetery?

With a tired whimper, she stepped forward and pulled open the iron door.

A set of stone steps waited inside, plunging into the black depths of the earth.

Naturally, her thoughts were drawn back to the temple and

all the unspeakable horrors she found there.

Deeper...

"Deeper," she repeated. "Right. So you keep saying." She pulled out her cell phone and looked at it. The battery was almost dead. If she tried using the flashlight, it wouldn't last long at all. She was going to have to proceed by the light of the screen alone. And even that she turned all the way down to its dimmest setting to make it last as long as possible. "You know, I kind of thought you meant 'deeper' in more of a 'profound' sense, not *literally...*"

She *really* didn't want to go down there. It looked scary as hell.

She took a deep breath and held it as she stepped through the doorway and peered down into the darkness below.

The faster she got this over with, the faster she could get back to her friends? Maybe?

She let the breath she was holding out in a defeated sigh and started downward. "I'm *so* not happy with you right now, Ghost Girl."

Chapter 37

Andrea wasn't sure how much time passed as she descended the stone steps, deeper and deeper into whatever fresh hell awaited her inside the ghostly tomb.

She felt so anxious being here that her stomach hurt. She felt sick. The cold, stone walls...the dank, earthy smell...the endless darkness... And she wasn't even sure how she came to be here. Was it like Tristesse Lane? Did someone bring her here? Had she fallen into some kind of trap? Or was this somewhere she was meant to be? Gina did say something about her unique abilities likely being the key to finding their way through All Trails Crossing. Was this what she was talking about?

It was so frustrating not having any answers!

"Are we there yet?" she asked, not daring to raise her voice above a whisper in case there were things nearby she didn't want knowing she was down here.

But the ghostly voice in her head had gone silent. Was she merely conserving her energy? She better not have stayed at the top of the stairs. This was *her* idea!

She trudged onward and downward, unhappy. How far had she gone, she wondered. Six or seven stories? Ten? A dozen? Her legs were starting to hurt. Much farther and she was going to have to stop and take a break.

And it didn't help that she was worried about Nicole and Gina. Where were they? When, exactly, did she lose them? They were right next to her. She found it hard to believe that they could've simply let her wander off, unaware. Did they disappear when the trees did? Did they stay in that forest while she stepped fully into the cemetery? Were they looking for her right now?

Why was everything so confusing?

Ahead of her, the steps finally came to an end. A tunnel continued forward into the darkness.

She'd been reminded of the Temple of the Blind, but the temple didn't look like this. Every surface of that place was smooth and clean, except where the Hounds prowled. The Sentinel Queen's children had acted as caretakers to ensure that it was kept in immaculate condition. Until they died out, anyway. And the tunnels leading down to the temple's entrance weren't like this, either. Those were mostly modern concrete. Even the oldest of those tunnels had been made of brick or stone. This looked more like a mineshaft carved straight through the bedrock of the earth, crooked and uneven. Every surface was rough, raw stone. And everything down here was *wet*. Water dripped from the ceiling and trickled down the walls. Fat, cold drops landed on her head and shoulders, soaking into her hair and tee shirt. The tunnel floor was slick with mud. The stale air reeked of dank and swampy places. Nevertheless, she couldn't stop being reminded of those other passageways. She expected to hear the machine-like droning of one of those awful hounds at any moment.

But step after step, everything remained eerily quiet. The only sound was the soft pitter-patter of dripping water.

What was this place? *Was* there some connection to the temple? Or were there just lots of places like this out there in the world? She really wished someone would just give her some answers already. It was so exhausting not knowing what was going on all the time.

She paused and shined her meager light back the way she came. It was *really* creepy down here. She wanted nothing more than to turn back and flee this place. But she was sure that would only be delaying the inevitable. If this was where she was meant to be, then she would only end up returning here, one way or another. It was better to face whatever was down here and get it over with. So she pushed onward, her shoes squelching in the mud with each step.

The minutes crawled by, each one feeling like ten as that hot, sick feeling in her belly grew ever hotter, ever sicker.

Then, finally, the tunnel ahead of her opened up, yawning wide into a vast, black emptiness.

She was still underground. The air was still stale and dank. And there was still that steady drizzle of dripping water from the cavern ceiling somewhere high above her. But now she could hear a steady trickling of water from somewhere nearby as well. An underground stream?

She hoped she wouldn't have to swim down here. Crossing those frigid pools of water down in the temple was pure torture. She very much never wanted to have to do that again.

She wanted to turn on her phone's flashlight—just for a few seconds—and take a quick look around, but she didn't quite dare to use up too much of the dwindling battery. It would be all for nothing anyway if the room was anywhere near as large as it felt, so she resisted the urge and crept forward, sweeping its stingy glow back and forth in front of her, barely managing to illuminate her path. She was especially careful to watch where she stepped, making sure there wasn't a sudden drop-off that she couldn't see. The last thing she wanted was to fall into that water. Or worse, over some open ledge into a bottomless chasm. Or a pit filled with deadly spikes, which sounded like some ridiculous trope from an Indiana Jones movie, but was dreadfully and gruesomely *real*.

The sight of Beverly Bridger's bloody body lying sprawled in that awful trap had haunted her nightmares for *months* following that night and still made her feel sick to think about even after all these years.

She paused and shined her light around again. She thought for a moment that she could hear voices murmuring somewhere nearby, but maybe it was only the gurgling of the water. Sometimes that sounded like voices. The fish tank in the living room at her parents' house used to sound like that when it needed water added or the filter changed. Maybe this was like that.

Or maybe not… There was something about this space that made her feel very much not alone.

She looked back over her shoulder, uneasy. She didn't like this. She *really* wished she didn't have to be here by herself.

"Now would be a good time to let me know you're still here," she whispered into the darkness. But still, that ghostly voice remained silent.

She could feel herself growing more anxious. Something about the emptiness of this huge space, the inability to see her surroundings... An icy panic was quickly creeping up on her.

She closed her eyes for a moment and took in a slow, calming breath. She held it for a moment, then let it out slowly through her pursed lips, willing it to take that fear and anxiety welling up inside her with it.

It didn't work. Like, *at all*. But it was worth a try.

She opened her eyes and forced herself to push forward, venturing ever deeper into that looming darkness, anxious of the million things she imagined were waiting for her there. But step by step, none of those things appeared.

After a few agonizing minutes, she realized that the ground beneath her feet had shrunk to a narrow walkway, only about ten feet wide, with a sheer drop on either side of her. She shined her light back the way she came, but her cell phone's screen only illuminated a very small area around her. She couldn't see where the walkway started. Was she simply too focused on where she was placing her feet to notice, or did the space around her change on its own? Was this even the same place she was a moment ago? Between Tristesse Lane and that awful hospital, then All Trails Crossing and that creepy, ghostly cemetery, it was impossible to know for sure anymore. One moment she was in one world, the next she was in another.

She didn't try to rationalize it. There was no point. She saw the Wood with her own eyes, its eerily empty sky, its hordes of insatiable undead. She walked with the spirits on their Journey of the Dead. And the Sentinel Queen even told her that no one, not even she, knew how many other worlds were out there, so the fact that places like these existed wasn't new information to her. But she never thought she'd come across so many of them in such a short period of time.

She peered over one side of the walkway, but there was only an empty blackness and that endless sound of softly trickling water somewhere below her.

A bridge.

There were bridges in the temple, too. Some crossed the perilous, hound-infested portions of the labyrinth and some seemed to look down over nothing at all. They were the places that teased her the most when she was down there, she recalled, places that were wide open, but undiscoverable. She remembered wishing she had a light of some kind to toss over the edge, a flare, a torch, even a disposable flashlight, just to see how far down it plunged, for just a glimpse of how deep into hell that frightful place really reached.

Now she stood staring down into another mysterious darkness, distracted, her cell phone's dull light fading almost immediately into nothingness. For some strange reason, she found herself imagining an impossibly massive serpent slithering through that unseen water, miles and miles of glittering scales passing beneath her like a tremendous freight train, and the thought for some reason filled her heart with a strange mix of wonder and dread.

Then, just as quickly, the sensation faded away and was gone.

Her overactive imagination? Or yet another glimpse of the strange and endless wonder that was this bizarre reality she'd found herself in?

She turned and looked out over the other side of the bridge, into the endless darkness, where her mind's eye showed her just a flicker of a huge, vanishing tail.

She squeezed her eyes shut and took another breath. No. Definitely just her imagination. Even the Temple of the Blind didn't have giant snakes crawling around in it. That would surely be too much for *anyone* to have to deal with. She was scared. And tired. That was all.

She continued onward, across the bridge that seemed to go on forever.

She felt strangely vulnerable here, with nowhere to go but forward and back, with a watery abyss somewhere beneath her feet that may or may not be infested with ginormous snakes. She felt desperately exposed. She couldn't help imagining that if someone were to suddenly flood this place with light, she'd find herself trapped on this narrow stone bridge while countless unthinkable things swarmed toward her from every possible direction.

And now she felt her gaze drawn up into the mysterious darkness overhead. She still couldn't see or hear anything, not in the pitiful light available to her, but she couldn't help imagining things moving around up there.

Lots of things…

She wasn't sure how much more of this she could take. Where was she? Why was she here? She wished someone would give her some answers.

When she aimed her light forward again, it fell on a tall, pale figure that startled a terrified shriek out of her and almost made her drop her phone. She fumbled to hold onto it and thrust the spear toward the figure as if she knew anything about defending herself with such a weapon even if it *had* a handle…

By the time she regained her grip and aimed her phone forward again, the figure was turning away from her and vanishing back into the shadows from which it appeared.

She stood there, staring after it, confused. She only saw it for a second or two, but it was enough to recognize several eerily familiar details about it. It was about ten feet tall, thin and naked, with grossly elongated limbs. And its face was utterly featureless. It looked just like one of those statues from the Temple of the Blind. It looked like a *sentinel*. But that was no statue. It was pale flesh, not gray stone. And she was certain she saw it *walk* away.

She stood there, her heart still racing, her entire body trembling as she processed it all.

It wasn't impossible, she reasoned. Although the sentinels in the temple were only statues, the *Sentinel Queen* was a living, breathing woman who claimed to have been the daughter of a *real* sentinel. And she certainly didn't appear completely human. Like the sentinels, she was unnaturally tall, her body elongated in all the same ways as those strange statues. And while she wasn't *entirely* faceless, she had only a small bump of a nose and a tiny slit of a mouth. The most compelling proof that she wasn't human, however, was that she possessed potent psychic abilities. When she spoke, it wasn't aloud, but directly into their heads.

And yet, it was still hard to imagine that those freaky statues were of real beings…

She wrinkled her nose as she pondered the idea that, sometime long ago, the Sentinel Queen's perfectly human mother met one of those guys and apparently decided he'd make for a good time. How was it even possible? Those things had freakishly huge…*parts*… Like *scary* huge! *Terrifying*! She remembered the entrance to the sex room and that gauntlet of obscene statues they'd had to walk between, each pair more *aroused* than the last, miming out their perverted warning of what awaited them ahead. At the time, she thought it was a joke. There was no way those things could ever have been real.

Yet she was quite sure she just saw one…

If this guy thought he was going to get to be *her* baby daddy, he had another thing coming! That was absolutely *not* happening.

She took another calming breath and pushed forward. "Hello?" she called, still too afraid to raise her voice much above a whisper.

She still wasn't to the end of the bridge, so it looked like her only choices were to follow him or turn back. And she still doubted very much that the second one was really an option. If she was here for a reason, then turning back would do nothing but waste precious battery life on her slowly dying phone.

It was a familiar feeling, venturing into the frightening unknown. She remembered following Wayne down into those tunnels that night… Looking back on it afterward, it was hard to really explain what ever possessed her to do such a thing. He was a complete stranger back then. All of them were. She had no way to know for sure that those people wouldn't grab her the moment they were too deep for anyone to hear her scream and do unspeakable things to her. It was a terrible world out there, filled with all kinds of sick people. And yet she just went along like nothing bad could happen to her.

Certainly, she'd wanted answers. Who wouldn't? A mysterious envelope appearing at her window... A secret meeting of strangers at the creepy ruins in the forest behind her house... A monstrous shadow looming over that old cellar door... And then that voice inside her head. More than anything, it was that voice. That wasn't just people acting suspiciously. That wasn't some kind of clever prank. That was something *supernatural*. She couldn't stand the thought of just going home after that. She would have spent the rest of her life wondering what it all meant.

And so she seated herself down in those woods and she waited. And when Wayne and Olivia emerged from beneath those mysterious walls for the second time, she joined them. And what followed was as thrilling as it was terrifying.

But at least she had a choice back then. She could have ignored it all and gone back home at any time. Or at least up until she'd gotten herself hopelessly turned around in that labyrinth, she supposed.

What choice did she have this time? Between the spear, Hotdog Creep and Gina's goddess, she'd been robbed of any choice in the matter right from the beginning.

She paused and shined her light around. Everything had changed again. She was no longer on a bridge, but in another tunnel.

The ground was muddier here. She could feel it soaking through her shoes and into her socks. And it was getting slicker, too. She was going to have to watch her step.

She continued forward, shining what little light her phone offered ahead of her. There was an intersection waiting for her. She was going to have to choose a direction. But almost as soon as it came into view, she was again startled by the pale, hunched shape of the sentinel as it darted past, moving from left to right.

She froze, a terrified whimper escaping her. She *really* didn't like this. This was the stuff of horror movies.

The sentinels were supposed to be the good guys, right? They were the ones who built the Temple of the Blind, who engineered humanity's escape from the dying worlds to the new ones, literally saving mankind from extinction. Their statues offered warnings and guidance throughout that strange journey.

They even stood *outside* the temple, under that empty, starless sky.

They were symbols of *hope*.

Right?

But what did she really know about them? Hadn't they also designed the trap that killed Beverly Bridger? And even if they *were* the good guys, that didn't mean that *all of them* were good.

What if this one had gone crazy?

Or what if the pale thing lurking in this darkness wasn't a sentinel at all, but something altogether different? Something dangerous? Something *evil?*

Somehow she crept onward, her breath held, her heart pounding, and shined her light around the corner, first one way, then the other. Nothing was waiting to grab her. Nothing tried to slash her throat. Nothing jumped out with a chainsaw to chase her.

And why should it? This was all part of the plan, right? This was where she was supposed to be? This was where the Keeper or Gina's goddess or whoever else was involved in all this craziness meant for her to be right now?

God, she hoped this was where she was supposed to be…

She followed the sentinel.

Seriously, why couldn't anyone just tell her what she was supposed to do? Why did everything have to be such a scary ordeal?

The floor beneath her was sloping downward, ever deeper into this dark place. And the farther she went, the steeper and muddier the passage became. It was getting harder and harder to keep her footing.

She saw no footprints in the mud. Did the sentinel really come this way? Or was this some kind of trap?

She didn't like this. Maybe she should turn around and try the other way.

But before she could take another step, her cell phone battery finally died. In an instant, she was plunged into a terrible and absolute blackness.

Chapter 38

Andrea stood in the darkness, blind, too afraid to move, her heart thudding against her ribs, so loud in the eerie silence that it seemed almost as if it could be heard across a crowded room. She couldn't seem to catch her breath. She couldn't remember ever being this frightened before, although she thought she probably had been. There were plenty of times down in that temple when she really thought she was going to die. But she simply couldn't get control of herself. All she wanted was to be out of this strange, black place and back with her friends. But how would she ever find her way out of this place in the dark?

She still didn't even know how she came to be here in the first place!

Breathe...

She turned around, her eyes wide open but useless. Was that the ghost girl again? Or was that only her own thoughts bubbling up through the suffocating panic?

Either way, she needed to calm down.

She forced herself to close her eyes. They weren't going to help her anyway.

She was hyperventilating. She needed to slow down and take long, deep breaths. She needed to get control of herself, physically *and* emotionally.

Inhale... Nice and deep... Then exhale... Slowly... Don't rush it...

She just needed to find a happy place. That was all. And there were lots of places she was happy.

...inhale...

She thought of Nicole. And of home. Of long nights talking and giggling in their apartment. Of easy, simple meals in front of the television. Of quiet evenings with their noses in their phones, sending each other amusing videos.

…exhale…

She thought of Olivia and Wayne, of the way they sometimes popped into the ice cream parlor when she was working, just to grab some shakes and say hi. Her beautifully genuine smile. His charming awkwardness. Their overflowing love they had for each other that anyone could see from a mile away.

…inhale…

She recalled the last time they all got together at Albert and Brandy's apartment, the six of them gathered together, eating pizza and drinking beer. Telling stories. Laughing until she couldn't breathe. Those were her favorite times, the ones she wanted to go on forever.

…exhale…

Her friends… She *loved* her friends. *So much.* She would do anything to make sure she saw them all again. But to do that, she needed to get control of herself and get through this.

And she was doing it. She could feel the panic draining away. She could feel herself calming down.

She could do this.

She took one last deep breath and let it out again. Then, finally, she opened her eyes.

"Right…" she muttered into the darkness. "Still can't see in the dark…"

But she was back in control. And that was what really mattered.

Except…

She crossed her arms over herself, confused.

Why was she *naked?*

Her mind was racing. How did that happen? *When* did it happen? Had she lost time somehow? She was wearing clothes just a moment ago. Sure, she was having a bit of a panic attack, but she was still fairly confident she'd have noticed something taking off her clothes. Strangely, she still had her phone clutched in one hand and the spear in the other. Why would anyone capable of finding her in this place take her clothes but not the spear?

She knelt down and felt at the floor around her feet with the backs of her fingers, hoping she might find them lying strewn about the floor, but even if they were there, she could search for hours in this absolute darkness and never find them.

It didn't make any sense. There was no reason for her to be like this. The only thought that came to her was that she was naked when she ventured into the Temple of the Blind. But this wasn't the temple. This entire place was dank and dirty, nothing at all like those clean, smooth surfaces. There was a persistent, mildewy sort of stench in the air here.

She stopped moving. Wait... That wasn't quite right... She couldn't smell the dank earth anymore. And the floor beneath her fingers and toes was neither muddy nor rough. She was no longer standing on a slippery slope but on a flat, even surface. It felt clean and smooth.

The hair on her arms was standing up. She placed the phone and spear carefully on the floor and ran her hands over it until she found the wall.

A neat, ninety-degree corner. Cool, slick stone.

She *knew* these surfaces...

The Temple of the Blind was gone. She saw it falling apart with her own eyes. Yet, here she was. Squatting in what felt exactly like one of those dark temple passageways. Butt naked. Just like she was that night...

Except back then she was given a choice. Wayne warned her and Olivia both before they even set out that venturing past a certain point would require them to be naked. He used it to try to dissuade them from going with him. He didn't want them getting hurt and tried to talk them out of it. Either of them could have turned around right then and avoided all of that embarrassment. But they both chose to move forward, their desire for answers outweighing their modesty to their own surprise. (And a little bit of terror at the thought of trying to find their way back through all those scary tunnels all alone.)

But why was she naked *now*? What purpose would that serve in *this* place? Of course, that was something of a silly question, she realized. After all, she never understood what the point was in being naked back then, either. They were never given a good reason. Even Albert had never been able to think up a really good explanation for it.

Had she somehow traveled back to that frightful night? Could she have traveled back in time somehow? Was it five years ago, when the temple still stood and the murderous Caggo still prowled this black labyrinth?

No, that didn't make sense.

She reached up and touched the ring in her right eyebrow and raked the stud in her tongue across the back of her teeth. She didn't have those back then. She was still wearing all of her jewelry, like she was that night, all her rings and bracelets and necklaces, but they were the same ones she was wearing when she left her apartment. She changed them up every day.

She grasped her phone and the spear and then stood up again. The motion sent an odd jolt of pain through her right knee and she rubbed at it in the dark, trying to remember when she hurt herself. But she felt nothing there. The sensation was gone as quickly as it came over her. Just a twinge of some sort? A brief cramp, perhaps? A pinprick of pain from all those stairs she had to walk down?

Spontaneous nakedness? Phantom pains? Giant, imaginary snakes? She didn't understand *anything*. Nothing made sense anymore.

Was this that sentinel's doing? Did he do something to her? Did he…

An awful thought crossed her mind. She thought of the Sentinel Queen, of how she claimed that her mother was human and her father a real, living sentinel…

And now that she was thinking about it, didn't the Sentinel Queen do something pretty much exactly like that to Wayne?

No. That was…*different*. She didn't feel violated in any way. She was pretty sure she'd know if she was, given the size of their… Yeah. She'd definitely know.

She shuddered and pushed the awful thought from her mind. That was ridiculous. Thinking icky thoughts like that wasn't going to do her any favors. Nor was she getting any closer to finding her way out of this place by freaking out about her clothes.

She needed to focus.

She turned her blind gaze toward the passage in front of her. She was *fairly* sure she was going this way when her battery died and everything changed…but then again, everything had changed. She had no way of knowing which way was which. And without any light, that sentinel wouldn't be able to do his creepy horror movie "follow me" thing.

But as she stood there, squinting into the darkness, she realized that there was something ahead of her. There was an open space. A chamber of some sort. Just ten or twelve yards ahead, she thought. She couldn't quite understand the sensation. She couldn't see it, obviously. And it wasn't something she heard, exactly. The only sounds were her own breathing and the rhythm of her pulse in her ears. It was more like something she felt on her skin, something similar to a faint movement in the air that stirred the hairs on the back of her arm, letting her know something was there. Except it wasn't exactly like that, either. She didn't *physically* feel anything of the sort.

And now that she was thinking about it, wasn't that what Gina told her, way back when all this began? That she could sense things others couldn't? She called her "a bridge between the living and the dead" and told her she was "exceedingly rare."

Cautiously, she crept forward, prodding at the cool stone with her bare toes with each step, still vividly aware that there were deadly traps in the Temple of the Blind.

With each tentative step, she became more and more certain that there was a room waiting for her there. A big, open space loomed in the silent darkness. And somehow she also understood that it was somewhere she needed to be.

Whatever was there, whatever that strangely compelling space was, it was the reason she was brought here. The nearer she came to it, the more *significant* it felt and the more she found herself drawn toward it. The feeling was growing more urgent. She had to make a conscious effort to stay patient and aware for traps.

It was right in front of her. Only a few more steps... She felt herself stepping out from between the narrow passage walls and into the wide-open space beyond.

She could *see* it. She was utterly blind in this darkness, but she found that she could see every surface. It was spread out before her, as clear as the image on a television screen, a room about the size of a football field, filled with thin, towering pillars that reminded her of the pine trees back in that creepy fog.

She stepped out into the room, taking it all in. Her wide eyes drifted from one pillar to the next, a mere force of habit, since there was no light to see by and she didn't need them anyway.

The temple didn't have any chambers in it with pillars like these...

She reached out and touched the nearest one. A strange, icy tingle seemed to wash through her.

The stones...

"They go deep," she whispered to herself in the silence. "All the way into..." In the utter darkness, her blue eyes drifted across the room again. "...somewhere else..."

A shiver raced all the way down her back and her knees wobbled a little beneath her.

She still didn't really understand what it all meant, but something about this realization felt almost *staggering*.

She withdrew her hand and turned her attention toward the far end of the room. There was a set of stairs waiting for her. They led up to a platform overlooking the pillared chamber. There was something up there. A stone archway set into the wall.

A door?

Distracted, she crossed the room, weaving her way through those mysterious pillars. Still clutching her phone and the spear, she reached out and dragged the tips of her fingers along each pillar that she passed, letting that strange, icy sensation trickle up her arms.

Peculiar, alien thoughts flickered through her head, like long-forgotten memories bubbling up from somewhere deep inside, only to pop and vanish the moment they broke the surface.

They weren't her own memories, she somehow realized, but snippets of other people's lives from long, long ago.

She wasn't really aware of crossing the room. Before she knew it, she was climbing those steps, her blind gaze fixed on that archway.

Was it a door? It was little more than a stone slab set into the archway. Staring at it—if that was what it could be called with no light to see by—filled her with a strange sensation that she didn't think she'd ever felt before. She wasn't sure how to describe it. Not exactly. The closest thing she could think of was that it somehow reminded her of the way warm sunlight felt on her skin. It radiated from that stone slab. It almost seemed to beckon her to it.

She wanted to feel more of that *warmth*.

That was, after all, why she was here. Wasn't it?

She hesitated as she reached the last step. *Was* this what she was here for? She turned and looked behind her, at all those looming pillars. She still didn't understand any of this, how she found herself all alone in that cemetery, how she lost her clothes, how that dank, muddy tunnel became the temple, how she was able to "see" the things in this strange chamber.

Was this where she was supposed to be? Or was this merely where someone wanted her to *think* she was meant to be?

Deeper...

She frowned and turned her blind gaze back on the door in front of her, on the source of that strangely compelling warmth. Up close, it appeared just like all those headstones that led her here. It had the same shape and the same rough, worn texture. It was just much larger. Sort of like the stone that turned into the vault that led her here.

Was she supposed to open it? It didn't have a handle. It was just a slab of weathered stone. Did she just...push on it, maybe?

She reached out with the hand that held the spear, her fingers outstretched, meaning only to touch the surface.

She felt the tip of the spear tap against the door. She heard a sound that wasn't a sound ring out in a note that never touched her ears but filled her head regardless.

Something happened…

The world around her became a blur of light and sound. Images flashed before her eyes. A thousand voices seemed to speak to her. Ten thousand thoughts raced through her mind. A long time passed in a single instant…or perhaps a single instant passed for a long time? She traveled a vast distance, yet she took not a single step. She was all alone, but she was also with her friends. She was afraid and she was happy and she was sad and she was angry.

And there was a voice. It rang out above all the rest of the chaos, faint as the flapping of butterfly wings, but at the same time booming like thunder, reverberating all the way down to the deepest depths of her conscious mind.

She stood there, enveloped by the warmth that poured from the stone slab in front of her, letting those mysterious words echo through her dazed mind.

Then it was over.

She shuddered and blinked up at the hazy sky.

What was she just doing?

"Hey! Snap out of it already!"

Nicole and Gina were standing next to her, staring at her. She was back in that foggy forest, right where she started. "Huh…?"

"Don't scare me!" sighed Nicole.

"What happened?" She turned and looked out into the forest. All those headstones were gone. There was no sign of them anywhere.

"You just…zoned out, I guess."

"It was scary," agreed Gina.

"Sorry…" She looked down at herself, confused. She wasn't naked anymore, thankfully. Was she ever? Was any of that real? She lifted the spear and the cell phone she was holding. "How long was I gone?"

But Nicole only frowned. "I don't know. A few seconds, I guess. You looked like you were way out in dreamland or something."

She never went anywhere? But she had to have been gone at least an hour. Maybe several. Didn't she? She checked her phone to find that it was dead. Did that prove anything? Probably not. It was almost dead already before she was separated from them. "I was back in the temple..."

"What?"

"There was a sentinel. A real one. Or...maybe the ghost of one?"

"What's a sentinel?" asked Gina.

"You never moved from that spot," said Nicole.

She turned and scanned her surroundings. "What's going on? I *know* I didn't just dream it. I followed the stones. I found that vault. You guys disappeared, and I was all alone."

"We've been right next to you the whole time," insisted Nicole.

"There were stairs and a muddy tunnel and..." She pouted. "Seriously? Did I just imagine all of that?"

"Maybe?"

"No," said Gina. "I believe her."

Nicole nodded. "Yeah. I mean, I guess stranger things have happened."

"Yes, but..." She pointed at Andrea's feet. "She said it was muddy."

Although the forest around them had been hot and dry since they arrived in All Trails Crossing, Andrea's shoes were covered in fresh mud.

Chapter 39

"That was freaking *bizarre!*" said Andrea.

Although the creepy headstones had vanished, she found that she was quickly able to spot more of those huge rocks and match them to the markings on the spear. They were back on the path again. One by one, she was making her way through the last of the spear's enigmatic clues.

"It *sounds* bizarre," agreed Nicole. "I mean you were only zoned out for a few *seconds.*"

"It was *definitely* longer than a few seconds."

"Was it, like, an out-of-body experience kind of thing, or what?"

"I'm pretty sure I had my body with me," she said, remembering how she suddenly found herself naked down there. Didn't she have to have a body for it to be naked?

"Whatever you did down there," reasoned Gina, "must have been important. The goddess told me to protect you. There must be something you can do that no one else can."

"Yeah…" Andrea looked down at the spear. She remembered that strange sound that rang out when she tapped it against that stone slab. She couldn't even remember what happened after that. It felt like several *years* flew by, but it only lasted a second. Was it just that her simple human brain wasn't capable of comprehending whatever it was that she experienced down there? She had this nagging feeling that someone told her something very important at some point, but she couldn't for the life of her remember what it was. It was like waking up from a dream and immediately forgetting it all.

This was one of those times, she supposed, when all you could do was hope it wasn't something that was going to be on the next test…

The map was almost all used up. There were only two notches left now. And even the fog was starting to lift. The forest had begun to transition back from that creepy pine forest to the much denser vegetation that was there before the fog rolled in. And the heat and humidity was starting to return.

Six more rocks loomed in the brush ahead of them. Andrea lined up the last two notches as they pushed their way toward them and found that the path passed between the fourth and fifth ones.

Only one left.

When they cleared the underbrush between those last rocks, they were all three immediately struck by a strong scent of water on the air.

"I guess we're by the lake," reasoned Nicole.

"Cedric's Cove is supposed to be somewhere along the shoreline," Gina reminded her.

She nodded. "That's what I was thinking."

The fog continued to thin as they walked and the sky brightened. At the same time, the sounds of the forest began to return. She began to hear birds and bugs for the first time since the fog rolled in. She even glimpsed a squirrel scurrying through the trees.

It seemed like an odd thing to notice, especially as tired as she was, but Andrea found herself recalling something Albert once said about there being no cobwebs inside Gilbert House, in spite of the fact that it had been gathering dust for most of a century. In fact, there were no bugs of any sort. Or any rats or bats or other creatures for that matter. And the temple had been the same way, even deep down in the darkest depths of the labyrinth where the Sentinel Queen's children didn't dare go.

It was as if nature, itself, instinctually knew to avoid such places.

She was starting to wish *she* had such an instinct…

As the last of that strange haze burned away completely, giving way to brilliant sunshine casting mottled shade across the forest floor, Andrea caught sight of a narrow stretch of pavement ahead of them. A country road carved its way through the woods here, and just on the other side of it: "Water," said Andrea, pointing with the spear.

The softly rippling surface of the lake was glittering in the sun as the gentle waves lapped against the shore. "Is it really Lake Huron?" wondered Nicole.

"Hard to say," said Gina. "Could just be a mirror image of it, not connected in any way. Or the same water could flow back and forth between the two. But I'm pretty sure we're not anywhere that would appear on any map." She looked up at the towering branches overhead. "This definitely isn't our world."

Andrea looked down at the asphalt as she walked across it. It wasn't just an old road in need of repaving. There were tall clumps of weeds sprouting from the many cracks. There were dangerously large potholes. To her left, an entire chunk of it had completely washed out and would have been impassable to cars. Clearly, no one had driven here in a very long time. If ever.

"It *almost* feels like our world…" said Gina. She turned and looked out across the lake. "But it's…small."

Andrea squinted up at the sun. "Is it just me, or it getting late already?" It was definitely the end of the day. If they were looking at the lake, then they'd be facing north. Unless this weird place was some kind of mirror universe where the sun set in the east, it definitely wasn't morning already.

Nicole checked her phone. "This says it's not even one o'clock yet." Then she frowned. "But…that doesn't mean anything, does it?"

"It doesn't mean much," said Gina, "no."

"It might be *tomorrow* night already…"

Gina nodded. It was certainly possible, it seemed.

But it didn't feel like early afternoon *or* evening. Andrea felt like she was slowly losing all sense of time. It felt like weeks since she woke up and started getting ready for the wedding. *So* much had happened. And yet it also felt like it was all one very long day…

She turned and looked up the road, toward the washed-out part. Then she turned and looked the other way. Two more of those very large rocks had been placed there and tipped up onto their ends, one on either side of the shoulder, creating a sort of gate for the road to pass through. She lifted the spear and lined up the final notches. "Cedric's Cove," she sighed. "We've reached the end of the map."

"We made it," said Gina.

"Fucking *finally*," growled Nicole.

Chapter 40

The three of them trudged up the middle of the crumbling road, between the two rocks and along the winding coastline, following the decrepit pavement. Three times it dipped into the lake. Twice only partially, allowing them to circle around the murky water without getting wet, and once vanishing completely beneath the surface, forcing them to choose between wading across it or attempting to circle around it through the dense forest.

Nicole charged straight through it. She just wanted to get this journey over with. Andrea and Gina followed her without a word of protest. They had no intention of being separated a third time. Plus, whatever unpleasant things might be squirming through the mud and silt settled on this flooded stretch of highway couldn't be worse than anything they'd encountered on Tristesse Lane. Besides, Gina had already warned them about stepping off the path. She wasn't taking any chances.

Beyond there, the water receded back to just along the shoulder of the road. The remains of a rusty barbwire fence was sticking up a few yards offshore, along with a fair number of long-dead trees and a row of leaning utility poles.

Around the next curve, they found a badly sagging barn with its stone foundation almost completely surrounded by water.

"It's like the whole area is slowly sinking," observed Andrea.

"Or the lake is slowly rising," countered Nicole.

"Or that."

"It still feels like layers," observed Gina. "I don't really know how to explain it, but it's like it started as one thing and then, over time, it just kept being added onto."

"That's so weird," said Andrea.

"You said most places like this mimic their surroundings," reasoned Nicole. "Maybe since this place moves around, it borrows elements from different places, every time the gate opens or whatever."

Gina nodded. "It's possible." *Anything* was possible, it seemed.

Andrea pointed up ahead. There was a long-faded sign mostly hidden in the underbrush. "City limits."

"Cedric's Cove," said Nicole, nodding. She couldn't decide if she was more relieved to finally be at the end of this awful journey or anxious about what nightmares they had left to deal with.

Around the next curve, they found it. The weed-choked gravel shoulder became weed-choked sidewalks displaced by many years of weathering from above and root growth from below.

They walked down the middle of the crumbling street, taking it all in. It was strange. Big, brick buildings stood surrounded by lawns completely reclaimed by the forest. Any awnings and flags had long ago rotted to tatters, but there was no litter strewn about. Some signs had fallen down and there was an abundance of bird nests, but there was no vandalism of any kind, no broken windows or graffiti, only the scars of the invading trees. The lake had crept up over some of the streets and buildings in the lower elevations, but there wasn't a single vehicle to be seen. Doors and windows were completely blocked by trees and vines and no foot traffic had worn paths through the overgrown grass. There were street signs and lampposts, benches and flower pots, utility poles and power lines strung from building to building, but no trash cans or mailboxes.

There was something eerie about that utter lack of human activity laid over a modern, man-made cityscape. It was as if some future alien race had tried to recreate the footprints of humankind, but forgot a hundred miniscule details.

"This place is creepy," whined Andrea.

Nicole scanned the rooftops of Cedric's Cove's Main Street and then glanced back at Gina. "Can you feel anything?"

"Like I said, it's just like our world, but very small." Her gaze drifted out toward the lake. "Within a mile or two of here, there's...nothing. And I feel lots of wildlife..." She turned her gaze toward one of the doorways. "And cats," she added, pointing at a longhaired tortoiseshell curled up in the shade there, watching them pass with its big, yellow eyes.

Andrea's face lit up at the sight of it. "Kitty!" She'd always liked cats.

"Lots of them..." she added, looking around. She could only see the one right now, but she could feel them all around her. "...but no people at all."

"There has to be *someone* here," argued Andrea. "We're here to find the Lady of Cedric's Cove, remember?"

But Gina shook her head. "I'm sure there's no one else here."

"So we're alone," said Nicole. On one hand, she could definitely use a break from all the weirdos they'd encountered. But there was something especially eerie about being the only people in an entire city...

"Not necessarily alone," said Gina. She was still looking out toward the partially submerged buildings. "There's *something* here. Something under us. I started feeling them about the time we passed the city limit sign. I don't think they'll bother us if we stay up here, but we should be careful to stay out of the water."

Andrea groaned. Of course there was something here. Why wouldn't there be something to scare them in a place like this?

Nicole scanned their surroundings again, then a thought occurred to her. She took out her cell phone. The battery was nearly depleted and there was no signal, which wasn't surprising, but it still worked. She opened the camera and took some pictures. "If this place really is some lost, wandering city, maybe we should make an effort to bring back some proof."

Gina nodded. "Good idea. My friends would probably appreciate that. They spent a lot of time looking for this place."

"It's the least we can do since they pointed us in the right direction," said Nicole as she turned and aimed her camera down the other side of the street.

Gina glanced around at it all. "I almost feel bad for not bringing them with us, but I couldn't risk putting anyone in unnecessary danger."

"That's what you keep saying."

"The goddess was clear on the matter when she spoke to me."

Nicole continued onward, still snapping pictures as she walked.

The Main Street buildings were mostly two-story shops and businesses, but behind those buildings were taller structures that peeked up over the rooftops. Many of the side streets, however, were under water. It was only as they approached the end of the street where the sidewalks ended and the trees took over that they found an accessible path leading to higher ground.

There was a grocery store with an eerily empty parking lot that was more wilderness than pavement. There was a little restaurant with its roof caved in and a towering pine jutting up out of the gaping ruins. They found a bookshop with no books in the windows, only empty shelves, which Gina found to be especially depressing. And there was some kind of sprawling factory surrounded by a half-collapsed chain-link fence.

There was even a strangely soulless-looking McDonald's half submerged in the invading lake, its bright, cheerful colors faded to shades of sickly brown.

And Gina was right. There were lots of cats. They peered back at them from the shade in alleyways, on concrete steps and from shadowy windowsills. Every now and then one would dart across the street ahead of them. There seemed to be an entire feral population taking advantage of the lack of human activity.

"So we're here," said Nicole as she stared at the rust-streaked shell of a water tower rising from the trees in the distance. "Now what do we do?"

"Yeah," said Andrea. "Where's this Lady of Cedric's Cove?"

But Gina didn't have an answer for them. She knew as much as they did.

"There's nothing else on the spear," said Andrea. She glanced over at Nicole's purse. The spear was inside it again, wrapped in the heavy cloth it first arrived in. It seemed safer in there. Besides, she'd lined up all the notches. All of the markings scratched into its surface had illustrated how to follow the path here. The only thing left was the message about piercing the gatekeeper's heart. There didn't seem to be any point in just waving it around. "We can't be expected to search every building for her."

"There's nobody in any of the buildings," Gina reminded her. "I'd feel them."

Nicole sighed. She was so tired and this seemed like such an enormous task. Cedric's Cove wasn't exactly a metropolis, but it wasn't tiny, either. They'd walked past dozens of buildings, and they hadn't even seen half of it yet.

"I'm not getting any ghostly stuff here," reported Andrea. Even the voice in her head had fallen silent again. Had she left? Was her job done? Or was she merely conserving her energy?

Nicole snapped one more picture of a church steeple looming in the distance and then her cell phone screen went dark. "Well, that's it for my battery. I'd say we're on our own, but I think we've pretty much been off the grid since we left home."

Gina gasped and stiffened. Her sleepy eyes were suddenly wide awake. "Oh no…" she squeaked.

"*What?*" asked Nicole. "*What happened?*"

"He's here."

"Who's here? Glum again? The barely-there?"

"No…" Slowly, she turned to face the building behind them. "*Him.*"

There, standing in the doorway, stood an all-too familiar figure of a man.

"Aw shit," groaned Nicole, exhausted. "Not *Hotdog* again."

Chapter 41

"My name," growled the muscular maniac, "is *Hochog*. Elias *Hochog*."

Nicole shrugged. "Ask me if I care, Sausage Party."

"Where did he come from?" whispered Andrea.

Gina shook her head. "He was just *there*. Like the way he vanished when he stranded us in that hospital. He can move between dimensions somehow."

The man stepped out of the shadows, those glaring gray eyes positively menacing. It was already well established that the guy wasn't right, but this time something was different. There was something *very* wrong about him now.

All three of them took an involuntary step backward.

"Anun Goar Nangup," he snarled at them. His white tee shirt was dirtier than it was before. The entire left side was stained black. His jeans were similarly discolored. He looked like he'd been through an ordeal of his own.

"Nobody knows what that means!" shouted Andrea. She was trying to sound brave, but her heart was pounding. This was the murderous maniac who tried to strangle her, after all. And who sent them to that God-forsaken hospital. She swallowed hard and then managed to add, "Is that supposed to be, like, Klingon or something? You some kind of Trekkie nerd?"

"No…" His voice was strange. He practically hissed the word at them. It had an unearthly sort of quality about it that didn't sound quite human. "*You* wouldn't know Him… You're not *worthy* to know His name…" He was still walking toward them, slowly closing the distance between them. That wrongness only increased as he approached. There was a strange stiffness in his walk. His left arm looked injured. And there was something about one of those gray eyes. It looked swollen. "Only *I* am worthy to know Him..."

"*Okay...*" croaked Nicole, taking another step backward. "I think Wiener Dude's officially gone to the special sausage factory with all the padded rooms."

Gina nodded. "Agreed."

"Mm-hm," squeaked Andrea.

The lunatic was still stalking toward them, getting closer with each stiff step. His left eye wasn't merely swollen. It appeared to be bulging from his face. Had he suffered some kind of stroke since they last saw him?

"He wasn't very happy with me for letting you escape..." he hissed. "Not very happy at all. He had to punish me *severely*."

Again, they stepped backward. There appeared to be blisters on his bare arm, now that they could see him better. The skin there was discolored. And his clothes didn't just look dirty. They looked partially *burned*.

"Who's 'he'?" asked Nicole.

"The Patient One," he replied in that awful, hissing voice. "He Who Waits. *Goar Nangup.*"

"Right..." recalled Andrea. "He said that stuff when he had his filthy hands around my neck."

"What, like some kind of god or something?"

"The *only* god!"

"And he did *that* to you?" pressed Nicole. The closer he came, the more wrong he looked. Especially that awful, bulging eye. It looked as if something was pushing against the back of it, something *inside his head.* "Because he sounds like kind of a dick."

"I disappointed him," he bemoaned, and there was such deep anguish in his voice this that it gave Andrea a chill to hear the words come out of his mouth. "I deserved *worse!*"

"Can we run?" whispered Andrea.

"*I* sure as fuck can," replied Nicole. She was backing away faster now, ready to run for it.

But Gina understood what she was asking: "He's not hiding any weapons. But we can't underestimate him. He looks injured, but he's still very dangerous."

"All the more reason to stay as far away from this freak as possible," said Nicole. "Go!"

The three of them turned and fled, darting down the first side-street and out of view as quickly as possible. Dangerous or not, he didn't look like he was in any shape to pursue them. If they could just put some distance between themselves and him, maybe they could find somewhere to hide.

Andrea looked back over her shoulder. "He's not following us!" But as soon as she looked forward again, the maniac limped out of a shop doorway ahead of them, blocking their path.

"Goar Nangup was there in the beginning," he informed them. "And He will be there in the end."

They turned and ran back the other way. "What the *fuck*?" panted Nicole. "Hotdog can teleport, too?"

"He must be able to pass between different points in the *same* dimension as well," said Gina.

"*Obviously!*"

"He gave me this power," he shouted down at them from a second-floor window as they passed beneath him. "What has any other so-called 'God' ever given?"

"Is he trying to kill or convert us?" gasped Andrea.

"Either way, I'm not buying!" shouted Nicole.

Gina was trying to follow his movements, but it was hard. "He just keeps disappearing and reappearing all around us. I don't know how long we can stay away from him."

This was insane. Now they were dealing with a *teleporting* murderer? Andrea couldn't decide whether she wanted to scream, cry or laugh.

Although, thinking about it, she supposed that *did* explain how he was able to surprise her outside the clubhouse after the reception. She was cross at herself for letting her guard down and allowing him to catch her off guard. If he could do this trick the whole time, then she sort of felt a little better about that. He was clearly cheating.

They cut across the sidewalk and ran down the next street.

"He gets what He wants!" Hochog shouted at them from the rooftop. "He *always* gets what He wants. You can't beat

Him."

There was a small city park ahead of them on the left that was half-submerged in the rising lake water. There was rusty playground equipment jutting out from the stagnant surface. As they ran past, a large waterfowl was startled into flight. And there was something about the scene that felt very surreal to Andrea. Something about the way the sunlight sparkled off the flying water drops and the racing ripples on the still surface. A literal splash of the natural world surrounded by an unnatural not-quite-right landscape that was somehow man-made and yet simultaneously untouched by man.

There was still no litter to be seen, not even in the water. There was driftwood and lake foam. There were fallen branches lying everywhere, but no plastic or aluminum or glass to be seen. Andrea couldn't help being surprised at the fact that the absence of *trash* could feel so utterly *wrong*.

"Everything is going to end!" Hochog shouted from behind them. "Nothing can stop it! Not us! Not the *Keeper of Lies*! It's inevitable! *He* is inevitable!"

The buildings on the far side of the park were also flooded, their foundations completely surrounded. The sidewalk in front of them and on the left side of the street were also under water.

Andrea didn't bother veering around it. It obviously wasn't very deep if the right side of the street was still above water. And it was only about twenty yards across.

But Gina grabbed her arm and halted her before she reached it. "Don't go in the water!"

She stood at the water's edge, her thoughts racing, and watched as something she couldn't quite make out moved beneath the surface, churning up mud and silt in its wake. "Right..." she gasped. She warned them that there were things in the water. "Bad water... I forgot..."

"The universe..." said Hochog from right behind them, startling screams from all of them.

They spun around to face him. He was only a few yards away, limping toward them, that gross, bulging eyeball making him look every bit as insane as the nonsense he was spouting sounded.

"*Every* universe..." he stressed. "Everything that was ever created..." He shook his head and grimaced, as if just thinking about all the things that existed disgusted him. "*Mistakes*," he spat. "Garbage. *Filth*."

They were backing away from him, careful to skirt along the edge of the water. The other side of the street was still dry. They weren't trapped yet.

"It never should've existed," he went on. "It's nothing but pain. Misery. *Rot*."

Nicole turned and fled. "This way!"

"You know it's true!" he shouted after them. "You've been to Tristesse Lane! You've seen for yourself what's left when you peel away the lies people use to mask the ugly truth!"

"Crazy Hotdog Guy's pulling out the deep philosophy now," panted Andrea. She could barely believe this was the same man who made her swoon at the reception. Did she really think, even for a moment, that *that thing* was attractive? Just thinking about that night made her feel sick.

"He's a complete whack-job!" decided Nicole.

There was an open manhole in the street ahead of them, its cover lying next to the curb several yards away as if something very strong had simply tossed it aside. Something splashed in the black water beneath it as they approached, startling Nicole and making her give it a wide berth.

"What's down there?" she gasped.

"I don't think we want to know," replied Gina. She couldn't tell what they looked like, but she could feel a great many eyes on them. They were peering out from storm drains and basement windows, lurking unseen in the stagnant depths. They wouldn't leave the water. Not in the daylight. But she sensed very strongly that they'd claim anything foolish enough to set foot in their domain.

"I don't like it here!" whimpered Andrea. "Total one-star review of this town!"

"I don't think Cedric's Cove has a Yelp page," said Nicole.

"Well it *should*!"

Gina grabbed them each by the arm and jerked them to a stop again.

Hochog was suddenly in front of them, sneering at them.

A sleek ginger cat in the nearby doorway arched its back and hissed at him, its tail puffed up, then fled down the street and disappeared.

Andrea stared at him as she backed away. Was it her imagination, or did he look even worse than he did when he first appeared? That one bulging eye was glazed over. That blistered arm looked even more discolored. There were great purple blotches on his neck that she was pretty sure weren't there before.

"Don't you understand?" he asked, his voice strangely calm, almost pleading. "Can't you see the whole picture?" He lifted his good arm and opened his hand toward them, as if he were offering them a truce instead of more of his crazy babbling. *"No one knew pain when He was free."*

"This is bad," whispered Gina. "We need to lose this guy."

"Yes, please," squeaked Andrea.

"Give Him the package," he said in that awful, hissing voice. "Help Him end all that pain."

Chapter 42

Nicole tugged at Gina's hand and ran toward the open doorway of a nearby shop. She'd wanted to avoid the buildings. She didn't like the idea of being trapped inside one. But they couldn't seem to get away from the psychopathic sausage outside. Maybe being out in the open was the wrong course of action. Maybe they were too easy to track.

But as she ducked into the gloomy interior and ran past the empty racks and shelves, she immediately began to fear that this was a terrible idea. What if they cornered themselves in a storage room somewhere?

What if this was exactly what Hotdog wanted them to do?

She glanced back, but he wasn't following them. He was standing right where they left him, staring back at her through the dirty window, his one good eye seemingly fixed on her.

She headed for a doorway in the back. There should be a rear exit. It was basic fire safety code. But it was darker the farther into the building they went. There was no electricity and no lights. And their cell phones were both dead.

She shoved her hand down into her purse as the light from the front windows faded and rummaged for the disposable cigarette lighter she still kept in there. (She quit smoking around the same time Brandy did, but she still kept a lighter in there out of habit because it was handy for more than just bad habits. Like now, for example.) It didn't put out much light, but it was enough to find their way down the short hallway, past a small restroom and a cramped office, into a much larger storage room where all the shelves were as empty as the sales racks in the store.

It was like the lack of vehicles on the street outside. This store looked deserted, but that wasn't exactly right because there was never anyone to abandon it. It was never a real store. No one ever owned or operated it. It never had anything inside it to begin with. It was very possible, she realized, that they were the first human beings to ever even set foot inside it.

What was this place, anyway? Who built it? Why?

Was Cedric's Cove even really a city?

Nicole shoved open the back door and stepped back out into the blinding day. They were in the alleyway between the buildings. Two cats were lounging in the cool shade, watching them, apparently unbothered by the noise, but Hotdog was nowhere to be seen. Maybe this was the key to losing the weirdo after all.

She tried the door on the other side of the alley and found it unlocked. They could slip through here, out the other side and then dart into another building, weaving in and out until they completely lost the lunatic's trail.

At least, that was the best plan she could think of at the moment.

"Where is he?" she whispered as she closed the door behind them and lifted the lighter again.

"He hasn't moved."

"What?"

"He's still standing right where we left him."

"What's he playing at?" wondered Nicole as she made her way toward the light of the front windows of whatever false business they were trespassing in.

"He's got to be up to something," decided Andrea.

"Definitely," agreed Gina.

As they ventured into the light, they found themselves in some kind of café. There were tables and chairs neatly arranged around the dining room, collecting dust and cobwebs. But just like everywhere else in this town, there were things missing. There were no menus in sight. No napkins. No salt and pepper shakers.

But there was also no Hotdog, which was all that really mattered.

As they approached the front door, however, Gina gasped and looked back.

Nicole and Andrea turned to look.

"He's gone again."

"Where'd he go?"

There was a loud knock on the door behind them, startling more screams out of them.

"You can't beat Him!" shouted Hotdog through the glass. "He is the only choice! Everything else is *suffering!*"

"No soliciting, asshole!" shouted Nicole as she backed away from the door.

He fixed his gaze on her and asked, "Do you *like* suffering?" Then he vanished, evaporated into thin air before their eyes.

In the same instant, a strong hand clamped down on her shoulder. "Then *suffer*," he whispered into her ear.

She screamed, terrified, and tore herself free of his grip. But when she turned to defend herself, Hotdog was gone. Andrea and Gina were gone. And she was no longer inside the empty café.

She was in a terrifyingly familiar hospital hallway.

"Oh no…" she breathed, her heart sinking. "No, no, no… Oh no…" She turned around, then turned again, scanning her surroundings. "Oh, God no…"

This wasn't happening. It *couldn't* be happening. She couldn't be back here again. She barely escaped with her life last time. She barely escaped with her *soul!* There was no way she could do it again! Not by herself!

She was still turning in a circle, still trying to convince herself that it wasn't real, that this wasn't happening again.

But it *was* happening. She was here. And this time she was all alone.

She needed to stay calm and think.

The spear. The spear was the way out. Maybe if she could just find that room with all the beds again… If she tried to do what Andrea did…

But when she reached for her purse, it was gone.

She'd lost it.

"No…"

Did Hotdog steal it when he dumped her in this place? Did he finally get what he was after?

Panic was quickly overwhelming her. She couldn't help it. It felt like there was a fire burning deep inside her belly. Her heart was racing. She couldn't quite catch her breath. She felt dizzy. Her chest hitched with the force of a terrified sob and tears welled up in her eyes.

"Oh god, oh god, oh god, oh god, oh god…"

It wasn't fair…

It *wasn't*!

Chapter 43

"*Where did she go?*" shrieked Andrea.

But Gina didn't know. She couldn't feel her *anywhere*. One second she was right there beside them, the next she was just gone. It happened so quickly, she didn't even have time to react.

All that was left was her lighter, lying on the floor where she was standing, dropped the moment she was grabbed.

"Nikki!" She ran back to the gloomy hallway. "*Nikki!*"

Gina turned and scanned the room around them. She felt him for just a second or two when he took her, too brief a time for her to react, then disappeared completely, along with Nicole. Was he only toying with them that whole time? Was he looking for the perfect opportunity to spirit one of them away? She should have been more alert. How could she let this happen?

Andrea pushed open the back door and squinted into the sunlit alleyway. "Nikki!"

"We have to stay together!" Gina called after her as she hurried to catch up.

She turned and hurried back to the dining room, passing her in the hallway. "Where is she?"

"I don't know. I can't feel her anymore." This was bad. She'd never encountered anyone who could move around like this before. And it wasn't just the way he moved. He seemed to be able to make himself appear anywhere he wanted, with startling precision. He was able to snatch Nicole away before she had time to warn anyone. Worse still, it seemed like he was able to track them. He could be right behind either of them in an instant.

She couldn't understand it. If he had the ability to do that all along, why did he waste all that time trying to trick them into trusting him? Why stand there shouting all that nonsense about his awful god at them?

Something about all this didn't make sense.

Andrea rushed across the room and looked out at the empty street outside. "We have to find her!"

"I know," said Gina. She took hold of her hand and squeezed. "But we have to stay together. Don't let him surprise us again."

"This is so frustrating." She wiped at her eyes with her free hand. "I don't even know what we're doing!"

"That seems to be how these things work."

"Where is he now?"

"I don't know. Not here. I can't feel him anywhere."

"Do you think he's with her?" Andrea looked out the window again. "Could he be hurting her right now?"

Gina didn't answer that. She didn't know, after all. Not for sure. All she knew for certain was that she wasn't here in Cedric's Cove anymore and neither was he. She *hoped* he just took her somewhere to separate them, maybe sent her back to the real world. Or at least back to All Trails Crossing. But he was clearly quite insane. He could easily be doing horrible things to her while they stood here trying to decide what to do next. And with no idea where they could have gone and no way to leave Cedric's Cove's bizarre little pocket dimension even if she knew where they'd gone, they had virtually no chance of saving her.

"Nikki..." sighed Andrea.

It was all so frustratingly unfair. Why did they have to deal with something like Hochog? Did the goddess really think she could handle him? Sure, she'd been able to see through his psychic mind tricks, but between the teleporting and his blatant craziness, he was utterly unpredictable.

But she couldn't just give up. "We have to keep moving," she said, as much to herself as to Andrea. "Stay alert. Don't let him surprise us again. We just...finish what we came here to do." She stood up a little straighter and tried to sound encouraging. "Find the Lady of Cedric's Cove. Maybe...maybe she can make everything right."

"I don't think we can," sighed Andrea. She turned and met her gaze. Tears were sliding down her cheeks. "We lost the spear. Nikki had it, remember? And he has *her*."

Gina stood staring back at her for a moment, her heart sinking. She was right. Nicole was carrying the spear in her purse. And they still needed it. It wasn't just to show them the path to Cedric's Cove. They were supposed to pierce the gatekeeper's heart with it...whatever that meant...

Was that why he took Nicole instead of one of them?

The idea that he'd merely spirited her away somewhere and killed her seemed all the more likely now.

And if he really did have the spear... Could that be why she couldn't sense him anymore? Now that he had what he wanted, did he just leave them here?

Thinking about it, they still didn't know what the spear was ultimately for. Was it possible they needed it to leave this place? Were they trapped here now?

"I think your goddess might've screwed up. She never should've sent it to me." She turned and looked out at that eerily silent street again. "And I never should've picked it up. If I'd just run away from it, then maybe she..." She couldn't finish the sentence. The words lodged somewhere in her throat.

But Gina shook her head. "No. That's not how it works. I told you, there were lots of things at that wedding that didn't belong there. They were watching. Taking possession of the spear probably saved your life. Nikki's too. You can't just ignore things like that. There are consequences." She reached out and took her other hand. "And I keep telling you, the goddess knows what she's doing. I've seen it before. It happened with my friends in Wisconsin. And you've seen it too. Down in that temple you told me about. Things seem impossible but they always work out. One way or another. You can't give up hope. Not yet."

Andrea closed her eyes and took a deep breath. She was right, of course. But it was so hard. And she was so afraid right now.

"Let's keep searching the town," said Gina. "Before he comes back. The Lady of Cedric's Cove must be here somewhere."

The front door was unlocked, just like the back door. She supposed it made sense. What would be the point in locking up a building with nothing in it in a city with no people? She stepped back out into the sunshine, her strange senses wide open for anything that shouldn't be there, and squinted down the empty street in both directions.

She might have liked it here if not for those unsettling things in the sewers. The idea of having an entire city all to herself wasn't unappealing. There were so few places in the world where she could truly be alone, after all. She'd rarely laid her head down at night without the presence of other people looming inside her brain. Knowing exactly where they were...what they were doing...and all too often what they were capable of. She learned at a young age the harsh truth of the world: that the capacity for human cruelty wasn't as rare as books and movies made it out to be and true kindness was the exception, rather than the norm.

The world was rotten. And it always had been.

But that didn't mean there weren't good people out there. Her roommates back in Wisconsin were good examples. And Violet and Corey, without whom they probably never would've found their way here. And of course Andrea and Nicole. They were good people, too.

She squeezed Andrea's hand again. She hadn't dared let go of her. And she *wouldn't* let go of her. She wasn't going to lose her, too. "Stay close. Don't let go of me."

Andrea nodded. She didn't want to leave the café. It felt like giving up on Nicole. But it wasn't like standing around in there was going to bring her back. And if that lunatic came back, that was probably the first place he'd look for them.

"We should make our way north," decided Gina. "Toward the lake. The flooded areas. We haven't been there yet."

"Because you told us to stay out of the water..."

"Sometimes the things you're looking for are in the last places you want to go."

Andrea frowned. "I guess so..." She didn't like it, but she

nodded. "Okay. I trust you."

The two of them set off again, and Gina sent a silent prayer to any God, god or "god" who might be willing to listen, that she didn't let anyone else down today.

Chapter 44

It was the northwest section of the city that was the most flooded. The streets there were completely submerged and the buildings had turned into islands, separated from each other by surprisingly clear lake water. The lowest buildings at the far end of the street were so sunken that only the tops of the doorways were visible above the surface. It was surreal to look at, Andrea thought. And creepy. Like some kind of dystopian movie setting. And somehow that complete lack of litter in the water still only made it look that much *more* surreal.

She wasn't sure how Gina thought they were going to get over there. It wasn't going to be possible to even approach most of those buildings without going into the water, which she already warned wasn't an option.

Even the cats seemed to be avoiding this part of the city.

"Do you feel anything?" asked Gina as they followed the waterline to the northeast.

Andrea glanced at her, confused. "Me? I don't think so… Should I?"

"I don't know. Maybe not. But since the spear was given to you, I was thinking that maybe the Lady of Cedric's Cove can only be found with your specific abilities."

She looked out over the flooded city. "I don't think I've felt anything since we got here. This place is completely dead." Then she frowned. "A *different* kind of dead, I guess?" This was all so confusing. It didn't make any sense to her. If she was so sensitive to spirits, then why was she only finding out about it now? Sure, she was only twenty-two, but that seemed to her like plenty of time to find out she had crazy *ghost powers*.

Ghosts…

A thought occurred to her then. What if she suddenly heard Nicole's voice speaking to her like that?

No. That was more than she could deal with. She couldn't think like that.

Nicole would be fine. She was one of the strongest people she knew. She'd come back to them no matter what. She was *certain* of it.

But she was certain of no such thing and she knew it. It was hard to lie to herself when tears kept welling up in her eyes…

Gina approached the windows of a building that was only partially submerged in the lake and peeked inside. This one appeared to have been an office of some kind. There was a waiting room and a receptionist's desk inside. But it was otherwise as dark and gloomy and empty as all the rest. "A lot of these buildings aren't safe," she warned. "Bad floors. Water damage."

"And those things in the water? Whatever they are?"

"The basements are like underwater dens." Her sleepy gaze drifted down to the dusty floorboards. "They gather down there. It's where they sleep. Where they drag their food down to eat it. And it's where they breed."

She shivered at the repulsive thought. "Gross…"

"Yes." She turned and scanned the buildings around them. "I can still feel the layout of my surroundings. I know which buildings have roof access. We might be able to see more from up high."

"Do you think that'd help?"

"Probably not."

Andrea wrinkled her nose. She definitely didn't like that plan, then.

"Honestly, I have no idea what to do." She turned and looked back the way they came. Her usually sleepy face was unusually tight. Her lips were pinched. Her eyes weren't teary, but they were misty. "My brain's telling me no one's here but us, so I don't know how to find the Lady of Cedric's Cove. But finding her is the only thing I know to do. It's why we're here. I'm really scared right now."

Andrea gave her hand a reassuring squeeze. "That's okay.

Me too."

"I'm sorry. I'm trying really hard."

"I know. We'll figure it out. I'm sure we will." And she almost believed it. It was, after all, no crazier than what she did five years ago. Crossing into another world… Encountering actual monsters… Surviving that terrifying fall… Walking with the dead on their final journey… Opening portals and saving her friends… This time was a lot like that. She'd crossed into *several* new worlds, encountered entirely *different* monsters, and conversed with the dead on a whole new level. She was stronger than she realized. But she was still so scared for Nicole…

She couldn't shake the feeling that it was her fault. Why did she let her carry the spear? She shouldn't have burdened her with it. It was *her* responsibility. It was given to *her*. If she'd been carrying it, would Hotdog have taken her, instead and left Nicole alone?

Gina rubbed her eyes and took a shaky breath. "Thanks… I'm sorry."

"Don't be."

"I'm feeling really tired…"

"Yeah, we've kind of been going nonstop for four days or something, apparently."

"Oh yeah…"

Andrea squeezed her hand again. "It's like you said. We just have to find this Lady of Cedric's Cove. Whoever she is…" She kept wondering that. Who *was* she? Why was it so important that they find her? And could she really help them get Nicole back? At this point, it seemed that all she could do was hope.

Gina stiffened and looked back the way they came. "Oh no…"

"What's wrong?" she gasped.

"He's back."

"Hotdog?" In an instant, her heart was hammering again. "Where?"

"Back in that building where we were when he took Nikki." Then her gaze shifted. "Now he's outside." She creased her brow as her eyes flitted from one point to another. "He's jumping around. I think he's looking for us. We need to hide." She tugged at her hand and hurried down the street, past the office, past the next building, then turned down the next street, where the water was up over the pavement but the slightly higher sidewalks remained dry for a hundred feet or so. "There," she said, pointing to a doorway ahead of them. "That building. I don't feel any of those water things in there. And there are multiple exits. If it's possible to hide from him, we might be able to do it in there."

But the words had barely crossed her lips when she gasped and looked up at the roofline across the street. "Oh no..." she squeaked.

Andrea followed her gaze and her heart sank.

Hotdog was there, staring down at them.

"What do we do?" she whispered.

But Gina didn't have an answer. All she could do was shake her head.

Again, it wasn't fair. He'd lost sight of them for a little bit. That should've been their chance to get away from him. But he'd already found them. Did he have some kind of psychic power similar to Gina's in addition to his stupid teleporting trick? And now that he knew where they were, there was nowhere they could run to escape him.

She gripped Gina's hand as tightly as she could and backed away, pressing her back against the brick wall of the building behind them. It was the only thing she could think of. Preventing him from getting behind them like he did when he took Nicole.

"Where is it?" he shouted down at them.

Andrea stared up at him, confused. Where was it? Where was *what*?

Then he was gone from the rooftop. He didn't disappear, exactly. It was difficult for her to wrap her head around what was happening when he did that. For a moment, he seemed to be gone. But strangely enough, at the same moment, he also seemed to be in two places at once. Then, before she was even fully aware that anything had happened, he was standing on the sidewalk opposite them, glaring at them with that one good eye.

Gina let out a startled whimper and crowded closer to her.

Hotdog lifted his good arm. Gripped in his fist was Nicole's purse.

The sight of it made her stomach roll over. She felt like she was going to vomit. "What did you do with Nikki?" she croaked, her voice cracking.

"*Where is it?*" he shouted again. Even from across the street, she could see the veins standing up on his muscular neck. His face was flushed with fury.

He turned the purse upside down and let the contents spill out onto the sidewalk at his feet. There wasn't much inside. There was some makeup, lip balm, gum, a couple pens and a handful of change as well as some earbuds and her wallet. Nicole had cleaned it out before they left, leaving important things like her credit cards and car keys at home so she wouldn't lose them—exactly like the lunatic was demonstrating right now—and making room for the spear.

Except there wasn't a spear.

Andrea stared at the scattered items at the man's feet, a hurricane of feelings churning inside her. Nicole. Her stolen purse. Her disrespected belongings. The missing spear. And of course the enraged lunatic who literally had them with their backs against the wall.

He took a step toward them. "Tell me where you hid it," he growled.

Her gaze dropped to Hotdog's foot. He was so close to the water's edge...

Did he not know about the things in the water?

Her mind was racing now. What if they could trick him into stepping into the water? Would the things in there take care of him for them?

"*Tell me!*"

"Go to hell," said Andrea. She was trying to sound confident, but her voice betrayed her and cracked. It came out in a clearly terrified creak.

Hotdog literally snarled at them, his lips peeled back, barring his teeth like some kind of wild animal. The look was so menacing, so overflowing with raw fury that it made her blood run cold.

But he took the next step.

His foot splashed into the water as he stalked toward them.

She almost laughed. He actually did it. He actually stepped into the water. He did what Gina warned them not to do for any reason. He was in the territory of the things in the water, now. How stupid could he possibly be?

Except...nothing happened.

He stalked toward them, splashing his way through the water, his face still twisted into that hideous snarl.

And why *would* anything happen? The water was only ankle deep. What kind of terrifying, man-eating abomination could lurk undetected in three inches of water?

Her heart sank. Boiling dread settled deep inside her belly. So much for that last-ditch prayer. All that was left to do was run.

But he wasn't going to let them do that again. He crossed the first third of the flooded street and then he was suddenly right in front of them. One powerful hand closed around each of their throats and the backs of their heads slammed against the brick hard enough to send stars dancing across their vision.

"*WHERE IS IT?*" he screamed at them.

Andrea struggled against the maniac's grip, but it was just as it was that night in the country club parking lot. It was like struggling against a machine. How strong could one man really be?

Was he ever really a man at all...?

Beside her, Gina was struggling as well. She was beating against his blistered arm, trying to make him loosen his grip, but it was like that first time. He didn't seem capable of feeling pain.

But in that hallway, he'd sure been able to feel pain. When she and Nicole kicked him where it was always supposed to hurt. Was that his weak spot?

As the world began to dim around her, she gathered as much strength as she could and thrust her knee into Hotdog's...well, hotdog. But to no avail. That one murderous eye didn't even twitch as he glared back at her.

Was that all just an act back there in that hallway? A clever ruse to make them think they could cause him harm?

"Anun amum ut mu," he spat at her. "Anun Goar Nangup. I am Him. He is me. Do you think a little girl like you can really hurt a *god*?"

Little girl? Why did everyone keep treating her like a child? She was twenty-two, dammit! But she couldn't form the words to tell him so. She could feel the strength leaving her body. She was going to pass out soon. And the moment she was unconscious, it was going to be over. He'd either murder her, or she'd wake up somewhere terrible, *wishing* she were dead.

Beside her, Gina's struggling was becoming weaker, too. She was fading.

They didn't have much time.

"This is the last time I ask you," he growled. He leaned closer to Andrea, that bulging eyeball looming right in front of her face. "Where is it?"

She had only an instant to register the shape sliding through the water behind him. It was little more than a bulge on the surface, like the ominous shape of an alligator gliding just beneath the surface of a murky swamp. Then something large and slimy closed around Hotdog's face.

He let out a terrible scream and released his grip.

Andrea and Gina both collapsed onto the ground, clutching at their throats and gasping for air.

Before them, Hotdog was being dragged backward into the water by several...*things*. They looked like some hideous cross between a human, a frog and some kind of freaky deep-sea fish, with slimy, greenish-black skin, bulbous black eyes and huge, needle-like teeth.

In spite of how shallow the water was, more were rising out of it with every passing second. They started off flat, like an empty skin, and then swelled like an inflating balloon as they stood.

She stared at the awful things swarming the screaming maniac, her heart filled with dread, terrified at the concept of being dragged away like that.

They were already sinking their needle teeth into his arms and legs. Strange and terrible... Like...some kind of...*pufferfish monsters*? Or something? Was the momentary lack of oxygen making her woozy or was this really just too much to wrap her poor, aching head around?

Then Gina was pulling her to her feet. "We have to run!"

Of course they did. She rose to her feet, still coughing, and stumbled after her.

When she looked back one last time, Hotdog had vanished again. And terrible, fish-like monstrosities were crawling out of the water and lurching after them.

Chapter 45

Nicole needed to stay calm. She needed to think. There might still be a way out. Even without the spear. For instance, it was possible the doorway leading out of here was still open.

It wasn't *likely*. But anything was possible. Right? She just had to find that room. The one they only found because of Andrea's ability to communicate with the dead...

She buried her face in her hands and took a deep, shuddering breath.

It wasn't fair. She'd escaped this place once already. She thought she was done with it. But here she was again. And the truth was that she wasn't going *anywhere*.

Every door she opened was either a patient room or a storage closet. Did she have any chance at all of finding that same office? Especially before that soul-stealing monster found *her*? She had no such abilities, after all. Gina and the Sentinel Queen had both told her as much.

She rubbed her eyes and then turned and looked down the endless corridor behind her. She could see the doors way down at the far end, just like she could see the ones ahead of her, but she knew that beyond all of those doors were only more hallways just like this one. How far did it stretch? She could be a thousand miles from where they were before. Or she could simply be going nowhere at all. Gina said that distance and direction were little more than illusions here. Every room she peered into looked just a little different from the others, but that might not mean they were different rooms. It could be like Tristesse Lane and Glimmering Sunrise Place, where all the doors were only illusions and all led to the same place. For all she knew, she might be opening the same three or four over and over again and walking in circles.

Hotdog had really screwed her over this time.

She leaned against the wall, exhausted. This might be it for her. There was a very real chance she wasn't going to be able to get out of this one. She hoped Andrea and Gina were safe, that the lunatic was happy now that he finally had his stupid creeper hands on the spear. But she didn't really think he'd be satisfied with that. He was a sociopath, after all. He probably wouldn't be sated until all three of them were dead.

She closed her eyes and sighed.

That blue nightmare version of her apartment... The emotional torture of Tristesse Lane... And even here in this place, when that monster had its shadowy, skeletal claws wrapped around her... She rubbed absently at the bandages wrapped around her wrist at the memory. It wasn't Andrea or Gina who helped her escape those places. Someone else was involved.

And she *really* hated it.

She opened her eyes and cursed under her breath. "Keith?" She looked one way, then the other, from one end of the stupid, ridiculously repeating hallway to the other. It was so eerily quiet here. "Are you here? Because..." She clenched her teeth. Why did it have to be *him*? "Because I really need your help again."

But Keith didn't answer her.

Was it even really him? The first time, she thought it was just a hallucination. Like the way she thought the barely-there was Albert. (God, how mortifying!) And when he gave her that needed push through the portal Hotdog opened in Tristesse Lane, she thought she only imagined that the voice was his. There was so much going on, after all. And even the third time, when he freed her from the hospital monster and shoved her through the portal, she wasn't certain. She never saw him those last two times. She only heard his voice and felt his touch. Maybe it wasn't really him.

"Anybody?" she tried.

But no one answered her.

Maybe three was all she got. Maybe she'd already used up all her get-out-of-jail-free cards.

She groaned and slid down the wall until she was sitting on the floor. She propped her arms on her knees and buried her face there.

"This fucking sucks."

She hated feeling so helpless. It was awful.

She lifted her head, her eyes suddenly wide. The hair on her arms and neck were standing up. Something was coming. Even without any special powers she could feel it.

She sprang to her feet, her heart hammering in her breast.

"No…" she whimpered. "No, no, no, no, no… Not now… Not yet…"

She couldn't describe what it was she was sensing. It wasn't something she heard or felt, beyond that prickly, icy sensation on her skin. It was more of a primal instinct sort of thing. A primitive sense of approaching danger. And it wasn't the first time she'd felt it. It was the same feeling she had in that room with the portal…

Her gaze was drawn to the doorway she'd been walking toward, the one at the nearer end of the hallway. It had suddenly grown much darker behind the glass there. Creeping shadows seemed to be slithering through the cracks beneath and between the doors.

A sob forced its way up from deep inside her, expelled from her like a hiccup.

She wasn't ready. Not yet. She needed to run.

But there was nowhere to go. There were only two options. She could run straight down the hallway, passing through doorway after doorway into more and more stupid, repeating hallways until she collapsed from exhaustion. Or she could duck into one of the patient rooms and try to hide, very likely only to end up trapped with no way out, backed into a literal corner.

Those doors were already creaking open. She could hear the faint voices of the tormented souls crying out from those oozing shadows.

"Oh my god…" She was backing away, too afraid to take her eyes off it. She didn't want to go out like this. She didn't want to be trapped in this place forever with that thing. "Somebody please help me... Please..."

She didn't have time to run *or* to hide. She didn't have time to take so much as a step.

The thing came at her at an impossible speed. A great, boiling wall of muddy blackness filled with skeletal hands and the tortured screams of the dead.

She shielded her face and screamed.

Her friends were what went through her head in those final moments. Andrea. Gina. Brandy and Albert. Olivia and Wayne. They'd all been through so much together. It seemed unfair that she had to reach her end alone.

She screamed for a long time.

Chapter 46

The creatures that crawled out of the water were the things of absolute nightmares...but they were surprisingly slow on dry land. Even as more and more of them rose from the waters, inflating like cheap Halloween decorations from *actual hell*, Gina was able to use her otherworldly senses to lead them safely away from the nightmarish fish people and into the safety of a dry building.

They were now hiding in a stifling third-floor hallway of an office building that had never seen a single time clock punched or heard a single sexist joke uttered over the water cooler.

"Is he dead?" whispered Andrea when she'd caught her breath enough to speak. She was sitting on the floor with her back to the wall. She was sweating. It was way too hot in here. All the summer heat was collecting on this upper floor.

But Gina shook her head. "He disappeared again almost as soon as we ran away. I think he got away from them."

"Seriously? God, I hate that guy!"

"Yeah. Me too." She wiped at the sweat running down her face. "Are you okay?"

"I'm fine. You?"

She rubbed at her bruised throat and nodded. "Don't worry about me." She turned and peered through the doorway next to her. There were several offices up here, most of them broken up into cramped cubicles. There was a window in there, overlooking the alley behind the building. "There're fire escapes," she reported. "They're safe. And there are stairs at both ends of this hallway. As soon as I feel him appear again, we should have multiple exit points to choose from."

"Except he always seems to know right where we are

somehow," grumbled Andrea.

"I don't understand it. I feel like he shouldn't have that kind of ability. It's like there's something giving away our position."

"There's a *lot* about that guy *I* don't understand." She still couldn't wrap her head around why he bothered saving them from Tristesse Lane if all he wanted was to kill them. And after he pulled them out of there, why did he try to convince them he was trying to help them? He must've known there was no way they'd trust him after he tried to *strangle her*. He seemed quite desperate to get his hands on the spear. He'd already proven that he was more than willing to kill them, so wouldn't it have been simpler to just pull a gun on them and kill them all while he had them trapped? (Not that she was complaining, of course.) None of it made any sense to her.

Gina wiped at her forehead and then leaned hear head back against the wall behind her. "He had Nikki's purse," she recalled, "but not the spear. It seems like he really thinks we know where it is."

"But we don't!"

"I know. I don't understand it. It's possible she was able to hide it somewhere before he could get his hands on it."

Andrea grimaced. "I *really* hope she's okay."

"Me too. But right now, we have to stay ready. As long as that man is alive, we can be certain he won't stop coming after us."

"Maybe those things hurt him bad enough that he died as soon as he teleported out of there?"

"That would be ideal, yes. But we can't count on it." She turned and looked down the gloomy hallway. "He didn't come back immediately. That could mean at the very least that he's hurt pretty bad. Either that, or he's up to something new…"

Andrea chewed her lower lip. "Do you think we could kill him?"

This surprised her. Those sleepy eyes widened at the suggestion.

"I mean, he's obviously a total psycho, right?" she gasped. "You said yourself he isn't going to stop. I mean we… We may *have to.*"

"You're not wrong," she agreed. "I'm just not sure we're any match for him. He's definitely a lot stronger than me."

Andrea stood up and glanced around. She lifted her shirt and wiped at her sweaty face with it, flashing her bellybutton ring and bra in the process. "We just need a weapon, right? If we can just surprise him…"

Gina stared up at her for a moment. "Um… There's nothing in any of these buildings, though."

She wiped the sweat from her neck and glanced around. "There must be *something*."

"Everything in this town is hollow. There's just basic furnishings."

She made a face at the empty hallway as she fanned her sweaty belly with her shirt. "Well that's just stupid."

"Sorry."

Andrea stepped into the office and looked around. She was right, after all. There wasn't any merchandise in any of the stores, only bare shelves and empty clothing racks. She hadn't seen any tools or cleaning supplies. The only things in *this* room were desks and chairs. There wasn't so much as a pen lying around. Maybe if she broke something? All she really needed was a club… Although thinking about it, Gina might have been right. They were both on the small side and Hotdog was a brute. Would either of them really have the strength necessary to bludgeon someone like him? Even if they both attacked him at once, they probably wouldn't be able to overpower him. Plus he had supernatural powers and was quite possibly possessed…

"There aren't even any fire extinguishers," observed Gina.

"*Seriously?*" Her dad would totally freak if he heard that. That was a serious safety violation, even if there weren't any people here to get hurt in a fire.

"There are a lot of things wrong here. The wiring in the walls is just *weird*, like it was done by someone who had no idea what house wiring even looked like. I don't think anything would work even if there *was* power. And there aren't any heating ducts or air conditioners."

A working air conditioner would be nice right about now. This awful heat was sapping what little strength she had. She knotted the tail of her shirt, but there simply wasn't any air flow in here. Maybe if they opened a window?

But as she crossed the room, Gina let out a startled gasp. "He's back!"

She froze. "What? *Where?*"

"Outside!" She turned and stared down at the floor, her eyes drawn automatically to the spot where she felt the man's presence. "I didn't think he'd be that close."

Andrea grabbed the back of a chair, considering it, but it was too solid to break and too heavy to wield.

Again, Gina jumped. "He's in the building!" she hissed.

"Already?"

"We have to get out of here!" She rushed past her and opened the window. "Fire escape!"

But as Andrea hurried toward her, she found that it was already too late.

He appeared behind Gina as if by magic, his frightful, muscular frame simply blooming into view.

Gina knew he was there instantly, but it was no use. She had time for her eyes to go wide with startled terror, but that was all. He hit her before she could even cry out and she dropped to the floor with a terrible, lifeless thud.

"*Gina!*"

Hotdog sneered at her. "That should take care of the annoying one for a while."

Andrea stood staring back at him. He looked terrible. His clothes were soaked with blood. There were deep gashes in both his arms. And there were horrible-looking claw marks on his face. That one, bulging eye was no longer bulging. It was an oozing bloody mess. It was horrific to look at, but she didn't dare take her eyes off him, not for an instant. She was sure that the moment she did, he'd move again. He'd be right behind her. And then it would all be over.

She didn't know what to do. Was this the end? Was he finally going to kill them? She couldn't get away. That much was clear by now.

"Tell me where it is," he growled.

She wanted to scream at him that she didn't know. That neither of them knew. The last time they saw it, it was in Nicole's purse. But her throat had tightened with fear. She couldn't seem to make a sound.

Why did he even want the spear so bad? What did it matter if he was only going to kill them anyway?

Hotdog took a lurching step toward her, limping on that bad foot. "You're going to tell me," he informed her. "One way or another, I'll make you tell me where you've hidden it."

He meant that. She understood perfectly clear that he intended to hurt her. *A lot.*

And there was nothing she was going to be able to do about it.

Chapter 47

Nicole screamed for a long time.

An eternity, it seemed.

Or at the very least for a lot longer than it should've taken the thing to tear her limb from limb...

She expected a lot more pain than this...

Gasping for air, great, wet sobs gushing up from deep inside her, she dared a quick peek at the hallway in front of her.

The monster wasn't there.

Her body trembling, her heart pounding with terror, tears streaming down her face, she turned and looked behind her.

The squirming black shadow was disappearing through the doorway at the far end of the hallway.

Her chest hitching, her lips quivering, she stared after it. It felt as if her brain had stalled out. She couldn't seem to form a rational thought. Why didn't it kill her? Was she really still alive? Or had she just died so quickly that she didn't know the difference? But if that were the case, why wasn't she trapped inside that blackness, screaming in agony like the other spirits it had devoured?

Seriously, what the absolute *fuck*?

"That's the last time," said Keith.

She turned, numb with shock, and faced him. He was standing right there in the nearest doorway, staring back at her.

"I won't be able to save your sorry ass again. I'm done. You're on your own from now on."

"What...?" She still couldn't quite process it all. When did he get here? *How* did he get here? What the hell was he talking about? "Are you...really you?"

He stared at her. He looked disgusted. Like *he* was one to

judge. "No," he told her.

She blinked at him. "What…?"

He thumped his chest. "This isn't me. I'm not here. *Neither of us* are here. There *is* no here. This place is a dream construct." He reached out and tapped the wall with the tip of his middle finger. Ripples raced out around it as if it were water. At the same time, everything around them became sort of transparent. She could see *through* the walls. Sunlight shined on the other side for a moment. A glimpse of Cedric's Cove, overrun by the invading forest and slowly sinking beneath the surface of the lake. Then she saw the gloomy hallways of Glimmering Sunrise Place. Then the moonlit lake behind the dance floor at Brandy and Albert's wedding. And finally a long, dark corridor of smooth, gray stone, exactly as it had looked five years ago… Then, for just a moment, they were somewhere new. A gloomy living room. A dusty armchair. A cat curled up on the seat, staring back at her with yellow eyes that seemed to shine just a little too bright. Then she was back inside the endless, dilapidated hospital corridor. "And that's pretty much what I am, too." He reached up and rubbed at his eyebrow. It was a familiar gesture, one she saw a million times when they were dating. It used to be charming. Just a little snippet of his personality shining through. It was something he did when he was nervous or tired. "Or I guess you could say I'm more like a dream *within* a dream? It doesn't really matter. It's complicated. And you wouldn't understand if I *could* explain it."

She made a face at him, her thoughts still churning. Was he calling her dumb? What was his problem? Why the hell did it have to be *him*? She never asked him to save her.

Except…she did, didn't she? Before she felt that monster approaching. In her moment of terrified desperation, she'd called out to him, specifically…

Fuck…

"Essentially, I was able to pull you out of that hospital and into this dreamscape. So, you're welcome."

"I don't… *What?*"

He sighed. "I don't have time to try explaining it to you.

And neither do you. Don't you have some friends who need you?"

She straightened up, surprised. Andrea and Gina? She turned and looked back down the corridor. "How do I...?" But when she turned to look at him again, he wasn't there.

And neither was she.

That empty, endless hospital hallway was gone. She was sitting upright on the floor in an empty shop, staring out a dusty glass door at the silent streets of Cedric's Cove.

She blinked, confused. It *felt* like a dream. It had that same sort of distant quality, like something that happened long ago.

But when did she fall asleep? *How?* This wasn't even the same building she was in when that lunatic surprised her. She'd never seen this shop before. It looked like some kind of boutique.

No. That wasn't important.

Andrea and Gina... Where were they? She had to find them before Hotdog did.

She jumped to her feet and ran out into the late evening sunshine, praying she wasn't already too late.

Chapter 48

The bloody maniac took another of those painful, lurching steps toward her. "Goar Nangup will have what He wants. He *always* gets what He wants."

Andrea stared at him. She was terrified. How did she end up on her own against this nutjob? She wasn't strong enough to fight him. Was this really how things were meant to turn out? How could Gina's goddess ever have thought that *she* could do this? It was ludicrous! She never should've left Briar Hills.

He took another step toward her. The motion of it twisted his already horrid-looking face into a tortured grimace. It looked *agonizing*. How was he even still walking? "Do you know what the cycle is? Do you even comprehend what you set in motion when you opened that door five years ago?"

She wanted to inform him that she technically wasn't even there for that part. She was in the other place at that time, deep down in that ghost-filled tunnel. All she did was open the portals that brought everyone home. That was all. She was just the *designated driver*. But fear was still holding her throat closed. She couldn't make a sound.

"The first universe was an utter failure. It fell apart as soon as it exploded into existence. A festering heap of rancid *garbage*. Any 'god' with half a brain should have stopped right then and there. It couldn't be done. It *shouldn't* be done. But no, a second universe was created, right on top of the first, only to collapse on itself as well. A third followed, with the same result. A fourth... A fifth..." He shook his head, his bloody lip curled in disgust. "Hundreds of them? Thousands? No one knows. But the filth of those failures still exists today, an *ocean* of toxic black sludge stretching for an eternity. It's right beneath our feet, slowly eating away at the foundation of this and every universe that has ever existed." His shoulders slumped, as if his weariness had finally caught up with him. "That's the fate of all living worlds. They all die. They all *rot*. And they all sink into that foul, black Oblivion." He reached up and tapped his forehead. "He showed me the truth. That's all everything is. Life. Death. *Everything* that was, is and ever will be. It's all just waste in the end. Garbage. *Shit*."

Andrea glanced down at Gina. She wanted to rush to her. She wanted to make sure the lunatic hadn't killed her when he struck her from behind. She desperately wanted to protect her. But she couldn't do anything for her as long as *he* was here. And she wasn't anywhere near strong enough to beat him.

But he wasn't paying attention to Gina. His attention was focused entirely on Andrea. He was moving *away* from Gina's motionless form, leaving her alone for the moment while he stood there on his insane-asylum-issued soapbox.

She took another step backward, toward the door. If she ran for it, he'd follow her. She was sure of it. He'd leave Gina alone. But how long could she avoid him? With his awful powers, he could be on her in an instant. And then he'd just come back to finish her off.

She needed more time.

"The Keeper's cycle does nothing but prolong the inevitable suffering that life forces us all into. Goar Nangup understood this. He spoke out against it. And they *imprisoned* Him beneath the foundations of the living worlds, sealed beneath the unbearable weight of all that very suffering that He sought to prevent. Those self-proclaimed 'gods' are as stupid as they are selfish. They're nothing but childish buffoons and shameless whores!"

Andrea took another step back. This was starting to sound personal. Was this still Hotdog talking or was this Goar Nangup, himself? At this point, nothing would really surprise her.

He took another of those lurching steps toward her. "But *you* can end the madness." He held out his good hand. "Just be a good girl and hand it over."

She stared at that bloody hand. If she said no, he was going to hurt her. She was as sure of this as she'd ever been of anything in her life. And if she handed the spear over to him, he was also going to hurt her. Because he'd already proved three times now that he was a murderous psychopath. But handing it over wasn't even an option. She didn't *have* the spear. If Nicole didn't have it, then she had no idea where it could be.

"*Now*," he snarled.

She didn't know what to do. It was looking like it was over for her.

"Run."

She let out a surprised squeak of a gasp. Ghost Girl? She was still here? She hadn't heard a peep out of her since that bizarre temple dream back in the ghostly cemetery.

But…this wasn't a voice inside her head any longer. She heard it with her ears, like she did back in those haunted hallways. And unlike back there, she wasn't the only one.

Hotdog's sneer melted away. He frowned. His one remaining eye rolled, scanning the room around him. "What was that? What are you doing?"

Then a shadow seemed to materialize out of the gloom behind him, much as he'd appeared behind Gina a moment earlier. It closed in on him, enveloping him in a strange, shadowy sort of pocket.

He let out a startled cry and spun around, his bloody arms raised to defend himself against something she could barely see, something that was little more than a refraction of the light around him. He staggered to one side, nearly falling over one of the desks.

Andrea took the opportunity and ran.

It was painful, leaving Gina there like that, but she couldn't help her by staying in that room and getting murdered by that creep. She needed to draw him away. She needed to keep him busy.

Ghost Girl was giving her a chance and she wasn't going to waste it.

Hotdog let out a furious howl as she fled back down the hallway and into the stairwell.

But she couldn't go far. She *wouldn't*. She had no intention of letting that monster have Gina. She'd lose him and then circle back around to her.

Or…that's what she *wanted* to do. But could she really lose him? He seemed to know exactly where to find them at all times. Any second now, he was probably going to do his teleporting trick again.

And indeed, as soon as she fled around the first landing, she was startled to see his bloody form lumbering up at her from the lower floor.

"Use as many tricks as you want!" he bellowed up the stairwell, his awful voice echoing off the bare concrete. "The cycle *will* end! It's His will! And nothing stands against His will!"

When she reached the third-floor hallway again, he was there, too, staggering toward her on his injured foot.

Again, she turned to run back down, but he was right there waiting for her, only a few steps below her, startling a terrible scream from her.

But as he reached out to grab her with his good arm, she glimpsed that strange, shadowy shimmer pass through the air around him again and something yanked his feet out from under him. He let out a furious shout as he fell hard onto the steps and slid down.

"Keep moving!" shouted the disembodied voice, because apparently, from a ghost's perspective, she looked like someone who might want to stop and take a picture?

She ran on up the stairs, past the third floor, all the way to the roof.

She rushed out into the humid, evening heat, squinting in the bright sunlight with her dark-adjusted eyes, and realized immediately that this was a terrible place to be. Now she was trapped up here. But the awful truth was that she was going to be trapped wherever she went. He wasn't exactly playing fair, after all.

She remembered Gina saying that the fire escapes were safe. Maybe she could scurry down one of those. But as soon as she turned toward the back ledge, he was there, blocking her path.

She screamed and backed away.

His mouth was covered with fresh blood from his hard fall on the stairs, making him look even more monstrous. "Why are you so much fucking trouble?"

"You're one to talk!"

He stalked toward her. "Why can't you see that the Keeper's way is the *real* evil in the world. He's responsible for *all of it!*"

Again, she watched that strange, shimmering shadow pass over him. Out here in the sunlight, she could see it a little better. There was a human shape to it, like a reflection in flowing water, churning and warbling somewhere between light and dark.

He let out a terrible shout and clutched at his injured arm, precisely as if someone had just dug their fingers into the wound.

Andrea lunged forward, just as she did back in that hallway, and drove her knee as hard as she could into his groin.

He let out another howl of pain and staggered backward.

Now was her chance. She turned to run back the way she came.

But his powerful hand closed around her trailing ponytail and yanked her back again. In almost the same instant, his fist struck hard against her face. She fell to the ground, dazed, one hand pressed against her bruised cheekbone.

That...didn't work at all.

"That's enough of that!" he growled. He was lumbering toward her, that one gray eye bulging with fury.

She tried to get up, but she was too slow. He grabbed her arm and jerked her to her feet, then thrust her back against the ledge.

Again, he let out a painful grunt. That shimmering, half-there form was crowding over his arm again. Ghost Girl, trying to help her. But this time, he thrust that bloody arm out and seemed to shove it away.

"Enough of *that*, too," he said. "So you can make friends with ghosts. No wonder you're such a handful." He leaned close to her, his nose almost touching hers. The stench of his blood and sweat washed over her, overwhelming. Nauseating. "Now *where is it?*" he snarled.

"Go to hell!" she spat.

"We *all* go to hell," he informed her. "That's the ultimate insult, after all. The punchline of this cruel joke called 'existence.' We suffer and we suffer and we suffer some more. And then we die and go to hell. Life is suffering. *Death* is suffering. *Existence is suffering!*"

He pushed her backward, past the ledge, so that she was leaning precariously over it.

She let out a terrified scream and looked down. It was a three-story drop directly onto the unforgiving sidewalk.

"But stupid little girls like you don't listen to people who know better than them, so I suppose I'll just have to show you."

He leaned closer, that awful, gray eye bulging manically. "It might not kill you immediately. You might lie there a while before you die. I hope so, anyway."

She let out a terrified whimper. She could feel tears streaming down her face. Was it weird that she had enough courage left in these final moments to hate the fact that he could see her crying?

"If you live long enough, I'll make sure you get to hear your little friend downstairs screaming."

Gina... The last time she saw her, she was lying unconscious on the floor, utterly helpless.

"Bastard!" she gasped.

"What does it matter if I am? But I want you to know that, just because of you, I'm going to make sure she hurts for a long, *long* time. And I'm going to make sure she *knows* it's because of you."

"Hey, Oscar Meyer!"

Hotdog turned around, startled. "What—"

But Nicole was already swinging the branch she picked up on her way here. It struck him square in his face, knocking him backward.

Andrea grabbed the ledge, desperate to catch herself before she could fall. At the same time, she felt something push her back onto the safety of the roof.

Ghost Girl?

Hotdog staggered backward, clutching at his face, screaming.

Nicole took a second swing. He struck the ledge and teetered backward.

Then he was gone. He screamed one final time as he fell. Then silence returned to the traveling city.

Her heart still pounding, unable to believe it could finally be over, Andrea peered over the ledge. She expected him to have escaped again, to have used his obnoxious teleporting ability to vanish just before he hit the ground. But he was there, lying motionless on the pavement, a pool of blood slowly spreading beneath him.

She *really* hoped he was dead.

"Are you okay?" gasped Nicole. She tossed the branch aside and took hold of her cheeks, staring at the black eye he gave her. "What did that son of a bitch do to you?"

"I'm fine," she gasped. "What about you? Where were you?"

"Bastard dumped me back in his horror hospital again, but I got out."

"*How?*"

"Long story. I'm just glad I heard you screaming or I'd never have found you in time. Where's Gina?"

"Downstairs." She was already on her feet, desperate to get back to her. "Come on."

Chapter 49

Gina came to quickly enough. She had a splitting headache, of course, but she didn't seem to be badly hurt.

Nicole and Andrea both lamented that their friend, Olivia, wasn't there to look her over, and she didn't blame them. Having a trained nurse along on a trip like this definitely wouldn't hurt. But for now she was just going to have to trust that she didn't have a concussion and that she'd be fine as soon as this awful headache eased up.

Nicole had somehow found her way back from wherever it was that crazy man sent her. That was good. It was one less thing to worry about, and that was good enough for her. She didn't feel like asking what happened to her right now.

Andrea helped her to her feet and the three of them made their way back down the stairs.

By the time they arrived outside, however, the crazy man who hit her was gone. All that was left was a bloody stain on the sidewalk where he landed.

"Not again…" groaned Andrea. "I can't deal with that guy anymore!"

"How did he survive something like that?" wondered Nicole. "Fucking freak isn't human!"

Gina rubbed at the knot on the back of her head and looked up at the western sky. The sun was already sinking behind the trees. "We need to hurry up and find what we came here for. Those things in the water won't stay there once it gets dark."

Andrea made an exhausted squeaking noise in her throat. "Seriously?"

"It doesn't matter," said Nicole. "I lost the spear. Hotdog took it when he sent me back to the hospital."

Andrea looked over at her, surprised. "Hotdog didn't have it. He had your purse, but the spear wasn't there. He seemed to think *we* knew where it was."

Nicole stared back at her, confused. "Then where the fuck is it?"

"Somebody else must've taken it," reasoned Gina.

"Who else *is* there?" asked Andrea.

"There are a lot of parties interested in the cycle," she reminded her. "All those people who were at that wedding with you, pretending to be someone they weren't." Then she frowned a little. "Like me, I guess…" She felt a little bad, looking back on it. She crashed that party just like the rest of those strangers. And then she dragged her into this nightmare. But if she hadn't been there, that lunatic would've killed her in that parking lot…

Andrea sat down on the street. She looked exhausted.

"Not like it matters," said Nicole. "You keep telling us that there's no one in this city but us. Whoever the Lady of Cedric's Cove is, she's not here."

She was right. They were the only three human beings in this city. She could feel quite a few cats nearby, all of them watching them, seemingly curious. But there was no one else here. They were essentially alone again.

"Maybe we're too late?" guessed Andrea. "Did we take too long getting here?"

But Gina shook her head. "I can't imagine it being anything that simple." Again, she turned and looked up at the darkening sky. "We have to be missing something."

"Like *what?*" pressed Nicole.

But Gina didn't know.

Nicole rubbed wearily at her eyes. She'd lost the spear. And they were no closer to finding what they came for than they were when they arrived. It was starting to feel positively hopeless.

Andrea stared at the building in front of her. She hurt all over. Her throat was still scratchy from where Hotdog tried to strangle her. And her arm was bruised where he grabbed her and tried to push her off the roof. And of course her eye was puffy and swollen now from where the creep punched her.

But slowly, her expression changed. Her eyes narrowed. Her lips curled into a thoughtful frown. "Hey...?"

Gina looked over at her, then followed her gaze.

The building she was staring at was an old theatre. The marquee was blank, of course. She very much doubted that anyone had ever even set foot on its stage. But it wasn't the marquee that she was looking at. It was the name displayed over it.

"The Lady of the Stage Theatre..." sighed Nicole. "Wait..."

Andrea stood up. "Is that...? Is that what we were supposed to be looking for this whole time?"

Gina stared at it. Was the Lady of Cedric's Cove not a person at all? Was it a *place*?

"I mean, it would explain why you can't feel anyone else here, right?"

It would, indeed. She walked up the steps and pushed open the door.

"How do we know, though?" wondered Andrea. "How can we be sure it's not just a coincidence?"

"It's not," said Gina.

Andrea and Nicole crowded behind her.

The lobby was spread out before them. Directly across from them was the ticket booth. There was another cat sitting on the counter there, watching them. Lying next to the cat, atop the neatly folded red velvet it came wrapped in, was the spear.

"But...who brought it here?" wondered Nicole.

Andrea crossed the lobby and picked it up. The cat jumped down as she approached and fled into the shadows. She watched it go, then turned and looked at Nicole. "What's going on?"

But Gina was already moving. She made her way down the darkened hallway to the theatre entrance. She was worried it was going to be too dark to see anything. Theatres didn't have windows, after all. But as soon as she pushed open the doors, she found that someone had left an old oil lantern burning on the steps to the stage.

There were more cats in here. She saw a few running from her path, but she could feel more of them watching from the shadows, hidden from view.

"This is kind of creepy," said Nicole. "Not going to lie."

Andrea nodded.

It *was* creepy. But all the evidence was suggesting that this was where they were meant to be. They needed to find out why they were here before something else showed up.

"Look," said Andrea as she stepped onto the stage. She reached out and grasped the curtain. It was the same fabric as the cloth the spear came in. She could even see where someone sheared it off.

"The rope, too," said Gina, pointing to one of the pull ropes that someone had cut.

"This is it..." marveled Andrea. "We finally found it..."

Gina found herself drawn backstage. There was a door back there. It was an oddly familiar door... She felt like she'd seen a door like that somewhere before...

Was it...in a dream once...?

No. Not once. She'd seen that door in her dreams a number of times, but she didn't remember it until just now.

What was this place?

She opened the door and stepped into a small room.

Another door was waiting for her inside, but this one was chained shut. A huge lock held it all in place, barring the way forward.

"Not that way, I guess," grumbled Nicole.

"No," said Gina. "I think it *is* that way."

"But it's kinda locked?" said Andrea.

She shook her head. "No. It's not locked. It's *gated*."

Nicole wrinkled her nose. "Um...? Same thing?"

But Gina pointed at the spear in Andrea's hand.

Andrea looked down at it, her blue eyes widening. "Pierce the gatekeeper's heart to open the way..." she whispered.

The keyhole on the lock didn't look like it fit a normal key. It was extra narrow and extra tall, like a very thin diamond.

Or like the shape of the spear's blade.

Gina met her gaze. "This is it. Are you ready?"

"For *what*?"

"I have no idea."

"Can we just get this fucking over with already?" asked Nicole.

Andrea glanced back and forth between the two of them, then took a calming breath and approached the lock. "Here goes nothing."

Chapter 50

It was like that first hallway back in Hotdog's creepy hospital, when he disappeared and everything changed. As soon as she slid the spear into the keyhole, everything was different. It didn't *change*. It wasn't one thing that turned into another. It was as if the theatre was never there at all, as if they'd always been in this new place, but just couldn't see it for what it was.

"I'm never going to get used to that," said Nicole.

Gina nodded agreement.

Everything was as bright here as the theatre was dark. The floor was shining white marble. The ceiling was a high, glittering sea of lights. And they were surrounded by countless *things*.

There were dolls of every sort, from finely crafted little porcelain girls to limp little ragdolls to primitive-looking things made from clay and straw. There were fashion mannequins dressed in gorgeous gowns spanning every imaginable era in history and some that looked like they stepped right out of someone's fantasies. There were bicycles. There was all manner of jewelry. There were stuffed animals, handmade toys and fancy old kites. There were breathtaking paintings and exquisitely life-like statues. There was fancy dinnerware and old radios. There were books and handmade quilts. There was a baby carriage and an old popcorn machine. There were antique tools and old travelers' trunks. A hair brush. A jeweled egg. An old telephone. A wooden sled. And much bigger things, as well. There were automobiles and boats parked among it all. There was even an airplane. It went on and on, countless things, as far as they could see.

"A museum?" asked Andrea. And yet, what sort of museum would be curated in such a haphazard way? Everything was laid out seemingly without any intended organization at all. Nothing was grouped together. There were no shelves or display cases. Everything was either sitting on the floor or on something larger that was sitting on the floor. And yet there was nothing about the room that appeared *messy*. Although there was no specific order, none of it was simply tossed about. Every detail seemed to have been very intentionally placed so that every detail was perfectly shown off.

"I like to think of it more as a 'lost and found,'" said a soft and gentle voice.

The three of them turned to find a woman standing among the strangely organized clutter. She was both very beautiful and very otherworldly. Her hair was so long it trailed the floor behind her, and was a strange, iridescent white that shimmered with all the colors of the rainbow when she moved. Her eyebrows and even her eyelashes were the same color. She was very slender, almost *sleek*, her body both lovely and graceful as she walked. Her skin was fair, almost milky, and in stark contrast, her eyes were big and dark. She was wearing a simple white, strapless dress that flowed elegantly down her slim figure to her bare feet.

There was something about her, Andrea thought, something beyond her unusual hair, something she couldn't quite put her finger on, something about her face, the subtleties of those lovely features. She wasn't exactly Asian or Caucasian or...well, *any* specific race that she could identify, really. Something about those slightly bigger than average eyes...the exact shape of her ears... She looked just a little bit different from everyone else she'd ever seen, but she couldn't quite say *how* she was different. She just looked...somehow *alien*.

"Things that are loved dearly by a person during their life collect that love," explained the woman, her voice delicate and pretty. "They store it up inside them. And when things are loved enough, they can never be truly lost, not even after the people who loved them are long gone." She smiled. It was such a lovely smile. Beautiful and disarming. "Such things find their way to me."

Andrea frowned. Maybe she was a little slow, but that legitimately sounded like the most poetic variation of "I'm a hoarder" that she'd ever heard...

"Who are you?" asked Nicole.

The woman walked right up to them, those dark, shining eyes washing over them. That lovely smile never faded. "Ada," she replied.

"I feel like I've been here before..." said Gina.

"Of course you have," said Ada, turning to face her fully. She had just a hint of an accent, but like her facial features, Andrea couldn't quite identify it. "I'm so happy to see you again. And I'm delighted to see you making more friends."

Gina stared at her. "You're...really her...?"

Andrea glanced at her. "Wait... Is she...?"

"The Great Beholder..." sighed Gina. "The goddess..."

"You're a goddess?" asked Nicole..

"Well, that's a little embarrassing, really," replied Ada. "People always call me that, but I'm no more a goddess than you are."

"Oh..."

"You have questions," she said.

"Yeah!" said Nicole. "Like, a *lot* of them."

"I'll answer what I can. But there are things I won't be able to tell you. There are rules." She made a face as she said this, almost a pout, as if she were a spoiled child. "And the Keeper really is such a grouch when it comes to rules. I suppose he has his reasons. But it really does make everything so much more difficult."

She turned and walked out among her enormous collection of things, her slender fingers caressing the fabric of an elegant gown as she passed it. "First, about *me*. I was born just like everyone else. A perfectly normal baby girl. For a while, at least. Lots of people are born with special abilities. The human race has been around for a long, long time, after all, much longer than the vast majority of people ever know. And we all share the same ancestors. There are so many secrets buried deep in our blood. And those secrets come to the surface every now and then. Usually it's just little things. A girl in Ohio has never broken a fingernail. A boy in California attracts stray dogs and cats wherever he goes. A woman in Georgia has never once in her life had a cold. You see these sorts of things every day. Whenever someone possesses an amazing natural talent, whether they have an angelic singing voice, or can paint the most realistic portraits you've ever seen, or even grow the most beautiful vegetables in their garden. But some people get more." She turned those big, lovely eyes on Gina again. "Like you, I knew things. Little things at first. Then more things. The older I was, the more I knew, until a single glance could tell me every possible detail about a person. That's how these things often work. The older you are, the stronger those abilities become. But some people live longer than others. Some people live *a lot* longer than others. Sometimes hundreds of years. They're out there now, walking around, doing their best to fit in with a world that should have left them behind long ago."

"Really?" said Andrea.

"It's true," said Gina. "I know someone like that. She's two hundred and thirty-nine, but doesn't look a day over twenty-five."

Andrea stared at her. "Seriously, whatever your story is, we need to hear it!"

"Yes," agreed Nicole.

"It's not really my story, though," she replied. "I didn't do much."

"I don't care," said Andrea. "I want to hear it."

Ada giggled. It was a lovely giggle, easily as lovely and disarming as the rest of her. "I hope you can get her to open up more. I want to see her find her happiness."

"I'm fine," said Gina, looking embarrassed.

"Very few people ever live more than a few hundred years," said Ada, mercifully changing the subject. "But a handful find themselves lingering for thousands of years. And a very, *very* few can linger much, *much* longer."

"You?" asked Andrea.

"When this is all done, it will be my *third* cycle."

"That...sounds like a long time..."

"You have no idea. After a while, you simply go mad. But if you keep living long enough, you eventually go sane again." She smiled back at them. "So don't worry about that."

"Okay…" said Andrea. She wasn't worried about it until she put the idea in her head, but okay…

"To my knowledge, no one's been around longer than me. No one *human*, I should say. But there are a handful of people who were born during the *last* cycle. And when you've been around that long, your talents become considerable. One glance at you and I know every detail of your life, even those you've completely forgotten. And through your memories, I see everyone you've ever seen and know every detail of *their* lives, and so on, back through time, itself."

"Wow," said Andrea.

"When you have that kind of knowledge," said Ada as she stopped and picked up an old baseball, "it's not so surprising that people start calling you a goddess."

"I guess not," said Nicole.

"And that's when you pick up silly names like 'the Great Beholder,' too." Ada turned and faced them again. "So many questions… Why don't we start with the leaf?"

"Leaf?" asked Andrea. She looked down at the spear in her hand and found that it had changed shape at some point between the Lady of the Stage and Ada's "lost and found." Nicole and Gina saw it, too. They both leaned close to her, surprised. It was slightly smaller than it was, and the markings and notches etched into it were gone, as if the outermost layer had melted off when she slid it into that lock… And it now had a series of grooves running out from the center to the edges of the blade. It did, in fact, now look a little like a leaf.

"The leaf is one of three very old keys, described in legends as pieces of the mythical tree Yggdrasil. They're called the Three Whispers and are said to have the power to unlock the way to an ancient city located at the center of creation."

"*What?*" asked Nicole.

Ada giggled again. "It *does* sound a little silly when I say it out loud, doesn't it?"

Andrea stared at the spear. Except it wasn't a spear. It was a leaf? Was it supposed to be a spear before? Or was it always a leaf? But it was also a key? Was the spear the key to *this* place and the leaf the spear to...some *city*? This was all so confusing...

Ada continued smiling at them. "And speaking of the leaf, you want to know why Elias Hochog didn't just kill you and take what he was after."

"That's right," said Andrea, perking up. That had been bothering her this whole time. Not that she wasn't relieved that he didn't just murder the three of them in that awful hallway and walk out with the spear...but it just didn't make any sense.

"First, you've already seen that he was quite insane. He sold his soul to the ancient god, Goar Nangup, who wants to break the cycle and eventually be free from his prison beneath the weight of the living worlds. He was granted incredible powers, but was corrupted completely. His psyche was fracturing. By the time he arrived in Cedric's Cove there was nothing left of his humanity. However, he also couldn't just take it. The Keeper's rules. If he killed you without first possessing the leaf, it would only transfer to another, and he'd have to start his hunt all over again. But he also couldn't take the leaf because something was protecting it."

"Protecting it?" asked Andrea.

"Unfortunately, I can't tell you exactly what that protection was."

"Can't because you don't know?" pressed Nicole, "Or can't because of the Keeper's stupid rules?"

"A little of both, I'm afraid."

"Oh..."

She turned her smile on Nicole. "You were wondering about the road to Cedric's Cove."

Nicole nodded. She had, indeed, been thinking about Cedric's cove. Was she really reading her mind? "Well...I mean Cedric's Cove is supposed to be a legend talked about by people who stumbled onto it, wasn't it? But if this place is so hard to get to, how did *those people* get here?"

"The Keeper sent them here," she replied. "If he hadn't,

there wouldn't have existed a legend for people to talk about and you never would've known how to get here when the time came."

"Well that just sounds convoluted," grumbled Andrea.

Ada's laugh was as lovely as her giggle. "That's the Keeper for you. He's not human, so I can't read him. And he's old and wise beyond the ages. Legends say he's even older than the elder gods, that he was one of the few who were here in the beginning. No one knows his ways but him, but he's always many steps ahead of everyone. Nothing happens without him meaning for it to happen."

"So he *meant* for us to have to deal with Hotdog?" challenged Nicole.

"Probably. After all, it worked out in the end."

"But he's still out there," said Andrea.

"That man is dead," Ada assured them. "Something robbed him of his ability to escape death at the last minute. Something is protecting you. A spirit. Clinging to you since you left that unfortunate hospital."

"Ghost Girl?"

"I can't see spirits. I only know as much of her as you do, but she's real. Your abilities to converse with the dead are real. Trust in your senses."

"Okay…"

"But also beware. That spirit wasn't the only one clinging to you. There's another… Something far stronger than a mere spirit, something I can't see. I think it's been with you for some time, possibly since the first doorway, watching you, biding its time, but it's able to cloud itself from my sight somehow. You'll have to be very careful. I'm pretty sure its presence was the reason Goar Nangup's slave was able to follow you. It seems to attract unwanted things. And it delights in your misfortune."

"Oh good," grumbled Nicole. "Just what we needed."

Andrea frowned. That wasn't the kind of news she needed. So now she was a monster magnet? "But Hotdog's for sure dead?"

"He did *not* survive that fall. What walked away and remains out there is only an empty husk. Only Goar Nangup remains. The man's abilities to toy with people's minds is gone. What comes back will be different and in many ways more dangerous. But you can handle it. I know because the Keeper is never wrong."

"If you say so…" she muttered.

"So is the Keeper your boss or something?" wondered Nicole.

"Something like that, you could say." She glanced around at all her many things. "He gifted me this place. It exists outside the flow of time, in a place called the Compendium. It's a safe place, where nothing bad can find me. In return, I use my abilities to help him with the cycle. I send people where they need to be to do the things they're meant to do." She glanced at Gina. "Like sending *you* to find and watch over Andrea, so she could find her way to me."

"I see," said Gina. "I guess. But I still don't understand it all."

"No. I suppose you wouldn't. And that's okay. You can't really understand *everything*, can you? The more you manage to understand in this big, crazy world, the more new things you find that you don't understand."

Andrea frowned. That made a weird sort of sense. She didn't think she'd ever really thought of things like that before. "And what about Tristesse Lane?" she asked. "The Keeper meant for us to go there?"

"Maybe. Or maybe going there was inevitable and he only meant for you to find your way out of it. Gwilym Glum was never going to kill you. He has nothing to gain by breaking the cycle. More than likely, he meant to hold you hostage. With two of the Twelve now gone, the remaining ten are getting restless. They're vying to improve their positions. My guess is that Glum wants Janon Tane's Job as the representative of the cycle and meant to trade you to the Keeper for it."

"That's…*what?*" sputtered Nicole.

Andrea didn't understand any of that either. Ten of twelve? Twelve what? Janon who?

"Yeah, it's a little confusing, isn't it?" said Ada. "A lot's been happening this cycle." She glanced at Gina. "You can tell them about Tane when you have time."

She nodded.

"And Alwyn Thrud hasn't been seen since before the last exodus…" she said, almost to herself. "Again, I can only see into the lives of humans. The Twelve are beyond my abilities, so I can't presume to know their minds, but *through* humans, I've witnessed their actions for *eons*. Some of them definitely have the potential to be very nasty. I wouldn't be surprised if there were a war brewing between them. And that could be a nasty business…" Her gaze had turned distant as she pondered these things, but now she turned those dark and brilliant eyes back on Gina. "But that's not important right now." She smiled at Andrea. "Trust in your abilities, and you'll be fine. You don't just hear ghosts. You can see into the places where the realms of the living and the dead overlap. You can see the things that are hidden to others."

Andrea shook her head. "But…why—?"

"Why, then, have you never interacted with such things before?" she asked for her. "That's very simple. You *have* interacted with them. All your life."

"What?"

"When you were just a girl, and you'd sit outside and stare up at the sky, watching the clouds flow together like a stream across the sky."

Andrea stared at her. "Wait…" Why did that sound familiar? She could remember it. A blue sky filled with wispy clouds, all slowly floating along, then emptying into what looked like a river of clouds snaking from horizon to horizon. But…wasn't that just a dream?

"Those were a manifestation of the spirit highways, visible only to a very rare few."

"Seriously…?"

"You'd be surprised how many spirit places you've walked right by without ever realizing it."

She couldn't decide if that was cool or freaky…

Ada turned her gaze to Gina. "And trust *your* abilities, too. You're keenly aware of your surroundings, to a supernatural degree. Don't be afraid to use that. But the other ability you have might be among the rarest I've ever seen."

"All those scary things I see and hear?" she asked.

"Those things aren't from the worlds of the living *or* the dead. Neither spiritual *nor* psychic. Those are something else entirely. Those are things from the *other* world. The world of the unnatural. The shadows. The undefinable." Those dark, shining eyes widened. "The world from which the Great Enemy and his Twelve Teeth were born."

Gina stared up at her, confused.

"That was why I sent you to Vertical Design," Ada explained. "You were the only one who could do that job. You were the only one capable of realizing what that place really was."

Andrea reached out and took her hand. They were in the same situation, it seemed.

Finally, Ada turned her gaze on Nicole. "And don't underestimate yourself, either," she said. "You may not have the abilities of your friends, but you did *not* end up in that temple by chance. The Keeper doesn't make mistakes. You have a role to play in all this. Trust me on that."

"If you say so," replied Nicole.

Ada swept that bright gaze across each of them in turn. "That's all I have for you. It's time to finish what you started five years ago."

"Five years ago..." sighed Andrea. "But we opened that door. The temple fell. It's over."

Ada smiled that lovely smile again. "True. But there's more than one door. And there's more than one temple."

Chapter 51

Nicole cursed. It wasn't a very ladylike curse. It was quite vulgar. But it also didn't have much force behind it. She was tired. She just wanted to go home. And now this goddess was telling them they were going to have to go find *another* temple? They barely made it out of the first one alive!

"The Three Whispers will open the gates that lead to the City Beyond Memory," explained Ada, ignoring the vulgarity, "where the second temple is waiting. And the second doorway."

"So we have to go find two more of these things?" whined Andrea, staring down at the leaf in her hand. The very idea was exhausting.

"Not at all," replied Ada. "The other two Whispers will take care of themselves. Don't worry about them."

"Oh… Okay, then… I guess…" The other two Whispers would take care of themselves? What did that mean? She hoped it didn't mean that they'd end up coming back twice more when this was all done.

"It's all very simple, really. You need only to travel across the vast expanse of the Wood and deep into an area known as the Denselands, where you'll find and open the leaf's gate."

"Is that all?" grumbled Nicole.

Andrea grimaced. The Wood? Seriously? That place was an absolute nightmare! Filled with flesh-starved zombies and man-eating trees and those disgusting carrion eaters that pooped all over everything and pushed innocent girls off cliffs! She *really* didn't want to have to go back there again.

"Don't worry," said Ada. "Getting there is the easy part. A ride has already been arranged for you."

"A ride?" She glanced at Nicole and Gina.

Ada picked up a small music box and held it in front of her. "This will work like the lock that brought you here," she explained. "One of my many treasures. Gather close to it and open it, and you'll all be sent back to Cedric's Cove, where you'll find the entrance to the lake road open to you."

"Lake road..." said Nicole. "Is that going to be something we have to search the city for, too?"

Ada smiled a reassuring smile. "All you'll have to do is make your way down to the lakefront. There will be a boat waiting there. It'll be able to take you most of the way."

"A boat to take us through the Wood?" asked Andrea, confused.

"There are lots of lakes and rivers running through the Wood," said Ada. "They're dangerous waters, but they provide easier travel than by land. The captain will know how to get you where you're going. And while he drives, you'll have a chance to rest up for the next part of your journey."

Andrea groaned. She just wanted to go home.

"And what happens if we say no?" asked Nicole. "What if we don't *want* to go to another fucking temple and get ourselves killed?"

Again, she gave them that sweet smile. "That's your decision. Unfortunately, it's not that easy. Just like Goar Nangup and Gwilym Glum, there will always be someone seeking to get their hands on the Keeper's chosen ones. I understand your hesitance, but it's far more dangerous for you to turn back than to continue forward."

Nicole cursed again. And again, it was a weary curse, without much bite to it.

"I'm very sorry. I wish I could keep you here and let you rest up. But you have to hurry. It'll be almost dark in Cedric's Cove now, and you already know the city isn't safe after dark."

"Those things in the water," recalled Gina.

Andrea shuddered at the memory of those foul, toad-like things inflating like gruesome balloons from the stagnant water and swarming over Hotdog's body, dragging him down.

Ada held the music box out to Gina. "Take hold of each

other."

Nicole and Andrea each gripped one of her arms.

"As soon as she opens it, you'll be returned to the street outside the theatre. You should have just enough time to reach the lake before they start crawling out of the water."

Andrea let out a frightened whimper. Couldn't they just wait until morning? She didn't like the idea of being sent back out there where those fish people were…

And what about Hotdog? What if he came back? She assured them he was dead, but she also pretty much said that his corpse was still running around out there, possessed by some kind of pissed-off eldritch god…

Gina stared at the music box, uncertain. "You're sure we can do this?" she asked. It wasn't something she'd ever gotten to ask her before. She'd always awakened before she could ask any follow-up questions.

Ada smiled. When people smiled, it didn't mean much to her. Lots of people smiled and didn't mean it. People pretended to be nice. People pretended to like her. But people lied. All the time.

Somehow, however, Ada's smile didn't feel like a lie.

Was that a part of her goddess power? Making people trust her?

"I haven't forgotten my promise," Ada told her.

"Promise?" asked Andrea.

Gina bit her lip. It was the first time the goddess came to her in her dreams. When she told her to go to Vertical Design.

"It wasn't just a *job*," said Ada. "It was the right path. *Your* path. The one that will take you where you need to be, to find what you've been looking for all your life. It's right in front of you."

"What is it?" wondered Andrea. "What have you been looking for?"

"It's…"

"It's kind of private," said Ada. "She'll talk about it when she's ready. Right?"

Gina nodded.

"But now it's time to go. Any longer and you won't have time to reach the water."

Gina glanced at Andrea and then at Nicole. They both nodded.

"Good luck," said Ada.

Gina grasped the lid of the music box and lifted it open. In an instant, everything changed again.

They were standing out on the open street under a darkening sky. The theatre's marquee loomed in front of them. Hotdog's bloodstain was drying on the pavement behind them.

"Yep," said Nicole. "That's still weird."

Andrea nodded. "*So* weird."

Nicole glanced at Gina. "So…that was the goddess you were talking about… She was…*nice.*"

"She's always nice," replied Gina. She was looking up at the sky, at the shadows the buildings were casting, getting her bearings. "That's north," she said, pointing down the street. "We need to go. Now."

"Right," said Andrea, shaking off the weirdness of the teleporting music box. "The scary fish people."

"Okay, I *really* don't like the sound of that…" said Nicole.

"It's worse than it sounds," said Gina, already moving.

"That's true," agreed Andrea.

"But the goddess wasn't lying. There's someone else here now. I can feel a man in a boat, waiting for us."

"If you say so," said Nicole. "We trust you."

As she set off after Gina, Andrea looked down at the spear in her hand. No… Not the spear. The *leaf…* "This is going to get a lot scarier before it's over, isn't it?"

"Probably," admitted Gina.

Chapter 52

Andrea expected the trip to Cedric's Cove's dock to be a terrifying gauntlet of murderous, toad-faced fish people trying to drag them down into the murky depths. But the streets remained remarkably monster-free as they made their way north to the lake's shore. There were no more unplanned trips to dreary cobblestone streets or gloomy apartment hallways or abandoned hospital corridors or scary, mist-shrouded woods or even a creepy cemetery that only she could see. There wasn't even a zombie Hotdog Creep waiting to ambush them.

There was nothing but eerily empty streets and the steadily rising noises of the approaching night as the crickets and frogs and night birds began to stir.

And there were cats. Lots of them. They were creeping from the shadows and darting across their path, watching them as they passed.

"Is it really safe to go to the lake, though?" wondered Andrea. "Won't that be where the most monsters are?"

"They came out of the lake originally," Gina explained, "but they don't go back to it. They keep to the sewers and the flooded basements. I don't know why."

Andrea couldn't help wondering if that meant that something far worse than the fish people was waiting for them out in those murky depths.

It was getting later and later. The light was fading faster with each passing moment, but Nicole came to a stop as the lake finally came into view ahead of them. "Has that been there this whole time?"

Andrea, too, stopped walking. Ahead of them, the street suddenly gave way to a long strip of smooth gray stone stretching out into the lake. In front of it, blocking the path forward, was a single statue of a very familiar, ten-foot-tall, naked figure with no face.

"I feel like we would've noticed that," agreed Andrea. It was no small detail. It stretched at least two hundred feet out into the water. She looked left, along the dark shoreline. Didn't they enter the city from right over there?

"It's what the goddess was talking about," said Gina. Unlike the others, she didn't pause. She was still walking toward the ominous-looking statue. "It's the entrance to the lake road. It's in a separate reality from the rest of Cedric's Cove. Double-hidden. Where no one would ever find it."

"Seems like overkill," muttered Andrea as she hurried to catch up.

Gina stared at the statue as they approached it, her gaze washing over its bizarre, elongated anatomy.

"Freaky, aren't they?" asked Andrea. "Sentinels. They were all over the Temple of the Blind."

"It seems kind of familiar for some reason. Like I saw it in a dream once." But she didn't have time to ponder the familiarity. She glanced back over her shoulder and said in a surprisingly emotionless tone, "They're coming."

Andrea looked back. She couldn't see anything in the growing gloom, but she didn't doubt her for a second.

Luckily, the boat was waiting for them up ahead, just as Ada promised. It looked like an old, discolored trawler, tethered to the end of the dock.

"I don't see anyone," said Nicole as they approached it.

"He's there," Gina informed her. "I can feel him below deck."

"I hope he's nice," sighed Andrea.

"I hope he's *hot*," said Nicole.

Andrea looked over at her, surprised.

"What? It's been a long day. At least give me something nice to look at."

"I couldn't really tell you if he's hot or not," said Gina. "Or if he's nice. He's just stocking the refrigerator."

"Fridge?" said Nicole. "Fuck whether or not he's hot, then. I hope he has *beer.*" She raised her voice as they approached the trawler. "Hello?" Then she glanced over at Andrea. "Or am I supposed to say 'ahoy' or some shit? I've never really done the boat thing."

"In here," replied a man from inside.

"He could be hot *and* have beer," decided Nicole. "I could do that."

"No getting drunk," grumbled Andrea. She glanced at Gina. "Drunk Nikki has a habit of getting naked."

"I don't mind," said Gina.

"So you keep saying."

"I'm just getting everything ready," called the unseen captain. Andrea could see him now, stepping up into the light. "Welcome aboard, and all that." He stepped up to the side of the boat and looked down at them.

For a moment, all of them stood there in silence, staring.

"What the fuck are *you* doing here?" shouted Nicole.

"I came all this way for *you?*" Keith shouted back at her. "Seriously?"

She stared at him, her thoughts racing. He even looked just the way he did when he saved her. His longer, unkempt hair. His stubbled beard. He looked like he'd aged several years instead of only seven months. But she didn't care about any of that. "Why the fuck are you *stalking* me?"

"Stalking *you?* Don't flatter yourself, princess. You're the one who's been prancing through my dreams for the past week like you own the place!"

"*What?*"

Gina turned and looked at Andrea. "They know each other?"

She nodded. This definitely wasn't what she was expecting. "That's her ex."

"Oh... Awkward."

"Yeah..."

Chapter 53

Some distance away, unseen in the crowding gloom of the descending night, a solitary figure leaned on a dusty windowsill, looking out at the lonely lights glowing at the end of the dock.

Feminine fingers drummed blood-red nails softly on the splintered wood as a strange and ominous energy filled the empty room.

"Fun...fun...fun...fun..." sighed a soft voice in the darkness.

She'd been waiting so long, after all. So very, *very* long...

And there they were at last. The Keeper's chosen few.

A wicked giggle drifted through the bones of the old building like a haunting melody.

A crack shot up the wall. Plaster crumbled and rained down from the ceiling. A windowpane broke. And somewhere underfoot, a joist splintered and sagged.

She didn't move from the window. She stood watching as the trawler pulled away from Cedric's Cove and into the unknown, her sharp fingernails excitedly digging into the rotting wood of the windowsill.

"This'll be so...much...*fun!*"

About the author

Brian Harmon is an independent author of horror fiction, suspense and dark adventure. He grew up in rural Missouri and now lives in Southern Wisconsin with his wife, Guinevere, and their three children.

For more about Brian Harmon and his work, visit
www.BrianHarmonBooks.com

www.ingramcontent.com/pod-product-compliance
Lightning Source LLC
Chambersburg PA
CBHW050031030726
47506CB00001B/209